JONES WAS MAD—

so mad at Mondragon that she didn't think much about the footsteps behind her, the footsteps that were coming up faster than those of a casual passerby should.

And then a hand came down over her mouth and nose and there was some foul-smelling rag in that hand. She couldn't breathe. She started to struggle. She got her nails into the arm around her arms, that single arm pinning hers to her side.

Jones tried to bite the hand through the cloth, but the cloth was getting bigger and bigger and wrapping her all over and she was losing any sense of where her body was, or even if there was ground under her feet.

She hardly knew it when she stopped struggling and slumped against the man dragging her toward a boat made fast against the pilings of the pier. She barely felt it at all when the man hoisted her onto his shoulders. She didn't feel it at all when he let her go and she fell three feet. She didn't even hear the thud as the man followed, or the cough of the boat's engine starting, or the voice with a foreign accent calling, " 'Ware; 'ware. . . ."

DAW Science Fiction
and Fantasy by
Hugo Award Winner
C. J. CHERRYH

**C.J. CHERRYH invites you to enter
the world of MEROVINGEN NIGHTS!**

ANGEL WITH THE SWORD *by C.J. Cherryh*
A Merovingen Nights Novel

FESTIVAL MOON *edited by C.J. Cherryh*
(stories by C.J. Cherryh, Leslie Fish,
Robert Lynn Asprin, Nancy Asire, Mercedes Lackey,
Janet and Chris Morris, Lynn Abbey)

FEVER SEASON *edited by C.J. Cherryh*
(stories by C.J. Cherryh, Chris Morris,
Mercedes Lackey, Leslie Fish, Nancy Asire,
Lynn Abbey, Janet Morris)

TROUBLED WATERS *edited by C.J. Cherryh*
(stories by C.J. Cherryh, Mercedes Lackey,
Nancy Asire, Janet Morris, Lynn Abbey,
Chris Morris, Roberta Rogow, Leslie Fish)

and look for SMUGGLER'S GOLD—
coming in October 1988!

MEROVINGEN NIGHTS

TROUBLED WATERS

C.J. CHERRYH

DAW BOOKS, INC.
DONALD A. WOLLHEIM, PUBLISHER

1633 Broadway, New York, NY 10019

DAW Book Collectors No. 744

First Printing, May 1988

1 2 3 4 5 6 7 8 9

PRINTED IN THE U.S.A.

In the twisting highways and byways of TROUBLED WATERS, you will encounter:

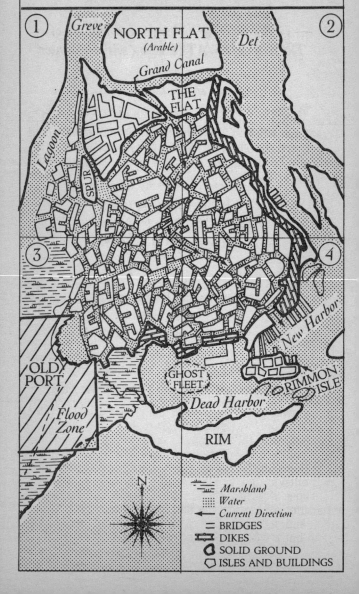

MEROVIN

① Greve NORTH FLAT *(Arable)* Det ②

Grand Canal

THE FLAT

Lagoon

SPUR

③ ④

New Harbor

OLD PORT

GHOST FLEET RIMMON ISLE

Dead Harbor

Flood Zone

RIM

N

≈≈ *Marshland*
⋮⋮⋮ *Water*
← *Current Direction*
= BRIDGES
⌷ DIKES
◖ SOLID GROUND
⬡ ISLES AND BUILDINGS

CHAPTER I

TROUBLED WATERS
by C. J. Cherryh

The winter came with spits of snow this year, not a great many flakes, but a chill all the same, down a cold wind; and that foretold bitter nights when there might actually be small sheets of ice in the still spurs of the canals, deep in cuts where no sun ever came. Wealthy Merovingen-above, its gray wooden towers thrust up into the light and the winds above the bridges, its windows subject to chill, drew velvet drapes and felt the change in the air and lit the oil furnaces. Merovingen-between, the burghers and tradesmen and scholars, stuffed the cracks in the settling middle tier walls and drank smuggled whiskey in tonics against the snuffles. Merovingen-below, the teeming undercity, under the bridge-shadows, on the sunless canalsides, endured the watery chill and the lean season, when very little of the hightown wealth came down the levels to the waterside, when less trade moved on the water and beside it, and less was the rule in everything—less to eat, less to do, less to hope for, except an early spring.

It was the gray season, the dead season, the long aching nights when a barefoot canal-rat put on an extra sweater or two, wore pants one pair over the other, if one was rich enough to have two—you put the holiest to the outside, to save the good as much as you could, unless they were too rotten, and then you put them inside, because they were good for warmth, but outside they would tear like old weed.

Those were the winters Altair Jones had known all her life: all her life she had had just enough between her and the cold, had gone barefoot all her days— who but a lander or a fancy poleboater would go shod

9

on the water, where wet soles could slip on a deck or soaked shoes and wet socks could give you worse than the snuffles? You worked barefoot while the sleet fell, because a poler's shifting feet stayed warm on the wood of the deck, and when you sat still on the rim of your hidey, your pole in rack, yourself hoping for another load to haul up or down the canals, you just tucked your blanket around you, wrapped your feet and your hands in rags, and tucked up and kept pretty warm, all considered, especially if you could find a spot of sun to tie-up in; and the nights, well, you froze a little and got through the winter storms somehow, just keeping warm as you could till morning: on bad nights your teeth chattered and your gut ached from hunger and from shivering, and if the storms came by day the wind would blow your stove out so you had dried fish if you had anything. But being a canaler who had spent every winter of your life on the water, you knew where the still spots were on a windy day and where every spot of sun fell at the best hours, and you lived, till you got too old and some night the cold got too much.

Winters were for dying in, if you were old and poor, and sometimes even if you were rich, when the snuffles went to the coughs and the coughs went deep: no few times each winter a solemn line of boats made its way down-current to the Harbor, to slide a body to its rest, splash, end of one life and, if the Revenantists were right, beginning of another, cycle begun again.

Being a half-hearted Adventist Altair Jones figured otherwise: if you died you were dead, and there might be ghosts, she never claimed not, but she never counted karma except as a tally of favors and grudges owed.

And she never figured on anything but luck, which had been on her side so long she had to worry.

An embarrassing lot of luck, ever since she had taken up with a hightown foreigner, one Thomas Mondragon, that all the world thought was some non-contract bastard Boregy, since Boregy had taken him in patronage; and a half-Falkenaer, since he was fair and blond, a real novelty in dark-skinned, dark-haired Merovingen, and that was like a Falkenaer; and certainly rich, since he lived in the middle tiers in a not-too-shabby isle, and came and went uptown in velvet and fine wool and talked like a hightowner.

But Tom Mondragon came and went in Merovingen-below too, and she had taught him to pole her skip and load cargo and read the weather at least enough to keep him safe from the worst. He was her lover, and he was, so far as she could learn, only hers, which scared her sometimes, he was so fine and so handsome. He asked her to his apartment, they made love in his bed, which was real brass, with white sheets, with quilts and covers against the chill, and damned if she could figure him.

He was not, Lord forgive him, Falkenaer or Boregy, either half or in part. Everybody on the canals knew *who* Thomas Mondragon was: he was Jones' man, and everybody looked after him without him quite knowing it, because he was all right, he had proved that right enough. But only a handful of people in Merovingen knew *what* Thomas Mondragon was, the secret being that he was Nev Hetteker, from up-Det, that he had escaped from the prison up there; and that he had been in that prison because he was Sword of God, and Sword of God was outlawed everywhere. Most specially he had been in that prison because Karl Fon, who was governor of Nev Hettek, was Sword of God too, and Karl Fon wanted to keep that secret. So he sent his friend Tom Mondragon to prison. And Mondragon got away and came south, but the Sword, on the orders of his friend, followed him to shut him up for good.

Nobody wanted trouble like that. So who took Tom Mondragon in? Altair Jones, a canal-rat. And who finally protected him? Anastasi Kalugin, the governor's youngest, pure and holy Revenantist, who had uses for a man with nothing to lose but a canal-rat he happened, Lord knew why, to be lovers with.

And Anastasi damn-'im Kalugin was one who knew; and Anastasi's pet rat ser Vega the banker Boregy was another; and maybe a couple in Boregy House, because the old Boregy had had secret dealings up in Nev Hettek; and folk in Gallandry House knew, because they had had the same. And maybe Anastasi's papa the governor knew: if you ran things you knew a lot of dark stuff that ordinary workaday folk never asked about.

She knew, of course, and so did the two Nev Hetteker boys, whose mamma had been Sword, Raj and that bridge-brat Denny, that Mondragon had taken in, Lord help them—they knew; and so did the Sword agents who had tracked Mondragon here, and who worried her plenty on dark nights—

Damn, politics was crazy. It kept Mondragon rich, but it was crazy and it was dangerous, and sometimes, even out on the canals that were life and breath to her, she added up all the odds against it lasting the way it was and had attacks of pure panic.

She was rich, wool socks, Lord, and all the food she could eat, and when the storms came she could be up to Mondragon's apartment—she was so rich she was outright embarrassed on the canals, and she got careless with her stuff, so damn careless she chucked a whole bundle of candles off her skip onto old Mintaka's, and a bundle of yarn too, when old Min was snoring off a drunk; (and she tried like hell to think of ways to get the Khouri-Liveys to take a couple of blankets, they were poor, their skip had had to have repairs before they headed into winter, and they had a new baby. But they were Revenantist to the deep and the bottom of them: they would not take the karma of a debt on them and on their baby; if they froze, they froze, but they would owe no one in their next lives. And they were canaler, which meant proud, and meant they took care of themselves and took charity from nobody, damn anyone who asked.)

Sometimes she thought that having money was the heart of all her unease.

Sometimes, lying in bed at night and looking at Mondragon sleeping by her by lamplight, so fine and so fair and so damn secretive about his business and his troubles—she knew for certain why she took to adding things up over and over again, and why she worried, because nothing like this could be and nothing like him could last, not in the dark of Merovingen-below, where she lived. He had come with the spring and lasted through the summer and the fall, and now was winter, when changes came: in her heart of hearts she knew that nothing that fine ever stayed.

Only the wind and the current and the seasons, and the rule of them was change.

She was Retribution's daughter, Retribution Jones, who had made a name for herself on the canals before fever got her, and before Altair had the skip to herself. Altair pictured Retribution sitting on the blunt bow of the skip, just so, as they went under bridge shadow, Retribution looking a lot like herself, with the same river-runner's cap, a little less disreputable in those years, shoved back on black hair; a woman with the same rangy build, baggy sweater, black breeches, bare shins and bare feet—her mama sat there on an empty whiskey barrel there by the bow, and shoved her cap back and shook her head.

The new paint job on the skip, mama would approve.

The bullet holes that made it necessary, mama would understand that too. Mama had run the dark ways all her life.

But Retribution Jones, in the dying sunlight on the Grand Canal, on gray choppy water with the skip heaving about and the wind making the poling hard, fixed her daughter with an imaginary dark eye and said: *Well, ye done it, ain't ye?*

Yey, mama, I done all right these months, too.

Where ye spending tonight, huh, Altair?

Ain't none o' your business, mama. Shove of the pole. A blast of wind came cruel and hard against her side, chilling right through her clothes.

Ain't none o' my business, yey, ain't none o' my business. Ye got yourself so fancy ye c'n paint the old skip black and hire out for a poleboat. To Boregy, like.

Shut up, mama.

Retribution's eyes were lazy and her mouth smiled, just ever so little, and she said: *Altair, ye're a fool, but he's damn pretty. Damn if he ain't.*

She grinned, and shoved hard with the pole, sending the skip gliding across the deep part of the Grand's bottom, there by Fishmarket Bridge.

Nice t' have ye back, mama. Damn if I ain't missed ye.

Retribution shoved the cap back, the same as she wore, and scratched her head.

I ain't been nowhere. Ye just ain't been listening. But then, a man'll do that, won't 'e? Been talkin' t' him, ain't got no time for your mama anymore.

You got advice, mama? Or you just here to keep company?

Hey, I give you my advice, Altair. I told ye: ye keep t' yourself and ye keep the boat under your own hand. And ye don't go makin' a fool o' yourself after any damn man, ain't worth the risk.

Ye're jealous, mama. Ye're outright jealous.

Ye're an ingrate brat. Mind your tongue.

The skip danced around the Foundry corner. "Ware, hey," Jones sang out, loud and clear, and passed a slower skip, cargo laden. The corner cut the wind off. It felt like warmth by contrast.

See that boat? Retribution asked. *That's that damn Sally Pick, there, loaded up heavy as she can push. Ye carrying anything?*

I carry plenty, mama.

Hell if ye do. Ye take this man's money. Ain't no way t' be, Altair. Ye mark me, ye earn your way in this world. There ain't no karma, but there's sure as hell debt, and I always kept ye clear of it. I didn't ask t' get a kid. But I done it right, I give ye ever'thing free and clear. I taught ye good sense, and ye got no business takin' nothing from no damn man, Altair. I didn't bring ye up that way. Hear?

I hear ye, mama.

I hear.

Whole town's crazy, mama. Fire in the sky, one night out over harbor, some damn great racket, and drunks going up and down after, raving that the sharrh is coming down in fire and thunder—

The sharrh being the ones who had claimed the whole damn world back from human folk, and come down on the Ancestors with fire and scoured the whole world of tech and machines, till finally they went away again, no one knew where.

That was what Adventists remembered: that they had had the stars and lost them, and some day human ships would come back victorious and take them all to

14

freedom from the hell that was Merovin; or something spiritual was going to come: Adventists argued about that, and humans on Merovin were going to rise up and start the Retribution themselves, after which the humans who had given them up for hopeless would come back and reclaim them.

That, Adventists said, was the meaning of the Angel who held his sword half-drawn on Hanging Bridge: that the closer that day got, that sword would move out of its sheath. But Revenantists said that the Angel's waiting was for the perfection of humankind on Merovin, even the Nev Hettekers, and *some* Revenantists said that good folk got reborn off Merovin, off among the stars; and others said they just got born richer, on Merovin, because nobody could leave until the Angel rose, until the Angel drew his sword and the Ghost Fleet came dripping and mossy from the bottom of Dead Harbor and launched itself into the sky, taking the righteous to the stars.

Hell if, when that fire had cut loose, people hadn't run to the Angel to see if it was still there, and if that sword was still sheathed. And finding it was, well, the priests were still arguing; people were scared, but canaler folk were saying now it was an explosion of some kind, that folk out to the harbor and on Rimmon Isle had smelled the burning, and that if it was sharrh they were damned odd sharrh.

Now people were talking about sharrists—who were another kind of religion, who talked about a testing, that the alien sharrh were good, fine folk who knew all the wisdom of the universe, and that as soon as human beings got enough like the sharrh, the sharrh were going to come back and welcome them like brothers.

Like hell, mama said, raking her hair back and setting her cap square.

Like hell, f' sure, mama, but ain't never been no shortage of fools in this world.

Revenantist Merovingen tolerated a lot of religions, solid, sensible Adventists, New Worlders like the Falkenaers, even the Janes (as long as they stayed quiet). Sharrists, now, sharrists were another matter: sharrists were damnfools and crazies, and if they were playing with fire anywhere near wooden Merovingen,

15

there was the gallows on Hanging Bridge for them and the whole of Merovingen above and below ready to supply the rope.

All of which meant nervous times, times in which odd meant dangerous and everybody was looking for strangers to lynch, while the blacklegs were fingering their sticks and looking for heads to break, and the gullible were flocking to the priests to pay their silverbit and be told how the world was safe for them to go on being the fools they were.

I seen fools all my life, Retribution said, fading now, in a stray bit of sun. *Ye can't change the world, Altair. Just watch out for it, that's all, and don't owe nobody.*

Mondragon ain't askin' nothin', mama. He ain't never. He ain't never done the things you say, I mean, sure, he worries, keep off the water, he says, wants me to come up to his fancy apartment and live. Ha. An' I tol' 'im no, and he took 'er at that, just my sayin' so. See? Ye just tell 'im an' he ain't pushin'.

Retribution stood up and flickered with passing bridge-shadow, a frown on her face. *Listen to ye. I talked about fools. Ye start talkin' about Mondragon. Who's the fool on this boat? Ain't me, daughter. —Ye keep that gun loaded?*

Damn sure, mama. Right back there in the drop-box.

I kept to smuggling, Retribution said. *Ain't never mixed myself in politics. Whiskey don't talk and ye know what a barrel's worth. Ye be careful, Altair. Ye be damn careful. Ye don't trust Old Det, he's mean and he's quick and he'll drink ye down for nothin', but ye know his ways and his currents. I ain't so sure about the waters ye been runnin' lately. I ain't so sure at all.*

Mama left. She always did when she had the last word, just faded right out in the sunlight, and Jones shook her head and thought—because mama nagged her—that maybe she ought to take the chance, Moghi was talking about hiring a man for the night runs—

I dunno, Jones, Moghi had said. *I used t' say . . . Jones can handle it, ain't no need to hire anybody else, Jones is always there. But I suppose that's the way of it, some feller comes along and a little money comes along an' maybe you ain't so hungry anymore.*

So what am I goin' t' do, huh? My barrels don't wait on no whim, Jones.

See? Retribution's voice echoed in her skull. *Told ye.*

Shut up, *mama.*

But it was true all the same.

Changes happened. Not all of them were what she wanted.

And she had no idea in the world how to hang onto Mondragon and onto the Trade at the same time. That was what worried her. It was like she was in two pieces. It was like she was riding two currents at once, and she couldn't see beyond a few weeks anymore.

CHAPTER II

A TANGLED WEB WE WEAVE
by Mercedes Lackey

Lies. That's what his whole life had been, lately. Lies and evasions and dirty little twistings of what scraps of truth he *had* told—

Raj's gut ached like someone had punched him, hard. It had ached like that for the last couple of weeks. His throat was so choked most of the time he could hardly swallow. And his heart—if it wasn't broken, it was doing a damned good imitation of *being* broken.

Rigel Takahashi—who called himself Raj Tai these days, and had good reasons not to own to the Nev Hettek merchant clan he'd been born into, reasons that involved the Sword of God and long-buried secrets—felt like he surely must be one of the most pitiable sixteen-year-olds in all of Merovingen. He was sad enough looking that Denny's friend Rif had commented on it; she'd told him to his face that he was drooping like an unwatered plant, and had wanted to know the reason. Which he hadn't dared tell her; he hadn't dared tell anyone.

Although he really didn't intend or want to be that way, his disposition wavered between sullen and scared-shitless. He spent most of his time moping around like a moon-sick idiot. His brother Denny had given up on him in disgust; Altair Jones and Tom Mondragon only knew he was pining over a girl and being unusually peculiar about it.

Tom was being more-than-patient, but condescending, and Raj was overly sensitive to that sort of thing just now. Altair, having failed to jolly him out of it, had taken to snapping at him, frequently. They repeated the same scene at least twice a day. It usually started with him glooming about in her path, and her stumbling around him, until she finally lost her temper—

Then she'd explode, canaler's cap shoved back on short dark hair, strong hands on hips, dark eyes narrowed with annoyed frustration—

Dammit Raj, can't you get the hell outa my way?

Even the memory made him wince.

She snapped, he sulked, they both got resentful, and Tom sighed.

The problem was, they didn't know the *half* of what he'd gotten into.

Raj, who was just "home" from work at Gallandry's, where Mondragon had gotten him a clerking job, huddled in a soft, plush-covered chair in Mondragon's living-room. He'd lit one lamp, right side of the sofa tonight—that was to tell Jones all was well—but had left the rest of the room in gray gloom. He was curled around the knot of anguish that seemed to have settled into his gut for good. Every time he looked up, the very room seemed to breathe reproach at him.

There was frost on the window—bitter cold it was out there. Here he was, warm and dry and eating good—he *could* have been out in the swamp, freezing his butt off, but he wasn't, thanks to Tom Mondragon. He could have been shivering in Denny's airshaft, or in their little, barren apartment on Fife—hell, he could have been *dead*, but he wasn't, again thanks to Mondragon.

Tom had taken him and Denny under his protection, who had damned little to spare for *himself*—had taken them in, and then taken them into his own home. He'd been feeding them and housing them, and keeping them safe because the town was in turmoil and that was the only way he could be certain they *were* safe. And now Raj had gone and compromised the whole damned setup *and* compromised Tom himself.

Jones was right. He *was* an ingrate.

He was more miserable than he'd ever been in his life; more miserable than the five years he'd hidden out in the swamp, because that had only been physical misery—more miserable than when his mother had been killed, because that was a clean-cut loss. This—

19

this tangle of lies and half-truths he'd woven into a trap binding him *and* Mondragon—this mess had him so turned inside-out it was a wonder he even remembered what day it was.

Oh, Marina— he thought mournfully, —*if only I'd never seen you.*

It had seemed so innocent, sending that love-poem to Marina Kamat; she wouldn't know who had sent it, so what harm could possibly come of it? But Marina had *assumed* it had come from Mondragon, because *she* was in love with Tom. *Not* surprising, that; Tom Mondragon was a *man,* not a lovesick boy. Thomas Mondragon was urbane and sophisticated, and to top it off, tall, golden-haired (in a city full of short, dark folk) and handsome as the Angel on Hanging Bridge. No girl would think twice about Raj with Tom in the same city. Raj didn't *blame* Marina—and truth to tell, he really hadn't expected her to respond to the poems so strongly.

But she had; and come to her own conclusions about them. She'd caught Raj delivering a second love-poem, and she'd got him so twisted around with the way she'd acted toward him that all he could think of was that she'd guessed about his own passion and she was being hightowner and coy. He'd been so dazed that he hadn't left her until long after dark—

Tom (and him still sick) and Altair and Denny had all been in a *fine* case over him then, worrying he'd been caught by the Sword or Tatiana's blacklegs or Anastasi's bullyboys, caught and maybe been tortured or killed.

And he was so full of Marina and how she'd guessed at the identity of the author of the poems and sought him out that all he could feel was resentment that they were *hovering* over him so much.

Only after he'd read her note, then reread it and reread it—then he'd begun to realize that she'd guessed wrong. She'd figured the author for Tom, and himself for his errand-boy. And she'd set him such a tempting little trap too—offered to have Kamat sponsor and fund him into the College, and make his dream of becoming a doctor come true, so he could be conveniently close to deliver more such messages. So tempting; he could at least see and talk to her, any time he wanted—he could have his other dream—all he needed to do was to keep up the lie, to keep writing those poems and pretending Tom was sending them. That was all. Just as simple as Original Sin, and just as seductive.

And now he was afraid to tell Tom, because he'd been a fool, and worse, got them tangled up with a romantical hightown *Family* girl, one with power and connections. He was afraid to tell Jones because— because she was Jones; she was capable and clever, and she'd laugh him into a little puddle of mortification and *then* she'd kill him, if Tom didn't beat her to it. And he *couldn't* tell Denny. Denny was put out enough over the notion of his brother taking a sudden interest in girls—"going stupid on him" was what Denny had said.

Hell, he'd gone stupid all right. So stupid he couldn't see his way straight anymore. And that was dangerous for him, for all of them, with the town in a dither over Papa Kalugin's damn census. And as if that weren't enough trouble, most of the towners were scared to death of the fireworks *somebody* had set off over Dead Harbor—fireworks that the low-tech Revenantist majority of Merovingen thought were a sharrh visitation at worst, and a sharrist plot at best.

That was Sword work, sure as death and taxes; and Tom was ex-Sword and knew too damned many Sword secrets. For that matter, so did Raj. The Sword was moving again. That was bad. There were certain bullyboys who might or might not be blacklegs that knew Raj's face, and Denny's. That was worse. Complications were *not* what they needed right now.

But complications were what he'd gotten into, and here he was not able to tell the truth, because the truth hurt so damn much, and he couldn't force it past the lump in his throat and the ache in his gut.

But he *had* to tell somebody; had to get some good advice before what was already worse got into disastrous, he could reason out that much. Somebody older, but not too much older; somebody with experience with Hightowners. Somebody who knew how Girls thought, romantical Hightowners in particular.

And somehow a face swam into his mind, surrounded with a faint shimmer of hope, almost like a halo.

Justice—Justice might help him think straight again. Justice Lee—he was a student; he was, Lord, smarter than Raj was by a long shot, and a little older, more experienced. He dealt with hightown Family all the time in the form of his fellow students. And he was old enough to know how to handle Girls. Maybe even how to handle *angry* Girls. He was Adventist—converted, but still Adventist at the core. He and Raj had struck a kindred note from each other from the first words they'd exchanged; *he'd* be willing to give advice.

Raj made up his mind to go find Justice right then and there, before he got faint-hearted again. Justice *should* be findable at Hilda's. Best bring a sweetener, though. He'd asked Justice to do more than was fair the last time he'd seen him. Lord and Ancestors—a lot more than fair.

Raj shuddered, remembering that night; it had been nearly as bad as the night he'd run from Mama's murderers. Justice had hidden him from killers; then taken some *very* dangerous papers back here to Tom when Raj couldn't get them to Boregy. Raj wondered if Justice had really known, *really*, down deep, how much danger he'd put himself in by doing that.

He jumped up out of the chair and padded across the soft carpet to the bottom of the stairway—listening carefully at the foot of the stair for the faint sounds of Mondragon dozing in his bedroom above. Tom had been sleeping a lot the past couple of weeks, which wasn't surprising given that the Crud had almost killed him. Just now Boregy and Kalugin seemed to be giving him a chance to rest and recover; and Tom, being no fool, was taking it.

Don't want their pet ex-Sword croaking on them while he's still useful, Raj thought bitterly.

Poor Tom; damn near everyone's hand against him—or would be, if they knew what he was—and now one of the kids he'd taken in had gone and messed up his life even more, and he didn't even *guess* the danger that kid had put him in. Raj felt like a total traitor.

Denny was in the spare bedroom downstairs, sprawled

on his back, half-draped across the foot of the bed and upside-down, trying to puzzle his way through one of Mondragon's books, and making heavy work of it. This one had pictures, though, which was probably what was keeping Denny's attention.

He writhed around at Raj's soft footfall.

"Den—I gotta go out; an hour, maybe. I'll be back by dark, okay?"

"Why?" Denny's dark face looked sullen; rebellious. Not only was he mad about Raj getting mixed up with girls, but Raj had had it out with him over obeying Tom and treating him with respect. Denny'd been smart-mouthed, and Raj had finally backed the kid up against the wall and threatened honest-to-God serious mayhem if Denny didn't shape up. Denny was still smoldering with resentment, and Raj *still* wasn't sure the lecture had taken.

"I gotta see Justice. I need to take some of May's Crud-weeds to him; I promised him some and I never brought them. And after what he's done for both of us—" Raj let the sentence dangle.

Denny's expression cleared; he nodded, and his brown eyes got friendly again, because it wasn't a girl that was taking Raj out, and it wasn't one of Mondragon's errands. "Yey. Reckon he c'n make somethin' off 'em?"

"Probably, what with half the College sniffling. He isn't much better off than we are, you know? He deserves a break."

"Just you best *be* back by dark," Denny admonished, shaking a tangle of brown hair out of his eyes only to have it fall back in again. "Or Jones'll have the skin off ye."

Talk about pot calling kettle! Raj bit back a retort. He dug a dozen packets of herbs out from under the bed, noting wryly that Denny was far more respectful of Jones than of Mondragon, even yet, after all Raj had told him. One of these days Denny was going to push Tom too far, and his awakening would be abrupt and rude. And probably involving any number of bruises.

"I'll be back," he promised, shoving the packets into his pack, huddling on his coat and shrugging the strap over his shoulder. "And probably before Jones is."

He slipped into the dark hallway, walking quietly out of habit, and eased the door open and shut so as not to wake Tom. The last rays of the evening sun were not quite able to penetrate the clouds, and Merovingen of the Thousand Bridges looked bleak, shabby, and ill-used. There was snow coming; Raj could smell it in the air, and shivered inside his two sweaters and canvas coat. The grayed-out gloomy bleakness suited Raj down to his toenails, and there was just dark enough that if he kept his head down and muffled in his scarf if was unlikely he'd be recognized. Foot traffic was light; what with the bitter wind blowing, anybody with cash was hiring pole boats even this early in the evening. That suited him too.

He'd almost made it down the water-stairs when somebody called his name. Recognizing the voice, he swore to himself, but stopped on the steps above the landing. Poling to his night-tie was Del Suleiman—clinging to Del's halfdeck was a kid.

Raj sighed and padded down the last three stairs to wait for Del to toss him a cold, stiff line.

" 'Lo, Del," he greeted the canaler, once he'd gotten the skip tied. "Got another one for me?"

Del nodded, face a comical mixture of relief and reluctance. "Papa sez 'er ear hurts—she's been cryin' since yesterday an' 'e can't get 'er t' stop. 'Er name's Kera."

No last name. Not that Raj was surprised. He rather much doubted that Del was even telling the parents exactly *who* he was taking their sick kids to. Bad enough to owe karma—to owe it to one of Altair Jones' pet bridge-boys—who were probably Adventist and were definitely going to come to no good end—would have shocked them senseless.

The ragged little girl huddled on Del's halfdeck was still crying; the kind of monotonous half-exhausted sobbing that tore what was left of Raj's heart right out of his chest. He eased down onto the bucking skip in the over-cautious fashion of one not very used to being on a small boat, then slid along the worn boards and crouched down beside her so that his face was even with hers.

"C'mere, baby—" he held out one hand coaxingly. "It's okay, Kera. I'm gonna help you—"

She stopped crying, stared at him for a minute, then sidled over to him, and didn't resist when he gathered her into his arms, trying to warm that thin little body with his own.

He murmured nonsense at her while he felt gently along the line of her jaw, and checked for fever. Gratitude and relief washed over him when he found neither a swollen gland nor a temperature elevated beyond what you could expect in a kid who'd been crying in pain for a day or more. With every kid brought to him, he expected to find one too sick for his knowledge or experience to help. Then what would he do?

Ah, he knew what he'd do. Tell Del the kid needed real help—and if the parents couldn't afford it, tell him about Rif and her Janist doctor. And let the parents decide whether it was worth the risk of having Janist strings attached to their kid's karma.

Or maybe kidnap the kid and take it there himself, and take the damned karma on his own life—figuring that was the way such things worked.

This one—like all the others so far, thank God— was an easy one. He used a few drops of Del's cooking oil poured into a spoon, and heated it to just-bearable over Del's candle, shielded carefully from the wind by both of them. Poured into Kera's ear, the warm oil made the hurt go away so quickly it must have seemed like magic to the child. A bit of clean lint stuffed in the ear to keep the oil in and the wind out completed the "cure."

He could see it in her face—the sheer wonder of the moment when the pain went away. Looking at him like *he* was the Angel. He blushed, and his heart melted a little more.

"Now—" he said softly (and mock-sternly), "—you have to promise me something. When the wind blows and it's cold, you keep your scarf tied around your ears, good and tight, you hear? Otherwise your ear'll start t' hurt again."

The tiny girl gazed at him from eyes so big they seemed to take up half of her tear-streaked face. "Don't got no scarf," she protested.

He sighed again, and reached under his coat collar to pull yet another of Denny's "souvenirs" off his own neck. That was the fourth one so far—two gone for bandages and one as a sling. Denny must surely think he was *eating* the damned things. It was a good thing they weren't the silk ones Denny liked to sport; the kid would strangle him in his sleep for giving them away.

He tied the scarf under her chin, making sure both ears were covered. "*Now* you do. Promise?"

She nodded, then unexpectedly threw her arms around his neck and hugged and kissed him, messily. He hugged her back, and she squirmed out of his grasp to go crouch at Del's feet. He knew he was still blushing a little, but was feeling better than he had all day, kind of warm inside. She was a little sweetie—a lot nicer than the last one, who'd kicked him. He got gingerly to his knees, and edged carefully back from the pitching boat onto solid land, tucking his chilled hands under his arms as soon as he got there.

Del cleared his throat, and Raj knew what was coming next.

"Dammit, Del, I've said I won't take anything about a million times—and I damn sure won't take anything this time, either! You folks haven't any more to spare than I do, and I haven't done a damn thing this kid's Papa couldn't have done if he knew how!"

"But 'e didn't, did 'e—"

"So you tell him, and he will." Raj set his chin stubbornly. "And don't you go bleating "karma" at me, either. I don't believe in karma. I refuse to believe God goes around toting up marks against people's souls like some cosmic accountant."

"That's as may be—" Del replied, just as stubbornly, "—but this baby's Papa *does* believe."

"Oh, Hell—" Raj sighed, pulled the rope loose, and stood up, holding it in both hands, braced against the tug of the sluggish current and the icy wind on the skip. Karma. Hell. The very idea revolted him, and he damn sure didn't understand the way it was supposed to work. But he had to have some way to get Del off his back, some way to make these people figure everything was evened up. If he couldn't think of something, Del would stop bringing the kids to him—Lord, then he'd lie awake *all* night between worrying about Marina and worrying about the sick kids—

Think, dammit.

Finally— "All right, I tell you what. If you people are so all-fired worried about karma, here's what you do. When there's a pennybit to spare, have the people I've helped put it in some kind of common pot against the day when I *can't* help one of these kids, and they need a *real* doctor. I s'pose you might as well hold the pot, Del, since you're always the one bringing 'em here. If they do that, I figure we're clear. Suits?" That should solve two problems—theirs, and his.

Del's face still looked stormy, but he must have reckoned that was the only concession he was going to get out of Raj. "Yey," he agreed, after a long moment of stubborn silence.

He signaled to Raj to toss back the tie, and poled back out into the current.

Raj headed back along the walkway, resuming his interrupted journey. His leather-soled socks made no sound on the damp wood as he kept to a warming trot; no bare feet in *this* weather, not for him or Denny; Mondragon had just about had a cat when he caught them without foot-coverings. Another undeserved kindness.

Sounds were few above the wind; the occasional murmur of voices from above, slap of waves on boat and building, the ever-present creaking of wood, canalers calling out to each other down on the water. Cold, God it was cold. *Weather for sickness, that's for certain; in the swamp, down on the canals, weather for dying, too.*

Funny, this business with Del Suleiman; it had started when he'd caught Tommy with a cut hand going septic, and forced him to let Raj clean it out. Then Tommy had brought him a kid with a bad case of the Crud. Then Del had gotten into the act. Always kids, though, never adults. Six, maybe eight of them so far.

Raj couldn't resist a sick kid—not even when they kicked or bit him.

Soft heart to match my soft head.

No matter. Raj knew damned well he could no more see a kid in pain and walk on without doing something about it then he could stop breathing.

Well, one thing, no matter how badly he'd messed things up with Tom, there were a half-dozen canaler babies he'd made a bit healthier.

He made Kass in good time; he'd have at least an hour with Justice before he had to head back. He was glad to get there; the overcast had given birth to flurries, and his nose felt numb.

If Justice was there—

Hilda's tavern was the likeliest spot to find him; Raj poked his head into the door and got hit in the face with the light and the noise. It was almost as bad as a physical blow after the chill gray of canalside. It took him a moment to adjust to it.

But when he finally did, he breathed a prayer of thanks to the Angel and St. Murfy—for at a table in the rear, book propped up in front of him and huge gold cat spread out like a rug on his lap, was a tall, thin, dark-haired young man wearing a College sash.

"—so that's the whole mess," Raj concluded miserably.

He slumped in his hard wooden chair, staring at his own clenched hands, surrounded by the clutter of artwork, books, and other paraphernalia of an art student's life that filled Justice Lee's tiny room. The lanky student across from him lounged on his unmade bed, chewing his lip thoughtfully. Raj had laid out the whole story—saving only Mondragon's identity, and what he was involved with. Justice already knew that Mondragon was a man with enemies—a *lot* of enemies. That was enough for him to add into his calculations, without him knowing enough for the information to be a danger to him.

At least Justice hadn't laughed at him.

"You've got yourself a problem, all right," Justice said, finally, putting his hands behind his head and staring at the ceiling. "A bad one. The Kamats are rising in influence; rising fast, from what I hear. They're moving into the Rimmon Isle circles. From the little I know, Marina Kamat would be a very bad enemy for your friend to have. And if you go through with this charade, she'll find out eventually; when she does, she'll want *his* hide as much as yours."

"I figured," Raj replied dismally.

"You weren't planning on trying to carry it off, were you?"

"For about five minutes, maybe," Raj admitted. "After that—dammit, Justice, it isn't *right,* that's all I can say. It isn't fair, even if I *could* make it work."

Justice smiled; a kindly smile. Like maybe he gave Raj a couple of marks for honesty. "How much of *your* hide are you willing to part with?"

The lump rose in Raj's throat, nearly choking off his words. "All of it," he said at last. "She's gonna hate me forever, no matter what happens. If there's a way to keep T—my friend out of it, I'll take it, and take my lumps."

"You got some place you could go to get out of sight for a couple of weeks? Long enough to let things cool down?"

Raj thought, as best he could. Not Mondragon's place, where they'd been staying. Not the apartment on Fife that he and Denny shared; that would be the first place a searcher would look. Rat and Rif?

They'd take him in—no doubt of it. But Rif was a Janist agent *and* a thief on top of that—Denny'd confirmed that, all of it. The two singers had been Denny's protectors and mentors in his early days on his own, Rat more than Rif, but he knew most of what there was to know about both of them. Rif had been "courting" Raj ever since she'd found out he wanted to be a doctor, dangling a secret Jane-run doctor school in front of him, like turbis-worms in front of a mud-pup. He was mightily afraid that his resolution not to get involved with any more fanatics would crumble under the slightest pressure at this point. It would be such a logical move; cut ties to Tom, get under the protection of somebody else, drop out of sight—and get his dream into the bargain. So easy—no, he wouldn't even think about it. "Easy" usually had strings at-

tached that wouldn't show up until later. And what if
the Janes used him to get at Tom or Denny—or Jones
and her canalers?

The swamp?

He gave that one a second thought, and then a
third. Maybe not such a bad notion. He could move
his hidey into old Ralf's territory, it would be open with
Ralf dead under Raj's knife. There was a fair amount
of food-weeds there, and some good fishing spots. It
was cold, sure; but he could take blankets and medicine out with him, he could tough it out for two weeks
or so. Maybe getting back to the basics of surviving
would clear his head out.

"I think maybe I got a place," he answered Justice
slowly. "Why?"

"I think if I were you, this is what I'd do—and first
thing is, you aren't going to *tell* anybody anything;
you're going to *write* to them—"

It was almost dawn; Denny was so dead asleep he
didn't even stir when Raj slipped out of bed. Raj
hadn't slept more than a few minutes all night, lying
there in the bed with every muscle so tight with nerves
it was ready to cramp. He dressed quickly in the dark,
putting on every bit of clothing he had here; not
daring to light a lamp lest he wake Denny. His pack
was back at Fife, already made up with the clothing
he'd left there and the blankets from his bed. There
were other things there, too; things he'd bought—a
spare knife, a firestarter, fishhooks and line and lures.
He'd been afraid to bring the pack here, or pack up
any of the clothes he kept here, lest somebody catch
him at it and try to stop him.

The swamp had been a real good notion, except that
he hadn't any money to buy the gear he needed to
survive. In the end he'd had to get back to their
apartment on Fife and retrieve his precious books and
sell them. He'd spent all the money he had saved on
trade-goods to swap with old May for the medicine to
keep Tom alive, and the books were all he had left in
the way of portable wealth. It had damn near broken
his heart all over again to part with them. But this was
his only choice; he couldn't live for weeks out there

without supplies and cold-weather gear, not in winter, and not when he knew Raver and May would have stripped his hidey of everything useful once they were certain he wasn't likely to be coming back to the swamp.

And maybe he'd have to stay out there for longer than a couple of weeks. The more he'd thought about it last night, the more logical *that* seemed. He'd just about talked himself into staying out there—unless his plan worked; the *other* plan he'd had, lying in the dark last night—

Now he crept to the bathroom, one careful, hushed step at a time. He had to get into Mondragon's medicine-chest for the last of what he needed.

He hated to steal, but there wasn't any blueangel left at any price down canalside, even if he'd had the money for it, and Mondragon had enough to cure a dozen fevers—or kill four men. Raj was glad there was a night-lamp left burning in here, else he'd probably have broken something and roused the whole house. The blueangel was right out in front, all the papers of it in a neat little row on the first shelf. Raj took about half of it; neither Mondragon nor Jones was likely to need it, and Raj might well before the winter was over. Blueangel was the only chance you had if you caught Hakim's fever. He stuffed the packets in his pocket, and stole out.

Now he crept quietly into the kitchen; ran his hands along the shelf until he found old bread and a bit of cheese by feel, then found the round, hard bulk of the tea-canister the same way. First thing Mondragon did when he wandered downstairs in the morning was to make tea, so that was where Raj's letter to him would go.

Dear Tom; I am a Bigger Fool than you ever thought I was. I've gone and got Both of us in Trouble, it began, and went on from there. It had been torture to write, and Raj wasn't entirely clear on what he'd put down. He'd fought down the ache in his gut and the swelling in his throat all through writing it, so it wasn't exactly a miracle of coherency. But it did lay out the whole sordid story, and finished by telling Tom not to go looking for him. He rather doubted Tom would want to waste time looking for such a fool as he was, but—better assure him that Raj was going to be hidden where nobody was likely to be able to find him.

Jones' letter was a lot shorter by about three pages; that was going to her mail-drop at Moghi's.

He wasn't going to leave a letter for Denny—Denny wouldn't have been able to read it. Although it caused him a physical pain as sharp as Ralf's knife to do so, he left a copy of Marina's letter folded up inside Tom's in the tea-canister, so Tom would be able to see for himself how Marina had woven a fantasy around him.

His throat and stomach were hurting again, but he forced the bread and cheese down. He wouldn't be getting any more of *that* in the swamp. He didn't dare take any food with him—no swampy stored food on his raft. To do so was to invite a *very* unpleasant death— being nibbled to death by a feeding-frenzy of skits. Anything he ate—not that food was real attractive at the moment—he'd have to catch or find *when* he wanted to eat.

He'd oiled the hinges of the door last night; now he eased down the hallway, and slipped all of the locks and bolts as carefully as he could. He froze half a dozen times, agonizing over the slightest sound, and finally inched the door open just enough so he could slip through. The sharp-edged cold hit him hard, waking him completely. He closed the door and relocked as much as was possible from outside, then went softly down the water-stairs and sneaked past old Min and Del and Jones' empty skip, all tied up at the bottom. The skips stayed silent, their occupants tucked up in all the blankets they owned, down in their hideys. Except for Jones, who was tucked up with Tom—

His stomach lurched. *Oh, Marina!*

Now came the hardest part of all—

He knew Marina would never be up this early; hightowners kept hours like Tom's. He trotted down the wet walkways, watching carefully for patches of ice, as the sun began turning the edge of the sky a bloody red. No fog this morning, but it was as cold as Kalugin's heart, and there might well be more snow before the day was over. He could see ice-rims along all the canals, and thin sheets of ice over the still spots, shiny as a hightowner's mirror. There were a few hearty souls about, even this early; canalers, folks on their way to work or coming home from it. The cold kept the stink down; the sharp breeze smelled mostly of smoke and wool. Once he thought he saw Rif's raven head with her bold red scarf tied about her hair to confine it. He quickly chose another way, then. Rif was damnably persuasive when she wanted to be. And he didn't want to be talked out of the only honorable course he had left.

Kamat's doorkeeper wasn't even awake—thank the Angel. Raj managed to slip his sealed letter to Marina through the mail-slot in the door. Five pages long, it was, and ended with a poem so she'd *believe* it was really him who had written the others.

Now she'd hate him forever. It couldn't be helped. It wasn't in agreement with Takahashi Honor that he leave Tom entangled in a lie, nor that he let Marina continue to believe that same lie.

So why didn't he feel better?

Now Fife, for his pack, then Moghi's.

Lying staring into the dark, he'd made some hard decisions last night. Given all the trouble he'd caused Tom, the best thing he could do for Mondragon was to cut his ties with the man. All of them, including the job with the Gallandrys, so not even *they* could hold that over his head.

He sniffled in the cold, his eyes burning and watering—surely from the early-morning smoke and smog—and rubbed his eyes and nose across his sleeve.

Smoke. Smog. Sure. Be honest with yourself, Rigel Takahashi, even if you've lied to everyone else.

This was hurting more than he'd ever thought it would. For a little while he'd had a family. A weird family, but a family all the same. It hurt to cut loose.

And he *had* to cut loose; and do it before he managed to do something that couldn't be gotten out of.

Denny could still be useful to Tom, and if Mondragon ever needed anything Raj could supply, he could send it surreptitiously through Denny. Honor could still be satisfied that way.

But he needed some way—if he ever was able to poke his nose back into town—to keep himself housed and fed. And maybe, maybe, save enough to sneak into the College on a changed name. If he could find something to make enough money. If Justice could find him a patron.

Well, medicinal weeds weren't all that grew in the swamp. And the way Raj had it figured, if somebody was stupid enough to want to rot mind and body with recreational pharmaceuticals, *he* might as well get the benefit of the money being thrown away. He only knew of one person, though, who might know where he could safely dispose of dangerous things like get-you-high weed. Moghi. Who scared the hell out of him.

Moghi's was just open; Raj went up to the front porch and through the door, open and above-board. He walked, barefoot (he'd stowed his socks in his pack), silent, and oh-so-carefully, across the wooden expanse of floor. He gave over Jones' sealed letter, then asked of the man behind the bar (Jep, that was—he remembered the name from a night in Moghi's shed that seemed like years ago), in a very soft and *very* respectful voice, if m'ser Moghi might be willing to talk with him on business. Jep left the bar in the care of one of the other helpers and vanished briefly. As it happened, m'ser Moghi evidently hadn't yet gone to bed—and was apparently willing to see the frequent bearer of so much of Mondragon's coin. Jep returned and directed Raj with a silent jerk of his thumb. The office.

The door to the office was beside the bar. Facing Moghi scared the liver out of him; to sit quietly at Moghi's invitation all alone in that cluttered cubbyhole while the dim gray light smudged the dirty window-panes, and stammer out his offer took all the little courage he had left. Moghi sat behind his desk, tall, balding—and *big,* most of it not fat—and looked at him hard and appraisingly, melting away the last of his bravery.

"You wanta sell drugs, huh?" he asked Raj bluntly. "Why?"

Raj could hardly think under that cold, cold stare. He stammered something about needing a lot of money, and didn't elaborate.

"What?"

"T-t-trinsedge, m-m-mostly," Raj stuttered; it was a fairly innocuous weed, about the same strength as whiskey. "A l-l-little jemgrass. W-w-wiregrass. D-d-deathangel, if I c-c-can catch them." None of those were really *bad* drugs, except for the deathangel—and God knew anybody hankering for that knew what he was getting into.

"That won't get you much in a hurry." Moghi continued to stare at him, jaw clamping shut on each word, eyes murky.

"Don't n-n-need it in a hurry. Just n-n-need to put it t-t-together."

"Huh." The way the big man kept staring at him, Raj imagined he could see all the way through him. He wondered what Moghi was thinking; the man's opaque eyes didn't reveal even a hint of his thoughts.

"Well, I don't deal."

"Oh." Raj's plan for independence—and the College—collapsed. "I'm s-s-sorry to have b-b-bothered you, m'ser. I g-g-guess it wasn't too good a n-n-notion."

He rose, awkwardly, and started for the door.

"Boy—"

Raj turned, a thread of fear running down his spine. Moghi wasn't anybody to trifle with. He wondered if he'd passed the invisible bounds beyond which Moghi allowed no one he dealt with to trespass. Moghi had a way of dealing with trouble, or potential trouble. It ended in the canal, with a rock tied to one ankle. Splash, gone. He wondered if he looked as deathly white as he felt.

"Don't you go making that offer anywhere else—"

Raj gulped. He wan't quite sure what the look on Moghi's face meant, but he thought he'd better answer the truth. Or part of it.

"I w-w-wasn't going to, m'ser," he replied. "You w-w-was the only one. I g-g-got more sense than t-t-to d-d-deal with anybody but you. M'ser. I got to be going, please, m'ser. You likely won't be seeing me again. Ever. That's a promise."

He meant that. It would be better for everybody at this point if he went back to the swamp and stayed there. Ties cut clean.

Moghi looked—funny. His eyebrows were up near where his hairline used to be. He looked a little confused *(Moghi? Confused?)* and oddly troubled, but let him go.

CHAPTER III

TROUBLED WATERS
By C. J. Cherryh

Jones had gone her way at dawn, about her usual time, and Mondragon had given her a sleepy kiss (he thought) and turned over and burrowed into the pillows, secure in the knowledge Jones was going downstairs under the witness of canalers, and that all the myriad enemies he had were not fool enough to take on the Trade.

The Sword wanted war, the Sword could get it personal if they touched a canaler, that was the truth. Even Anastasi knew his limits—and so did every thief and pickpocket in Merovingen, that was the miracle of it, that let that skip stay untouched down there in a city in which not a rag or a scrap fell without someone scavenging it.

And let a man sleep at night with the notion that his door was safe as a governor's guard could make it.

So he headed for a little more sleep, in soft sheets and feather pillows. On bad nights he remembered nights huddled in a defensible corner of a stone cell shivering his teeth loose. And much worse than that. But not on a peaceful morning, not with the light to tell him where he was: Jones always left him the lamp on; and he always fell asleep with it: he never told Jones why.

He always got his best sleep in the morning. And he got at least a half hour of it before he heard the squeak of that deliberately set board in the lower hall and the creak of the one in the front room, and shortly after that, the opening of the door that meant one of the boys had gone out.

Damn. The mind started working. He started wondering about Raj moping around, started worrying about Jones being out of sorts, he started going over the whole damn mess with Anastasi, and that was too much. He was awake. If he lay there any longer he had the whole list of problems in bed with him, and he shoved it all out, put his leg over the side and almost changed his mind when he felt the chill outside.

But he gathered up the courage and threw the cover off and staggered up to find his balance and his bathrobe.

Lord. Cold boards.

He staggered out into the hall and down to the kitchen, waking up a little, shivering and congratulating himself on his moral fortitude: get up, get the whole business uptown settled, maybe free himself up to spend the little time that would keep Jones happy.

Maybe go out to the Rim with her, the way she asked him to, go out and sit and freeze on a spit of sand, fishing and beachcombing and dealing with canaler-folk doing the same thing in the slow season.

The prospect made him nervous: canaler-folk at close range and in numbers made him nervous; being out of Anastasi's reach made him nervous, Anastasi being the suspicious bastard he was; and he was, Lord knew, only getting over Merovingen's latest gift. But Jones swore the sea wind was clean and fine, that the canalers were on holiday, that everything would be safe and that there, above all else, no Sword agent could come near him.

If it cheered Jones up—

Lord knew she was due her rest too. If that was her idea of it—

He fussed about the cranky oil stove, dipped up water in the brass pan and set it on for tea, unwrapped the two-day-old cakes, standing on one foot because the tiles were cold, and wondering where in hell he had left his slippers this time.

He got out a cup and a spoon and opened the tea canister.

The letter inside gave him a chill.

Sword? was his first thought.

But he fished the papers out of the tea and spread them on the counter and blinked them into focus in the dim light, lit a candle once he had recognized the penmanship, and skimmed it, madder and madder as he got into the bit about "writing Poems and making like they came from You" . . .

But the mad evaporated when he got to *you won't have to worry about what I'm going to get you into next, not any more . . .*

When I'm gone . . .

Please keep Denny out of trouble . . .

Dear Altair Jones:, the note said.

I am Sorry more than I can say for Causing you such a great Deal of Trouble. I can only say that I'll Never Be in your Way again. Don't get mad at Tom—it wasn't any of it his Fault and he never had anything to do with the Lady. Please take care of Denny when I'm Gone.

—Raj.

"Bad news?" Moghi asked.

"Where is he?" Jones asked, shouted. "Moghi, where'd he go?"

"I dunno, Jones. He come in here tryin' to sell me drugs— You know how I don't take to that. I run him off. He left the note with Jep."

"What's he mean, *gone*, f'Lordssake? What's he talking about? —*Drugs?* What in *hell* does he think he's doing, Moghi?"

"I dunno, I ain't opened your mail."

Drugs. Money. "When I'm gone . . ."

Sword of God. No, some damn connection of Denny's, somebody's put the lean on Denny, or on him, but it ain't a guarantee it ain't Sword, either—

"Damn 'im!"

She headed for the door. She was out it, headed across the bare icy planks toward her skip, when she recollected: *he never had nothing to do with the Lady. . . .*

What lady?

Marina took her morning tea, sitting in the large chair in front of the fire, wrapped in her dressing gown, her feet in warm slippers. "Thank you," she said to the servant who set down the service, and she saw, with heart skipping a beat, that there was a folded letter with it, on *His* paper.

She snatched it up, opened it without recourse to the silver letter-opener on her desk or a notice to the porcelain mug of tea the servant set on a napkin on the fragile table beside her.

Most Gratious and Beautiful lady Marina Kamat—
Without even intending to, I have Tricked you in a Cruel and Unforgiveable way. I, who you thought was only the Hand that delivered Another's message to you, am actually the True Writer of those messages . . .

Marina reached after the tea and missed. The mug went over, fell, spilled and shattered on the stones.

"M'sera?" the servant exclaimed, dashing back into the room. "M'sera? What's happened, m'sera?"

CHAPTER IV

A TANGLED WEB WE WEAVE
by Mercedes Lackey

The marsh and the wind swallowed up sound, and the weeds closed them almost in a little room, which was just as well. Raver howled with laughter, his eyes vanishing in his wrinkles; Raj prayed at the moment that lightning would hit him and reduce him to a cinder. It would hurt a lot less than what he was feeling now. He tucked his cold, wet feet up under him, huddled under his coat, and wished he was on the Moon. Or dead. Or something.

"Shet ep, ye old bastid—" May scolded sharply, her face crinkling up in anger as she pushed a stray bit of gray hair under her knit cap; Raj had brought her that the last time he'd come. "Hev some pity an th' boy. Maybe it's baby-love, but it hurts all th' same—an' a young 'un ain't never hurt that bad before." She turned to Raj, huddled on one corner of the raft. "Raj-lad, don' ye let 'im get t' ye. I ain't sayin' ye did right t' leave—but I ain't sayin' ye did wrong neither."

Raj made a helpless gesture. To *these* two, his protectors and friends, he could tell everything—and he had. It had lessened some of the burden, at least until Raver had started laughing at him. "I—May, after the mess I got him in, I *can't* face Tom, and I can't keep being a burden on him, either."

"I thought you was workin' fer Gallandrys. Real work, I mean, not make-work."

"I was."

"That don't sound much like bein' a burden t' me."

"I—" he hadn't thought of it quite that way. Sure, he and Denny had been living on Mondragon's bounty lately, but they'd been keeping watch over him while

41

he was sick. *And* helping get him out of the tangle that illness had put him in. And it had been his savings and Jones' that had bought part of the medicine that had kept Tom alive. He'd bankrupted himself for Tom's sake, and hadn't grudged it. He'd lost several more weeks' salary too, staying with Tom to watch him and watch out for him, and hadn't grudged that either. Maybe he *had* been pulling his own weight.

"An' who's gonna take care a' them sick canaler kids if ye'er hidin' out here?"

That was one thing he hadn't thought of. Not likely Del would take them to some strange Janist—Raj was karmic risk enough.

"Don' ye go slammin' no doors behind ye," May admonished him gently. "Now, gettin' outa sight till that Hightowner space-brain kin ferget yer face, that's no bad notion. But stayin' here? No, Raj-lad; ye don' belong out here. Jest stay long enuf t' get yer head straight—then ye go back, an' take yer licks from that Tom feller. Ye learnt before, ye can't run from trouble."

May was right. That was *exactly* what he'd been trying to do—he'd been trying to run from all his troubles, and rationalizing the running.

"Yes, m'sera," Raj said humbly, feeling lower than a mud-pup's tail.

She shoved his shoulder; but not in an unkindly fashion. "Get along wi' ye! M'sera! Huh!" She snickered, then turned businesslike. "Where ye gonna park yer hidey?"

"I figured edge of Ralf's old territory, right by the path in, over by that big hummock with the patch of thatch-rush growing out of it."

"Good enuf. Get on with it. We'll keep an eye t' ye."

Raver waited until Raj was off down the trail and into the reeds; out of sight and hearing. Then he slipped off the raft onto one of the secret paths of firm ground that wound all through the swamp. He generally moored both his raft and May's up against one of these strips of solid earth—they weren't really *visible* since most of them were usually covered in water about ten to twelve centimeters deep.

"Where ye goin'?" May asked sharply.

"Gonna see t' our guest," Raver replied. She shut up at that; shut up and just watched him with caution. Raver had changed in the past couple of weeks.

Yes indeed, he had. Or rather, begun acting more like the person he really was.

He balanced his way along the narrow, water-covered trails, so used to following them he did it unconsciously, so used to the cold water he never noticed his numb feet. Raver—no, *Raven*—had been changing.

For the first time in years he was himself—Raven Singh; misplaced Janist agent.

Fool Janist agent. He hadn't been prepared for the reality of Merovingen-below. He'd been mugged on his first night in Merovingen, and dumped in Dead Harbor after; he had wandered amnesiac for months among the other crazies in the swamp. That had been ten—no, twelve years ago. It had taken a long time for Raven to return; years, and a lot of swamp-water and self-medication with hallucinogenics to shake loose the memories.

And when he had, then he'd cursed the fate that left him so stripped of all possessions and contacts as to have to *stay* here. He'd picked up with May about two years before Raj had come to them; she'd had the gift for healing he lacked, though he had the knowledge. Together they'd formed the only source for medicine the swampies knew, and he'd done his best to follow the healing path among the crazed and the impoverished losers who lived here. And hoped Jane would make his path clear or get him the hell out of there.

Then had come the night the sharrh had appeared over Dead Harbor.

He grinned mirthlessly. *Sharrh, my rosy rear.*

Fireworks was what it had been, he'd seen fireworks before, in a small way, at celebrations upriver. Fireworks it was, oh, yes, set off by a Sword agent to put the fear of whatever in the Revenantist citizens of Merovingen. He knew; he'd seen it all, with the agitator silhouetted pretty as you please against the pyrotechnics and the fire he'd touched off in his boat.

Oh yes, and he'd gotten his little tail well-scorched, had Ruin al-Banna; he'd been dying when Raven had fished him out, burned all over and being dragged down by the sea-anchor he'd gotten tangled with. It would have made a pretty wager, whether shock or drowning would have gotten him first.

Neither did. Raven and May had; they'd patched him up (probably better than his own people would have), kept him dosed against fever, and hidden him away on one of the firmer reed-islands, under a hidey made to look like a reed-hummock, a hidey like May and Raven and Raj kept over their rafts. Raven had fed him more than just healing herbs; after all these years he knew everything the swamp had to offer in the way of psychogenics. Raven had him babbling his little heart out within the week. Then Raven had begun another project—the careful conversion of a former Sword of God terrorist into a Hand of Jane. It was, after all, mostly a change in orientation, not in purpose.

This, without a doubt, was what Jane had intended when She'd caused him to be stranded out here. Blessed be. Ruin—now renamed Wolfling after the appropriate ceremony of rebirth—would serve Jane far better than he, Raven, would ever have been able to. He himself had been a simple self-taught animal breeder before he'd seen Her Light. Ruin had been an assassin born and an agitator from the start. And sometimes before you could heal, you had to—surgically remove. That was a truism for governments as well as individuals. Wolfling would be a damned useful scalpel in the Hand of Jane if he could be turned.

But before he could be judged truly converted and turned over to the agents in town (and now, thanks to Raj, Raven knew who one of them was, at least—a singer-thief named Rif), there were a few things Wolfling would be doing for Raven. . . .

Raven approached the islet cautiously through the mist, making no sound in the water; he'd left Wolfling trancing-out on the heavy dose of bethany-root he'd fed to him.

His caution was needless; Wolfling was deaf and blind to everything around him. Except Raven's voice.

* * *

Ruin was having another vision. This one was, like the others, beginning with a face; a woman's face. She started out young, then flickered from girl to woman to crone and back again. It was Althea Jane Morgoth, of course. She had come to instruct him again. Ruin felt both exalted and humbled; and excited, with the kind of near-sexual excitement he'd felt before only when completing an assignment for the Sword. But he wasn't supposed to be thinking of that. He was supposed to be making himself worthy to be a Hand of Jane.

"Wolfling—" said Jane, her hollow, echoing voice riveting his attention upon her. "You have built up a terrible tower of debts to be repaid before you are judged worthy. Are you ready to begin that repayment?"

"Yes—" replied Ruin thinly, bowing his head as her eyes became too bright to look upon. Those eyes—they seemed to see right into the core of him.

"So mote it be."

There was a sound like a great wind, and Ruin was alone in the dark.

Or was he? No—no, there was someone coming. Or forming, rather, out of the dark and the mist. Another woman.

For a moment he thought it might be another avatar of Jane, then with a chill of real fear he recognized her. Angela Takahashi—once Sword herself, and dead at the hands of the Sword these five years gone. He knew she was dead; he'd been there when her lover, Mahmud Lee (as high up in the Sword ranks as Chance Magruder), had given the order to terminate.

For although she had been the only Sword information-drop in Merovingen, she'd also been loose-tongued and incredibly stupid; the kind of woman good only for one thing. She'd known about the planned Nev Hettek coup; she'd have talked, especially if her ex-lover hadn't pulled her back home. Lee had made sure she would never get the opportunity.

She didn't look too stupid now—

Ruin al-Banna, a voice said inside his head; *I see you—*

He blocked his ears, but it did no good. The ghostly voice cut right through him; the almond eyes did the same. She was stark-naked, well-formed ivory flesh floating in a cloud of smoke and fog and midnight-black hair, obliquely slanted black eyes cold as the grave—she aroused no desire with her weird nudity; he'd never wanted a woman *less*.

Ruin al-Banna, would you be rid of my curse upon you?

"I never did anything to you!"

My curse is upon all who still serve the Sword. My curse shall follow you wherever you go—Her eyes grew until they filled his entire field of vision, black, and like looking into hell. He felt ghostly hands running down his arms, leaving chill trails behind them. *When you sleep, I shall be there—waiting. When you wake, I shall follow; in all your comings, your goings, I shall be one step behind you, making you careless, making you nervous, until one day you will make a mistake—and then my fingers will close about you—*

"Wait!" he yelled, panicked now, fear that he had never felt in dealing with the living and the soon-to-be-dead shutting around his heart and squeezing it like a hand. "I'll do anything you want!"

The eyes receded, and again she floated before him in her cloud of smoke and hair and magic. *Then guard my sons.*

That caught him off-guard. "Huh?" he replied stupidly, unable to fathom the puzzle.

My sons live, Ruin al-Banna. Guard them. Keep them from harm. Keep the Sword from their throats. Only then my curse will leave you.

"I don't—I mean I don't even know what they look like, how to find them!"

There— she pointed, and something began forming out of the smoke and the dark beside her. The foggy image of an adolescent—sixteen, seventeen maybe. A dead ringer for Angela. *That is Rigel—he calls himself Raj. And there*— Beside the first, a boy about four years younger; Mahmud Lee as a kid. *That is Denny—Deneb. Guard them, Ruin. Your life on it, or my curse forever.*

He had barely sworn to it, when she faded away, and his grasp on consciousness went with her.

* * *

Raven was pretty well pleased with himself; that had been one of the better vision-quests he'd sent Wolfling on. The former Sword hadn't fought him, had responded beautifully to all the suggestions. Bethany-root was obviously going to be the drug-of-choice in dealing with this convert.

Wolfling came to gradually. He wasn't a particularly pretty sight, with half his head bandaged, and the rest of him splotchy with newly-healed skin. He coughed a good deal too; gift from the sulfur in the fireworks he'd set off, and the water he'd breathed. But he was functional, and functioning, and healing faster than Raven would have thought likely. He set up slowly, uncurling from his nest of reeds and rags and old blankets. He blinked at the sun, at Raven, eyes not yet focusing properly.

"Well?" asked Raven.

"I got—a thing—I got to do—" the man said through stiff lips, eyes still mazy with the drug.

"Jane give you a job, huh?"

"But I don't—I don't—I gotta take care of a couple kids—" his pupils were still dilated, but there was a certain despair in his voice. Raven kept his satisfaction shuttered behind his own stony expression as he crouched down next to Wolfling among the reeds. Jane's Hand should reveal nothing. Only Jane revealed.

"So?"

"But—how the hell am I gonna find her kids?"

"*What* kids? Whose kids?"

"Takahashi. Rigel and Deneb Takahashi." If Wolfing was confused about why *Jane* would be concerned over the welfare of two *Adventist* kids, he wasn't showing it, but then Wolfling had never been strong on logic. "How the hell am I gonna find them?"

Raven spread his arms wide with his hands palm-upward and looked to the sky, taking on dignity and power as he deepened his voice. This was the part he played the best—he knew, thanks to the suggestions he'd planted, in Wolfling's receptive mind, that the former Sword now saw him haloed in a haze of dim white light. Every time he took that particular pose, Ruin would see him glowing with the power of Jane. "Praise be th' Lady Jane in Her Wisdom, an' blessed be Her Hands what work Her will. Strange are Her ways, an' mysterious." Now he lowered his eyes to meet Wolfling's. "She has ye in Her plan, Wolfling; She's had ye there fr'm th' start of th' world. She's jest bin waitin' fer ye t' see Her. Rigel Takahashi is right here, Wolfling; in th' swamp. He's hidin' out, an' he's scared. He damn-well needs protectin'; he's a good kid an' this here is a nasty place. But he's nervy an' he's touchy; he don't let nobody near him but them as he knows, like me an' May. You wanta watch him, fine. That's Jane's will. But if ye show yerself, he'll run, I c'n promise that. If he even *guesses* ye're there, he'll run. You wanta keep him from runnin' further an' right inta more trouble, ye stay outa sight."

As Wolfling nodded understanding, Raven rose, and stepped off the islet into the knee-deep, murky water of the swamp. Wolfling followed, showing no more discomfort than Raven. The Janist grinned; the convert was coming along nicely.

"Come on, then. I'll show ye where t' keep watch on 'im without him knowin' yer there."

CHAPTER V

TROUBLED WATERS
by C.J. Cherryh

"I dunno," Jones said to Mondragon, still trying to make some sense out of the script-letters in the pages Mondragon had given to her. The wind ruffling the pages and the skip pitching and grinding against the stone edge of Foundry southside was no help. Mondragon had made a deal shorter work of the letter she had been bringing *him* when she had found him running for *her* usual morning route.

What lady? had been high on her personal list of questions. But a scared kid dealing drugs and talking about *gone* was right up there at the top, and she had *not* even gotten to the matter of the lady, except the letter did:

Dear Tom, it started off, and something about being a fool—(*yey*, she thought, *ye got that right*) and *writing* something *to m'sera Marina Kamat*—

"Kamat? What's he talkin' about?"

"Where'd you get this?"

"Jep. Mondragon, that damnfool kid was in there at Moghi's tryin' t' sell *Moghi* wiregrass an' deathangel. Lucky Moghi ain't broke his head for 'im, but Moghi said he was spooked, outright spooked—"

"Who was? Raj?"

"Moghi said 'e was all white and nervous-like, he said somethin' about never seein' 'im again—"

"*Who? Raj?*"

"Raj."

"God."

Mondragon looked as undone as she had ever seen him. *Not* a matter about ladies. She figured that. Or if it was it was bitter serious, and a life was first. *Then*

49

she'd kill him. "Is it Sword business? Somethin' o' yours?"

"I don't know. No. Not my business. Not Sword. The damn young fool—"

She shoved the papers back at him. "I ain't made sense of it. *You* tell me. What's he done?"

"Sending letters in my name to m'sera Kamat. Writing her poetry. . . ."

Jones stared at him with her mouth open. "Poetry?"

"Jones, he's a kid, he's got himself in a mess— He started writing the lady poetry in *my* name— A Kamat. Hightown. He's got *me* in a damned mess, but he's gotten scared, he's left me this damn thing—" Mondragon rattled the papers in his fist. "—and he's talking about *Take care of Denny when I'm gone*. He's dealing drugs with Moghi—what in hell does he want money for, that he wouldn't come to me?"

Jones drew several quick breaths, madder and madder, and feeling a knot at her own gut. "Well, he *ain't* likely t' come t' you after what he done, is he?"

"We're not talking about a damn fool mistake, Jones, we're talking about money he's raising on the sly—for *what?*"

Jones frowned at him. "He come up with that medicine."

"When?"

"When you was sick, dammit. I dunno how. He come up with it."

"I figured he took something from the apartment."

"Ain't none of us took from you, dammit, we ain't thieves!"

"*For medicine, dammit, what's stealing about that?*"

"Ye don't take without you ask, Mondragon, an' ye don't give what ain't yours t' give. Damn right he ain't took your stuff. He ain't took a penny. No more than me. Even Denny ain't. He's got that much, he ain't stealing from ye."

"Oh, good *God*, Jones,—"

"Maybe he got sera Kamat t' give 'im money. Maybe he raised it somehow's else. Drugs is drugs, ain't it? He got the healin' kind. Maybe he's payin' for it with the other. Boy like that, somebody give him the healin' ones if he'll run th' other; and he ain't tellin' either of us, ne? Lord knows."

"What in hell has it got to do with Marina Kamat?"

She lifted a shoulder, huddled against the chill of the wind. "Hey, possible *her* folk could be after 'im. Or whoever's givin' him the drugs. I dunno, it *don't* make sense. He sure don't know what he's doin', goin' t' Moghi. Moghi went easy with 'im. Somebody else—"

"He's talking about *gone*, Jones."

"Ain't unlikely if he's messing with Kamats and drugs and such."

"*Somebody* went out after you did. —Get me over to Gallandrys. Use the engine."

She scrambled, hopped up onto the half-deck and flung up the cover to start the engine.

It balked. It would, in weather like this. "Damn near faster to pole," she muttered, on the fifth crank.

It caught, a thunderous popping echoing off Foundry walls, and she put the tiller up and ran the pin through that held it while Mondragon cast them loose.

A TANGLED WEB WE WEAVE

by Mercedes Lackey

Raj's hands ached with the cold as he worked without really thinking about what he was doing. He was trying to hold his mind in a kind of numb limbo, as numb as the rest of him was getting. He was doing his best to avoid thinking, just to exist. The cold and damp were making his nose run, and the slap of water, the hushing of wind in the weeds, and the little sounds he was making while working were punctuated by his sniffles.

His raft and hidey had been where he'd left them, and as he'd expected, they'd been stripped. The hidey was still in surprisingly good shape, all things considered; Raj was grateful. He hadn't had much good luck lately.

With the water-level in the swamp at winter low, it

had been cruel, hard work to pole the raft out of his old territory and into Ralf's, especially trailing the hidey on its bigger raft behind him. Ralf had ruled one of the best territories in Dead Marsh; right where the Marsh met the Rim and both met Dead Harbor—the very edge of the old spaceport, so they said. There was an unobstructed view of the city across the water, and a nice stock of food-plants, as well as two really good fishing holes and a couple of real, solid islets— the tops of huge chunks of concrete that had gathered mud and plants on them. Raj's arms and back were screaming with pain before he got his home to its new location, and if he hadn't been working he'd have been three-quarters frozen. As it was he was soaked to the skin, and glad of the change of dry clothes in his pack. He had moored the raft up against the islet nearest the Harbor and on the pathway from the Marsh Gate to the Rim; with the camouflaging hidey over it, it would look like an extension of the island.

The sun was a dim, gray disk above the horizon when he'd gotten set up properly, and he was sweating with exertion; even his bare feet were warm. He'd been up since before dawn, and by now it seemed as if it should be nearly nightfall, not barely morning.

From the islet he gathered rushes and sedge to weatherproof the hidey against the winter rains and wind. Then it was nothing but drudge-work; crouch over the framework and interlace the vegetation into it. Grass, then sedge, then reeds, then grass again, until it was an untidy but relatively windproof mound. With only his hands moving the wind was chilling, so he'd lost all the heat he'd gained by the time he was ready to thread new tall weeds into the top of the brushy hummock to renew its disguise. It was well toward midmorning when he'd finished to his satisfaction.

He was exhausted and cold all the way through, still soaked to the skin, and more than ready for the sleep he'd lost last night. But he hadn't forgotten his old lessons. He made more trips to the center of the islet for old, dry grasses, stuffing the cavity beneath the hidey with them. He crawled under the basket-like hidey and stripped, putting his soggy clothing between his "mattress" of dry grasses and his bottom blanket to dry while he slept. Then he curled up into his grass-and-blanket nest to shiver himself into almost-warmth, then sleep the sleep of the utterly exhausted. It was a far cry from the cozy bed he'd left for Denny in Mondragon's apartment, and if he hadn't been so cold and tired, he *might* have cried himself to sleep.

Denny hadn't worried when he'd awakened to see that Raj's side of the bed was empty. Raj had been going to work early, the past few weeks, working in a frenzy of earnest activity all day, and leaving late. Old man Gallandry himself had come down out of his office to see the handiwork of his new clerk. Too bad Raj hadn't been there at the time; he'd been out at lunch, and nobody thought to mention it to him when he came back. Of course, the other clerks were probably jealous—half of 'em were Gallandry hangers-on anyway, worthless cousins who weren't expected to accomplish much for their salary.

Denny thought he knew why Raj had been working so hard; he might be hoping to get an advance on his wages. He'd spent all the cash he'd saved on Mondragon, and in a week the rent was due on their apartment on Fife. A runner earned about a quarter of what a clerk earned—Denny couldn't pay it. And if Raj couldn't raise the ready, it was back to the air-shaft for both of them, unless Mondragon would let them stay on. Which wasn't real likely. Jones was getting an impatient and irritated look whenever her eyes happened to fall on them. She'd been snapping at Raj for being underfoot, and it was clear to Denny that they'd worn out their welcome once Mondragon had recovered from the Crud. He had a fair notion that it was Mondragon overruling Jones that was keeping him and Raj in the apartment.

And that despite Denny's being smart-mouthed with the both of them.

With Raj too, which Raj hadn't much noticed, but he *had* noticed Denny's wise-ass attitude with Mondragon. *That* had gotten a rise out of him, more than Denny had intended.

He'd backed—no, *slammed*—Denny into the wall night before last; and his face had been so cold, so tortured—Denny hadn't understood that, not by half, but Raj was hurting inside over something, *that* much he could tell. And Raj had never turned *that* expression on Denny before—and Lord, it had scared him a little. More than a little.

You hear me, Denny, you hear me good. You're messing with a deathangel, I'll tell you once and not again! Tom's a gentleman, he's quiet—but he's killed more people than you have hair, and you'd better think about that hard before you smart him off another time. I dunno why he's puttin' up with you, but I won't, not anymore! I'll beat you blue next time—because I'd rather you was beat up than dead, and if Tom forgets himself some day, that's just what might happen. If you don't believe me, you think about what you told me about Mama; you just think about why They call Themselves 'Sword of God' and who murdered Mama before you open your mouth to Tom again.

He'd sulked the rest of the day and most of the next, not speaking to Raj. But he *had* thought about it, and and he'd come to the reluctant conclusion that Raj had been right. Even if he *was* more'n a bit touched about some girl. And he'd started to make friendly noises at his brother again.

So all in all, he didn't think twice about Raj being gone. But when Raj wasn't *at* work, and didn't show up there by the time Denny got sent out on his first run, he began to worry just a little.

He came around the corner of Gallandry on his second run of the day and saw a familiar skip tied up at the base of the stairs with a lurch of foreboding. No mistaking that particular tilt of a canaler's cap—that was Jones' skip down there, and Jones in it. And where Jones was—

"Man to see you, boy," was the curt greeting at the door; sure enough, behind Denny's supervisor stood—

Tom Mondragon. Wearing that impassive mask that said "trouble."

"Denny," Tom barely waited for Ned Gallandry to get out of earshot before starting in, and Denny backed up a pace or two, until his back was against the office wall. "Denny, have you seen your brother this morning?"

Denny decided to play innocent. "Ye mean he ain't here?" he replied, making his eyes big and round.

Mondragon was not fooled, and the flash of annoyance in *his* eyes told Denny that he was *not* in the mood for this sort of nonsense.

Aw, hell—Raj's in trouble—

"You know damned well he hasn't been here," Mondragon hissed, grabbing Denny's arm before he could dart out of reach. "Your brother's in a mess— now I want to know *what* it is and *where* he is."

"I dunno, m'ser Tom, honest—" Lord and Ancestors, the strength in that hand! Denny belatedly began to remember what Raj had told him when he'd read him the riot act—about what Tom was—and what he could do. And he began to wonder—

What if the man had turned his coat a second time? If he was planning to use Denny to get Raj, and sell Raj back to the Sword? Raj was worth plenty to the right people.

Paranoid, that was plain paranoid; there'd been no hint of any such thing.

But—if the Sword threatened Jones? Would he buy safety for Jones with Raj's life? He might, oh God, Mondragon might.

"Boy, I want you back in the apartment—" Mondragon was saying. "I've made it right with the Gallandrys." Denny had missed what had gone before; God, this did *not* sound good. There was no threat that Denny could read in Mondragon's face, but dare he take the chance that he *could* read an experienced agent? Denny was sizing Mondragon up now, with the eyes and attitude that he used to measure duelists, bridge-gangs, and blacklegs. He went cold all over, for he read *dangerous* in every move, and nothing in those murky green eyes.

Mondragon still had his arm in that iron grip, and was pulling him out the door with him. Denny's mind was going like a scrap of drift in a strong current. He couldn't take the chance that Mondragon was telling him the straight story; no way. He had to get away from Mondragon if he could.

Besides, if Raj was really in trouble, Denny could likely help him better than some Nev Hetteker or even a canaler like Jones could; he *knew* the town, and knew most of the dark ways. And there was always Rat and Rif to call on if he had to.

They were out on the balcony now, Denny playing docile, and Mondragon took that at face value. He relaxed a bit, and loosed his grip just enough.

Denny whipped around, putting all his weight behind a wicked blow with his elbow, and he'd aimed it a bit lower than Mondragon's midsection—aimed at something more personal.

Hit it, too; dead on target.

Mondragon was wide-open and completely taken by surprise; he might have expected Denny to pull loose, but he plainly never expected an attack from a kid less than half his size.

He doubled over with a painful wheeze, and dropped his grasp on Denny's arm.

Denny lit out like a scalded skit, heading around the balcony and straight for the bridge.

Mondragon recovered faster than Denny had figured he would, running after him. But Denny had gotten a good ten feet worth of head start, and that was all he needed. He made the bridge supports and jumped for the crossbeams, swarming up into the scaffolding like one of Merovingen's feral cats. From there he made it to the rooftops, and as he knew from long experience, there was no way an adult was going to be able to follow him up there—not unless the adult was another roof-walking thief like Rat.

It was colder than Kalugin's heart up there, and doubly-dangerous with the wind so strong and unexpected patches of ice everywhere, and smoke blowing into his face when he least expected it. Denny didn't stop for breath, though, not until he'd gotten halfway across Bolado. Then he slumped in a warm spot between two chimneys for a bit of a rest and a bit of a think.

Raj *was* in trouble; that much was beyond all doubting, no matter the source. Either with Mondragon or on his own. And Denny was going to have to see what he could do about it—if he could find out what the trouble *was*.

The last person Raj had talked to—that he knew

of—was Justice Lee. Denny reckoned he'd better pay *that* feller a little visit.

So best to lie low for a little bit, then get across Bolado to Bent and then to Kass. He'd been to Justice Lee's room once; and Denny figured he knew of a way into the rooming house that wasn't by the door, and a way into Justice's room that was right in his pocket.

TROUBLED WATERS
by C. J. Cherryh

"I couldn't catch him," Mondragon muttered, coming back down the steps, and Jones reset her battered brown cap on her head and frowned up at him.

"Boy knows something," Jones said.

"Boy doesn't trust *me*." Mondragon landed aboard, making the ship rock. "Dammit, Jones. Dammit to hell, where would he go?"

Jones shook her head, steadying the skip with the pole, and gave a heavy sigh. "I dunno. I dunno. There's a singer I know—might know."

"We haven't damn well *time* to go asking around over town. The boy's desperate, Jones, for God's sake, he's threatening to *kill* himself—"

"He goes dealin' f' drugs with Moghi, he's goin' t' save 'imself th' trouble. Damn that brat Denny! He ain't got th' brains of a fish. Ye let me find Rif—"

"*Rif!*"

Jones winced. "Yey. Raj's got some odd friends."

"All right. Find her. But drop me at Moghi's."

"Mondragon, ye don't go t' Kamat! Hear me, ye don't go t' Kamat! That's money, that's trouble, that's *real* trouble!"

"Moghi," he said firmly. "You ask around. *I'll* get Moghi on it."

"Moghi ain't no charity, he'll tell ye." She put the pole in and turned about, easy on the wide canal.

"Damn kid. Damn Raj. Double damn Denny. Rif c'n find 'im if I c'n find Rif. Ain't so easy. Damn 'im."

See, Mama said, taking shape on the bow, scratching her head and settling her cap to shade her eyes. Mama was in no way to feel the chill of the wind that cut through a body, coat and all. Retribution looked serenely disgusted with her daughter. *See, ye take up with landers, and lookit th' mess.*

Yey, mama, Jones thought to herself, and gave a furious shove of the pole as Mondragon took up the boathook to help out to starboard.

Ain't no karma, Retribution said, *'cept th' one ye get for meddlin'.*

Yey, there is, mama. There's the one ye get f'r bad-talkin' a boy till he runs off an' kills hisself. Damn, I knew he was carryin' somethin' heavy, I didn't need t' cuss 'im, did I, mama?

Kid ain't yours. Th' world ain't yours t' worry for, Altair.

Shut up, mama.

'Least I got somebody, which you never.

Mama vanished. It was an unfair cut.

I kept you safe, mama came back to say, having the last word. *How're you doin', daughter?*

CHAPTER VI

BY A WOMAN'S HAND
by Nancy Asire

Justice pulled the collar of his threadbare coat up around his neck, juggled his books in one arm, and headed toward Hilda's Tavern, the cold north wind blowing at his back. A heavy layer of clouds hung over Merovingen; the resultant dim light made late afternoon seem more like early evening.

Crowds filled the walkways of second level Kass: shoppers headed home with their purchases; students, dispersing from the College to their homes and rooms; and other folk who had reason to be about in the chill. Dodging two saffron-cloaked priests, Justice made for the tavern door, shoved it open, and stood for a moment in the rush of light and warmth, the sounds of conversation and laughter, and the smell of the large oil stove.

Shutting the door behind him, Justice shook tiny balls of sleet from his coat, fumbled one-handed at the buttons, and shivered in memory of the cold outside. Something soft and heavy bumped into his legs; he glanced down and smiled at the large golden cat rubbing against his boots.

"Come on, Sunny," he said, and started toward his room which lay behind the common room of the tavern. Exam time for the next couple of weeks. Desperation was in the air. The study session he had just come from at the College had left his head full of questions and answers, rules and exceptions to those rules. Nodding to several acquaintances, he skirted the tables, his mouth watering at the smell of dinner.

"Something for ye later?" a woman's voice called.

He glanced toward the kitchen and waved at Hilda,

who had planted her considerable bulk by the doorway. "Sure. I'll be out shortly."

She turned back toward the kitchen, ready, no doubt, to place his order without him needing to tell her what he wanted. Limited funds meant limited variety, but everything that came from Hilda's kitchen was more than merely edible.

Justice slipped behind the heavy curtain that divided the common room from the hallway leading to the small rooms he and other students occupied. Sunny danced between his feet, meowed once, and trotted tail-up toward a closed door. Only one oil lamp was lit in the hall, and by its dim light Justice was just able to see the keyhole into which he inserted his key.

The door swung inward on inky darkness. Justice set his books at his feet, scratched Sunny's head as the cat sat by the doorway, and reached to his left for the lamp. In a moment, he had it lit, set it back down on the small table, stepped into the chilly room, and shut the door. Sunny rubbed up against his legs again, turned toward the bed and his usual resting place, and froze.

Justice whirled around, his hand already on the hilt of the dagger he wore at his waist. The brightening glow of the oil lamp revealed a small dark-haired lad sitting on the edge of Justice's bed, wrapped tightly in one of the heavy blankets that lay folded at the end of the bed.

"It's me," the boy said, dark eyes enormous in the dim light. "Denny. Raj's brother. 'Member me?"

"I do," Justice said, easing the dagger back into its sheath. He drew a long breath, his pulse still pounding in his ears. "How the hell did you get into my room?"

Denny shrugged beneath his blanket, and wiped the dark hair from his eyes with one hand. "Secrets," he said. "Don't ye worry. Yer room's safe. Ye got one good lock on that door."

"Huhn." Justice took his coat off and hung in on the wall-hook. "Not good enough to keep *you* out." He walked across the tiny room, and eyed the oil heater on the floor with some longing. Though his room was windowless, the air still felt cold, especially since he had not had sufficient time to warm up after coming in from outside. "What do you want?"

"Raj." Denny unwound from the blanket. "Have ye seen 'im?"

Justice kept his face perfectly still. "Not since yesterday. He brought some more medicine to me."

Denny's face clouded. "Truth?" he asked, a particular note in his voice betraying what Justice sensed as real anxiety. "Not today?"

"No." Justice reached down, picked up Sunny, and stood scratching the cat's ears. "Has he gone missing?"

"Yey," Denny murmured, his eyes downcast. Then, as if he feared he had said too much, the young boy bit down on his lip and met Justice's eyes.

"I'll keep an eye out for him," Justice said, trying to keep his voice calm and friendly. "Maybe he's just late getting home. . . ."

"He didn't come t' work!" Denny blurted. His eyes shone in the lamplight. "He trusted ye . . . *I* trust ye! I thought maybe . . . maybe he'd come here."

"Not today," Justice replied.

Denny's face fell; he unwrapped completely from the blanket, let it fall on the bed behind him, and straightened his shoulders.

"I'll be goin' home, then," he said, getting to his feet. "Sorry if I startled ye by bein' in yer room. I didn't want anyone watchin' me."

More enemies? Ancestors knew how many shadowy figures trailed Denny or his brother Raj, or for what shadowy purpose. After his nighttime ride to Petrescu, Justice did not want to know.

"No harm done. I'm having dinner in a few minutes, Denny. Would you like some?"

A flash of emotion lit Denny's dark eyes, just as quickly gone. "No. I'd better get home myself 'fore I'm missed. Thank ye . . . thank ye all the same."

"I'll tell Raj you're hunting him if he *does* show up," Justice promised. He frowned at Denny's threadbare clothing. "You'll freeze on the way home. Do you want—"

"I been colder," Denny said, lifting his chin a bit.

Justice shrugged, knowing something of the pride that ran through both brothers. He turned, opened the

61

door, and stepped back to let Denny leave. The boy did not move; licking his lips, he cast a forlorn look up at Justice.

"Come with me, will ye? They'll stop me out there 'less I'm with ye."

That was truth. How Denny got back into the rooming house hall remained a mystery. Not much escaped Hilda's sharp eyes.

Justice nodded, gestured Denny into the hall, cut off the oil to the lamp, and followed the young boy. Setting Sunny at his feet, Justice inserted his key into the lock, turned, and heard the comforting sound of the tumblers falling into place.

Not, he reminded himself as he turned toward Denny, that this would make any difference to this lad.

Make a difference.

Besides Raj, he wondered what did.

TROUBLED WATERS

by C.J. Cherryh

Mondragon handed the note to Williams at the Foundry Bank and sweated while the banker went back to open the massive ledger which was chained impressively to the rear wall. He was not an uncommon client of Foundry Bank's sort—dark blue sweater, blue pants, mariner's heavy blue coat, the weight of which made the heating uncomfortable.

Lord knew the bank had seen him in better and in worse, and *knew* his drafts came off Boregy. When he rang at the bank's iron-guarded door the teller had had qualms, but Williams had let him in, even at closing.

Try not to look nervous. The last thing he needed was for old Williams the banker to send a runner to clear the check with Boregy's bank on White.

Old Williams riffled massive pages, adjusted spectacles and came back respectfully. "Yes, ser, but that will run your balance down to, approximately, 3.10 Ss. Just to advise you, ser. I'll stamp your check. To whom do you want it?"

"I need it in cash," Mondragon said.

"We have a policy against large withdrawals in cash. For the customer's protection, ser. This neighborhood—"

"Cash," Mondragon said. "My check is good. This is *Boregy* business, ser, please understand me. We are in a hurry."

Old Williams gnawed at his lip and finally went and countersigned the draft and made out his receipts, then called his teller to hold the desk and went into the back, where the vault would be.

It took a while, an interminable while for Williams to come back and count it out, 200 sols gold; and to make out his several papers for cash withdrawal and to have Mondragon sign his name on each.

"I hope you've got an escort," old Williams said.

"I've got an escort." Mondragon took the heavy, paper-wrapped packet like a lump of fish and tucked it inside his coat, pausing to nod an ordinary courtesy to the old banker, while the teller carefully unlocked the door to let him out.

"Is that the man?" the teller said, peering out the barred glass before he opened the door.

"That's him," Mondragon said; and slipped out quick as the cold draft came in; out and into the care of one of Moghi's own.

Across the bridges to Ventani High level then, up in the cold and the sporadic sleet, and down and down to harborside, past the second-hand shop to the shadows by Fishmarket Bridge.

The back way in, by the alley.

Moghi counted the coins, stacked them up like shining towers on his desk and looked at Mondragon. "All here. You got a real fondness for that boy, 's all I'll say."

"At these prices," Mondragon said, "I expect results."

Moghi jabbed a finger at the desktop. "Bottom rate. You want I put *my* boys on it, they do top job, but they ain't got no guarantee that boy's alive. This is risk money, m'ser. *You're* the risk. Understand?"

Mondragon tightened his mouth and said: "I understand you very clearly."

"Ye better. You an' your hightown friends. This money better have no trace-stamp on it."

"There isn't any. It's clean. There's no Boregy money, nothing they can trace."

"You got it, then. Go out front. Drinks come with the deal."

He nodded bleakly, got up and went out to wait in the front room.

So it was one more lie. The important thing was a kid out there somewhere in the city, scared and desperate.

He took Moghi's whiskey, he sat down at the corner table to drink the chill and the sick feeling away. He ate a tasteless dinner, Jep's cooking.

Jones was out looking. Every canaler in the Trade was at least keeping an eye out by now, since afternoon. Rif and her Janist friend Rat were looking, all of it in desperate quiet. Trade was off in Moghi's tonight. There was a trouble-feeling about the place, and only the canalside regulars were in, looked around once and twice to miss other regular faces and then, with the canny elusiveness of the knowledgeable on canalside, had a drink and vanished, quickly.

No sign of Raj. No sign of Denny.

There were, Lord knew, none of his *own* connections he dared so much as name the boy to. No way in hell he could help, except hire it done.

So he hired it. Paid Moghi, for Merovingen's shadowy underworld to do the looking. Moghi's expense would be halfway reasonable—counting the places Moghi could look, and the *kind* of help Moghi had to pay and pay off and (sometimes) silence.

But if the boy was dealing drugs, if he *hadn't* stopped with Moghi and gone on to peddle them elsewhere—it meant the underworld was the place to look.

Or harbor-bottom.

If it was not Kamat themselves who had taken the boy. And silenced him, to put an end to an embarrassment.

A bridge-boy, an orphan—against the Kamats. He thought about presenting himself at Kamat, about confronting the Househead and m'sera Marina Kamat and asking questions.

But Kamat had ties to Boregy.

And if *Boregy* had started asking questions, and those questions had come up with a boy writing letters that linked Thomas Mondragon with Marina Kamat, to Kamat's embarrassment and the possible collapse of delicate negotiations *between* Kamat and Boregy, because of him and because of a very expendable boy—

He had a second glass, against the chill. A few of Moghi's lads strayed in to report, with cold-stung faces, and to drink down a pint before they went out again.

The night fell, the night passed, to a tavern cold and virtually lifeless—open the night long, for the traffic that came and went by the back door, to report and get new orders, none of which had turned up a damned thing. Lanterns burned, lanterns burned out. Mondragon spent the night leaning on the table, head on arms, waked from time to time as no-news came in; and from time to time drank himself back to sleep again. In rare charity, Jep left the bottle on the table, set up another for himself, where he kept station at the bar.

By morning, headache added its own misery, and Mondragon's stomach rebelled at the greasy stench of Jep's cooking; but he tried an egg—fresh, Jep swore it; and dry toast. And he got the toast down, and the tea, in a room so cold the tea and the egg both sent up clouds of steam and his hands felt like ice.

He heard footsteps spatter up the porch, from the direction of the porch-edge and the water, looked up as the door opened.

Jones.

No luck. He saw that in her face—saw the little hope in hers die when she looked at him. She came back to the table, took the whiskey-glass full of hot tea Jep handed her and said:

"Ain't no word. They say Moghi's lads is out all night. You done 'er?"

Mondragon nodded.

"Damn," Jones said, and rested her elbows on the table and shoved her cap back, resting her head against the heels of her hands. "That damn *fool*— Mondragon, ye don't suppose—Anastasi—"

He shook his head. "I've got no reason to think," he said, in that whisper she had used. "No reason. It's Kamat worries me."

"Ain't no one seen 'im there. He doctored this kid f'r Del this mornin' . . ."

"Doctored a *kid?*"

"Sick kid. Del brung 'er to 'im. Raj's been doin' a little practice on th' side. Fixin' up kids. He ain't takin' any money. Wouldn't have it. Del offered. That *ain't* a boy dealin' drugs, Mondragon. I dunno what he's in, but he *ain't* a bad boy—"

"He's a damn *fool!*"

"An *honest* fool. Listen, Mondragon." She put her hand on his on the tabletop. "It ain't impossible he's got friends hidin' 'im. Somebody into 'im fer big karma. Doctorin' those kids—he might have a big 'un he could call."

He tried to think so. He kept thinking about Kamat, about Boregy.

And Anastasi Kalugin, to whom he had sold things . . . that no money could buy, only the safety of one canaler-girl.

He had brushed too close to the Sword lately—too close and too often. He had reported those contacts, dutifully. But perhaps Anastasi worried that there were more than that—worried, in his twisted, many-turning way, that his agent Mondragon was reporting some of them and not all, and that he had doubled again.

Or that his agent was, after all, working for Karl Fon—that everything was a set-up, under the deepest cover.

Anastasi would not, he thought, lay hands on Jones. Jones was his price and Anastasi knew it. But the boy—

"I'll go out again," Jones said. She rubbed her eyes. "Jep! Gimme some eggs. 'Bout three. Put 'er on my tab. —This yours?" With a backhanded wave at the whiskey bottle.

"Yes." He poured a shot into her breakfast tea, and fought his own nausea, seeing her take it down. But she was chilled through. The cold still burned her face. "I'll go with you this time. . . ."

66

"Ne, ye stay here, Mondragon. One of us should be here—"

"I'm not doing any damn good here!"

"All right." The eggs arrived, a greasy mess from which Mondragon averted his eyes. Toast followed. Jones took into it with a vengeance, whiskeyed tea and all.

"What *about* Del?" he asked. "Have you asked about friends? Anyone Del would know?"

"I asked. I asked." Jones swallowed an enormous gulp and washed it down. Two more bites. "Ain't no way he holds out on me, not him nor Mira nor Tommy. I got karma on 'em. Plenty." Two more gulps, the plate clean. Jones took off her neckscarf, wrapped the toast in it and stuffed it in her coat pocket. "Come on, then," she said, and Mondragon heaved himself for his feet, headache and all; and grabbed the whiskey bottle.

As the door opened, bang! and Tommy-the-ex-bar-boy came running in.

"Jones! We got a lead!"

CHAPTER VII

A TANGLED WEB WE WEAVE
by Mercedes Lackey

Old habits woke Raj with the first hint of dawn—he'd been so exhausted he'd managed to sleep most of the afternoon before the cold of the wind woke him. Then he'd spent a good part of the night with his teeth chattering hard enough to splinter, until exhaustion put him to sleep for another hour or so. He stuck his head out from under the hidey, still shivering, and peered around in the gray light. No fog this morning, though the sky was going to be overcast. He pulled his head back in, and checked his clothes where he'd put them under his bottom blanket. As he'd hoped, they were dry, water driven out by the heat of his body. He beat the worst of the dried mud out of them, and pulled them on, wrapped a blanket around himself, pulled his coat on over it all, and crawled back out into the day.

Unfortunately, weather-proofing the hidey was his only task. He was more cold than hungry, his stomach was too upset; nothing needed doing except to boil some water so it was safe to drink. It looked like it was about time to have a good long think.

He hopped from the edge of his raft onto the edge of the islet—which was an exposed and weathered ledge of concrete, and a lot more solid than many a landing back in town. He wriggled his way in to the center, having carefully to pull his blanket and clothing loose when branches snagged them, lest he leave tell-tale bits of yarn behind, or rip holes in clothing he didn't have the wherewithal to repair. He was looking for a place where he would be well hidden by the weeds—at least hidden from the casual observer. He finally found a dry spot, one well padded by the accumulation of many years of dead reeds, and made himself a little hollow to sit in. He reckoned it would do well enough; he hunched down to the unpleasant task of confronting everything he wanted most to avoid thinking about.

Take it one step at a time—

All this time, he'd been casually saying to himself "Tom will kill me for this." Looking at the mess he'd made of things in the cold light of dawn, and soberly recollecting his own lecture to Denny—*might* he?

He might, Raj thought reluctantly. *And justified. If the Kamats take offense—he could hand Richard my head, and get himself out of it. I've made myself into a pretty expensive liability.*

But *would* he? Raj looked at it from all the angles he could think of, and finally decided that he probably wouldn't. Mondragon never did anything that drastic without having several reasons for doing it. To be brutally frank, Mondragon was too much of a professional to waste anything, even the time and effort it would take to dispose of a stupid kid. And Jones *might* get upset if Mondragon took Raj out. But just to be on the safe side—

Justice had suggested he hide out here about two weeks, then come back into town. *Get hold of Denny first—give him a note for Tom. Use the old Sword codes, and flat ask him if he thinks I'm better gotten out of the way, permanent-like. Then make a counter-offer. Say— say that I'll do what he wants me to do; come in, stay here, or leave Merovingen altogether.*

The last wouldn't be easy, or desirable from his point of view, but he'd do it; he couldn't go north— but south, maybe? Or maybe hire on a Falkanaer ship?

That was a possibility. They'd seemed pretty rough characters, but basically good people, when he'd met a couple at Gallandrys. They wouldn't *hurt* him—

But he had a fairly shrewd notion of what some of the duties of a very junior (and passable-looking) sign-on might well include, and he wasn't altogether sure he could stomach the job. Better that, though, than dead. No such thing as a "fate worse than death" in Raj's book—except maybe a fate involving a lengthy interrogation at the hands of Sword, Signeury, or Kalugin —or Tom Mondragon.

But Denny—if he left Merovingen, he'd have to leave Denny. No good could come to a thirteen-year-old kid in a strange place like the Chattalen, or more-or-less trapped on a Falkanaer ship.

That would leave him more alone than he'd ever been.

He swallowed hard, and wiped his sleeve across his eyes. So be it. For Denny's sake, he'd do just about anything. Including take on that lengthy interrogation.

But figure Tom wanted him back in; in a lot of ways that was worst case. *Okay, I go in, I take my licks. God knows what he'll do. Probably beat the liver out of me. Be worse if he didn't, in some ways. He won't be trusting me with much, anyway, not after the way I've messed up. Don't blame him. I wouldn't trust me, either.*

So. Be humble; be respectful. Take orders, follow 'em to the letter, and *earn* the respect back. Even if it takes years.

Thank God he'd told the truth—at least he'd cut the thing with Marina short, before it had landed them in more tangles than could be cut loose.

Give up on the notion of College—too close to the Kamats, especially with Kamat cousins going there. Hang it up; stay content with being Gallandry's third-rank clerk. At least that paid the bills.

Stay clear of anyplace Marina might show, unless Tom ordered different.

Keep clear of the Janes, too. That meant Rif and Rat and Hoh's tavern—again, unless Tom ordered differently.

Going back meant more than facing Tom—it meant figuring a way to pay the damn bills with no money. Rent was paid until the end of the month—but that was only one week away. Borrow? From who? Jones didn't have it to spare. *Not* Tom—

Raj gnawed his lip, and thought and thought himself into a circle. *No choice. Has to be Tom. Or beg an advance from Gallandrys. Have to eat humble pie twice. Charity. Hell.*

Sometimes it seemed as if it would be a lot easier

just to find one of the gangs and taunt them into killing him; God knew it wouldn't take much. But he hadn't fought and fought and fought to stay alive this long just to take the easy way out.

Last possibility—that Tom would tell him to stay. That Tom would trust to the swamp to kill him, rather than killing him outright. Well, wasn't that what Raj had figured on doing in the first place?

All right, if he told Raj to stay in the swamp—well, Raj would stay. At least this time he'd arrived equipped to do a little better than just survive. Not much, but a little. So long as he could keep clear of the gangs, he'd manage. And he and Denny could go back to the old routine—at least he'd be near enough to keep in touch.

Now—the Sword—have I screwed up there too?

Denny waded through mud and freezing water; over his ankles, mostly, sometimes up to his knees. His legs were numb, his teeth were chattering so hard he couldn't stop them, and his nose was running. He kept looking over his shoulder, feeling like he was being watched, but seeing nothing but the waving weeds that stood higher than his head. There was a path here, of sorts, and he was doing his best to follow it. If he hadn't been so determined to find his brother, he'd have turned tail and run for home a long time ago.

Justice Lee hadn't told him anything—not directly. But Denny had Rat's training in reading people, and Lee was as open to him as a book would have been to Raj. Raj had told Justice his problems, and Justice had given him some kind of advice; that was the most obvious answer to the art student's evasions. So; given that first—there had been advice, and second—Raj was missing—and third—Justice wasn't too surprised that Raj was missing—

Huh. Uh-*huh*. Only one answer fit that profile. Justice must have advised Raj to go hide out. Denny had gotten a flash of inspiration right when he'd figured that out, and hadn't waited to try to pry more out of the reluctant Lee—instead he'd gotten Lee's escort to the door, then he'd lit over the roofs again—

It had taken him half the night to reach the apartment on Fife—

To discover Raj's belongings stripped, right down to the books. And *only* Raj's things, which ruled out thieves. Stuff gone, plus hiding out added up to *swamp* to Denny.

So he put on every sweater he had, and two pairs of pants, and made for the roofs again.

He had to get down to the walkways by the time he hit Wharf Gate, and by then he had the notion that it might just be a good idea to let Jones and Mondragon know where Raj had gone, and that Denny was headed out after him.

Damn fool Justice, he'd cursed, more than once, *Damn swamp almost killed Raj before this—hell, it could do it now! Damn fool towner, I bet Raj tol' him where he was goin,' an' I bet he was thinkin' livin' in the swamp's like livin' on the canals—*

So he'd looked around for a canaler, knowing that canalers stuck together, knowing that what he told one could be halfway across town by midmorning.

"Hey!" he'd yelled at the first head that poked out of a hidey to peer at him, bleary-eyed, in the dawnlight. "Hey—you know Jones?"

"Might," said the canaler; old, of dubious gender.

"Look, you find Jones, you tell 'er Raj's headed out into Dead Marsh and Denny's goin' after 'im." Then he added, shrewdly, "There's money in it."

The whole canaler had popped out of the hidey then, and the creature was jerking at his tie-rope as Denny had continued his run to Marsh Gate and the *path* Raj had told him about.

Raj had talked so casually about walking in. Denny was finding out now that it was anything but easy. For one thing, you could hardly tell where you were going, what with the weeds being so high. For another, it was hard to follow this so-called path; and it was prone to having deep washouts where you least expected them. He was wet to his collar, and mired to his waist, and it was a good thing wool clothing stayed warm when wet, or he'd have been frozen into an icicle by now. The swamp was eerily silent, with the only sounds being the splashing and sucking noises of his own passage, and the murmur of breeze in the reeds. It was *damned* cold. And it smelled to high heaven. Worst of all, Denny wasn't entirely certain that he wasn't lost.

"Raj?" he called, hoping he was far enough in that his brother could hear him. "Raj?"

Wolfling crouched in the cover of the weeds on the little muck-and-reed hummock Raven had led him to, watching the boy. Or rather, what he could see of the boy, which from this angle was only the top of his head. So far, this business of guarding Angela's kids had been absurdly easy. He'd stayed under cover most of yesterday, watching the boy work on his hidey until he seemed finished, then waching the hidey after the boy crawled into it to sleep. Then Raven had come to get him; fed him while May changed the bandages on his face and arms, then told *him* to get some sleep. When dawn arrived, so had Raven—the Janist had given him something to chew on ("Keeps the cold away" he'd said) and sent him back to his hiding-place.

So far all that the boy had done was to make a pocket-sized fire and boil a can of water for drinking. Other than that, he'd sat on the island for the past hour or more, hidden in the reeds, not moving. Wolfling chewed the bitter-tasting, woody stuff Raven had given him; it made his head buzz pleasantly, and did, indeed, keep the cold away. He wondered what the kid was up to. Meditating? Neither Raven nor Angela had said anything about the boy being mystical. But it was a possibility, given Jane's interest in him.

Well, whatever, it was certainly proving to be a lot easier than he'd thought it was going to be.

He was too well-trained to start at the sudden sound of a shout, but it startled the hell out of him. It was the voice of a young boy calling out a name, echoing out of the depths of the swamp.

"Raj?" It was so distorted so he couldn't really tell what direction it was coming from "Raj?"

Belatedly he remembered that "Raj" was also "Rigel" —and refocused his attention on the boy just in time to see him slide off the islet and into the reeds, fast as a lizard and nearly as silently. Wolfling saw the weeds shake once—and the boy was gone.

Ancestors!

That was *Denny's* voice, echoing among the islets out there on the path from Marsh Gate to the Rim—and if Raj could hear him, it was damn sure so could others.

Raj slid off the islet, skidding on sharp-edged, rustling grass, slipping on icy mud patches. He splashed down onto the path, ignoring the knife-like cold of the water, and then began moving as quickly and quietly as he knew how, passing through the reeds the way Raver had taught him, and hoping to get to his brother before anyone else did. He made scarcely more noise than a snake, keeping his feet under the icy water to avoid splashing, slipping between the clumps of dry, rattling weeds rather than forcing his way over them. Denny's one hope was that at this time of year, most of the *bad* crazies were either out on Dead Harbor on rafts, or deeper into the Marsh than this.

He burst into a tiny clearing unexpectedly, knife at the ready, practically on top of the kid.

"Raj!"

Denny flung himself at his brother, heedless of the knife Raj held, looking well and truly frightened. He clung to him as they both teetered in ice-rimmed, knee-deep, mud-clouded water. Raj returned the embrace, relieved almost to the point of tears to find him safe.

"Denny—" He hugged him hard. "Thank God—thank God you're okay!"

"Well, ain't that cute—a fam'ly reunion—"

Raj looked up from the kid clinging to him to see that they had been surrounded on three sides.

It was the Razorfins; a gang of crazies, but all canny-crazy types. Mostly younger than the general run of the swampies; late teens to early thirties. Rumor had it they worked for Megary—when supplies of disappearable bodies in town ran low, bodies tended to start disappearing from the swamp. There were about ten of them, ragged, dirty, and predatory. They had spaced themselves in a rough ovoid, standing on high spots at irregular intervals between the reed hummocks at distances from fifteen to twenty feet from the two boys, except on the side bordering Dead Habor. Feral eyes gazed hungrily at them from within tangles of filthy hair and beard.

They were in very deep trouble.

Raj slipped his spare knife from his belt, feeling the hilt like a slip of ice in his hand, and passed it wordlessly to Denny. Then he shifted his own knife to his left hand and felt in his pocket for his sling and a stone. He got the stone into the pocket of the sling one-handed, and without taking his attention off the gang. With the sling loose and ready in his right hand, he shifted his weight from side to side, planting himself a little more firmly in the treacherous, half-frozen mud. And prayed his numb feet wouldn't fail him.

"Hear ye finished off old Ralf, Raj."

One of the least ragged of the gang members stepped forward a little, and Raj recognized the leader, MacDac, by his shock of wild reddish hair.

"Hear ye got pretty good wi' that sticker." MacDac made a gesture with his own thin-bladed knife toward Raj's knife-hand.

Raj's hopes rose a little—if he could somehow convince them to go one-on-one with him, they *might* have a chance. Denny would, anyway, if he could talk the kid into running for it while the gang's attention was on the fight.

"Good enough to take *you,* MacDac," he said, raising his chin defiantly. "You wanta dance?"

"Maybe, maybe—" the filth-caked, scrawny gang-leader replied, swaying a little where he stood, knee-deep in muddy water, wisps of greasy hair weaving around his face.

" 'Smatter? You *scared?*" Raj taunted, as the blood drained out of Denny's face and his eyes got big and frightened. "I'm not a kid anymore, that it? 'Fraid to take me on *now?*"

"Raj—" Denny hissed, tugging urgently at his soggy sleeve. "Raj, I don't think that's too smart—"

The gang-leader hesitated—and his own followers began jeering at him, waving their arms around and making obscene gestures. Under cover of their cat-calls, Raj whispered harshly aside to the kid.

"Denny—don't *argue.* For once, I know what I'm

doing, dammit! When you figure they're all watching me, you light out for Marsh Gate—"

"No! I ain't leavin' ye!"

"You damn well do as I say!"

"No way!"

"Shet up!" MacDac roared, effectively silencing all of them. He sloshed forward a pace or two and grinned. "I ain't afraid, Raj, but I ain't stupid, neither. I ain't gonna get myself cut up fer nothin'—not when we c'n take both a' ye, an' make a little bargain with Megary."

He sloshed forward another step—his last.

Raj's right hand blurred, and MacDac pitched face-forward into the mud, wearing a rather surprised expression, a rock embedded in his temple.

There was a moment of stunned silence, then the rest of the gang surged forward like a feeding-frenzy of skits.

Wolfling lost the boy as soon as he slid into the reeds. It took him longer than he liked to get to the place where the boy had vanished—if this had been the city, even a weird city like Merovingen, he'd have had no trouble tracking the kid, but here in this foul wilderness he was at a total loss. He floundered around in the mud, feeling unnaturally helpless. Fine Hand Of Jane, *he* was. He couldn't even keep track of a dumb kid!

Then he heard the shouting; enough noise that he had no trouble pinpointing the source even through the misleading echoes out here. It sounded like trouble, and where there was trouble, he somehow had no doubt he'd find the boy.

But getting there—it was a painfully slow process; he literally had to feel his way, step by cold, slippery step. Weeds reached out for him, snagging him, so that he had to fight his way through them. The noise echoed ahead of him, driving him into a frenzy of anxiety as he floundered on, past treacherous washouts and deposits of mud and silty sand that sucked at him.

Until he was suddenly and unexpectedly in the clear. He blinked—there was a boy—no, *two* boys, standing at bay, side by side on a hummock of flattened reeds. They were holding off—barely—a gang of mud-smeared, tattered crazies. One boy was Rigel—"

Shit!

The *other* was Deneb!

Wolfling saw Jane at work, it was too much to be coincidence; first the vision, then Rigel just *happening* to be holing up out in this godforsaken slime-pit—and now the *other* boy turning up—

But the boys weren't doing well; they'd accounted for one of the crazies (now floating face-down within arm's reach of Wolfling), but the others were going to overpower them in a few minutes. Rigel had an ugly slash across his ribs that was bleeding freely and soaking into a long red stain along the front of his mud-spotted tan sweater. And even as Wolfling moved to grab a piece of driftwood to use as a weapon, one of the crazies started to bring down a boathook, aimed at the younger boy's head.

"Denny!"

Wolfling saw the horror in Rigel's eyes as the boy saw it coming, and before Denny could turn, the older boy shoved him out of the way and took the blow himself.

The deadly hook missed, but the boy took the full force of the pole on his unprotected head. The pole broke—the boy went to his knees—

And Wolfling waded into the fray from behind, roaring in a kind of berserker rage, wielding his driftwood club like the sword of an avenging angel. He connected with at least two skulls with enough force to cave them in; got enough purchase in the treacherous mud to kick in a few ribs as well. Then the rest, panicked by the unexpected attack from the rear, faded into swamp, leaving behind three floating bodies and a sudden, absolute silence.

The younger boy had flung himself at his brother when Rigel had gone down, and was holding him somewhat erect—he looked around with wild eyes when the sudden quietude registered with him. He fastened on Wolfling, paled—

And put himself as a frail bulwark of protection between the Janist and his semi-conscious brother.

Wolfling was struck dumb by a thought that approached revelation.

Those two—they'd die for each other. Rack might've killed for me—but he wouldn't have been willing to die for me—

It was hardly to be believed, that kind of attachment —but there it was, and unmistakable. Those two boys would willingly die for each other.

He held himself absolutely still, not wanting to frighten the younger kid further.

They might have remained that way forever, except for Rigel. The boy began struggling to his feet, distracting his brother, so that Wolfling was able to transfer the crude club he held to his left hand and take a step or two closer. At that, Deneb jerked around, knife at the ready, but the older boy forstalled him, putting a restraining hand on his shoulder.

Wolfling met the disconcertingly direct eyes of the older boy with what he hoped was an expression of good-will.

"N-no, 'sokay, Den—"

The words were slurred, but there was sense in the black eyes that met his.

"—'f he meant us trouble, he wouldn't 'a' waded in t' help us."

Rigel used his younger brother's shoulder to hold himself upright, and held out his right hand. "D-dunno who you are, but—thanks."

Wolfling looked from the outstretched, muddy hand, to the candid, honest face, with its expression of simple, pure gratitude.

No one, in all his life, had ever told him "thanks." No one had ever been grateful to him for anything.

He stretched out his own hand almost timidly to take the boy's, finding himself moved to the point of having an unfamiliar lump in his throat.

This boy—was *good*. That was the only way Wolfling could put it. Honest, and *good*. Small wonder Jane wanted him watched over. Wolfling had never known anyone he could have called good—

And—so Wolfling had often been told—the good die young.

Not this one, he swore angrily. *Dammit, not this one!*

Rigel swayed in sudden dizziness, and Wolfling sloshed through the churned-up mud to take his other arm and help keep him steady; Deneb tensed, then relaxed again when he realized that Wolfling was going to help, not hurt.

"Which way from here?" the Hand of Jane asked.

Raj fought down dizziness as he grayed-out a little; heard the battered, bandaged stranger ask, "Which way from here?"

"We gotta get 'im outa here—back t' town," Denny replied, hesitantly. "There's prob'ly people lookin' fer 'im by now—an 'e ain't in no shape t' stay out here, anyway."

Raj gave in to the inevitable, too sick and dizzy and in too much pain to argue. "Th' path's—through those two hummocks," he said, nodding his head in the right direction, and setting off a skull-filling ache by doing so. The three of them stumbled off down the rim-path, making slow work of it—especially since they had to stop twice to let him throw up what little there was in his stomach. He concentrated on getting one foot set in front of the other; that was just about all he was up to at this point, that, and keeping from passing out altogether.

But he was survival-oriented enough to be aware that now that they were in the clear, they were attracting the attention of the rafters—some of whom were more dangerous than the Razorfins. He tried to warn the other two, but his tongue seemed to have swollen up, and it was hard to talk. Some of the rafts began coming closer—

But South Dike was on their left side now, crumbling and water-logged brick-and-wood, looming up over their heads. And Marsh Gate was in view.

There was a shout from up ahead; shooting through Marsh Gate like a miracle incarnate was a small boat. An errant beam of sun glinted off blond hair in the bow, and there was another, darker figure waving at them frantically from the stern.

And there was ominous splashing growing nearer behind them.

The stranger on Raj's left suddenly dropped his arm, and Raj and Denny staggered as Raj overbalanced.

Then things got very blurred and very confusing.

The stranger bellowed behind them, and there was the sound of blows, and cries of anger and pain; Denny began hauling him along as fast as they could stumble through the weed and muck. Then he was in waist-deep water, with the sides of a skip under his hands, and he was simultaneously scrambling and being pulled aboard; Altair Jones was cursing under her breath beside his head.

And then a gun went off practically in his ear.

He got aboard somehow, just tumbled onto the bottom slats and lay there, frozen, and wet, and hurting; shivering so hard he could hardly think, with shouting going on over his head, and another shot, and the motor roaring up. Then they were into shadow, under the arch of Marsh Gate, then deeper shadow as they passed into the canals themselves.

It was over.

Jones shut the motor off, letting the skip coast, while Denny got a blanket around him and helped him to sit up. It was a good thing Denny was supporting him; he was shivering so hard now that he couldn't sit on his own.

"He all right?"

There was worry in Jones' voice; *that* surprised him.

"He need help? Lord—he's bleeding, ain't he! Tom—"

Mondragon was down on the slats beside him, without Raj seeing how he got there. He shut his eyes as much to hide his shame as to fight the waves of dizziness. Amazingly gentle hands probed his hurts.

"Cut along the ribs, looks worse than it is. But this crack on the skull—"

Raj swayed and nearly lost his grip on consciousness and his stomach when those hands touched the place where the boathook pole had broken over his head. The pain was incredible; it was followed by a combined wave of nausea and disorientation. The hands steadied him, then tilted his chin up.

"Open your eyes."

He didn't dare to disobey; felt himself flush, then pale. The green eyes that bored into his weren't the dangerous, cold eyes he'd seen before, but they were not happy eyes.

"Concussion, I'd judge."

"So what's that mean?" Altair asked, harshly.

"Mostly that it's his turn to be put to bed, and he isn't going to be moving from there for a while. You—"

Tom was speaking to *him* now, and Raj wanted to die at the gentle tone of his voice.

"—have caused us a good deal of trouble, young man."

"I—I didn't mean to—I just—I just wanted—" He felt and fought down a lump of shamed tears. No, no, he *would* not cry! "—I made such a mess out of things, I figured you was better off if I went away somewhere. I didn't *mean* to bring you more trouble! I tried t' find some way I c'd get you out 'f it, and get out from under your feet, and when that didn't work I just tried to do what was right."

"If I had thought differently," Mondragon said, slowly, deliberately, "you'd be out there entertaining the crazies right now. There are more than a few things I want to have out with you, but it's nothing that can't wait."

Then he got up, and took a second pole to help Jones, ignoring Raj's presence on the bottom slats.

But that wasn't the end of his humiliation. Every few feet along the canals, it seemed, they were hailed, either from other boats or from canalside.

"Yey, he's okay," Jones called back, cheerfully, "Yey, we got 'im."

Apparently *everybody* in town knew what a fool he'd made of himself. There were calls of "Hoooo—so *that's* the loverboy? Eh, throw 'im back, Jones, 'e's just a piddly 'un!" With every passing minute, Raj felt worse. Finally he just shut his eyes and huddled in the blanket, ignoring the catcalls and concentrating on his aching head.

Because, as if the humiliation wasn't enough, there were more than a few of those on canalside who *didn't* shout, shadowy figures who Mondragon simply nodded to in a peculiar way. And Raj recognized one or two as being Moghi's.

Moghi—that meant money—

A damned *lot* of money. Out of Mondragon's pocket. Raj wanted to die.

The ribald and rude comments were coming thick and fast now, as they headed into the Grand. Jones was beginning to enjoy herself, from the sound of her voice. Mondragon, however, remained ominously silent. Raj opened his eyes once or twice, but couldn't bear the sunlight—or the sight of that marble-still profile. The third time he looked up (still hoping for some slight sign of forgiveness), his eyes met something altogether unexpected.

Mondragon had shifted forward, and instead of his benefactor, Raj found himself staring across the water at another skip.

There was a girl in that skip, helping to pole it; curly brown hair, a generous mouth, a tip-tilted nose—merry eyes, wonderful hazel eyes—

Oh, she wasn't beautiful, like Marina Kamat, but those eyes held a quick intelligence worth more and promising more than mere beauty.

Those eyes met his across the Grand, and the grin on that face softened to a smile of genuine sympathy, and then into a look of utter dumbfounded amazement.

Which was maybe not surprising, if she felt the shock of recognition that Raj was feeling; because even if he'd never seen her before, he *knew* her, knew how the corners of her eyes would crinkle when she laughed, knew how she'd twist a lock of hair around one finger when she was thinking hard, knew how her hand would feel, warm and strong, and callused with work, in his.

In that moment he forgot Marina Kamat, forgot his aching head, forgot his humiliation. He stretched out his hand without realizing he'd done so—saw she was doing the same, like an image in a mirror.

And then he grayed-out again; when his eyes cleared, she was gone, and there was no sign she'd ever even been there. And he was left staring at the crowded canal, not even knowing *who* she could be.

Before he could gather his wits, they were pulling

up to the tie-up at Petrescu. He managed to crawl under his own power onto the landing, but when he stood up, he didn't gray-out, he blacked-out for a minute.

When he came to, he had Jones on one side of him, and Mondragon on the other, with Denny scrambling up the stairs ahead of them. They got him up the stairs; Lord and Ancestors, *that* was a job—he was so dizzy he could hardly help them at all. Mondragon had to all but carry him the last few feet. Then he vanished, while Raj leaned against the wall in the hallway and panted with pain.

Jones, it was, who got him into the bathroom; ignoring his feeble attempts to stop her she stripped him down to his pants with complete disregard for his embarrassment. She cleaned the ugly slash along his ribs, medicated it with something that burned and brought tears to his eyes, and bandaged him up; then cleaned the swamp-muck off of him as best she could without getting him into the bathtub. Then she handed him a pair of clean britches and waited with her back turned and her arms crossed for him to strip off the dirty ones, and finally bundled him up into bed, stopping his protests with a glass of water and a couple of asprin.

He was so cold, so cold all the way through, that he couldn't even shiver anymore. And his thoughts kept going around like skits in a cage. Only one stayed any length of time—

"Jones—" he said, trying to get her attention more than once, *"Jones—"*

Until finally she gave an exasperated sigh and answered, "What *now?*"

"Jones—" he groped after words, not certain he hadn't hallucinated the whole thing. "On the Grand—there was this girl, in a boat—a skip. Jones, please, *I gotta* find out who she is!"

She stared at him then, stared, and then started a grin that looked fit to break her face in half. "A girl. In a boat." She started to laugh, like she'd never stop. "A girl. In a boat. Lord an' Ancestors—I may go Revenantist! Instant karma! Oh, Ancestors! Damn, it's almost worth the mess ye got us in!"

She leaned on the doorframe, tears coming to her eyes, she was laughing so hard.

Then she left him, without an answer.

Left him to turn over and stare at the wall, and hurt, inside and out. Left him to the cold, to lie freezing in a cold, cold bed, as cold as his broken heart, as cold as Mondragon's face.

Left him to think about how he'd lost everything that really meant anything—especially Mondragon's respect. About how the whole town knew what a fool he was. About how he'd never live *that* down.

And think about how everything he'd meant to turn out right had gone so profoundly wrong; how he owed Mondragon more than ever. Left him to brood and try to figure a way out of this mire of debt, until his head went around in circles.

He was going shocky, he knew that somewhere down deep, but he didn't much care anymore. He wouldn't ask for any more help, not if he died of it. Maybe if he died, if they found him quiet and cold in a couple of hours, and not going to be a trouble to anybody ever again, maybe they'd all forgive him *then*.

He entertained the bleak fantasy of their reaction to his demise for a few more minutes before he dropped off to sleep.

Denny hadn't missed one of those subtle little signals Mondragon was passing to those shadow-lurkers canalside. Denny knew those shadows, knew them for Moghi's. Knew how much they cost. Was totaling up that cost in his head, and coming to a sum that scared the socks off of him.

All that—for Raj?

Oh, *hell*.

He had begun doing some very hard thinking along about the time they hit the Grand. He'd made up his mind by the time they reached Petrescu.

Mondragon had helped get Raj as far as the bathroom, then let Jones take over while he headed for the sitting-room. He stood looking out the window in the dim sunlight, arms crossed over his chest, handsome face brooding and worried. Denny made himself a silent shadow following him.

"M'ser—" he said quietly, as soon as they were alone.

Mondragon started—barely visible; controlling an automatic reaction of defense. Denny's quick eyes caught it all, and his evaluation of Mondragon rose considerably above the already high marks he'd given the man.

Damn—he's good. If he can pull his reaction after all this—he's damned good. Better'n anybody I've seen.

"What?" the man said shortly; obviously not in the mood for any nonsense.

"M'ser," he said soberly, as Mondragon regarded him over one shoulder. "I—I'm sorry about the—" he gestured, flushing, "—where I hit ye."

"You're *sorry?*" Mondragon was actually speechless.

"M'ser—lissen a minute, hey? I didn' know what t' think. Thought maybe ye might ha'—well—Raj might be worth a bit, t' the right people."

"Thought I might have turned my coat again, is that it?" Mondragon looked very odd; bitter, a little amused, and *maybe* a little understanding.

"M'ser, I don' blame ye. I was thinkin' maybe somebody's been leanin' on ye. If I was you, reckon I'd swap a kid fer Jones, if I had to—hard choice, but—that's th' way I'd be doin' it." Denny kept his eyes on Mondragon, and thought he saw a little less of the bitterness and a little more of the understanding come into those eyes.

"So—hey, I thought, ye didn' have Raj, ye might use me t' get Raj. So I let you have it where it c'd count, so's I could scat."

"I'm afraid, boy," Mondragon said quietly, "that this once you were wrong."

Denny preferred not to think about what that peculiarly phrased sentence might mean if he examined it too closely.

"Look, m'ser, I tol' ye—ye got a hard choice t' make, ye make the best one ye can. Happen I was wrong this time, but I'm sorry, hey? Now—" Denny got down to business. "I think m'brother cost ye more'n ye could afford, ne? I got eyes—an' I know what Moghi's rates are—"

Mondragon's own eyes narrowed speculatively, but he said nothing.

"M'ser Tom, I use t' figger there was one person worth spendin' anything t' keep alive, an' that's Raj. Now I figger there's two."

He felt, more than heard, Jones come in behind him. That was all right; nothing he was going to say now that he didn't want Jones to hear. "Well, maybe three, 'cept Jones back there c'n take care a' herself, *I* reckon. But t'other one's you."

Mondragon turned to face him fully, a small hint of surprise showing in the depths of his eyes, as he shifted his weight to one foot. "So?"

"It's this, m'ser—Raj, he's *good*, ye know? Ye maybe know Raj, he got a message from Granther. Well, I got one too. 'Cept mine was a hair different. I *ain't* good—Granther knows it. 'You take care a' Rigel,' he said. 'The good 'uns need us bad 'uns t' keep 'em safe.' "

Mondragon's right eyebrow rose markedly.

"I'm guessin' you got somethin' like that notion, ne? M'ser, I—" he waved his hands helplessly, "—I guess what I wanta say is this. You got inta somethin' deeper'n ye like fer us—fer him. I'm guessin'. I figger ye need a mite a' help. Well, from now on, you say, and I'll do. Whatever. However. Fer as long as ye like. An' there's some things I ain't too shabby at."

The eyebrow stayed up. Mondragon made no pretense that he didn't understand what Denny was talking about. "And if I say—no noise?"

Denny remembered a certain window, and a certain escapade which no longer seemed so clever, and the shadowy men on the canalside walkways, and shuddered. "Then it'll be quiet, m'ser. *Real* quiet. Babies wouldn't wake up."

"And how long can I expect this sudden fit of virtue to last?" Mondragon asked, with heavy irony.

"It'll last, m'ser, long as ye got use for me. Though happen—" Denny grinned suddenly, engagingly, turning on the charm he knew damned well he had in abundance. The only *useful* inheritance he had from his mother. "Happen ye'll have t' crack me over th' ear, now an' again. Rat used to—'bout once a week."

Mondragon's eyes narrowed a little as he studied Denny. The boy held steady beneath that merciless gaze, neither dropping his own eyes, nor shifting so much as an inch. Finally Mondragon nodded in apparent satisfaction.

"You'll do as I say? *Exactly* as I say? No arguments?"

"Yes, m'ser. No arguments, m'ser. I c'n spot a professional when I see one, m'ser. Happen ye could teach me more'n a bit, ne? I learn quick, even Rif says so. One other thing, though—Raj, he went an' spent all th' rent money on yer medicine, an' both of us had t' take leaves t' help out here, so there ain't nothin' saved." Denny was *not* averse to rubbing that in, just to remind Mondragon that they'd already bankrupted themselves for *him*, and that debt could work both ways.

He got a bit of satisfaction when this time he definitely saw Mondragon wince.

"So we either gotta stay here, or hit th' air-shaft again. Happen th' air-shaft ain't no bad notion; ye gotta get over th' roof t' get in it—hard fer folks t' sneak up on ye."

Mondragon shook his head ruefully, closing his eyes for a moment.

"Mercy—" he mumbled, "—*what* have I let myself in for?"

He cast a glance behind Denny. "Jones, you've got some stake in this too—"

Denny didn't look around, but heard Jones flop down in a chair behind him.

"Happen it's no bad idea," she said, "keepin' 'em here. Lots of comin's and goin's—maybe not all by doors—confuse th' hell outa watchers."

Mondragon looked over at Denny again, and Denny had the peculiar feeling of seeing someone quite near his own age looking at him out of those adult eyes for one brief flash.

"Hey, air-shaft ain't so bad," he gave a token protest. "I lived there three years. Better'n the swamp."

"I'd rather you were where I could see you."

Denny shrugged. "Well, ye want us t' stay, we stay. But we got jobs, we'll kick in."

"Ye'd better." That was Jones, behind him.

"Well then, Deneb Takahashi, I think we may have a bargain." Mondragon grinned unexpectedly. "Even if my bones tell me it may well be a partnership made in Hell."

Denny just grinned right back. "Hey, not fer *you*, m'ser. But fer people actin' unfriendly-like? 'Gainst a team like the three of us, you, me, n' Jones, m'ser Tom? They ain't got a chance!"

It was nearly sunset, and Raven had spent most of the afternoon in fruitless argument. Raven had been less than pleased with his convert's plans. He ranted at Wolfling until he was hoarse—but Wolfling had apparently been chewed out before this, and by experts; he simply held his peace until Raven ran out of words and then repeated his intentions.

Wolfling had confessed that he had panicked at first, when he'd seen *who* was picking the boys up. He told Raven and May that he'd broken out of the knot of fighting crazies he'd engaged (who by then were so busy beating on each other they hardly noticed his absence) and struggled vainly to get to the skip before it could carry the boys off.

But the skip's motor had coughed into life and carried the whole party back into the shadowed bowels of the city.

Then (so he said, with glittering eyes), recollection had come to him, and he had edged past the brawl back into depths of the swamp, comforted by this new evidence of Jane's intervention. As he had told Raven earlier, Mondragon was *former* Sword; a man with an assassin's knowledge, a snake's cunning, an eel's ways, a duelist's defenses. As Wolfling saw it now, if the Sword was after the boys, what better protection could they have than that of the man who knew most about the ways the Sword operated, and from first-hand?

But—Jane had charged him with watching over the boys—and Mondragon was only one man; he couldn't be everywhere at once, and he couldn't spend all his time awake. So. That meant that it was Jane's will that Wolfling should return to the city—

"I'm goin' back in," Wolfling said simply, for the hundredth time. "Jane put it on me, the job's not done till *She* says. She said to watch the boys, so I'm watchin' the boys."

Raven sighed, finally conceding defeat. "Cain't argue wi' Her," he admitted reluctantly. "But you got any notion *where* ye're goin'?"

Wolfling nodded, slowly. "Know where Mondragon lives; know lots of watchin' holes around Petrescu."

"Ye just contact them agents, if ye run inta trouble, hear? Rif—that's th' main one. Singer—"

"—works outa Hoh's tavern, lives second floor Fife. You told me that already." Wolfling did *not* add what he had told Raven once before, though *only* once, and only when drugged—that he probably could teach this supposed agent more than a few things about covert work. The convert had little respect for female agents; according to him, most of them were damn little use out of bed. He was obviously itching to get out and moving—Raven had given him another drug; one that was meant to clear his mind, but which had apparently also fired his feeling of purpose to a near-obsession. It was pretty clear to Raven that every moment Wolfling spent dallying was only making the urge to get into place stronger.

"All right, get movin'," Raven growled. "I kin see ye ain't got no more interest nor purpose out here."

Wolfling did not wait to hear anything more.

Perhaps he should have.

"May," Raven said, looking after the way his convert had gone, "Get yer things. It's time we got back inta town."

CHAPTER VIII

THE PRISONER

by Janet Morris

Some drunken canalers were singing, *"Sharrh light, sharrh bright/ first sharrh I see tonight/ wish I may, wish I might/ kill the sharrh I see tonight,"* when the dirty, dark stranger crossed Moghi's threshold, found himself an empty corner table, and ordered beer from the bar.

Nobody took much notice of the stranger, not this winter's eve in Merovingen, in the wake of the todo last night, with so many people bleary-eyed from search and drink. There was risk in the air. The canals had gotten to stirring untimely; it was winter, when pickings were short, and Adventist, interventionist tempers ran a shade wild. Discreet, proper Revenantists put a proper distance between themselves and the singers, fearing Adventist Melancholy, Adventist craziness. Bounty hunting was not beyond possibility, since Iosef Kalugin the governor had put a price worth a poleboat on the perpetrator of what the governor's office called a sharrist plot, and the Revenantist College of Cardinals had offered to match that price.

The snow fell and melted on the boards outside, and neither sharrh nor sharrist crazy would step in a canal-rat's trap. People laid grandiose plans and discussed what odd things they had seen; they planned to become rich.

Sharrh-hunting was not in Altair Jones' plans. She had other things besides strangers and strange lights in the sky to worry about—things like Thomas Mondragon, who stared mournfully at her over his whiskey. If the sharrh had really returned from the ends of the universe to blast Merovin to cinders for its sins, then how come, when the lights in the sky had come, no Retribution had followed?

"They're chasin' willy-wisps," she said to Mondragon, who was curing a headache the hard way, the way he had tried it that afternoon, and come, still fuzzed, to Moghi's where, as Mondragon put it, he had good credit. "So're *you*, dammit. How much'd ye spend? Do I got to ask Moghi?"

"Two hundred."

"Silver?"

"Gold."

Jones' mouth was open. She shut it. And took a drink herself. You could buy hightown lives for that. She shook her head in shock and said: "Where'd ye get it, Mondragon?"

"I told you I wasn't hurting for money. You wouldn't believe me. It's *nothing*, Jones. Tell those damn kids they don't pay me back, there's no way they can pay me back—"

"Nor *me!*" Jones snapped, short of temper. "Two *hunnert,* f' Lord's sake—"

"It's *nothing!*"

She felt sick at her stomach. Rage at Moghi. A desire to break Raj Tai's neck. The understanding, finally, that when she talked about doing a little smuggling to help out the expenses—

—it was damn useless. *She* was. Measured against that, herself and her skip and everything she owned or ever hoped to earn on the water in her whole life—

A lump swelled up in her throat. "Well, maybe then you better pay them boys *back*. They give ye medicines, they spent themselves poor f' ye. Like *me*. Ye owe me a bit, too."

"All right. How much?"

"*Your damn neck!*" She couldn't stand him when he was like this. She wanted to throw something at him, so she threw the taunt.

Jones didn't understand all the intricacies of Mondragon's dealings with his patrons, the Boregys, who were thick as thieves with Merovingen's governor's third heir, Anastasi Kalugin. She didn't understand that any more than she understood the lights that had come from heaven and begun the sharrh-hunts and touched off the Melancholy on canalside and the religious revival on the upper tiers of the stilt-city. She didn't pretend to understand how Mondragon, this handsome aristocrat from Nev Hettek, had become involved with the revolutionary, outlawed Sword of God there, or with the Sword's agents here in Merovingen.

But she understood Thomas Mondragon. He was a duelist. He was a gentleman, hightowner, a blueblood. He was an outcast, for all of that. He could never go home and that, too, Jones understood, having no home to speak of but her boat. She also understood that Mondragon had killed people, maybe a lot of people, back in Nev Hettek—and perhaps since he'd gotten here. That he'd become a traitor in the eyes of the Sword. That he was bound up in the political gaming between Karl Fon, once secret leader of the Sword of God, now respectable governor of Nev Hettek, and Merovingen's aging Iosef Kalugin.

And she understood that Mondragon got his money that way, and that he got a lot of it, but, damn, *that much*—nobody could come by honest, nor anything like it. Nobody could imagine money like that.

It's nothing.

Hell!

"Well," she said, "maybe I should take to huntin' th' sharrh, tie one up with bows and all and give 'im t' the governor. Maybe I should try some other line o' work, so's I c'n buy ser Mondragon a drink now 'n again, huh? ser hightowner."

"Hush, Jones, keep it down, for God's sake—"

"What ye *done* f' money like that? Huh?"

"Jones, you're drunk! Shut it up!"

"I ain't drunk." She stood up and her chair squealed back under her legs. "Don't you call me drunk! See these hands? I got blisters, *I* got blisters all over town after that damn boy, an' you sittin' here, nice as you please. I *ache,* an' the' whiskey's got me warm, which is th' cure I got, I hurt so much I could curl up an' die, curin' your damn mess, and you don't tell me shut up, you don't take that tone with me t'night—"

"Jones—"

The rickety chair went all the way over as she stalked blindly away from Mondragon and their table, toward the door and the wintry night. Moghi's wasn't a place he should be chasing her out of; Moghi was *her* boss, *her* livelihood—except Mondragon threw money like that at him.

Yes! m'ser!

She went, fast as she could, her back straight and her heels hitting the floor boards hard. Drunk, hell. She didn't look around, not to the right or the left or behind her. She couldn't risk another glance at Mondragon, or she was going to put her fist into Mondragon's pale, cold face.

Damn 'im!

She wove at the doorway, her vision swimming. She hoped Moghi and Jep hadn't heard Mondragon treat her like some beggar child. She hoped no one had. Out the door, between the two piles of salt that protected Moghi's threshold this winter. She almost kicked one over. Little piles, no taller than her index finger, carefully poured just where the door shut.

Everybody was getting crazy, since the sharrh had come. If they had. Nobody'd found a sharrh, or been found by one. There'd been no cleansing fire, no alien presence, no mutilated corpses—except those of the unfortunate lizards and swamp swimmers that folk had dragged in harborside, to show to the priests—

But although nobody knew what the alien sharrh looked like, anybody with a lick of sense knew they wouldn't be paddling around in the swamp or holed up in some burrow. They were the *sharrh*, who had reduced Merovin to a techless, isolated ball in an endless night, afraid to rebuild its communications and defenses, afraid of electrics, even—because the sharrh had blasted the world and gone away, not occupying it, evidently content that the world stay vacant; and if people on Merovin lit large lights and looked like heavy industry to alien eyes, then the sharrh might come back—and this time there wouldn't be any people left when they'd gone.

So if the colored lights shooting across the night sky last month had been sharrh, then how come nothing was destroyed? How come the Kalugins had put prices on the heads of sharrists? How come Cardinal Ito Boregy had held special services directly after, and demanded special donations? If the sharrh were really here, then no amount of "donations" from the faithful was going to make them go away.

And, come to think, how come the census-taking was still going on like nothing at all had happened? "Hrmph," she said to the night, down the steps now and headed for canalside, where her poleboat was tied up in the dark of three-tiered Fishmarket Bridge.

She didn't think much about the footsteps behind her, until she headed down the stone part of the walks. Then she started telling herself, Well, maybe it's Mondragon, come to apologize. But then, maybe it *was* Mondragon, just taking the long way home. He was still living at Petrescu, though he'd never take the shortest way home, like anyone else. Not Fishmarket Bridge or Little Ventani Bridge, no; Thomas Mondragon would cut all the way around by Hanging Bridge, where the Angel Michael's statue was, where the Sword of Retribution was still only partly drawn.

So she didn't turn around, or give any sign that she'd noticed the footsteps. Could be just regular traffic, too. Jones wasn't the only one who'd tied up at Fishmarket tonight. She was beginning to regret that she had, as the cold wind bit her. She could have come in closer, but she was still trying to do things Mondragon's way—don't fall into routine; don't be too obvious; do everything a little strange—you want to go here, go there first; you want to hide, do it in plain sight.

Jones was almost ready to turn around and wait for him to come up to her and apologize. She was slowing down to make it easier for him. She was considering how hard it'd be for him, that apology, and how maybe she should throw herself into his arms and make it easy for them both. . . .

She heard the footsteps coming closer, as she slowed. She was figuring what she'd say and what she wouldn't, how she'd be content with a hug and a kiss and no wordy apology. Words between them were always risky. She'd just let her man say what he wanted, keep his pride—

The footsteps behind her came faster, not slower. Maybe it wasn't him at all, just a stranger who'd go on by. . . .

A hand came down over her mouth and nose and there was some foul-smelling rag in that hand. She couldn't breathe. She started to struggle. She got her nails into the arm around her arms, that single arm pinning hers to her side.

Jones tried to bite the hand through the cloth, but the cloth was getting bigger and bigger and wrapping her all over and she was losing any sense of where her body was, or even if there was ground under her feet.

She hardly knew it when she stopped struggling and slumped against the man dragging her toward a boat made fast against the pilings of the pier. She barely felt it as the man hoisted her onto his shoulders in a fireman's carry and started climbing among the slippery bridge-supports. She didn't feel it at all when, overbalanced, he let her go and she fell three feet onto some sacks stacked on the runabout.

She didn't hear the thud as the man followed, or the cough of the little engine as it started, or a voice with a foreign accent calling, " 'Ware; 'ware."

Jones, sprawled on grain sacks and covered with a moldy blanket her captor had tied there, was dreaming that Mondragon had caught up with her on the walk, and they were back at his place, making amends the way they always did. . . .

Chance Magruder still couldn't believe his luck as he headed his runabout and his captive toward Megary, the slaver's stronghold.

But then, Magruder didn't believe in luck, other than the luck he could make. Magruder was Nev Hettek's Ambassador to Merovingen, Minister of Trade and Tariffs from Karl Fon's revolutionary Nev Hettek government to this Kalugin-ridden pesthole of a city. He was also a Nev Hetteker spy, the chief tactical officer in Merovingen of the Sword of God. And the Sword had a bastion in Megary, as well as a handy way to get rid of unwanted privy parties. This woman, Jones, a confederate of Mondragon's, was bound to be of some use, living or dead.

Either Jones would know the answers to the questions he needed to ask somebody, or the economical act of taking her captive would provide the answers to other, equally pressing questions, such as whether the Megary Sword could be trusted, and where their loyalties lay; and who would come looking for her. Should worse come to worse, Magruder could cut Jones' throat, throw her in a handy canal, and see who did the mourning and who did the blaming—and who was blamed. Or he could tell Megary to sell her and see what happened.

It was a decent night's work, even if she wasn't in Mondragon's business up to her filthy Merovingian neck. He'd watched them together in Moghi's, and if there was a good time to separate this pair and ask questions, this was surely it. It didn't take an expert to see that the two were disaffected with one another, that Mondragon was showing plenty of strain, and that the young woman was ripe for just the sort of maneuver Magruder had in mind.

No, it didn't take an expert, but Magruder was one, nevertheless. And he was, as much as he could ever be, desperate. Magruder had an agent in Merovingen who was at terrible risk, and he intended to protect that agent, one Mike Chamoun, at all costs.

Chamoun had been badly compromised, and when the kid had come to Magruder finally with the truth, it was nearly too late. The trail of treachery and double dealing had led, not unexpectedly, straight to Tom Mondragon, ex-Sword, professional traitor, leech on the neck of Vega Boregy, and involved in Boregy's own high-level machinations up to his eyeballs.

Boregy and Mondragon were supporting Anastasi Kalugin in a bid for Poppa Iosef's powerbase. Chamoun, who'd married Boregy's daughter, Cassie, was supposed to be the Sword's agent in Boregy House—Magruder's agent. But Mondragon and Boregy had tried to use Chamoun to create a second channel to the Sword in Nev Hettek, cutting Magruder out and turning the Sword against him.

And if that weren't enough, unbeknownst to Mondragon and Vega Boregy, the Revenantist College had put out a kill order on young Chamoun. Magruder knew because he was sleeping with Iosef Kalugin's daughter, and that daughter, Tatiana, had heard it from her father.

It was such a damned mess that Magruder would have to kill Chamoun himself, if this ploy didn't work. It beat waiting for somebody else to make a bad job of it, and maybe interrogate Chamoun in the bargain. It beat having to wonder who was using whom in this snakepit. It beat every plan Magruder could think of, with the single exception of using this Jones girl to get a handle on Thomas Mondragon.

And it was a longshot. Thomas Mondragon had reached that point in a man's life where almost nothing could touch him: Mondragon didn't give a damn what happened to him. Magruder was betting that, deep down in the aristocratic soul of the New Hetteker named Mondragon, there was still a bit of him that would care what happened to an innocent girl suffering in his stead. If Mondragon cared enough about Altair Jones, maybe Jones and Chamoun and Mondragon himself wouldn't have to die by the Sword's hand. By Magruder's hand.

Maybe.

Megary was the best place to try to turn a maybe into a certainty. Jones was wide awake by the time he put in there, her eyes huge over her gag, her shivering limbs struggling with her bonds.

It had been a long time since Magruder had wagered so much on a flimsy bit of guerrilla theater. He didn't like doing it now. But sometimes matters of life and death could come down to the quality of a single human soul, and this was one of those times. If this girl could be shown the right things, asked the right questions, and forced to the right actions, then she'd save three lives—one of them her own.

But Magruder couldn't even tell Jones that. He had to run her through his hastily-constructed maze and see if she learned to push the right buttons. It wasn't a cheery prospect. And it was going to take time; at least a week. Time Magruder didn't really have, if Boregy and Mondragon were playing factional games inside the Sword of God.

Hoping to hell that Altair Jones knew more than she should, and would tell him what she did know, Magruder tied up his boat, hoisted the writhing burden onto his shoulder, and struggled up the quayside toward Megary. She knew where she was, now. She was yelling as loud as she could, around her gag.

It was muffled but he knew what she was trying to say. He just couldn't listen. Magruder hated abusing innocents. He couldn't get it out of his head that this girl was one, no matter that she'd been keeping company with Mondragon. For her sake as well as her lover's, he had to hope he was wrong.

The fate she thought was in store for her as she fought helplessly on his shoulder—that of being sold as a slave—beat the hell out of what Magruder would have to do to her if she turned out to be useless in any way but as an object lesson.

You ought to be able to fight your wars between combatants, but that wasn't the way this war was going. Fon wanted control of Merovingen, and Anastasi Kalugin wanted Nev Hettek. Even if Magruder had to whack this girl, the traitorous Mondragon, and Magruder's own agent, Mike Chamoun, it was a lesser loss of life than if crazy Anastasi got his wish and put Merovingen footsoldiers in the field against Nev Hettek.

Magruder had to keep telling himself that, because he was making war on innocents, women and children and fools. All three of which, Altair Jones was as she struggled to bite him through her gag, or to wriggle off his shoulder, or to slip her bonds when he handed her over to the slavers who answered his knock.

She got a good look at him as he said to them, "Don't do nothin' to 'er, yet. She's mine. 'Fore we sell her, I got questions t' ask 'er. Hold 'er till I get back."

But that was no problem. Magruder wanted her to see his face. To remember that face, the single hope she had of not being sold off as a slave, the only thing between her and what Merovingians considered a fate worse than death. To make sure she did remember his face, he leaned down close to her, took her chin in his hand, and forced her to meet his eyes. He said, "Don' give 'em no trouble, hear? I can't be here every minute. I'll be back and we'll talk, is all. Don't you be afraid."

In the torchlight of Megary's high doorway, there could be no doubt that she saw his face, and that those wide eyes of hers would remember it. Which, of course, was why Magruder had gone to Moghi's in disguise: Chance Magruder, Nev Hettek's ambassador, was well known. Jones might have seen him, or might see him later if she survived; the man Jones saw, stubbled and dye-dark with wad-filled cheeks and a putty nose, wasn't anyone she'd ever seen before.

But she'd see him again, and again, before her time at Megary was done.

CHAPTER IX

STRANGE BEDFELLOWS
by Lynn Abbey

A cold, sleety wind followed Ashe into the shadows beneath Kamat Bridge. His fingertips left ice patterns on the bronze doorknocker and he tucked his hands beneath his armpits while he waited for the door to swing open. Another day when the sky was the same color as the Det and both were aching cold. Time was coming to accept what Kamat offered: a uniform, a two-room flat and meals in a common kitchen. Independence exchanged for security; it seemed a good idea when winter coated Merovingen with a dull, gray rime.

He swung the knocker again, and added a curse for good measure. It was six bells and high time for the mid-door of the house to be open. He'd had nothing for breakfast and the churning in his gut made the ache in his fingers worse. Still, he'd hammered a third time before Eleanora Slade opened the door.

"Took you long enough," he complained as she pushed the heavy door shut behind him.

"We're short again today. Three sick that we know of, and another four that haven't showed up yet."

Ashe grunted and stamped his feet to get the blood moving again. He shook the beads of melting ice from his jacket and hung it on a peg beside the others in the vestibule.

"Quiet night?" he asked as a canaler might ask about the winds or the tide.

Eleanora said nothing. The woman didn't gossip with the other servants and employees, though she was the point of a good deal of their whispered conversations. They all knew she wasn't like them, for all that there was a Kamat ensign worked onto her starched white collar. She poured the tea in the private study, then sat and drank it with Richard Kamat who was the master of all this. She did nothing improper—Angel knew there were enough eyes alert for any sign of *that*—but she wasn't like the rest of them, and Ashe wondered, as she walked away from him, why he had even bothered to ask.

"Anything special I should know?" he called after her in a less conspiratorial tone.

"They've come to put new beams in the larder below the kitchen, so the back middle stairs are blocked," she replied before continuing on her way.

Ashe made a mental note of that and calculated his reroutings. Merovingen's island houses were little worlds unto themselves. Riddled with stairways and corridors, Kamat House—like every other House in the city—made a mockery of geometry. Family lives and businesses were twisted and crushed together until no map could do them justice and the mark of a good retainer, like Ashe, was his ability to know at least three ways to get to any room or cul-de-sac on the island.

With a fleeting, self-satisfied smile, Ashe went up the stairs to the main hall of Kamat House where a box partly filled with envelopes waited for his attention. The mail would be delivered even if he hadn't shown up for work, but everyone from Richard Kamat on down knew that he would deliver it faster and more efficiently than anyone else. He sorted the mail in his fingers, adjusting his course as each envelope slipped into place.

Lower house mail came first—mostly bills and trade broadsheets—then the mid-house mail: a scrawled letter for Cousin 'Lexsandra from one of her classmates, an invitation for Cousin Gregory from one of his college societies; and finally the interesting mail for the family itself. Ashe shot his cuffs beneath his sweater before rapping on Andromeda Kamat's door.

"Mail for you, m'sera."

There was a hesitation, and a faint scuttling sound as if the dowager of the high house weren't quite ready to receive her servants. Ashe brushed a hand across his forehead to be certain it did not shine with perspiration and shifted his weight silently from one foot to the other.

"Come in, Ashe."

He entered silently, as a House servant should, and kept his eyes focused discreetly—rigidly—on the patterned carpet between the door and the small redwood table where m'sera Kamat kept her pens and paper. But he missed no detail of the room. Ashe saw how m'sera's breakfast was untouched and cold; how her daughter, Marina, sat all cramped and anxious on the chaise; how m'sera held a scrap of cheap paper against her thigh.

The writing was folded to the inside of the paper—not that it mattered. Ashe could not read script, but he remembered well enough, and he remembered delivering that scrap to the young m'sera three mornings ago. The night porter remembered that a scruffy youth had delivered the scrap to the house, and the underhouse chambermaid guessed it was the same youth who had dined with the young m'sera during the dowager's recent absence.

Ashe laid the vellum on the table and left as discreetly as he'd entered. There was a story here to dissect and reconstruct over tea in the underhouse kitchen. He walked a bit faster and took the stairs to m'ser Richard Kamat's rooms two at a time. Richard heard him coming; the door was open when Ashe reached the landing at the top of the octagonal tower. Ashe's face was faintly red as he handed the envelopes to the house's master, but Richard—discreetly—took no notice of it and Ashe escaped much as he had arrived.

Richard listened to the rhythm of the servant's retreating steps for a moment. It was a tight, two-faced realm that he commanded within Kamat's walls. The more loyal a retainer was, the more that retainer was addicted to gossip about the family in the lower rooms. Something faintly scandalous echoed from Ashe's heels, something that he, as Househead, should probably be aware of. Ruffling his mail Richard wished, and not for the first time, that he was half so good at smelling out scandal within the other Houses as his servants were within his own home.

He opened the letters in the order he had received them—which was to say, in no order at all. It was karma, then, that the most important communication was the last. Richard read it twice then let it fall to the desk where the red wax imprint of the Boregy crest shone like blood in the winter light, and the graceful signature of Vega Boregy smiled insolently up at him.

"Well, Murfy take all," he muttered, knowing that no one could hear him, "if that's not the limit of arrogance."

It was a short letter, informal in style and grammar, as if Vega were sharing an inconsequential thought with a friend. And therein lay the arrogance, for Boregy was no friend of Kamat, though it was not an enemy, either . . . yet. Boregy brokered political power along with its bank notes, but it had never before taken any notice at all of Kamat. Boregy wasn't even Kamat's principal bank; Hosni Kamat, the house's founder, had decreed that no banker should ever have more than twenty percent of their assets.

Richard had come to power in Kamat nearly fifteen years ahead of schedule and he'd had less than a year to accustom himself to the ways of power. He had not contemplated revising any of his grandfather's policies in the near future—but he was contemplating now and praying—to Murfy, if no one else was listening—that Kamat's collective karma lay solidly on the plus side of the ledger.

Have given the matter some thought, Vega Boregy had written. *The mercantile houses should have their own security force. Our bank would back a prospectus offering should it come from a major depositor. Are you preparing such a prospectus? Keep me informed.*

Richard had learned to swim one morning when he was four years old. The memory was very clear in his mind, and it was his only crystalline memory of his grandfather. Hosni had taken him downstairs to the huge vats where the wool was rinsed, then the old man had thrown him in. Richard could still conjure up that water's taste. He was smiling unconsciously, and looking very much like the portrait of Hosni Kamat that hung in the dining room, when he reached for his pen and ink.

Iosef Kalugin had rewritten the rules of Merovingen when he let his children brawl their way toward power. Perhaps he thought his conservative, Revenantist city would sit idle, as timid about political change as it was about encroaching technologies. And perhaps it was, but Kamat knew what its founder had known: there was a time for caution, and there was a time for risk.

Dear Vega, Richard began without hesitation. *I had, in fact, been considering which bourse would underwrite my prospectus for the* Samurai. *Your timely offer has spared me the choice. I am today directing my agents to commence transfer of Kamat assets—*

Richard heard footfalls on the stairway. He blotted the ink and slid another sheet over the top of it before he heard a knock. There were some things one did not let the servants find out before one had informed the family.

"Come in."

He'd expected a servant—Ashe or one of the others, perhaps even Eleanora Slade—but it was his mother who came through the door, with Marina a nervous shadow in Andromeda's wake. Briefly, angrily, Richard wondered if Boregy would have had the audacity, along with the arrogance, to contact Andromeda directly.

Andromeda pulled one of the leather wing chairs closer to her son. "Dickon, I think we have a problem . . ."

Richard let his breath out slowly, made a show of clearing his desk to give them his full attention. He hid all traces of the Boregy matter. Whatever was troubling his mother and Marina, it wasn't business—not if they were calling him Dickon. Yet it couldn't be trivial, either, or they would have waited until later in the day.

"So tell me and I'll see what I can do about it."

"Ree has gotten herself into a situation—"

Marina looked away as her mother unraveled all the details of her involvement—one couldn't call it an affair—with the rootless orphan she knew only as Raj. It was all so ludicrous. A hightown woman, like herself, stumbling blindly into love because of a doggerel poem. And it was dangerous as well.

"You see, Dickon," Andromeda explained. "She thought the notes were from Thomas Mondragon."

Despite himself, Richard jerked his head up and stared at Marina in disbelief. She started to cry and the older brother in him wanted to rush to her chair to tell her everything would be all right. He didn't.

"Thomas Mondragon," he repeated. "Have you taken leave of your senses completely, Marina? The damned Sword of God nearly got you killed at Nikolaev; they're smuggling our cargoes; and you're exchanging love poems with one of their agents!"

Andromeda leaned forward, recapturing his attention. "Now, Dickon, it's not as bad as all that. We've every reason to believe that young Mondragon is on the outs with the Sword—"

"Then he's drawn them here after him. It's all the same difference."

"Well, be that as it may, Dickon, yelling at Marina won't change what's been done. She thought the notes were from young Mondragon and she thought the boy was his messenger. She made certain . . . ah, *promises* because of that—"

"Oh, Lord—what promises?"

Marina shifted uncomfortably in her chair. "He's a bright boy, Dickon."

"I know he's smart enough," Richard interrupted angrily, thinking she meant Tom Mondragon. "It's you I'm worried about."

"Not Mondragon," Andromeda corrected as her daughter's lips quivered. "The boy, the messenger, the one she promised College sponsorship to medicine . . . so he could continue delivering the messages." Marina cringed as her motives were revealed, but Andromeda rushed on. "The boy himself saw the dishonor of it, but, being only a boy, he's handled it poorly and run away to the swamps rather than face his shame."

With that, and as Marina hid her own face, Andromeda Kamat laid Raj's scrawled note—and his earlier poems—on the desk before her son. Dutifully, Richard read them, then laid them aside.

"Well," he said after a dramatic, almost melodramatic, pause. "What am I supposed to do now, Mother?"

Andromeda trembled with the exasperation of dealing with her grown children. This was hardly the time or situation for Richard to display the first signs of sarcasm. "I expect you to understand what this means," she said with grim earnestness. "A boy to whom Kamat has made promises has taken himself off to the swamps where he will, in all likelihood, meet an untimely end. An untimely end, do you hear that?"

Richard did; and he knew that he had no options. Still, he was riled past mere annoyance, and something would have to suffer his displeasure. "What? Should I fear public opprobrium because an orphan dies in the swamps? Will the cardinal care? They're probably all Adventists, anyway, Mother. Linked up with Mondragon. They don't believe in karma any more than you do—"

"Richard!"

His mother's voice went shrill. Her face flushed scarlet and Richard found his anger evaporating quickly. Nikolay Kamat's death had scarred and crippled Andromeda. She was frail where she had once been elegantly slender; hysterical when she had been vivacious. Richard had sent her out of the city for her health while the weather was stagnant and just recently suggested she come back.

There were a dozen or more comments swirling in Richard's head, each more scathing than the last. He swallowed them all. Karma or no karma, he was not prepared to have his mother's relapse on his conscience.

"All right, I'll try, but I'm not *promising* anything myself. If this Raj did—does—live in Mondragon's shadow, he's hardly likely to show up in any of the registers. People like him disappear even when they don't want to; it's an upstream swim to find them if they don't want to be found. . . ."

Both women nodded, but Richard was not deceived. Neither had any idea of life's rigors in Merovingen-below. They thought that because he could talk to the canalers in their own jargon, he could pluck the boy out of his hideout. It was a trust that settled uncomfortably around his shoulders, but it was better than the alternatives.

"Now, I want you both to promise me that you'll let me handle this. I don't want either of you lifting a finger, whispering to a servant or, Murfy forbid, thinking you'll wander Below yourselves."

"But Richard, I'm the only one who knows what he looks like, or has any idea where else he might have gone . . ." Marina looked up at her brother.

"Then tell me, and make me a sketch. I'm serious about this, both of you. No promises and I won't lift a finger."

"We promise not to search for the boy ourselves," Andromeda said quickly. "But what will you do when you find him?"

"*If* I find him," Richard corrected, "then I'll tell him Kamat's promises are good—no matter who makes them."

He glowered at his sister and she thought the better of further comments. They left after Richard said he'd be down to Marina's rooms in an hour to get the sketch he'd asked for. He said he had a few loose ends to tie up before commencing his search, but in reality he slipped down the hall to his sparsely-decorated bedchamber and changed his clothes.

"You don't look like you're going Below," Marina criticized when he appeared in tailored woolens.

Richard took the sketch, studied it, and folded it carefully into his waist pocket. "I have a few other things to do first," he insisted.

"You'll be a marked man if you go Below wearing that signet—" Andromeda emerged from one of the wing chairs. The lapis ring wasn't the House signet, but it was official enough to move Kamat money from one bank to another—a fact which clearly was not lost on the dowager.

'I won't wear it Below. It's just . . . as I said, I have a few other things to do first.'

Andromeda stared into her son's eyes until he turned away. "I'm sure you'll do what you think best."

The ice in her voice was cold comfort to Richard who muttered his good-byes and beat an ungracious retreat. One of the many things Nikolay had not had time to teach his son was how to control the privileged members of his household. Richard could not lie to them, not artfully or creatively as a Househead must; he could only repeat his clumsy half-truths with rising intensity until one side or the other backed down.

He would search for the boy, although Angel knew there was little enough hope of success there. He'd make some inquiries among the canalers and jobbers who regularly congregated in Kamat's slip waiting for work. But not now, not today. If there was karma, then it was, like all things, relative, and the karma attached to the Samurai was infinitely greater than the karma of an orphan.

Richard let the front door slam behind him. A boatman in the Kamat slip shouted up, offering his services to the Househead. Richard waved him aside and scuttled across the St. John bridge like a shamed dog.

"He won't help," Marina muttered, her voice filled with childish disappointment. "He lied to us."

"No more than we did to him," her mother corrected.

The dowager wrapped her thin fingers around a bell cord. She yanked it three times in quick succession before facing her daughter.

"How did we lie to Richard?"

"By omission, Marina dear, by omission. I told him what we would not do, but I did not tell him what we would do. Your father and I loved you too much— each in our own way. You both have much to learn."

There was a knock on the door. Andromeda called the servant in.

"Your service, m'sera?"

He was a large young man with broad shoulders made larger by the bulky First-bath sweater he wore.

"M'sera Marina will be needing you to ferry her about the city this afternoon. She will be looking for the gentleman I described to you earlier."

The retainer's hair was dark and curly, his face was bland and regular, his skin was the sallow gold so common in Merovingen, and yet he was an altogether memorable figure—which struck Marina as very odd, since she could not remember having seen him before around the House. She looked at her mother who replied with an enigmatic smile.

Perhaps there was indeed more to learn about House life than she had hitherto imagined. "We'll be looking for Raj?"

"No, Ree, you'll be looking for Thomas Mondragon."

It was only with the greatest of efforts that Marina kept a flush from burning across her cheeks as her mother—her oh-so-proper, discreet and timid mother—explained an itinerary to an obviously loyal Kamat servant neither she nor—and Marina was certain of this—Richard had ever laid eyes upon before.

"You understand, Kidd, that I'm holding you personally responsible for my daughter's well-being?"

"Yes, m'sera."

"Very well, now get the boat ready." Andromeda was silent while Kidd left, then she turned to her gaping daughter and appraised her appearance from boots to hair. "That will never do, Ree."

"What will never do, Mother? What in Murfy's name is going on? How am I supposed to go looking for Tom?"

"It's what you want to do, isn't it? It's your heart's desire; it's written clearly on your face. I think I saw Thomas Mondragon before I married your father—he was only a toddler then—but I knew the Mondragons, or of them. Sword of God he may be, but he's Mondragon first. If the boy's missing, he's missing because of Tom as much as he's missing because of you. We might not have karma in Nev Hettek, but we've honor—and that's enough for a Mondragon."

The color rose in Marina's cheeks at last. She *did* love Thomas Mondragon—in a blind, romantic way. Her imagination could conjure all manner of consequences to locating Tom and searching with him to find the boy.

"What should I wear?" she asked as Andromeda led the way toward the wardrobe.

An hour later, more carefully turned out than for a Kalugin's ball, Marina descended the inner stairway to Kamat slip where Kidd was waiting.

"Petrescu," she said, scarcely recognizing her own

voice. Her heart was pounding against her ribs; she felt deliciously alive and eager for adventure.

"Yes, m'sera."

Petrescu! Petrescu's spires were visible from her own bedroom. Marina had watched the boy, Raj, run across Foundry Bridge toward it. Had she known she might have kept watch beside her window and caught a glimpse of her hero on the seat of some poleboat going about his business. She did not ponder how her mother had, in a few short hours, flushed out the elusive Mondragon's home; she only marveled that Andromeda had given the venture a romantic's blessing.

Yet, like most dreams, meeting Thomas Mondragon was better imagined than lived. Marina's face was pale and her hands both cold and damp by the time Kidd expertly cut the current and sluiced around into Petrescu slip.

"Will you wait here?" Marina asked as he tightened the bow line.

"Yes, m'sera."

Marina nodded and waited for him to assist her from the boat to the walk and the stairs. It was not the sort of hightown gesture she usually affected, but her legs had gone rubbery and she needed his rock-solid arm.

Andromeda Kamat's information was both precise and accurate. Marina found herself on the second-tier walkway before a nondescript, unmarked door. She purged the air from her lungs and inhaled deeply. Her hands steadied and the knots in her throat loosened, then she tapped on the door.

Nothing. But then Marina Kamat wasn't used to knocking on doors. People knocked on her door, servants knocked for her, but mostly she had never gone where she was neither expected nor invited. Below her the water splashed noisily between boat and isle-rim. Kidd was watching her; she could feel his eyes. He was laughing at her—laughing silently and without expression the way all servants did. Marina steeled herself and fairly threw her fist at the door.

This time there was sound beyond the door: feet scuffing along floorboards, a throat being cleared, a spy-hole clicking open and shut. Marina smiled automatically when she heard that, but her lips were thin and she could smell her mother's ashes-of-roses perfume rise around her.

The door swung open. It was Tom Mondragon—and she was left speechless. Her hero looked as if he'd been sleeping in his clothes—possibly sleeping off a binge in them. His pale gold hair tousled disarmingly across his forehead. The arm he held against the door-jamb seemed to keep him upright while the other hung limply at his side. He did not stare, but blinked as if he did not believe his own eyes. Fortunately, Marina found her tongue before he found his and she introduced herself as Andromeda had suggested.

"I am Marina Cassirer Kamat; I've come about the boy, Raj . . ."

He pondered that for a heartbeat or two, and Kidd on the landing a heartbeat longer. A cat might have smiled as Mondragon did as he invited the Kamat heiress into his home and closed the door behind her.

"We've got him back, a bit worse for the wear but nothing permanently damaged. Your concern is appreciated."

All the lines Marina had rehearsed flew out of her head. If Raj was safe, there was nothing she could say. Or so it seemed.

"Cassirer—that's an unusual name for Merovingen, isn't it?" Tom asked softly.

Marina fancied herself a kindred spirit of the lower classes—or at least the middle classes. She affected cut-off breeches and baggy sweaters when Andromeda did not intervene. But she knew next to nothing about life beyond the security of the Houses. She thought Mondragon was still fuddled by alcohol and sleep. She thought he was making polite conversation.

"It's a Nev Hettek name. My mother's from Nev Hettek."

"Come in, then. Sit down."

He led her to the sitting room. Marina's heart was pounding again, but the notion that she was further and further from the boat where Kidd stood guard never wandered across her mind. Still, some warning must have turned in her subconscious.

"We had a devil of a time finding you, Thomas

111

Mondragon. You're quite the shadow. I guess that's why . . ." She blushed, and a scent of musk and roses grew around her. "Well, you *do* know what happened?" She pulled Raj's poems and his final note from her pocket and held them out.

Mondragon took the tattered sheets. His expression remained sleepy-wary as he read the melodramatic letter, but it changed when he encountered the poetry.

" 'But if, despite of all my lies/ There is forgiveness in your eyes/ Then as my sorrowing soul dies/ I shall most welcome Death.' " The corners of Tom's mouth crinkled upward and he shook his head slightly. "I could never write like this, Marina Cassirer Kamat." He handed the packet back to her.

Marina looked down as she took them, but it did no good. She blushed violently. The edges of her ears were warm and, she was certain, brilliant carmine. "I feel so utterly foolish. I—I should go back home. I'm as hopeless as the boy."

She retreated a step, but Mondragon's fingers clamped around her arm and she stopped.

"Raj gave me a pretty scare, disappearing like that. I had no idea what he was up to, not even an idea how much he dreamed of medicine and the College. I'm not sure I'd have seen things his way. I might have been inclined to take Kamat's stipend and continued the lie, if I'd felt as he did—about medicine, that is."

Her heart could pound no harder, and, as no one could actually die of embarrassment, Marina found her composure slowly returning. "That wasn't a lie—not if he's as talented as he claims he is. Kamat stands by its promises."

"Karma?"

"Honor."

The unreadable veil of expression across Tom's face changed its texture. Marina believed she'd risen a bit in his estimation, and for once she was not completely mistaken.

"We'll sponsor Raj to the College." A bit of fire and sincerity had returned to her voice. "We'll give him whatever he needs: his books, his board, and enough silver in his pocket so he needn't apologize to anyone."

"Raj wouldn't like charity."

For a moment Marina forgot the Angel-faced man who touched her arm. It was her House they were talking about—her honor—and there was nothing romantic or embarrassing about it. "It wouldn't be like charity. Kamat takes care of its own; even the Below knows that. There'd be a place for Raj when he was finished." She stared straight into Mondragon's eyes. "We pay for a man's labor, not his soul, and we don't use him up."

The pressure on Marina's arm increased for a moment, and changed, as did his expression. "Kamat? Kamat . . . woolworkers and dyers, aren't you?"

"First-bath."

He nodded, taking note of the midnight silk she wore so casually, and the subtle weaving of silver which traced her collar.

"A man is lucky, then, if House Kamat is his patron or employer."

"We think so. My great-grandfather herded sheep above the Det Valley."

Tom released her and she took a moment to brush the wrinkles from her sleeve. Kamat was not the wealthiest House in Merovingen, though it issued no public debentures and registered no unsecured liabilities with the Signeury. Only the wiliest of Houses guessed, or remembered, that Kamat's greatest assets were not within the city at all. They had never divested themselves of the vast flocks or tracts of land that had first given them the price of an island home in Merovingen.

"We remember our origins and our word. I'll tell Raj that myself, if he's here. He can apply at the College whenever he's ready."

Mondragon shook his head, and caught her again, this time more intimately above the waist. "He is at the age where a man's pride is his most cherished possession. He wouldn't know how to thank you, and it might keep him from accepting your offer. But he'll accept it; I can no longer give him my shadow."

Marina's eyes asked the question.

"One of your Det Water fevers, I'm afraid; plus looking for Raj, and . . ." his voice trailed off, leaving Marina to guess what was left unsaid.

The Kamat heiress guessed quickly, and wrong, since there was nothing that she could recognize to say another woman made her home here. "And you have no relief from your patron, yourself—"

Tom's eyes shot to the right: a small gesture, and one Marina might have missed altogether if it had not been cousin to the one Richard had used before leaving her room. In neither case could she see behind the hiding, but she knew to move carefully.

"I wouldn't presume to offer you anything. If you'd been seeking company in the Houses, it wouldn't have been half so difficult to find you. You probably think I'm a schoolgirl goose anyway."

"A schoolgirl wouldn't have found me. I have to admire you some for that."

Marina cringed inwardly. This was Andromeda's arena, and Marina couldn't dredge up from her imagination how her mother would turn all this to advantage. "And I admire you," she murmured awkwardly.

He smiled at her, radiantly and expertly. "I know. You shouldn't. I'm a marked man, and a very poor one. I've nothing to offer the noble House of Kamat."

That was a lie, and quite possibly he knew it. There was no mistaking the tension in his fingertips, pulling Marina closer. Close enough that she could feel his warm breath on her face and lose herself in his eyes.

"You hardly know us. A wise man doesn't make presumpt . . ." Her words froze as he tucked a lock of hair behind her ear.

"Who said I was wise?"

Thomas Mondragon was everything she'd dreamed a man should be. His arms were perfect; his kisses were perfect; upstairs, in his bedroom, even the tingle of the coarse linen sheets as they rasped across her spine was perfect. His lovemaking proved that she was right to have waited until the perfect man came along—and she did not consider it at all strange or improper that she could not possibly have been the first for him.

In point of fact, Mondragon took it rather poorly that Marina had surrendered her virginity to him. House women usually shed that sort of nonsense before leaving school. How else was a woman to know if she wanted to get married or not? How else would she perform her ancient duty to create the next generation? In Merovingen, romance had little to do with sex, Andromeda said it was somewhat different in Nev Hettek, where schoolgirls spent more time reading novels than learning religion.

Marina lay in the arms of a Nev Hetteker. She could have asked and gotten the truth of it for once and for all, but she didn't. There was no need to clutter up such a singular afternoon with philosophy. He was content to let her slowly explore the realms she had avoided. Occasionally, between kisses and caresses, he would remind her that he was House-less here, a Boregy adherent poorly maintained, with nothing to offer in return, and she was at pains to insist that she already owed him a debt larger than she could repay in a lifetime.

"We'll see," Mondragon replied, tracing the blood-flushed aureole of an upright breast. "A lifetime can be very long."

Shadows filled the windows and hid their faces before Tom saw fit to remind Marina about the man she'd left guarding the landing.

"Someone will be wondering after him, if not you," he chided as he trailed her shirt across her skin.

Marina grabbed the silk and broke the moment's magic. "I'd like to wash."

"There's a basin on the shelf. I told you I'm poor. Go back to Kamat for your porcelain tubs and hot-water pipes." Her face dropped. Mondragon was moved to sit again on the bed beside her. "I'm shamed to live like this—and know that this is better than it will be. The rent is due, Boregy is put out with me, and Petrescu wants lunes, not soggy, twice-steeped tea—"

She had come expecting to endow the search for Raj. Her mother had supplemented her allowance with a half-dozen fingertip-sized gold gram coins. No promises; no accounting—as if Andromeda had guessed that her largesse might not flow toward its original purpose. Marina folded her collar and cuffs, then reached for her breeches.

"I suppose," she began, thinking herself very clever, and artful, "that if Raj can't come to us for his pride, then someone else shall have to watch over him." She fished the pieces out, but had to pull his hand toward her and pry his fingers apart before she could place the coins on his palm.

He stood before the window, hardfaced and silent in the waning light.

Pride, Marina reminded herself, the romance novels were filled with prickly, fragile masculine pride. He was a Mondragon, and that counted for more than she imagined he could forget. His house was gone—betrayed and slaughtered, with him taking the blame, (Andromeda had that from her aunt, Fortune, who'd married into the Fon clan for a time). He could hardly feel good with Kamat gold burning in his hand, however much he needed it.

She buttoned her breeches and laced her boots before going to him. "I know about a man's pride," she whispered. "I really do."

"You should be more careful," Tom replied, still staring out the window.

"My brother will welcome any child I might bring into the House," she said lightly and confidently. "It simplifies his life somewhat."

Mondragon dropped the gold into his pocket, then leaned against the window frame. His arms bulged beneath his shirt and his neck pulsed in the chiaroscuro light. "Life isn't what you think. I'm not what you think. Nothing is, not this afternoon, not anything. If you've any sense at all, Marina, run away before you get hurt."

That, too, was something men said when they were in tight straits, when they wanted someone more than they dared to admit. She stood on tiptoe to kiss his hard, cool cheek. "You run away, then, and I promise I won't look for you. Is that fair?"

He shook his head wearily, but said that it was.

In romantic novels, the heroine always knew when and how to leave a tryst. Following their oft-read examples, Marina finished dressing, left an earring casually beside the basin (for retrieval the next time she came) and slipped quietly out of the apartment.

"You all right?" Kidd asked the moment she arrived at waterside.

Marina realized that for all her care, her hair was still mussed and her shirt unevenly belted. She attended to those details quickly and assured Kidd that she was, indeed, all right.

"I was beginning to get real worried. 'Bout two hours ago a kid comes out of there like his tail's on fire. Took the stairs two at a time, up the bridge-beams, and lit out onto the roofs, I think. Didn't know what to make of it."

"Raj?" She felt guilty suddenly, remembering the boy's lovelorn poetry and that she and Tom had not troubled to be quiet.

"Little kid, maybe eight or nine. Glad you're all right, m'sera. We should get going."

Marina sat down in the boat feeling serene and elated, both at the same time. She ached a bit and felt that her walk was somehow different—mature, no longer schoolgirlish. There was an emptiness above her thighs she had never felt before: a constant reminder of what had been and what would have to be again.

While Kidd poled the boat into the current, she imagined a little scene where she told Richard that the next Kamat heir would have Mondragon blood. Richard looked pleased; he congratulated her for her wise and attractive choice. Then she imagined telling Tom (his room was nicer—he was living in Kamat, working for Richard, or so seemed likely). Tom's face was unreadable; not even her imagination could make him smile broadly.

A cold wind blew across the canal. Marina wished she had her own bulky sweater rather than her mother's lacy wrap around her shoulders. Her belly was ice cold and she hunched forward, catching Kidd's eye as she did. The servant looked away.

Richard was at the slip talking with a knot of canalers whose boats were riding low under bales of Kamat wool. He still wore his good clothes, but that was not as uncommon for him as it was for Marina. He stared at her as she climbed out of Kidd's boat, and she stared back. They were different as night and day, yet too close for secrets. Marina saw that he, too, moved differently, as if his body were not the familiar place it had been in the morning; and she was confident that he noted the change in her. Yet Richard had had his flings since before College.

"The boy's been found," she said, needing something to break the silence between them.

He nodded and relaxed his shoulders. "Good. I'm glad. Nobody seemed to know anything anyway."

"I had the most amazing afternoon, Dickon—"

"I'll see you at supper, Marina."

He *had* changed. There was no doubt about it, and the mystery of it cast a pall through her sitting room. It wreaked havoc with her thoughts as she strove to commit the tryst to the scented pages of her diary. She'd begun the diary, after all, when her brother had become more absorbed in business and could spare less time for his little sister's dreams.

Marina was ready to replace her brother's face with her lover's in her dreams—but she wanted to choose to do it.

Far below Richard's octagonal office a canaler shouted out the start of the first night watch. By custom, the family ate supper midway through the watch, but timing would be the only customary aspect of tonight's dinner. Richard's hand trembled as he poured an amber dram of brandy. He threw his head back and caught the liquor at the back of his throat. It burned, and the burning steadied his nerves.

He poured a second dram and savored it in the proper fashion.

The meeting with Vega Boregy had gone well. Difficult, but well. Boregy was as smooth and polished as his hardwood desk; it would have been terribly easy to play the student to his mentoring—and, Angel knew, Vega had tried to grease the skids. But Richard felt he had resisted, felt he had gotten a fair deal for his House.

Kamat had, in effect, become a Boregy client, yet that had not entailed a downward step in Merovingen's all-important hierarchies. Boregy was banking and finance; Kamat was mercantile with solid interests far beyond Merovingen. The man had been impressed when Richard showed him an annotated, and abridged, tally of his House assets. For three generations Kamat had operated alone, lest it be swallowed. Clientage was, perhaps, the inappropriate word; alliance felt better—so long as Richard kept his wits securely about him.

He swallowed the second dram.

Aye, there's the rub, Richard quoted the ancient play in his mind. *To keep my wits about me, when I don't know what I'm doing.*

He picked up the decanter and carried it to the fireplace where Eleanora Slade waited quietly in a wing chair. "Sip it slowly," he advised her as he filled her tiny glass. Brandy of this age and purity seldom escaped the private cellars of the great houses.

Eleanora's eyes filled with tears after the first swallow. She stared at the bit that was left and wondered why anyone would trouble to acquire the taste for it. "This is a celebration?" she asked in the blunt way that Richard had come quickly to cherish.

"A reward for work well down; and the strength to do more work tomorrow."

She shook her head and handed the glass back to him. "You must work very hard, but I see your point. Why will you call them Samurai?"

Richard emptied her glass and threw it at the fire. For a moment the flames hissed and burned hotter. It was an old custom, and one that had nothing to do with fire-wary Merovingen. Shepherds carved their mugs, then burned them when their rotgut liquor soured the wood.

"My father had a book: THE BOY'S HISTORY OF HONOR. It had hand-colored pictures and I remember reading it, oh, a dozen times or more. The Samurai were men of honor a thousand years before mankind ventured into space. They served the great houses, but they were more than employees. They were part of the house and they defended it as if it were their own. There was no distinction between a house's honor and a Samurai's honor. I always remembered that.

"It's what we want in our new security force: honor. Honor to each other, honor to the houses, and honor to Merovingen. Not like the blacklegs who started out as pirates, smugglers and thugs, and who haven't changed very much."

Eleanora slipped her shoes off and tucked her feet beneath her in the chair. "I understand that, but, Richard, there are only a few sorts who will be interested in patrolling the warehouses and docks night after night—and most of them would make better thugs than samurai. How do you plan to separate the wheat from the chaff?"

He smiled and kissed her lightly on the forehead. "You've touched the heart of the problem: how indeed? And I'll tell you just as honestly, I just don't know." One of the many bells above the door jingled, announcing that supper had begun its journey from the kitchen to the diningroom. "The family awaits. Wish me luck; I'll be back when it's over."

"You don't need luck Richard. You'll do yourself proud without it."

He kissed her again and, as he descended the spire, reappraised what it would take to get the rest of the clan to acknowledge her as an equal. He was getting used to the politics and intrigues of Househeadship—he was even starting to enjoy them—but he wasn't going to bring those problems into his bedroom or his heart.

As usual, Richard was last to the diningroom, having traveled the farthest. Andromeda and Marina were already standing beside their chairs at the far end of the huge, empty, table. He gasped his greetings and thumped solidly into his chair; Andromeda rang the silver bell beside her plate and the meal began.

They exchanged pleasantries and gossip over the appetizer—sculler prawns in aspic—but the conversation waned more quickly than Richard had expected, as if his mother and sister sensed that there were more important things to discuss than Beri Raza's twins and preparations for the Festival of the Angel next month.

The soup was still steaming in its tureen when Richard began the enlightenment of his family. Some of it was already known, but bore retelling: the anarchy that flowed in the wake of the rivalry among Old Kalugin's children; the wanton smuggling at the warehouses, much of it by the hand of Nev Hettek and the wink of the blacklegs; the rumble of discontent that had been heard Below since the Sword of God and the fever settled into the city. Richard laid it out with careful, uncontestable logic; the women nodded as their spoons rose and fell.

"Merovingen has passed the point where balanced karma can be restored without change. Even Old Kalugin knows that. It's like the Det herself; she eats at her banks and each season we shore everything back up, but when she floods, there's no turning her and it's the city that adapts." Richard summed up the past and the present before plunging into the future.

"And since everything must change before balance is restored, Kamat will change too, but this time we'll be in the van—not the rear."

He told them what had been decided at Boregy. A new security force—self-incorporated, but funded and controlled by the great merchant houses—was ready to emerge, and Kamat was the driving force behind it. A new force in Merovingen to balance the corrupt blacklegs, the Sword and other nameless sowers of anarchy. And as it succeeded, Kamat's fortune and karma would rise.

There would be fifty of them at first, working the warehouses in round-the-clock shifts, but the force would grow much larger as its counterbalancing power was felt and appreciated. They would be called Samurai and, as Richard had explained to Eleanora, their honor would be paramount.

"The blacklegs will make trouble," Andromeda cautioned. "They won't stand down for your men of honor, Dickon. What will we do then, if we're the ones who start it?"

"If there is fighting, there will have been fighting whether we created the Samurai or not. And if there is fighting, it is better to be in a position to win from it."

"But what if we don't win," Marina asked.

"Then we leave the city and shear sheep."

"What about First-bath? What about our obligations?"

Andromeda nodded approval of her daughter's question. "Yes, Dickon, what about everything we stand for?"

"I don't intend to lose, Mother."

Richard's voice held a finality that had not been

heard at this table since Nikolay's death last Greening: the voice of a Househead issuing orders. Andromeda sat back so suddenly that the butler asked if something were wrong with the meat. She stared at her son, whom she loved but had never directly influenced, and saw a stranger.

"You're the head of Kamat now," she said, more to herself than to him. But she was no fool, and she did not add that her husband, Nikolay, would never have embarked on such a course.

Marina's curiosity moved to fill the void in the conversation. "Will the Samurai be Kamat people? I'm sure cousin Gregory would love to be involved."

Richard shook his head. "It's not the sort of job for blood, though I'll rely heavily on Kamat at the start. But it's not strictly a Kamat enterprise. The other mercantile houses will have to get involved as well."

"Will they?" Andromeda re-entered the discussion. "We compete, we don't cooperate. And no one's likely to take a step if it means crossing the Kalugins."

"The Kalugins are hardly monolithic, Mother. You can't turn right anymore but another Kalugin's on your left. However, the Signeury's agreed to seal the prospectus and I've good cause to believe we've got a Kalugin or two on our side."

Vega Boregy had, in fact, assured Richard that Iosef, himself would approve the chartering documents. And Anastasi had been aware from the beginning, though Richard wouldn't admit that to anyone who didn't already know. Let Anastasi choose his own ground for proclaiming his tacit involvement and support.

Andromeda was unreassured. "Money. Is it all Kamat money? What about Boregy, or Kalugin itself? Are we talking all the risk?"

Tension seized hold of Richard's shoulders. There was a fine line between what the family had a right to know and when it insulted or challenged the Househead. He told himself Andromeda's question was legitimate, but he distrusted its tone. "We only consolidated our liquid assets, Mother, we didn't commit them willy-nilly to an unchartered enterprise."

This time when Andromeda sat back in her chair she let the butler take her scarcely touched plate away.

"Remember that you're young yet. You ought not move so quickly. They aren't above using you as the proverbial stalking horse."

"I'm ready for Boregy and Kalugin—but I'm not ready for treachery at my back." It was not a wise thing to say, not the sort of thing that Nikolay would ever have said, and it hurt this sister and mother more than it outraged them.

"We would never oppose you, Richard," Marina whispered, looking at her mother's stricken face, not her brother.

"I count upon it."

Richard gestured for a servant to remove his plate. The butler came forward to fix the tea while a girl barely out of her teens struggled to get the silver dessert service safely from the sideboard to the table. Conversation, even thought, stopped while forks clicked against each other and the pudding raced for the edge. The butler caught the bowl just as it became airborne, everyone sighed with relief and the tension—even the family's tension—was broken.

The mood was lighter when Marina spoke again. "I told you they found the boy. He's all right, but I guess he won't be starting at the college right away."

Richard swallowed hard; blancmange was his favorite dessert and he was always inclined to race through it. "How'd you find that out? I was having no luck at all with the canalers."

Marina caught a cautioning glance from her mother.

"I inquired among my friends at the Children's Charitable League," Andromeda said quickly. "They knew."

Richard nodded absently, and Marina tried, without success, to place the Children's Charitable League among the many genteel organizations her mother belonged to. She gathered that Andromeda did not want Tom Mondragon mentioned at the table and meant to change the subject. Although, since Tom was practically the only subject in her mind, her execution fell somewhat short of her intentions.

"Dickon, I think you should consider hiring Tom in your Samurai. He needs a job, Boregy is hardly supporting him in decency, and he'd certainly be qualified."

"Tom?" Richard asked, unaware of the rigid mask that had descended across his mother's face.

"Tom Mondragon. I saw him this aft—"

Words failed for Richard, and so did everything else. He choked on a piece of fruit. The butler surged forward, determined to save the Househead's life regardless of his dignity. Richard shook free of the heimlich hug and scalded his mouth with tea.

"Marina!" he gasped, making her name three distinct raspy syllables. "Of all the harebrained, lunatic, irresponsible things to do! My god—Thomas Mondragon's practically the reason we *need* the Samurai. Lord, I'd sooner recruit Megary than Mondragon. The man's a complete scoundrel."

Marina put her napkin to her face and bolted from the diningroom with loud sobs. Andromeda folded her napkin carefully, then unfolded it and started again.

"What do you know about this?"

"There's no way to deny infatuation," she said without looking at her son. "The only was is to ride it out. She would have seen him sooner or later."

"I'd guess that seeing him didn't stop the infatuation, did it?"

"The Mondragons kept an exemplary household. I'm sure that whatever else he is, Thomas Mondragon is well turned-out—"

"He's not some House-blood come looking for an heir. He's god-be-damned Sword of God, Mother!"

Andromeda Kamat, daughter of the Cassirer of Nev Hettek and related to the governor of that city by haphazard liaison, looked up with hard, flashing green eyes. "Then he's just the sort of man you're going to need!"

She was out of her chair and stalking toward the door before the butler twitched.

CHAPTER X

TROUBLED WATERS
by C. J. Cherryh

"I dunno," Moghi said. "I ain't seen 'er. What'd ye say t' her, anyhow?"

"I don't damn well remember," Mondragon said. It was like that with their quarrels. "Look. Watch her boat. Put it in drydock. Put it on my tab."

"I ain't so sure about your credit," Moghi said.

"You *owe* me a shade more for the two hundred," Mondragon said, keeping it cold, very cold. "You got away with a killing, Moghi. Your lads out hardly a night. I don't think it's like you haven't seen money from me lately. And Jones one of your own."

"Shit," Moghi said, and spat and turned away, walking across the boards. But he gave that wave of his hand that signaled acceptance. "Jep, have the boys put that there boat up." He reached the office door—no patrons at this hour, in the half-hour before Moghi's regular opening for breakfast. Mondragon had used the back way—being one of the few Entitled. And Moghi turned and fixed him with a cold stare of his own. "Ye better straighten it out wi' that 'un," Moghi said. "Ye don't mess with mine, m'ser. Ye break it clean or ye make it up, but ye don't fight in my place, ye don't raise no row. It ain't Jones that done it. She's one o' mine, she *knows* the Rules. You pushed 'er. An' I ain't likin' this. Ain't like her. Ain't like Jones to leave that boat."

Mondragon stood still in the middle of the room, with panic gnawing in his gut.

He knew, damn, he *knew* what could keep Jones away, what hurt could keep her out of sight, hidden away.

Dammit to hell! What does she want?

Me to come searching for her, that's what she wants.

Wants me to beg.

He walked for the door, met the lock and swore, unlocking it, and walked out into the cold, hands in pockets, toward Hanging Bridge.

Trying to make me worry.

She wants me to worry until I turn the damn city upside down for her, spend two hundred gold for her, that's what she wants!

She's a damn kid. She's seventeen. At seventeen you can be a fool.

I yelled at her. I shouldn't have yelled, oh, damn, I shouldn't have yelled.

It's money again. We always fight over money. Two hundred sols, I say. It's nothing.

It's more money than she's ever seen. Ever will see, on the water. And, damn, it's nothing, *I say.*

Damn, damn, damn, *and if somebody saw Marina Kamat and told her—*

He felt the heat of shame on his face, burning in the wind. *Two hundred sols* isn't *nothing. Kamat isn't* nothing. *There's no choice. I sell what I have to.* She wouldn't. *But I can't afford that kind of pride. Can't afford to think about it, you just do it, that's all. Whatever pays the bills.*

It was Boregy money that had hired Moghi's men. Money Boregy had put in his account to pay the rent, to keep up his gambling in a certain gaming house, to buy up a certain few clerks' debts, and buy a certain few souls—

When Boregy finds out—

If Boregy has found out, if it's Vega who's got her—

He'd say by now. He wouldn't kill her. He wouldn't do that. He'd tell me—tell me how to buy her back.

And I would. Anything.

"Min," he said, softly in the dark, crouching close on waterside by the aged skip, where the oldest woman on the canals lived her life. Mintaka tied up every night by Petrescu: Jones had sold her that right, for Min's own sake. And the old woman, alcoholic and muddled between now and twenty years ago, was Jones' friend for life—the way she had been Retribution's, so Jones said, and never could remember which of them was which. "Min, it's Mondragon. Can I come aboard?"

"Mondragon?" In the wan, cold light of upstairs windows on Petrescu, he saw the rag-curtain of the hidey part, and a tousled gray head poked out. "Thet Mondragon?"

"Yey, Min." He stepped into the skip and crouched down in front of the hidey. "You seen Jones?"

"Ne, ne." Min grunted and heaved more of herself out, hauling her blankets with her. "She ain't wi' your business?"

"No. Not mine. Not Moghi's. I asked. Min, she's mad at me. I hope that's what it is. I'm hoping she's hiding somewhere, but I'm afraid for her. Please. If you know anything, if you know anybody who might know anything—tell me."

Min wrapped her blankets about her, a gray, whiskey-smelling lump in the dark. "Mad at ye?"

"Lover's quarrel, Min."

"Awwwwww." Min hunched up with interest, blankets under her chins. Min was a romantic. "What ye gone an' done, huh?"

"Min, I—" Tell Min anything and it was one end of Merovingen to the other by morning. "I yelled at her. I got mad, I yelled, I—"

"Been messin' wi' m'sera Kamat?"

O my God . . .

"Do you know where she *is*, Min? I know you wouldn't break a promise to her. I know you wouldn't betray her. But it's dangerous for her to be out alone right now. I've got enemies, Min. They could try to get her. I'm scared to death they *have*, do you understand me? You wouldn't lie to me, would you, Min?"

A shake of Min's untidy head. "Ne, Mondragon." Not *m'ser* Mondragon. Just Mondragon, canaler-style, which came like a guarantee of truth. "I ain't seen 'er. I thought she was wi' you, or off on some business o' Moghi's— But ye go 'round wi' that m'sera Kamat, she won't take to that, no. Ain't no wonder she'd be mad at ye. So'm' I."

"I'm begging her, Min. If you know where she is.

It's for *her* sake, Min. If she wants anything—I'll do it. *Tell* her that."

Min shook her head slowly. "I ain't seen her. That's the truth. Ain't seen her. I dunno where she is."

"Find her and tell her. Will you do that, Min? Will you pass the word to the Trade? Something's happened to Jones. She's in trouble. Just tell me she's safe, and I'll settle whatever's between us later. Anyone finds her—just so they can tell me she's all right, I'll give them whatever they ask."

"Ney. Jones's *Trade*."

There was outrage in the old woman's voice. Reproof. Mondragon ducked his head, and said: "Yey, Min. But I love her."

A knobby, warm hand reached out and clumsily patted his cheek. "If I was younger I'd give 'er a fight f' ye, boy. I would. Ye go. I'll ask Del an' Mira and that Tommy. They'll ask too. We'll look."

"Thanks, Min." He knew better than to give her whiskey. *Nothing* would get done. He knew better than money, too. So he hugged the old woman, smelly blankets and all, and got himself off her skip and out of her way, home, upstairs, because there was the chance Jones would come back, there was the chance the boys could find out something—

He was beginning to panic. He had nothing left in trade—except the delicate matter of Marina Kamat, which might afford more money than Marina Kamat was willing to part with: there was the money. Boregy might pay for information he could get . . .

Or there was Jones' life and health, which might be at stake—which might mean the affair with Marina Kamat was the only coin he had to trade in, with Boregy, with Anastasi—

With his other enemies, who were capable of anything.

THE PRISONER

by Janet Morris

When Jones had tired of throwing herself against the door of her cell, she'd wept in frustration, curled up on the moldy straw bedding. There was a bucket in here for a toilet, and that was all. Nobody came when she called.

Once food came through a slot in the bottom of the door—stew and bread. She didn't eat it. They didn't take it away when the slot opened again. Somebody's gruff voice said she didn't get anything else until she'd eaten that.

She dumped it in her slop bucket, as if anybody cared.

The empty tray was taken, and eventually more food came. This time she ate it, because daylight was coming through the slit near the ceiling of her cell.

That daylight went, eventually, and came again, food with it, and went again, before anyone said another word to her. She had far too long to regret and to fume. Mondragon had done this to her—she never should have fished him out of the water that time.

She'd done it to herself, her mother would have said. And that made her angry. Fooling around with Merovingen-above, that was what had gotten her here. She wasn't going to make anyone a good slave, didn't they know that? Whoever they were, couldn't they figure that out?

She yelled at the slit, the next time food came, that she'd kill anyone who came near her. No one answered.

Someone had searched her; what she'd had for weapons, and all she'd had of value, was gone. She sat a long time, and her anger bled away that day.

The following night was one wherein all the horrors of slavery that her imagination could find were tortures as real as the straw on which she sat or the tiny red bugs she'd found crawling on her when morning light last came through the slot.

That night, no food came with sunset. Good, she

thought. I'll starve myself. Nobody will want me. They won't be able to sell me. I'll starve myself to death. But her stomach growled and she was getting very thirsty. And no one had ever come to clean her bucket, which was filled with her first meal here and her waste products. It smelled so bad in her cell she could hardly breathe.

She began to worry that they'd forgotten about her. She'd die here, and nobody would ever know. She went to her door and pounded on it. She yelled herself hoarse. She took her slop bucket and threw it at the door.

Then the smell was really horrible, and the foul mess was all over everything, and spreading in slow rivulets toward her straw pallet.

Why hadn't she realized that the floor of her cell wasn't level? Pretty soon, there wasn't going to be a dry spot in here. She sat up all that night, in unnatural fear that a rivulet of rotten stew and human waste was going to touch her.

By morning she was exhausted, shivering, huddled in a corner with all her straw piled up under her and her feet pulled in against her buttocks, staring blankly at the door which hadn't opened for so long.

Then when it did open—all the way!—she didn't believe her eyes.

Magruder imagined he knew everything his prisoner was feeling: the way the light streaming through the open doorway at his back dazzled her eyes; the way the decent food he'd brought smelled to her; the way fear and anger and eagerness and relief bounced around inside her head like a pack of penned hunting dogs trying to get out to run.

He imagined he knew because Magruder had been imprisoned himself. Captured. Incarcerated. Interrogated. Tortured physically as well as mentally. Having been through the process, he considered himself an expert on the reactions of a subject in this sort of situation.

As for the interrogator's role . . . he knew that one too. You don't rise as high in the hierarchy of revolution as Magruder had without learning how to get the information you need from the unwilling. Sometimes you could even get it from the unknowing.

But always, when faced with the countenance of the prisoner, Magruder was startled by the sameness of those faces. Male or female, young or old, a prisoner was a prisoner and they all looked alike. The glassy eyes, the defiant mouths, the pinched wan faces of the terrorized never differed. And their responses fell within a predictable range.

The young woman called Altair Jones was predictably startled, predictably confused, and predictably hostile. She was also predictably relieved that she hadn't been forgotten.

And she was frightened: a huge shadow was coming toward her with a fragrant tray of food and unknowable motives. She was weak and disoriented and ready for exactly the kind of chit-chat she wouldn't be expecting.

Magruder put the tray of food down between them, ignoring the shit and chunks of blue-green meat and the maggots crawling on them. He sat cross-legged in the mess she'd made as if it didn't exist. He picked up one of two plates on the tray and pushed the remainder toward her.

She didn't move to take it.

He took a bit of fresh hot bread and said, as he chewed, "Sorry it took me so long to get to you. These slavers ain't playin' along. Once they saw you, they forgot the deal we made. I just need to ask you some questions. You answer 'em, I think I can get you back out of here." He reached for the tray, took one of two mugs of hot mulled cider, and sipped it.

The huge-eyed girl before him just watched. Her fists were balled in her lap. Her mouth was thinning with the effort it took not to grab the food.

"C'mon," said Magruder in his best Merovingen-below patois, "eat up, m'sera. Amends, an' all."

"Amends!" It came out of her explosively, then she clamped her mouth shut once more. A fist came up and with it she knuckled her eyes, eyes burning bright with tears of struggle and fury.

But her silence was broken, and with it her resolve to silence. Magruder showed no sign of triumph, he simply chewed and sipped, returning her glare with as soft a look of compassion as he could manage.

Eventually, he said again, "C'mon, m'sera, I went to lots of trouble, gettin' this in here. I can't help you if you won't let me."

"Help me? You did this to me, crud!" Invective followed, and a flash of her hand to the tray, where she grabbed the hot bread and threw it at him.

He caught it casually, to let her know he could, and to let her know something else: he put the bread back on the tray and said, looking at it, "This is about your friend Mondragon. It's him got you here, not me. Up to your hips in his business, you ought to have expected somethin' like this—"

"Liar! You dunno nothin' about me and Mon—" She nearly launched herself at him. Instead, she bit her lip and he half expected to see blood flow.

"Mondragon's been usin' you a long time, everybody knows that. You don't see him tryin' to batter his way in here to break your butt out, do you? Come on, eat this. Like I said, I'm sorry this got started. I just needed to talk to you. I didn't expect these Megary fools to get so set on turnin' a profit."

"I'm not eatin'," she said. She pushed the tray toward him. "Not gonna be fat and pretty for 'em."

"Talk to me, and maybe that won't happen. Tell me what Mondragon and Boregy're doin' and—"

Then she did launch herself at him, and he let her come, grabbing her wrists and fending off all of her bites and most of her kicks and blows. She needed to let her rage break through, and he knew how it felt to be helpless.

She struggled against him until she was out of breath, and then she gave a strangled sob and slumped down bonelessly.

The food he'd brought was now fouled with the slop on the floor, and he said, "I wish you hadn't done that. I can't get you no more food now. I'll bring you something tomorrow night," and let her go.

She rubbed her eyes. She was sitting in the middle of the mess she'd made. She picked at the ruins of the first decent meal she'd had a chance to eat for days, and she seemed suddenly like a kid on the beach looking for something she'd lost in the sand.

That was the moment when Chance Magruder realized that this interrogation was going to be tougher than he'd expected—on both of them.

She sat there in the mess for too long before she crawled back to her straw, crossed her arms over her breasts, and raised glittering eyes. "I ain't tellin' you nothin'. You did this to me. Why?"

"I answer your question, you answer one o' mine," he bargained. She inclined her head minutely. He took it as assent, saying, "Deal, then," and answered hers: "Money," he lied. "Somebody paid me . . . maybe the College, maybe some Kalugin agents, I dunno. Somebody wants to know what you know about Mondragon's connection with the high houses. I needed the money." He let his eyes drop.

She flared, "Money? You did this for . . . Crazies that hired you didn't tell you I'd had scrapes with Megary before? That Mondragon's had . . . dealings with these Megary bastards—" She bit her lip again and this time the blood came, drawn by strong white teeth. "I'll never get out of here. There's no use me talkin' to you." She turned her head away and her shoulders were shaking.

He stood up. "Y' owe me one honest answer, remember." This wasn't the time to push her further. He'd pushed her quite far enough. Now he just had to worry her. "I'll be back," he promised too loudly, as if he weren't sure he could promise it at all. Then, with what he hoped would ring true as false bravado, he added, "Anybody bothers you, you tell 'em I said I'd be back to talk to you again."

And he left her stunned there, slumped against the wall, looking after him dully, too shocked even to demand to know the name of her protector.

The man didn't come back the next day. She screamed through the slit when it opened to take the tray she'd shoved over there that, "It's a mess in here and somebody better come clean it up!"

But nobody did, and she dreamed about roaches and rats when she slept. When she woke, she had to

133

stamp her feet to make the roaches and rats disappear. She wanted the man to come back and then she didn't when she could finally hear him outside her cell, arguing with somebody.

The two men out there went at it—the voice of the man who'd brought her the good food, and somebody else. She couldn't catch sentences, only words. By the time she'd swallowed her pride enough to crawl over to the door where she could hear, no longer caring what he'd think if he caught her with her ear to the door, the men weren't yelling at each other any longer.

She heard footsteps, though, as both of them went away. And she spent that whole day wondering what the snippets of conversation she had heard might mean. She knew they'd been arguing about her. She was sure she'd heard something about a slave ship, and the voice of the man with food saying "She's mine till I say otherwise. You been paid."

But she wasn't sure.

She huddled in her corner for what seemed like forever, and then there were footsteps again. This time she was certain it was just the regular guard with another foul meal, but it was him!

He wasn't as big as she remembered him, but he was just as dirty. He had pale eyes, and she hadn't noticed that before either. They were looking at her mournfully. And he didn't have any mulled cider or fresh bread with him. He was empty-handed.

He sat down in the slop-and-maggot mess as if it weren't there and said to her, "You owe me one straight answer, m'sera Jones."

She shrugged one shoulder. He hadn't brought her any food. She felt betrayed. She tried not to look at him, but she couldn't. She'd wanted him to come back. Now that he was here, she wanted him to leave.

"Just tell me if you think Mondragon cares enough about you that I could go to him for money to get you back out of here."

So that was it! "Slime sucker! You think Mondragon can ransom me? You did this for cash? Thomas ain't got no money! None of us does!"

"But the Boregys do . . ."

"Boregy's ain't about to help him get me . . ." She

stopped, bit her lip. Since it was where she'd bitten it before, she winced when the sharp edge of her tooth opened the old wound. "What's your name, scum? Y' kin tell me that."

"Pace," he said, and rushed on as if somebody'd opened a dike in him somewhere: "Look, Jones, don't you see this is politics? Bigger than you, bigger than me? We're just pawns, is all. Who'd know the Boregys wouldn't pay for you? Not me. I just did the snatch. Followin' my orders. Somebody wants Mondragon to be a good boy, like he ain't been. Want me to talk to him? Maybe he can help you, and you just don't know it? Maybe it's worth a try." He reached into his shirt and came out with a leather-wrapped packet. "Write him a note? Here's all you need. Tell him you're alive, and t' pay the bearer. That's all you gotta do."

"No," she said. What if he couldn't—or wouldn't pay?

"What's the matter, can't write? You dictate it and I'll write it for—"

"I can write. And read." Defiantly her head came up. She licked her bloody lip. "But I ain't writin' nothin' for you, Pace, so's you get Thomas in deep in what—" She stopped, tried to still her questions, then blazed: "What's to say you won't get money outta him an' keep it, and still let Megary sell me?"

"I came back like I said, didn't I?"

"You didn't bring me nothin'."

"Bring you . . . ? Oh, food. I can get it, I think." He stood up and headed for the door.

"Wai—" She bit off the word, but he turned, still holding the packet. She didn't want him to go. He was her only link to the outside. "I'd write a note to Moghi," she managed.

The man calling himself Pace came back and hunkered down before her. He said very softly, "Moghi? These politicos ought to take their own medicine, Jones. Don't you think Mondragon'll try to help you? I would, if you were mine. Do whatever it'd take." He was untying the knot on the packet, getting out paper and a charcoal wrapped in cloth.

"You don't understand . . ." It sounded miserable. She wanted to explain about the Sword agents, the trouble Mondragon was in, the way that trouble was isolating him from everything and everybody. But she couldn't get out a word of it, not when she was sitting in this stinking cell and here was somebody trying to help get her out of it.

"Then explain it to me," he said softly, holding out the white square of paper now, already smudged from his dirty hand.

In the end, she wrote the note to Moghi, making Pace promise to leave it with him for "Whoever wants to know . . ."

And Pace was real happy, he said. But he didn't look happy. It was like he was worried the note wasn't going to do any good.

After he left, the food he promised came, though, and she ate it all like it was the key to salvation—very slowly, savoring every bite of bread and every sip of cider, trying to close her nose against the stench of her body and her cell and the rot that nobody, not even Pace, cared enough to clean up.

Tatiana Kalugin's bed was the only place Magruder could get the stench of Jones' cell off him, though he religiously showered and scrubbed himself raw every time he came back from Megary to the Embassy through the servants' entrance.

Tonight, not even Tatiana's beauty or her magnificent suite on the Rock was enough to do it. When he left here, he was going to deliver the Jones girl's message.

"What is it, Chance?" said Tatiana, all honey and musk and skin like suede in his arms.

A chill pierced him with her words. He was slipping. It was one thing to be distracted, another to show it. Tatiana Kalugin was arguably the smartest of the ruling family, his only ally among them, and the most dangerous of his enemies because of all the aforementioned. If she even thought he was holding back with her, hiding more than professional power players always must hide, he'd lose everything here. End up in one of the Signeury interrogation modules, so much more agonizing and sophisticated than the Megary cell where he was keeping young Jones.

Magruder was no coward, but he was claustrophobic, and he was in the middle of a protracted interrogation himself, which made him less willing even than usual to consider the consequences to himself if he should fail here. So he said, "I keep worrying about what old Ito's planning for Mike Chamoun. A kill order from the College, that your daddy's agreed to, isn't anything to take too lightly—"

"I told you, Chance, I'll take care of it. I know you consider yourself the boy's protector. You've got to realize that I consider myself yours, in matters Merovingian." She ruffled his silver-streaked hair. "You've got to trust me, though it's foreign to your nature."

"Yeah, and you me." He swung off her, put both feet on the floor. He had to play this right, or it would be the beginning of the end of this relationship, the most important tactical one he'd cultivated here. He had to make his distress seem plausible, since he couldn't hide it. He had to make sure that the protective instincts she spoke of were roused in his defense, or else she'd figure out he was playing her false. And that would be the end of Chance Magruder.

"We'll manage," she said. "For these stakes, we must." She came up on one elbow and he glanced at her beautiful, mature body half out from under the sheets. "Once I've tamed Anastasi's warlike instincts, you and I are going to forge a relationship with Nev Hettek that will be worth all it's cost so far."

Once I help you ace your brother and succeed your father as sole despot here, you mean, he thought but couldn't say. "If we lose Mike Chamoun—and we can, with him out doing census work in the lower tiers, vulnerable to Ito's henchmen—then it's back to square one."

"Would it really be that bad? If a Sword of God attack during Festival Eve didn't destroy our budding diplomatic relations, how could the loss of one riverboat captain?"

"You've got to take this more seriously, Tatiana. He's a Nev Hetteker; I'm his ambassador. We know threats have been made against his life and a hit sanctioned by Merovingen's highest officials. If it happens, it's your government executing one of my citizens, without trial or due process of any sort. This while he's hip-deep in a shipping merger and a marriage to one of your most noble houses to facilitate the paperwork . . . you bet it's worse. It contravenes all the progress we've supposedly made here. If you're saying you're really not certain you can protect Michael, I'm going to suggest to him and his bride that they come live in my embassy compound until the threat's over. It's either that or face Ito and your father and tell them we know what they've got in mind."

She came up behind him and her hands started kneading his shoulders. "Ssh, Chance, let me handle this. I promise you, no one's going to execute your Chamoun boy. Or, if they do, they'll have my justice to reckon with. Which wouldn't be a bad trade-off, you know? To be rid of Ito . . ."

He knew she was smiling that smile colder than a duelist's. He didn't try to see her face. He hung his head and shook it, simultaneously leaning back into her expert massage. "I want Chamoun safe. We'll get Ito another day, another way—or Ito will get Ito. That's usually the way with these fundamentalist types. Promise me you won't close your eyes to this just so that you can take a cardinal's scalp in the aftermath."

She sighed a deep, unpremeditated sigh. "Yes, all right. You drive a hard bargain, Chance Magruder. Now come back here and prove to me you're worth it."

He wasn't going to have any trouble doing that.

When he'd proved that fact to both their satisfactions, he left for the Embassy.

By the time he'd changed there and slipped out the servant's entrance in his disguise, it was pitchblack, the dead of night.

Nobody was out tonight but smugglers, Anastasi's police, and drunken sharrh hunters. Or so it seemed, until, as Magruder swung up onto Ventani pier, a rapier's tip was waiting for him there.

He had a choice. He could step back, dive into the canal, away from the sword. But he knew the sword and the man behind it. The only thing he didn't know was whether the man knew him, or Mondragon was just so spooked by Jones' disappearance that he was out looking for somebody to blame.

Magruder should have known better. Mondragon was Sword-trained. A putty nose and some berry-juice dye weren't going to fool him for long.

"Magruder! You bastard, where is she?"

Magruder spread his hands away from his sides casually. "A note from her—in my inside pocket. You want to take it yourself, you ought to put that blade down. There's no return address, and you'll never find her on your own. Not when I hid her."

The sword came down, just enough for Mondragon to feel up Magruder for the letter. "It's for Moghi," Mondragon said uncertainly.

"She didn't want to implicate you even that much—or she thinks you don't care enough about her, or couldn't help her if you did—she said that much."

"She wouldn't tell you anything."

"She didn't tell me much. But she told me enough. And you're telling me the rest. I'll release her, Mondragon, no sweat. You just shut down that second channel to Nev Hettek and quit trying to put my head in a noose."

"I can't do that," Mondragon said, lifting his eyes from Jones' terse, ungrammatical note. "There's other people pulling strings here."

"Anastasi Kalugin, Vega Boregy, right?"

Mondragon only blinked.

"Ito Boregy and old man Kalugin as well?"

"Not that I know."

"Well, then your girl's dead."

"So are you."

"You'll have to wait on that, don't you think?" Magruder said easily. "Until you see if you and I can make some kind of secondary deal?" Mondragon's swordtip wasn't back at his throat. Yet.

"Like?" said the wraith in the night, hardly more than a pale shadow in the darkness.

"Like you do a little dance for me. Protect Mike Chamoun, keep him out of the middle of this—"

"How am I supposed to do that?"

Getting desperate, Tommy, from the sound of your voice. Best not to let the opposition know what you're thinking. Or are you just plain past where you can do any thinking? "I don't know, Tommy. How'd you tangle Chamoun up in this in the first place?"

"Couldn't be helped. Look, Magruder, there must be a way."

Good boy. There's always a way, Tommy. "Then you find one. Shut down the second channel—no more using Chamoun to run your suicidal parallel operations. You want to kill yourself, that's fine with me. As far as I'm concerned, you should have been dead when I first found you. But don't take my assets down with you. Make your Boregy and Kalugin contacts think Nev Hettek shut you down, or that I'm too solid to be hurt by this sort of thing, or whatever you like."

"It won't work." Now Mondragon's sword did come up.

It wavered an inch before Magruder's face. He knew better than to focus on the weapon. He focused on the eyes of the man behind it. He said to Mondragon, "It better work. I took your girlfriend. I can take your other friends. Anytime. All the innocents you've got mired in your affairs like it doesn't matter who gets hurt—they'll all suffer. You've got to realize, Tommy, nobody gives a damn about your carcass anymore, because it's clear you don't. But that doesn't mean we can't reach you. Anywhere. Any way we want. Whenever we want." *Now put that weapon away.*

It worked. The sword came down, found its scabbard. Just as Mondragon was sheathing it, some big mother of a yacht went by, and in its running lights, reflected over the water, Mondragon looked like the angel on Hanging Bridge come to life, with his sword half-sheathed.

Then the boat was gone, the light was gone, and the sword was at Mondragon's side.

"Someday, Magruder, I'm going to even up with you."

"Maybe in another life," Magruder grinned. "If you turn Revenantist so you can have one. In this life, you ain't been winning real regular. Now, write a nice note to your girlfriend, and we'll turn her loose, oh . . . tomorrow night, sometime."

"I can't show any results by then—"

"You think I don't know that?" Magruder took a step forward, away from the edge of the pier. Mondragon retreated before him. "You owe me, Tommy. You always will, from now on. You're going to be a good boy and a good Sword informant. From now on, if you have to pretend to use Chamoun, you use him to get messages to me. And don't try to leave Merovingen. Or get the girl out. Next time I take her, you're going to wish you got her back in pieces this time."

"She's not . . ."

"Hurt? Not physically, not really. I'm even willing to let her think that her hero coughed up cash to rescue her. That's what I'll tell her. It's what she wants to hear."

"A magnanimous gesture. It doesn't suit you, Magruder."

"I don't make gestures. You're getting rusty. I close traps. She doesn't know I took her—she doesn't know who did, or why. If you're smart, you won't tell her any more than that you got the note, and paid somebody named 'Pace' what it cost. If you're not smart, what's left of your life is going to unravel before your eyes. Now, write something for her."

Mondragon said nothing more, just backed up until he was under one of the oil lamps hung on the pilings of Ventani pier, and wrote his note.

When he'd finished, he handed the packet to Magruder and stomped away, toward Moghi's.

Magruder waited until the ex-Sword agent was swallowed by the shadows of the tiers before he left for Megary, where the prisoner waited.

When the man called Pace came again, Jones felt as if she'd been waiting forever. She was resentful that he'd stayed away so long, and gladder to see him than she'd ever admit.

For his part, he didn't sit down across from her this time. He tossed her the packet on which she'd written.

Her fingers were stiff with the cold and the damp; it was nearly dawn, from the way the left upper corner of her cell was lightening. Pace had brought a lamp.

When she'd opened the packet, she found she had to go over to the lamp he held in order to read it.

She'd never been so close to the dark, dirty man. She was so aware of his proximity that it interfered with her reading. She mouthed Mondragon's words slowly, and then said them aloud, " 'I've made a deal. You're free. Meet me at Moghi's as soon as you can. Th.M.' "

"See there," said the man called Pace, "your boy-friend cares more about you than you thought."

"How did you— I mean . . ." Jones wanted to hug the big man, stopped herself, took three quick steps back. He was her captor. Her jailer. She should hate him. But he was also her rescuer. She jammed her hands together, tangling her fingers. "That's it, then? I can go? How do I get—"

"I'll take you," he said softly, and she'd never been more grateful or more relieved.

Out of Megary. Out of Megary into the gray fog of a wet dawn. You couldn't see farther than the tip of your outstretched hand, but Jones would always remember walking through the holding pens of Megary, and up, and out.

The sea wind on her face. The smell of salt and canal, not rot and feces. The launch that Pace had brought, bigger and faster than the runabout he'd had last time.

There was a funny look to his face, even in the fog. He said, "You're better at this than I am. Why don't you pilot this thing back to Moghi's?"

She was glad to do that, anxious to be away, afraid until Megary was swallowed by the fog that somehow the slavers would come chasing after them, even though Pace seemed sure everything had been arranged.

" 'Ware," she cried when a hull loomed close. Her voice was shaky, thick, choked with emotion she didn't want Pace to hear. " 'Ware!' "

Water raced under the launch; the fog wouldn't burn off for hours, not in the winter cold. She shivered as she steered. The cold and the wet and the water and the danger were freedom, and she loved it. Half-obscured by the weather, the man called Pace sat in the bow, hunched over. She wanted to say something to him, she really did.

But what did you say? He'd done her no favor. He'd blackmailed Mondragon. Maybe it wasn't his fault, like he said. Maybe he was just like her, just caught up in things. So if she wasn't angry at him, then that just showed that being free was such a gift it made up for everything else.

It had to.

When they reached Ventani pier, he said, "Out."

That was all. He didn't even move from the bow.

She pulled in close. Grabbed a piling, found a ladder rung.

Even while she was climbing out, somebody dropped into the boat from the pier above.

Pace must have been expecting it, for he didn't move from the bow.

The new man in the boat took the helm, and Jones barely had her feet on the ladder's rungs before the launch was pulling away below her.

She watched it disappear into the fog, feeling somehow that she should have said good-bye. Then she shook her head and climbed. She headed down the pier for Moghi's. When she found Thomas Mondragon, he was going to have a lot of explaining to do.

CHAPTER XI

TROUBLED WATERS

by C. J. Cherryh

Up the board steps to Moghi's . . . toward the skewed rectangle of light that showed there. . . .

"Jones!" a male voice said. "Jones!"

She turned, saw young Jimmy Singh clambering up from his skip. Singh pointed, toward the waterside.

"Ye got a man looking f' ye—"

She looked, saw her own skip at tie-up. Saw the man in black standing in it, looking her way. Dark cap, blond hair escaping under it. Damnfool.

She crossed the boards and landed barefoot in the bow, with a force that made the skip bob and heave and that shot fire through her feet. And stood there with her own shadow blotting out most of him and his face pale and scared in the light from Moghi's lantern.

Damn 'im!

"Let's go home," Mondragon said. "All right?"

"Yey," she said. And stalked over the clutter—*clutter!* in *her* well—and snatched up the boathook from the rack. *He* had the pole. She shoved the boathook at him. "Gimme th' pole!"

"Yey," he said quietly, and traded, and went up to the bow. "I'd better tell Moghi you're all right. I promised I would."

"*Do* 'er," she said harshly; and stood there leaning on the pole while Mondragon climbed up onto the porch and went inside.

The pole felt good in her hands. The wind smelled clean—the *city* wind smelled clean—after the stink of the cell. She kept seeing the walls. She kept hearing the silence and the echoes, when there was the sound of the water to hear.

He came out again. Moghi's shadow filled the doorway. Others were behind him, canalers, she reckoned.

"Ye all right, Jones?" Moghi asked.

"I'll talk," she said, "t'morrow. 'M takin' my man home. All right, Moghi?"

"Yey," Moghi said in a curiously quiet voice. Or everything seemed quiet. She waited while Mondragon got aboard again, and pulled the bow-tie free.

Then she put the pole in, and backed, and Mondragon took up the boathook and shoved with it off the porch. They swung around into Grand current, and she snapped: "Hey, *hin!*"

So he skipped to it.

Without a word.

"Ye're safe," Min blubbered. " 'E was worrit, gel. Real worrit."

"Yey, Min," Jones said, and patted the old woman's arms. "Do me favor, Min, ye spread it 'round, gimme ternight wi' m' man, ne?"

Min grinned her gap-toothed grin and bobbed her gray head. "Hoooh, yey!" Min said. And grabbed up her pole to get moving.

Mondragon waited on waterside, and walked up with her, up the stairs to the apartment—with his key, inside.

The *boys* were there, Denny quiet, Raj—

Raj damned quiet, damned worried. Embarrassed-like, and sober.

She put *that* together and her face went hot. Like they figured what would have happened to her, like they *imagined* what would have happened to her, in some cell somewhere, before Mondragon bought her out. And she stared back with her jaw set and said:

"Clear out. I'm all right. *Clear out!*"

"Jones." Mondragon rested his hand on her shoulder, pressed hard. "Boys. Get to bed, *Now*."

"Yesser," Raj said, a breath; and grabbed his brother and went, down the hall, fast.

"They ain't *touched* me," Jones said, rounding on Mondragon.

"Jones," Mondragon said.

"They *ain't!*"

"It's not important—" he said. And she hit him in the face, a roundhouse blow he did not even try to stop. He only recoiled, and wiped his mouth, and said: "I meant—if they had—it wouldn't be your fault. I wouldn't care, you understand me? *I wouldn't think the less of you!*"

"What'd you *pay* f' me?"

"Jones—"

He reached for her arms. She hit his hands away and backed up, sick at her stomach.

He just stood there. Just stood.

"Jones," he said. He was hurting. She knew that. So was she.

"They *didn't* touch me."

"You want to hit me again? I don't *care*, Jones. I don't damn well *care!*"

"I stink. I want a bath. I want that smell off me." She shoved past him and got as far as the hall. And knew she was wrong, knew there was pain behind her. She stopped there with her hand on the banister, said, without looking at him: "Megarys. I was at Megary's. You been, once. They ain't never touched me."

"I can't say the same," came from behind her. She didn't understand that. She turned and looked at him, hardly able to get a breath, confused.

"Jones. What *happens* to you doesn't matter. What you *do* matters. Hear me?"

She listened to that, several times through. And felt like she was going to give away at the knees, the knees gone to water and trying to shake under her.

"I'll take my bath," she said, and turned and walked away, down the hall, where, she thought, it was a cold bath, next the kitchen, the washroom.

But there was water heated. The boys must have seen to it. The boys must have known—where she was. The damn boys must have made up their own minds what had happened, how she was, everything—hours ago.

She saw Moghi in the doorway, the people behind him. Half damn Merovingen had to know. Like Min. Del. Mira. Everybody making up their own minds.

She poured hot water into the tub. She peeled out of her filthy clothes and got in and ducked her head between her legs, scrubbing and scrubbing, and trying not to remember the cell, while her eyes were shut, underwater.

"Jones . . ."

She yelped as she brought her head up. She covered herself like a damn fool and sat there staring at Mondragon standing in the open doorway, her heart pounding, herself so weak she could slip down and drown.

He came in, he pulled the wooden chair over, he soaped up a washcloth and did her hair and her back, and she shut her eyes and let him, leaning with her chest on her knees, with Mondragon dipping up warm water to wash her hair clean, with Mondragon's hands gentle on her back.

"How much'd you pay?" she asked. Because it bothered her.

"Nothing," he said. And after a moment, after the cold that left: "It was Sword, Jones. It was Sword worked the deal. That's what I paid."

She twisted around, looked up at him, his face pale and serious in the lamplight. Her heart was thudding in her chest.

"What'd you do? What'd you agree to?"

"Anything. Everything. I lied. But that's the price, Jones. They knew I'd lie. They know I will. They know—there's only one way to hold me to it. That's you."

The whole world swung round and stopped on that point, that one, clear as day point. Who. And why. And threat all around them.

"What about Anastasi?"

Mondragon shrugged and began to wash her back again.

"What about Anastasi?"

"Anastasi failed me. Anastasi swore he'd protect you. He swore his reach was long enough. It isn't. It damn well isn't. Jones, for the next few weeks—I'm asking you—"

" '—stay off the water.' *Dammit*, Mondragon—"

"Dammit all you like." He wrung out the cloth, and worked over her shoulders gently, gently. "Jones. It's not all the trouble I'm in. There's Kamat. I'm being

147

blackmailed. There's Boregy. You know *where* I got the two hundred gold? Boregy money. I stole it."

She started to shiver, her teeth to chatter. "Ye're a damn *fool*, Mondragon! What've ye done? What've ye *done?*"

"Shush." He put his hands on her shoulders. "Shush, Jones. *Don't* shout. It's not something I want to tell the boys. You, I can depend on."

"*Me?*" She twisted around again, and climbed up on her knees. *Damn him,* she thought. *Damn him—*

"Come on," he said, and pulled her up and helped her out; and wrapped her in a towel. "Upstairs."

"I can't," she said. Her teeth were still chattering. "I can't. I can't."

But he got her there. He got her into bed and got in with her and held onto her until the shivers got smaller and she worked herself up against him, arms clenched around him. Her hair sopped the pillow. He held onto her and finally he said:

"Jones?"

She knew what he was asking. She pulled him over and he made love to her, carefully, except she was the one who started the roughness, and he did, then, because nothing else was real. Nothing seemed real, not this place, not him, not the room, except when pain got through the memories.

"I know," he said. "Dammit, I *know*, Jones. It's all right."

She woke up when Mondragon stirred from bed. "You're all right," he said hugging her against him, kissing her on the brow. "You're in my bedroom. Upstairs. Petrescu. Sleep in. I'm going to fix breakfast."

She looked at him, a hazy impression as her eyes drifted shut again, opened and swept desperately around him, to be sure. But it *was* his bedroom. It *was* Mondragon. She tried to go back to sleep.

But trying, she remembered the other place. Remembered Megarys, and the cell, and tired as she was, sleep got away from her, leaving her afraid to shut her eyes again.

So she rolled out of bed and hunted her clothes until she remembered she had gotten here in a towel. So she got into the wardrobe and found some of Mondragon's—a sweater, easy. Pants were harder come by, but she found one of his second-hand, canalsider sort that would fit, barely, and stumbled downstairs into the hall to the kitchen, looking for morning tea and the toast that wafted its scent clear upstairs.

The boys were there, with Mondragon. "Out," he said to them; "Yesser," they said, and grabbed up their toast and gulped their tea and went.

"Sit," Mondragon said then, pointing at the vacant chair by the cupboard, and she sat down in the warmth of the kitchen and took the cup of tea he put into her hands, trying not to slop it after he had given it to her. "How are you doing?"

"Not bad," she said, and let go the cup with one hand to scratch behind her ear. "Damn bugs."

He made a sympathetic face. "I know." He put a plate of toast on the shelf of the cabinet beside her, went back and brought a cup of tea for himself, back to the other chair by the cupboard. "My old friend Karl Fon—got me out of prison now and again. Used to bring me to the government house—feed me breakfast. Tell me he was sorry." He gave a grimace that turned into a visible shiver, and a one-sided smile. "It was always good for a bath and breakfast. Ten times as bad going back."

I don't want to hear this. Don't. Mondragon—

But he was silent a while. "I don't want you to go out for a while," he said. "Not—forever. Just till I know it's safe again. Just till some of the worst of it's over."

Panic coiled around her, loss of the open air; loss of safety, one thing and the other. "I was drunk," she said. "They never could have caught me—"

"Please. *Please*, Jones."

"I never give 'em *anything!*"

"I know. You'd try not to."

"*I didn't!*"

"I believe you. But if they put the pressure on, you would; I would; I *have*, Jones, at least—at least to save my life. Because nothing else made sense at the time. Eat. Drink your tea. I want you to go back to bed and stay there today. Everything's all right. Your skip's safe. I'll bribe Min. It's not your worry, what happens. I'll solve it—"

She remembered about the money, then. Boregy. Kamat. "Damn that Raj!"

"It's beyond his fault. Don't lay this on him. It's my problem."

"What ye goin' t' do, Mondragon?" Her voice came out a thin croak, close to tears. "What in *hell* ye goin' t' do with this mess?"

"Jones." Mondragon reached out and caught her wrist hard, "Jones, listen to me. I slept with Marina Kamat to get the rent—to keep Boregy from knowing I couldn't pay it—which would have meant Boregy knowing everything."

"*I'll gut 'er!*"

"No. It's *money*, Jones, it's fast money, it's not blood money . . . I'd have done it for a good meal, if I was hungry, Jones, that's the way I am. I didn't have to kill anybody for it. That's *cheap*, Jones, you don't know how cheap that is in my trade. No blood on it. You know what I'm telling you?"

She was shaking all over. Tea went all over her knee, the one hand out of control, and she set the cup down with a rattle. "What ye done f' *me*, Mondragon? What d' they want ye t' do?"

"Double on Anastasi. Ultimately."

"Lord . . ."

He got up, he pulled her to her feet and hugged her to him till her bones might crack. Her teeth chattered, she was shaking so. Her knees would hardly hold up.

"Mondragon, they're goin' t' kill ye. Ye got to lie low. We c'n go out t' th' Rim, just pack up here—it's winter anyhow. We give out ye been sick—"

"Jones, Jones, you think a man who looks like me can disappear in a town?" He ruffled her hair, held her close, rocked her back and forth. "I'll be all right. Listen to me. It's you they can get at. You're all I care about. Be smart for me. It's not going to be forever. I can get this worked out. I've slipped out of tight places before this, but you've got to be smart, you can't take chances, you can't put yourself where they can get at you."

Prison. Prison cleaner than the Megarys. Prison with

him with the keys, and that not so terrible, but prison all the same. Locked up behind doors, under a roof, off the water—

"How ye goin' to pay f' this place?"

"Same way I have. Whatever I have to do. I have to think, Jones, I couldn't think until you were out of there, I couldn't do anything . . ."

"Ye take me with you. I ain't waitin' here. I ain't waitin' in any damn shut-in place. I c'n ferry you here an' there. I can't stand roofs, Mondragon!"

"I'll set you up with Moghi—you hang around there, damn him, he owes me that much. I don't want you alone anywhere. I'll set the boys up to room at Gallandrys."

"How ye goin' to come by all this *money*, f' Lord's sake?"

"Same way I got the rent. For the rest—" His hand strayed over her hair again. "I sell Kamat to whoever wants to buy information; I see the Sword to Anastasi; I set up with Anastasi to sell certain information to the Sword. Anastasi's a lot of things, but he's not stupid. He won't take it amiss I'm being leaned on. I'll score him good for letting them snatch you—he's not supposed to let that happen. He failed me; I slipped on him. But I can come back with him. I can make money off this mess, Jones, I can stay alive in this mess, it's just going to move quick and delicate for a while, and I can't have you and the boys rattling around in the middle where someone can lay hands on you. I'm sorry. I'm sorry for everything. I didn't want to involve you in this business. God knows I never wanted to tell you. But I won't let you walk into it blind. No more. I won't tell you *what* I'm doing. Maybe I just lied to you. You don't know. You'll never know. —Except I won't lie to you about being in danger, I won't lie to you about what I care about, I won't lie to you about taking care of you. Everything's for that. *Everything's* for that, Jones. That's not a lie."

She leaned there against him a long time, feeling the strength all drained out of her, and the sense, and everything. She hardly had the strength left to hold her arms around him, to hold herself on her feet. Her throat was sore and her knees were watery as her gut, and tears leaked from the shut eyes and made her nose stuffy. Nothing like m'sera silk an' fancy Kamat, no. Her nose's stuffed up. She sniffed. And sneezed so hard she shook him.

"Damn," she muttered against his chest. " 'M sorry, 'm sorry . . . I walked into 'er, Mondragon, I know 't. Ain't goin' to be stupid again."

Megarys is going to die, she thought. *I got to go on the water again, got to go back in view of the Trade and all, I got to face people and they got to know what happened—*

I'm Trade, dammit, and Megarys is going to die for this.

"Jones." Mondragon rubbed the back of her neck. "You want me to put you to bed? Come on. Let me get you upstairs. I'll bring your toast. Bring you breakfast in bed. All right?"

"I'm all right." She found the strength to push away, and find her chair and sit down. Her feet were cold. She curled them against each other, picked up the tea-mug and slopped it, her hands were shaking so. "I think I'm comin' down with the Crud, my throat's sore."

"Oh, God. . . ."

"Ain't nothin'. I'm *Merovingian.* I grew up on Detwater. Crud ain't nothin' but a nuisance. A little blueangel. If I was on my skip, I'd—" Her hands took to shaking, *not* from the fever. From everything. She slopped tea left and right. "Damn, Mondragon!"

He got the cup away from her. "You're going upstairs," he said, and hauled her up and got his arm around her and helped her, out and down the hall, up the stairs—he had tried carrying her once in his life, but she was a canal-rat, all bone and muscle, and she had tensed up and made him fall with her. So he didn't embarrass her, trying to do that—

—until they got inside his bedroom. Then he picked her up so fast she grabbed him in shock, scared he was going to fall. But he dumped her neatly into bed, and started unfastening her breeches. She hardly cared. "Leave th' sweater," she said, when he started with that. She groped after the covers. " 'M *cold*, Mondragon."

He covered her to the chin, arranged her hair with his fingers.

"You want t' light th' lamp f' me, Mondragon?"

Because rooms bothered her. And dark rooms were worse, but damned if she would plead that with him. She nerved herself to get up and do it after he left, if he said no. But he did it for her, and adjusted the wick, and stood looking down at her with his face so still and worried.

Like I was one damn mess too much for him.

"I ain't goin' t' get the Fever. I'm fine. I got th' sniffles. Go on." But the thought of him leaving, going out on the walkways, with all his enemies—made her gut ache. "Ye tend your business. I'll warm up a bit an' get my own tea."

"Denny's on the roof."

"Huh?" she blinked, tried to focus on whether she had missed a minute or two.

"Denny's on the roof. Keeping lookout. That's his *job* for the next little bit. He'd got a friend going to see Raj over to work, and Raj isn't going to *breathe* without my say-so and without knowing his escort's there. Denny's got himself a coal-pot and a blanket, and he or one of his friends is going to sit up there and keep watch on everything that comes and goes. But I'm not going anywhere for a few hours. People I deal with don't get up with the sun."

A few hours. That was better. Denny on the roof was comforting. She lay there with the covers up to her chin and clean pillows under her head and blinked at him. Damn, he was so pretty. Do anything for her. *Had.* Damn Marina Kamat. *I'll gut her. I will.*

"You be all right till I bring the tea?"

"Fine," she said, calm, collected. Warm now. The sweater and two quilts and the room being warmer with the cooking downstairs all helped, except her feet were still like ice—but a canaler's feet were always cold, except when she was working. "I'm all right. Git."

He got. She lay still, comfortable, loved, full of resolve about how she was going to do, how she was going to do everything he said for a while, because he was smart, he understood how to navigate with Boregys, it wasn't so terrible, it was just business he did all the time, nervous-making as it was. The best thing she could do was keep herself exactly where he said and keep herself from being a target and never, never do anything to upset him: he needed to think, and if he was sleeping with Marina Kamat, that was all right, because that was money and he was a man and there wasn't any way he could get a baby and louse up his life like mama had done getting her—

—'cept mama had shot that man that did that to her.

—'cept he *could* get a baby, with Marina damn her guts Kamat, and it would be *his* and *hers,* and she would want to kill that woman then, because if Marina Kamat got a baby from him, then there was no being shut of her, ever, because say what he liked, it would be *his.* A kid was a kid, and if it was Mondragon's and he laid eyes on it, he wouldn't ever forget it.

Damn her!

And she was stuck in his bed and her boat down there with Lord knew who watching it. Lord, if it was Min and he bribed her with whiskey, they could steal *Min's* boat from under her and Min wouldn't notice. *He's got to have more sense than that. You give her yarn, Mondragon, never whiskey when you want her to do somethin' except sleep. Whiskey's for after.*

I got to go on the water again. I got to, and ever'body lookin' at me last night, all starin', wonderin' what happened and where I come from—

I could say I was mad and hid out . . .

No. That'd make people mad, people don't like to feel like fools.

I got to say. I got to say about the Megarys. Megarys can't lay hands on one of the Trade and get away with it, that ain't right, no way!

They'll think I got raped, that's what ever'body in the whole damn town'll think, and they won't believe not, not if I say it till the Angel flies. So what? So my mama was. She done all right. She shot that man. She had me. She brought me up right, and wasn't anybody in the Trade wanted to get aslant of her.

Ain't no shame, if it happened. Shame's if they get away with it.

Megarys is rough. Megarys is a way to get some people hurt, people with kids on their boats and all.

What do I do, mama?

What do I do about it?

She tried really hard, this time, to see mama sitting there. It was hard to bring her. She lifted her head and tried till sweat ran, and finally she *was* there, dimly, in the corner chair.

But Retribution Jones took possession of it then, folded her arms, leaned back, and put her bare feet out.

Hell of a lot warmer in here, Retribution said. *Smells better, too.*

Mama, he bought me out.

Yey. He ain't done bad.

She didn't trust it when mama got friendly and agreeable. Like it wasn't mama, and she couldn't trust it.

They ain't touched me, mama.

Ain't nothin' you did. They *didn't, is all.*

Odd, something said, in the back of her brain.

Mama, it ain't like I'm not going on the water again. Mondragon understands. He ain't keepin' me. I just don't feel so good t'day.

. . . an' I'm scared, mama.

Retribution frowned.

You goin' to take into me about Mondragon and that Kamat, mama? It ain't like you to be so quiet. . . .

Don't be dead, mama. . . .

Mama stood up. Like she was leaving. But she came and leaned on the end of the bed, and her face was like Jones had never seen it, grim and shadowed, and her eyes like light, like the fire of God.

Like mama was going to come over the end of the bed and take her by the throat.

You get 'em. You get 'em, Altair, you don't come whinin' t' me! You got a name in th' Trade, an' it's my name, and you ain't runnin', Altair. You get yourself back on the water, you hold your head up, you tell it like it happened an' you make 'em believe *it, Altair.*

They won't, mama.

They will *when you clean your mess up, because* you *say, an' it's* your *word, an' it damn well better mean*

*somethin', Altair, it damn well better mean somethin',
an' it don't mean shit until you straighten yourself up
and look folk in the eye and take Megarys f' layin' a
hand on you! That's the cost of it. Ye don't whine t'
me, ye do it! Ye do it!*

Mama left. Left nothing but the end of the bed and
the bare wall where she had stood. That and a heat
that made her sweat, and a strength that had her head
up even with her shaking, had every muscle in her
hard and tense.

*Can't do it yet, mama. I got a man in trouble. I got
to wait.*

There was no anger from the shadows. Just a comfortable, biding mad.

And the sound of Mondragon coming up the stairs.

He brought her tea. He settled the pillows behind
her.

"Your color's better," he said, and took her hand
before he gave her the cup. "Hands are warmer."

"I'm doin' fine," she said, and pulled her feet up.
"Sit. Sit an' talk t' me, huh? Tell me what you think I
better hear."

He sat. He talked to her. There was blueangel in
the first cup of tea. She tasted it. Her nose was
starting to run for good and all, and she sniffed and
wiped it on her hand, drank her tea and listened,
sober and plain, while he said how he had looked for
her, and how he had thought she was mad at first, and
was still worried, and then got scared, and worried
sick. How he had gone to old Min and asked for help,
because Min was the only canaler he knew was going
to understand without blaming him.

"I'd have slept with *Min*," he said. "if it could have
gotten you back."

She thought that was halfway funny. If it was not so
grim all around it.

And then he said, with a terrible look on his face:
"I'd rather, than deal with the Sword."

"They're tryin' t' get ye *back*," she said. "Back up
that river. Mondragon,—whoever you deal with—don't
trust 'em. Don't trust 'em f' nothin'."

"I don't," he said. "But don't ask me who I'm

156

dealing straight with, Jones. For your sake—I don't want you to know that."

"Don't go back on Anastasi," she said. The cold feeling was back at her stomach, a lump of sickness. The empty cup in her hands nauseated her with the memory of the blueangel-taste. "He's th' one c'n save ye. He's th' one Boregy swings on. That's more power 'n all the rest, in this city. Politics an' money. The governor's son and th' banks. Don't trust Kamat. I'm tellin' ye, not because I'm jealous, because there ain't nothin' right about that set-up, an' that woman don't run the House. If you get aslant of who does, they'll turn on you, they'll do you hurt, an' if ye took their side against Boregy and Anastasi, ye ain't got nothin' left. . . ."

"Don't ask me what I do. Don't ask me who I deal with. But you've got damn good sense." He took the cup, bent and kissed her on the forehead. "Get you another?"

She shook her head, jaws clamped. "No. 'M fine." The shivers wanted to come back. The fear did. She gave him a jaws-clenched smile, her stomach trying to turn inside out. "Ain't goin' t' worry about ye. 'M scared silly, Mondragon. Ever' time you go out—I'll be scared. Ye take care. All right?"

"All right," he said.

Which was as much as she thought she could get.

STRANGE BEDFELLOWS
by Lynn Abbey

Richard sat alone and uncomfortable in a barely reputable tavern at the Ventani waterline. Mohgi's. It had a certain reputation with the hightown thrill-cravers, and Marina had assured him it was a place where Thomas Mondragon could be found—eventually. Moghi himself had agreed, or he hadn't disagreed which in this sort of place passed for agreement, and said he thought Mondragon would show sometime before third watch.

Richard toyed with a brandy he'd ordered but could not bear to drink. Three short days, and nights. The Samurai offering was two-thirds subscribed before it had been published in the daily mercantile report. Kamat's partners and subordinates had come aboard first: Balaci, Yakunin, Wex, but others had followed. Even Zorya, which also finished wool, and craved the secret of First-bath dye like a starving man, had anted up the minimum fifty sols.

Vega Boregy had opened his private club to his new ally, inviting Richard to dine with Ito and Exeter, Romney and Rosenblum: men and women who had been power in Merovingen when Kamat still chased and sheared sheep by hand. They praised him to his face and asked the same question: When do you start hiring?

He gulped the brandy and wiped his mouth. His old nurse's purgatives tasted better than the sheepdip Moghi poured. Lord, sheepdip probably tasted better. Richard guessed he'd have an ulcer from the brandy or from nerves if Mondragon didn't show soon.

"M'ser Kamat?"

Richard beheld Thomas Mondragon staring down at him. Unlike Marina, he knew danger when he saw it, and knew he'd been wise to come unarmed. Mondragon might hesitate to kill an unarmed man. There was no doubt he *could* kill, no doubt—looking into those unreadable eyes—that he *could* have been Sword. Richard could go through the motions with a sword, but he was no duelist and he'd never shot a gun. He could defend himself nicely with a canaler's pole, but he could scarcely use a pole in a tavern—even one as rowdy as Moghi's

"Have a seat."

Cat-supple and still staring, Mondragon eased into the chair opposite Richard's. "I got your message. I have no intentions, honorable or otherwise toward your sister, m'ser Kamat."

"I assumed you didn't, but Marina has intentions toward you."

"She came to me. I told her it was unwise—"

"As you took her money."

"Which is long since spent, m'ser Kamat. Gone and spent; you won't see it again. Not from me. State your intentions, if you think I'm in your debt."

The man was cold as a sharrist hell. His eyes were veiled; his posture so relaxed it bordered on insolence. And there was the whisper of threat behind his every word. Richard tried to imitate him.

"My sister has never loved a man before."

"I gathered that much."

"I don't want to see her hurt."

"Then you should have locked her up, m'ser. She's reckless and unwise, and attractive in the bargain. It's a combination that makes for hurting."

Imitation wasn't working. Richard couldn't outcold the Sword. He let his anxiety rise naturally to the surface and leaned forward on his elbows.

"What did she promise you, Mondragon? She thinks you'll be her lover; she thinks she wants your child. You're not the man for that sort of thing, I think. So is she an utter fool, or did she promise you something? Gold?"

"She promised me everything, Kamat; I took the gold because I needed it."

"You care nothing for her?"

"I care nothing for anyone. You know that; you told me so yourself."

"But you'll still need gold."

Mondragon said nothing. He did not look away from Richard's challenge, but he did not answer it. As with Moghi, the lack of disagreement tokened agreement.

"You might understand, m'ser, that I wouldn't interfere with my sister's lovers, and, as you imply, a certain amount of pain is one of love's most exquisite pleasures. Still, I would prefer that lust, if not love, be the only currency involved."

"What are you getting at, Kamat?"

"I don't want my sister paying for your feigned affection."

"So you'll pay instead? You Kamat are such a *considerate* family."

The barb cut close to the bone, and Richard winced visibly. He had thought nothing could be worse than sitting in Vega Boregy's office, feeling immature and inferior while the older man spun his webs. He'd been wrong. Sitting with a man not too many years his senior, and feeling the same thing, was worse.

"I found myself covering my sister's promises to the boy: We will sponsor him. Regrettably, it seemed a similar notion to consider her promises to you the same way."

"That would, I think, be *very* unwise." There was no trace of humor in Tom's voice.

"She tells me you're poor. That the gold went to cover your rent—"

"Among other things."

"And certain parties would take it amiss if you went back to your regular trade, I dare say."

There was no humor in Richard's voice, either, and Mondragon's expression went absolutely blank.

"I have a proposal to make to you, m'ser Mondragon. Marina suggested it first, and I thought it foolish at first, but I think there might be some wisdom to it after all. You may have heard that Boregy's bank has underwritten the charter for a new security force in Merovingen."

Tom remained impassive. "So?"

"They're fronting mercantile money: Kamat money and gold from a fair sampling of other houses. Enough gold to employ fifty men on annual contracts, and more later."

"I'm not interested."

"I've got to hire those fifty men and, on careful reflection, I expect that certain men who cramp your style will present themselves to me. Now, I won't know them by sight, and you haven't been able to find them—"

"If there were such men, I'd hardly consider sitting down in front of them, Kamat."

"You've spent little enough time in a Merovingen hiring hall, then. No one would see you, but I'd be most grateful if you could assure me that I'd hired no Nev Hettek ringers for the Samurai."

Tom's facade slipped a little. "You say Boregy and

your peers are behind you? I wouldn't think that's enough to set up another security force when the blacklegs are in all the right places."

"Even on the Rock there are places the blacklegs are not invited to go, and places where the Samurai will be invited."

"You seem pretty sure of yourself for a man who knows nothing about security."

Richard tipped his mug and found he'd drunk all the so-called brandy. His mouth was gluey and his tongue felt thick. For a heartbeat he thought he'd been drugged, but it was just the adrenalin pounding through his system. He had mentioned needing additional expertise to Vega Boregy; the man hadn't blinked. He knew Boregy had ties to Anastasi now, and it was rumored that Mondragon had ties to Anastasi Kalugin as well. If he could get Mondragon to take the bait, he'd have hired expertise, all right, but who would it really be working for?

"We're merchants, m'ser, every season we risk ruin and collapse. Perhaps you haven't been here long enough to see a House fall, or a new one rise to take its place. The only security we want is for our docks and our warehouses. And, I assure you we know the value of gold."

"I'll consider it, Kamat, but my back grows itchy when I sit in one place too long." Mondragon pushed his chair from the table. "I'm not cheap to hire, and I follow no one's rules."

Tom did not offer his hand, and Richard ordered another brandy once he'd left the tavern.

It was Sunday, the day when wealthy folk went praying or slept late. It was a day much like the others for the rest of Merovingen. The sun was shining and the wind was, for once, quiet. Ashe paused at the end of St. John Bridge and took a final drag on his tabac before flipping the butt into the canal below. He was about to light another when he noticed a messenger on Kamat Bridge bearing for the front door.

Sunday mail was always private, always personal. Ashe pushed away from the rail and headed for the mid-door. The day underporter, reeking of Satterday gin and Sunday incense, let him in.

"Messenger coming," Ashe explained, tossing his jacket on the peg. "Saw him from the bridge."

The dayman grunted and went back to staring across St. John Bridge. Ashe heard the big bronze bell upstairs. The messenger was in the vestibule with Eleanora Slade when he completed his climb.

"I'm here, no need for you to deliver that," he informed her, deftly inserting himself between them.

"I'm to deliver it to m'sera Marina Kamat, personally," the youth said.

"The family's in the diningroom," Eleanora replied. "You'll not go in there."

"Then I'll wait. I got my instructions clear."

"I'll handle this." Ashe dug into his pocket for a silver libby; he'd get it back from the butler, later; the butler'd be reimbursed from the cook, and the cook would shave his from the household allowance. The tied and sealed message fell easily from the youth's hands.

"You'll deliver it yourself?" Eleanora asked.

"Of course."

Richard, Andromeda and Marina were drinking tea when Ashe followed the butler into the diningroom.

"A message for m'sera Marina from Petrescu," the butler announced, taking the paper from Ashe's hand.

"Petrescu?" Marina asked breathlessly. She broke the seal and let the string fall to the floor. Her face began to glow with happiness as she scanned the lines. "It's from Tom," she said—as if the other two hadn't guessed. "He says," she paused, her forehead wrinkling slightly, "he says to be remembered to you, Richard, and . . . oh, Mother—he's invited me to dinner! What shall I wear?"

"You're on your own, Ree," Andromeda said with an indulgent, but slightly thin-lipped smile.

Marina left the diningroom at a run. So did Ashe and the butler, though only after they'd been dismissed. Andromeda and Richard locked stares and the tea between them grew cold.

CHAPTER XII

SAYING YES TO DRUGS
by Chris Morris

Mike Chamoun was a riverboat captain from Nev Hettek, nothing more. Whenever he went aboard his beloved *Detfish*, he could believe that again. Even to stand on the *Detfish*'s poop was more honor, privilege, and unattainable luck than a poor boy like Chamoun would have dreamed of, a year ago in Nev Hettek.

But this wasn't Nev Hettek, and it wasn't last year. It was this year in Merovingen, and Chamoun wasn't the son of a poor Nev Hettek Adventist family any longer. He was Michael Chamoun, scion of the instant dynasty called Chamoun Shipping; husband of Cassiopeia Borey and resident of Merovingen's noble Borey House; officer of the census by special decree of Tatiana Kalugin Herself; convert to Revenantism under the personal tutelage of Uncle Ito—Cardinal Tremaine Ito Borey.

He was also the favorite pawn of Nev Hettek's Ambassador in Merovingen, one Chance Magruder, and more. Michael Chamoun was a Sword of God agent, a revolutionary, if you liked; a terrorist, if you didn't. He was, in plain fact, a Nev Hetteker spy under deep cover in the very bosom of his enemy—in Borey House.

If that weren't trouble enough, Michael Chamoun was slowly falling in love with the wife he'd married for the Cause, young Cassie. He hadn't meant it to happen. It wasn't supposed to happen. When he'd came here, he'd still been in love with the unattainable Rita Nikolaev.

Maybe, he told himself fiercely, he still was. That

163

was the reason for this meeting, the real reason Chamoun was on the *Detfish* tonight. He was going to tell Chance, when Magruder got here, that Chamoun wasn't anybody's boy anymore as far as personal stuff went—that he was going to see Rita, and do what a man did in a situation like this.

He had to. He was too damned confused. He'd gotten in too deep here and had to straighten his thinking out, at least. Before he made some foolish mistake—or another one—that cost people's lives.

Dockside, the *Detfish* had only a skeleton crew, and Chamoun moved dreamily off the poop toward the captain's cabin. When he'd come here, he'd brought Sword agents other than just himself and Magruder. Dimitri Romanov had been with him, and Rack and Ruin al-Banna, the vicious twins. Now all but he and Magruder were dead. It ought to be a sign to Magruder, who was trained to calculate odds in such things.

But Magruder was making himself scarce, and the last time Chamoun had seen him, the meeting hadn't gone well. Michael had been forced to explain that he'd gotten himself compromised by the ex-Sword Mondragon and Vega Boregy, his wife's father. That Chamoun was up to his ears in a second channel meant to sever Magruder himself from the Sword of God.

It hadn't gone down well. Chamoun wasn't a tactical genius, a strategic planner like Magruder, but he knew he had to do something to restore Chance's confidence in him. People Magruder didn't trust—like the al-Bannas, like Romanov—didn't live long.

Chamoun had to tell Magruder how he felt, and what was going on in Boregy house . . . especially with his wife, Cassie . . . before it was too late.

Down three stairs and into the captain's cabin went Chamoun, surreptitiously fingering a flashlight at his belt. He'd given one to Cassie when he'd asked her to marry him. Merovingen didn't have enough tech to power up a radio. That was what the Kalugins wanted from Nev Hettek: knowledge. Tech was black magic here, where the Revenantists were sure that the vengeance of the sharrh was going to find them out if they so much as put in a wireless.

The flashlight lit, Chamoun slid between the narrow bed and the cabin's chairs to light an oil lamp. He wasn't using his own electrics, not with the generators down while the *Detfish* was docked. It didn't do to draw attention to yourself, not here.

Mike Chamoun had found that out during one of his conversion lessons, when Ito Boregy had given him a drug-induced glimpse of Michael Chamoun's purported previous life. The result of that memory (true or false, it didn't matter) of Chamoun's former life as a member of the Merovin Space Defense Force, had made Ito Boregy Chamoun's mortal enemy. And made Cassie Boregy an explorer on the astral plane.

Every night that Cassie could get the drugs and wheedle Michael into helping, she'd been going into trances and trying to remember a life of her own beyond the sky—some wisp of reality that belonged to Merovin's history before the sharrh had come and destroyed everything. It was illegal. By Revenantist standards, it was probably immoral. And if her father or Ito found out, Michael Chamoun was going to be Cassie's *ex*-husband, quicker than you could say "trip to the Justiciar's dungeons."

How he was going to explain about the previous-lives stuff to Magruder, Chamoun still couldn't fathom. His fingers found the oil lamp. Flashlight in his teeth by its stalk, he struck a match and lit the lamp.

Then he turned and there, on his bed, sprawled on one elbow, was Magruder, watching him casually—if you didn't worry about the pistol he held.

"It's me," Chamoun said unnecessarily, his hands spreading of their own accord.

Magruder said, "So I see," in his husky voice and swung upright in a motion that ended with the pistol going back to its home next to his spine. "What's up? I've got a diplomatic reception—" he bared his teeth, "—in an hour and a half."

Chance was around Chamoun's size, but rangy—stringy, almost. He always looked uncomfortable in his Merovingian velvet, and tonight was no exception. In that sharp, weathered face with its broad forehead and flaring jaws was all the fielded power of the Sword of God. Sometimes, when Chamoun had been away from Magruder for a while, he forgot that checked lethality and started thinking of Magruder as an ally, a benefactor, a friend.

Tonight, one look at the man from Nev Hettek who was here as Minister of Trade and Tariffs, as His Excellency the Ambassador, telegraphed a clear message to Chamoun: caution.

Magruder brushed graying hair impatiently off his forehead when Chamoun didn't answer. "Come on, Mike. Sit down and tell me what the blazing trouble is. Didn't you hear me? I'm on a tight schedule."

"Sir . . ." Chamoun started to reply in Nev Hetteker fashion and stopped, correcting himself in answer to Chance's scowl. "Ser," he amended as he took a seat on the map table opposite Magruder; he needed to speak perfect Merovingian dialect, now, to prove to Chance he had his wits about him. "I've got . . . problems."

"So I gathered. Lay it out, boy."

"It's . . . well, Cassie first, si—Chance. She's been trying to do regressions ever since Ito drugged me into telling him I was a space-based soldier in—"

"Not this again." Magruder leaned back on the bed, balancing on his elbows. "Next you'll be telling me those fireworks we set over the harbor have got you convinced the sharrh have come again, like the rest of these crazies."

"You gotta know this stuff, Chance. You told me, once—whatever I thought was important." Once in a previous life, Chamoun had been someone named Mickey, who'd died fighting the sharrh. He knew he had; there was no way to convince anyone who hadn't been through it that he had, though. "Whatever you think of the regressions, just try to understand that if her father finds out Cassie's eating deathangel every night, Retribution's going to break loose in the household."

"You're her husband. Forbid her."

"Chance, you don't understand. You can't forbid Cassie . . . Anyway, I'm going to go see Rita, maybe she can help me."

"I bet." Sarcasm laced Magruder's response. "I told

you, kid, I don't care what you do with your spare time. Just don't blow off your marriage."

"I . . . Great. Yeah. Fine." Chamoun was sorry he'd asked for this meeting. Magruder was watching him too closely. The Ambassador's reactions weren't their usual, protective sort. Something was really wrong and Michael was making things worse, not better.

"Fine? You think you're doing fine?" Magruder shifted just enough to slide the fishknife from his belt. He started paring his nails with it. "I just finished cleaning up your last mess—with Mondragon and Vega Boregy. I thought, I'll admit, that was why you'd called me—that something had happened vis a vis the second channel. Has it?" Eyes as blank as a dead man's centerpunched him.

"I . . . don't know what Mondragon's up to. Nobody's had me carrying messages to Megary and back, that's all I know."

"That's something, anyhow. Another mess like that one, and I'm sending you back to Nev Hettek—on family business or something; I'll think of an excuse. You're more—"

"Chance!" Michael objected.

"You're more use to me," the Ambassador continued implacably, "as an absent husband than as a dead one. Ito's still after your scalp, and you and your wifey are playing druggie games? Not real welcome news, kid."

When Magruder's diction slipped, his violent side was roused, Chamoun knew. There wasn't a single person or group or natural phenomenon in all of Merovingen, including the canal-spawned diseases of this pest hole, as deadly as Chance Magruder.

Chamoun reminded himself of the night he'd married, when Magruder had pledged to take care of Chamoun: his troubles, his enemies, his body and mind. He clung to that thought now. He had to, or he'd start wondering if Chance had decided he was expendable. If he started wondering that, he might as well go back to Nev Hettek and face the music. If he could get that far. An angry Sword tribunal could brand him a coward, a fool, a failure. But they wouldn't kill him out of hand—not him or his parents.

Magruder would.

As if reading his mind, Chance said, "You've got your parents to think of, Mike: lots of people depending on you. Go see the Nikolaev woman if you think it'll help. Put your foot down with your wife. And if Mondragon so much as shows up at Boregy House, send for me. Next time he's there, I want to accidentally be there too."

Magruder put away his knife and got up, stooped in the low cabin. His hand went to the small of his back, where his pistol was. "By the way, you're doing a nice job with your census taking. Tatiana thinks the world of you."

The parting shot was like a behavior-modification morsel thrown to a guard dog after a grueling session, Chamoun knew. He watched Magruder until he'd gone. Then he put his head in his hands and stared through spread fingers at the deck. Why couldn't he talk to Chance? How come he couldn't make Magruder understand what was dangerous here, and what wasn't?

Chamoun knew in his heart that Cassie's mind-games were more dangerous than Mondragon's maneuvering, that Ito's enmity could wipe out more than simply Mike Chamoun. Ito was capable of undoing everything the Sword was trying to do here, starting with Michael Chamoun's life.

But then he thought back over what Magruder had said and realized that the Sword cell leader had offered him a way out—a way he might not like, but one that was survivable.

Instead of making him feel better, the realization made Michael Chamoun feel worse. Magruder was implying that Chamoun was in a mess not even Magruder could unmake; that the only solution was to pull Mike Chamoun from the playing field. The final resolution of that lay in the behavior of Michael's wife, Cassie Boregy. And Cassie was acting just like any spoiled child with a new toy, never mind that that toy was mind altering drugs in conjunction with hypnotherapy.

Suddenly, Chamoun's problems didn't seem like a handy excuse to see Rita Nikolaev and find out if he still loved her. Suddenly the night was darker and the

Detfish's cabin smaller, and the winter chill of the Merovingen harbor bit through his clothes to scrape his very bones.

Cassie Boregy was all alone in her blue bedroom and she was very angry. She had everything prepared. She'd been looking forward to tonight. And then Michael had to go out—so he said. Deathangel wouldn't keep forever. It wasn't fair.

It also wasn't fair that Michael had had such a great revelation. He was an unbeliever, really; he was only converting because of her. Yet Uncle Ito had taken Michael under his wing and guided him to a soul-ennobling experience, and now no one would help Cassie do the same.

If Michael Chamoun, a mere Nev Hetteker, an Adventist tech-lover, could find that in his soul lay a great hero of the war against the sharrh, then what wonderful deeds might lie in Cassie's own forgotten past? There had to be some.

God would not be so mean as to give Michael a past as a space warrior against the sharrh and give her nothing but vague memories of sculleries and babies and wood-chopping and water-carrying. Somewhere in Cassie's soul, the noble heroine she knew must be there was hiding. It just couldn't be that the Nev Hetteker she'd married had been a hero in a previous life, and she a common fishwife.

So she kept searching. She searched with Michael, night after night. She knew it was boring him, but he should have a little consideration. All he had to do was take notes, while it was she who risked her sanity and her health taking the deathangel so regularly, trying to expel her soul from her body and send it through time and space.

And now he was openly more hostile. He'd just said he was going out to Rita's, of course, to hurt her. There was no reason for Michael to deal directly with the Nikolaevs. He was trying to make her think that he'd gone to talk to Rita about Cassie's "addiction" to deathangel.

That was obviously not the case. Michael was only trying to hurt her, to manipulate her, the way her father often did. Men were all alike. Or else Michael wouldn't be treating her just like her father would, if Vega had known what was going on behind closed doors in her bedroom.

She paced the room. She touched her ormolu-festooned furniture. She sat before her dressing table and combed her gold-streaked hair with a silver brush. She looked at herself in the mirror calmly, waiting for the deathangel to take affect. Soon enough, she'd see whether Michael hadn't been somehow holding her back, guiding her mind away from its true goal, toward the mundane revelations that seemed to be all she'd ever gain from the regression process.

As soon as the mirror began to look like a wavy pool of clear water, she began reciting the regression formula. She knew it by heart. She didn't need Michael to tell her that she must find a previous life of interest and value to her present self. She didn't need Michael to tell her to listen only to his voice. She could listen only to her own voice.

She talked to herself in the mirror until she stopped talking. The deathangel in her system made it seem that she was still speaking aloud, but she wasn't. The person before her in the mirror was changing, and the scene that the mirror displayed was beginning to spin.

She wasn't aware that she dropped her hairbrush, or that she gripped the white enameled dressing table with both her hands. She didn't see her own eyes widen, and take on a glassy, unblinking stare. She didn't see anything at all, from that moment onward, that was in the outer world of sight and sound and taste and smell.

She was somewhere else. The person who she was looked into a cracked mirror, and that mirror reflected flames behind her. The ground itself was burning. The city around her was blazing. And she was sitting in a vehicle whose doors she couldn't open.

Outside her, a mob was rocking the car she was in. She knew it was a car, and she knew that the mob was out of control. She also knew that in the front seat of that car her driver lay sprawled, shot to death. She was trapped alone, helpless.

The mob closed in, until she could see nothing

through the mirror but their dark bodies pressed against the car's windows, and faces full of hatred screaming at her—distorted faces full of hatred for the techno-barons who'd brought the retribution of the sharrh down upon them all.

She found herself clasping her stomach. She was pregnant. Didn't they know out there that she was pregnant? She screamed back at the crowd that it wasn't her fault, that she wasn't to blame for the sharrh's coming. But her family owned a controlling interest in the largest of the Merovin conglomerates, and the rioters were not about to listen.

The crazed mob was rocking the car now, back and forth, back and forth. More and more came to join them. Suddenly the car was being pushed forward, and then it canted to one side.

She screamed, "No!" when she realized they were lifting the car. She pounded on the glass, but the faces pressed to it didn't soften. She tried to open first one door, then the other, to no avail. Against the weight of the crowd, they were as good as locked.

Her car was completely off the ground, now. The crowd had lifted it, and was carrying it toward the flames.

As she realized what they were doing, she screamed louder and louder. She screamed that the sharrh's coming wasn't her fault; she screamed that technology hadn't done this to them; she screamed that she would give them all her money and all her possessions, if only they would let her and her unborn child go.

But the mob didn't listen. Women's faces, distorted against the glass, cursed her. Men leered. And closer came the flames.

The car rocked so now, from the lurch of the crowd as it picked up speed, that she was thrown about on the back seat. She grabbed for the front seat's head-rest, holding on.

Then she saw how she would die.

The mob was running with the car toward a great fire, and a smaller bonfire set in the middle of the street. She screeched in horror, and started to scramble over the back seat into the front seat. The windscreen was cracked; perhaps she could punch it through and escape that way.

As she straddled the seat, she remembered her driver, with his brains splattered over the upholstery. Then her knee hit the dead man's chest, and she slipped in his blood.

The car tilted crazily. Then it fell, throwing her against the dashboard. When she scrambled up, holding her head, trying to blink away the dizziness and look through the cracked windscreen, the crowd was no longer around her.

Fire was everywhere. Through it, she thought she could see faces contorted in fury as the mob watched the car burning in the middle of the bonfire.

She was coughing; she was hot; everything around her was hot. She was burning up. The upholstery caught on fire—little puffs of smoke that caught and blazed. The car's doors were too hot to touch, and the door-upholstery was plastic, which gave off choking fumes as it melted.

She was coughing her guts out, and she felt her baby die just before the flames all around the car reached its petrol tanks and she felt nothing more but a single spark of white obliteration that seemed to explode her into a universe of eternally blazing stars.

Nikolaev House was as far west as you could get on Rimmon Isle; it faced New Harbor on the north and Dead Harbor on the south. You could see Ramsey-head and beyond from its docks. The elite mercantilists wanted to keep watch on their customers, one and all.

Michael was out with Rita Nikolaev on her private balcony, a place he'd never thought to be. Not alone with her.

But alone with her he was, and his body and mind were sending him conflicting signals. She was as wondrous as ever he remembered her; she was everything his flesh desired. And Revenantists . . . well, they were freer with their bodies than Adventist women were, or Nev Hetteker women would ever be, since both common sense and morality differed here. An Adventist woman worried about disease and pregnancy;

Revenantists didn't. Both were karmic penalties, to be embraced even if they killed you. Everything here was a matter of politics: you negotiated even with God. Did what you pleased, so long as no one found out.

Yet Rita was a friend of Cassie's—an older friend, a wiser friend, a more experienced friend. And Cassie was in need of a friend whose opinion she respected. Could Chamoun do what his body prompted—reach out and put his arms around Rita Nikolaev's slim waist, pull her against him, take advantage of the privacy she offered and the invitation he was almost certain he saw in her eyes . . . ? Do all that, and then say, "Look, will you help me talk some sense into my wife?"

"Now tell me what it is that's troubling you, Captain Chamoun," said the Nikolaev woman teasingly. Cassie's friends all still called him "captain"; Rita made it a joke they shared. She was older than Cassie by centuries of experience, it seemed, though by not more than a few years. Maybe she knew about all her previous lives. Maybe there was something to this Revenantist creed, to make a woman so arch and proud, so calm and competent, so sure of herself though she was no older, no more experienced, than he.

He felt like a bumpkin, a rube, standing there before her, tongue-tied and hesitant.

When he didn't respond, she moved closer, looking up into his eyes with a probing intelligence that had made a slave of his heart the first time he'd seen her, so long ago in Nev Hettek. Those eyes were grave, all humor gone: "It's serious, then? I'm sorry. We're safe here, no matter what we need to discuss." She touched his arm. "Nothing you say to me will go any farther. We're about to become business partners, after all.'

"Huh? Oh, right." Merger details. He'd paid no attention to any of that. Vega Boregy and Magruder and the Nikolaevs were hammering out some kind of shipping agreement. Chance had kept him out of it, or he'd been too busy with the census, or with Cassie. . . . "But that's not it," he blurted. Rita was so damned *close* to him. The lights from Ramseyhead seemed to reach across New Harbor to halo her beautiful head.

"Then what is it?" She took his hand. Hers was

warm and dry. She led him to the balcony's rail and there she sat on the railing, swinging her velvet panted legs as if she had no idea of her effect on him. "Come on, Michael," she smiled encouragingly. "It can't be that bad."

"I'm no Revenantist, to know how bad it is. You decide." Begun, he rushed on: "Cassie's doing death-angel every night, trying to remember a previous life. It's—"

"A what?" Rita Nikolaev's head came up. Her eyes narrowed as she fought to keep a straight face.

"You don't understand," he said. For she didn't. She was still holding his hand, and tugging on it. He let her pull him closer and then he was looking down at the part in her hair. To it, he said, "Cardinal Ito gave me a deathangel-induced regression, and I told Cassie. Ever since then, she's been trying to do the same thing. I—"

"The same thing? Who were you, Captain Chamoun, in your previous life?"

"Oh, no. I'm under sentence of death for that as it is, according to the College."

She chuckled. She thought he was joking. Somehow, it seemed funny, telling it to her. The whole thing seemed funny; ludicrous, even.

He found himself wanting to sit beside her on the rail. He dared it, and their thighs touched. But that beat looking her in the eye, with her sitting there, legs spread in her pants, so close he could have moved in between them, put both arms around her, and . . .

"Anyway, she wants to find out she was a hero of the battle with the sharrh. And she won't stop. I need you to help me make her quit it. How much deathangel can you eat, before something goes wrong?"

"Lots," said Rita authoritatively. "More than you'd imagine. But every so often, somebody decides he can fly, or swim to the Rim . . . You were right to come to me, 'Captain.' "

"Mike's fine. Everybody's so formal here. My friends at home call me Mike."

"Mike, then." She wasn't one of his friends at home. The single syllable sounded very un-Rita-ish, too harsh in her fine mouth.

He looked at her and she was staring at him. "Will you come back with me to Boregy House, Rita? Tonight? Talk to Cassie with me?"

"Why did you come to me, Mike? Not to someone else, or some member of the family?"

"I hadn't seen you since you were at the house with Mondragon." The memory still bothered him. "Maybe I wanted to find out why you were keeping such bad company." He didn't know where that had come from; it just slipped out.

"Thomas? Thomas has problems, that's all. You must have gathered that. I can't even remember how we happened to be together that night—ah, yes I do. I'd come on my own, and Thomas was there, so as a gentleman, after the card game, he offered to escort me home. Considering that the Sword of God murdered my sister, it was a natural thing for him to offer. He's a swordsman, after all."

"He's a duelist," Michael corrected. *He's Sword himself, or close enough.* "I wouldn't let him escort Cassie from the parlor to the dining hall."

"Ah, I'd heard Adventists from Nev Hettek we:e old fashioned."

"Protective of our womenfolk, yes."

"*Womenfolk?* Protectiveness is charming; provincialism is offensive." She pulled away from him enough to end the contact between his right thigh and her left.

It was easier, then, for him to remember why he'd come here. "Will you come with me to see Cassie? Now?"

She looked at him boldly, and there was a measuring aspect to her glance. "Yes, now," she said, as if slightly disappointed. "Since you insist."

And then he realized he'd just missed his chance, perhaps the chance of a lifetime, as Rita Nikolaev slid off the railing and faced him, hands on her hips, saying. "Well, Mike, what are you waiting for?"

There was no recapturing the lost opportunity—not now. But as he left the rail to follow her, he said, "Considering what happened to your sister, and that I'm taking you out so late, you'll have to let me bring you back here, afterward."

"Perhaps," she said haughtily, though he thought he heard a promise there. "If you're good."

Cassie was floating somewhere, between death and a new life. She liked the place where she was, all brown and soft and womby. It was a place where there were many lives, and no pain. A place where God was all around, and human affairs no more important than the affairs of ants.

So when a voice, and then another, started calling her stridently, she resisted.

She didn't have to listen to those voices. She had only to listen to her own voice. Hers was the single voice of reason in the universe she inhabited. Hers was the only voice that could command her. And her own voice was telling her she didn't have to leave here, no matter what anyone said.

There was no strife here, no jealousy, madness, or grief. There was no misery, no poverty, no disappointment. There was no failure, no treachery, no deceit.

But there was love, of a sort. There was the love of nature, the love of the process called life itself, though she wasn't sure such love was worth the price. She kept hearing the voices of other entities, but she knew those entities were imprisoned in their bodies. What did they know of the fullness of life? Of the expanse of a point? Of the width of a straight line? Of the event called being?

She had lost a body, a life, an unborn child. She wasn't ready to go back to that world of flame and pain and horrors inflicted upon her by her fellow man. She wasn't ready to be born again, to suffer again, and to die again, just to get to . . . here. Again.

Where was here? Where was she? Was she dead? Discomfort began to invade her peace. Distress prickled her person. Uneasiness disturbed the sea of endless, velvety dark around her. Was she dead?

Death was frightening. She remembered it. If she'd died, then she must be dead, since she wasn't alive. At least, she wasn't alive in the sense of a life full of incidents that one could remember.

The voices kept intruding, calling her name. One voice would call, then another. One voice she heard was male; the other, female. This differentiation disturbed her rest further. Where she had been, there was no real difference between male and female . . .

And yet there was. Male was aggression, bright transformation, artifactually creative and destructive because of that. Female was diplomacy, dark receptivity, transmutationally creative, and modifying because of that. She saw herself as a female, the femininity deep in her being. She was like a great pink/red/orange/purple flower, then a flower of the sea: a jellyfish of gorgeous hue, trailing long tendrils in the water, while her middle expanded to accept the nourishment her tendrils found . . .

"No!" she said, and sat up. "No!" she yelled, and put her arm across her eyes.

She was being pummeled by ice-cold water. She coughed amid the spray, and struggled against whatever was holding her. She was freezing cold, fully dressed, and being held in the shower against her will by her husband and Rita Nikolaev.

She shouted and cursed. She struck out and hit Michael across the mouth.

His blood mixed with the shower's spray and dribbled down his cheek, pink and dilute.

Rita was telling Michael loudly to ". . . get her out now. We've got to walk her around. Walk her! Don't let her go back to sleep."

She fought them like a wet cat, but it was no use.

She was back in the world, stuck in her body, which walked between her torturers like an automaton.

She wanted to vomit, so she did, all over all three of them. They wouldn't let her stop walking even then.

And Michael kept saying to her through his cut and blue lips, "You gotta promise me, Cassie, you won't ever do that again!"

And Rita was telling her how foolish she'd been, to try such a thing on her own.

Cassie ignored them both. They could walk her freezing body; they could souse her with water and hold her under the shower again, to get the vomit off. But they couldn't take away what she'd learned. She'd died by a mob's hand in the wake of the sharrh's invasion. She hated those who'd murdered her and her unborn baby.

When they walked her past her window, she looked out onto Merovingen, across the high towers, to the city of tiers spread out like a maze in the night. She hated them back, now. All the superstitious and the foolish, the uneducated and the poor. They were her enemies, everyone in Merovingen-below. These were the descendants of the mob that had burned her alive, and they could not be trusted.

Neither could the Nev Hetteker she'd married, or the woman who'd come here in the dead of night to shake her from her sleep. They were all her enemies. They'd turn on her in a moment—the moment that the sharrh came again.

Michael caught her eye and said, "What's the matter, Cassie? What did you see?"

"Nothing," she lied. "Nothing at all."

"Then you'll promise," her husband pressed, "that you'll stay away from that deathangel. This is too dangerous. We almost lost you, and for what?"

And Rita said, "She'll be all right now, Mike."

The other woman had been her friend. But friends didn't take that proprietary tone with one's husband. Not that it mattered. No one could be trusted. Cassie knew, now, what she must do. She must make herself impregnable; she must find ways to protect herself from the inevitable burning to come.

The sharrh were here again and in their wake, once they'd made themselves known, would come the mobs with their torches. It was just a question of time.

When the time came, Cassie must be ready. Boregy House must be ready. And the mob, the subhuman inhabitants of Merovingen-below, must be discouraged. They must learn fear, before they were too powerful to control.

"I want to see my father," she said, shaking off Michael's grip. "Now. You've done enough. You too, Rita. Thank you, but I'm fine now. I must change."

Her tone stopped her husband and her friend in their tracks. They exchanged glances.

Then Michael said, "Whatever you say, Cassie. I'll wait until you've cleaned up. Then I'll take Rita home."

178

"Now, I said," she repeated. "Leave me." It was a command, to ignore it would be to create an incident.

The possibility hung between the three of them almost too long. Then Rita smiled smoothly, "Whatever you wish, Cassie. Perhaps you'll join me for lunch tomorrow?"

"Perhaps," said Cassie brusquely. "But now, you'll have to excuse me. . . ."

When they were gone, whispering together as they went, she stared after them through her door's crack. Then, slowly, she began with numb fingers to unbutton her blouse.

She *was* going to see her father, to offer herself wholeheartedly as a serious adherent. Borey House had to be impregnable, before the inevitable riots began.

Rita Nikolaev's mouth tasted sweet and cool in the night air. Her fancyboat rocked under them softly, tied up at Nikolaev pier. His hands seemed clumsy, numb from the cold, as they fumbled with the buttons on her blouse. He was certain that if he ceased kissing her, those lips would tell him to stop.

So he didn't, even though it was she who'd initiated the kiss.

If he'd thought about it, he'd have realized that it was she who'd begun the conversation that had kept him here, in her boat, when he should have been decorously walking her to her door.

"Poor Michael," she'd said, and touched his cheek with the back of her hand. He'd shifted and his lips had found her palm, and her fingers his own eager mouth . . .

"Poor Michael," she'd repeated. "You don't understand what's going on, do you? Don't fight it, it's karma. It's all karma. Our lives are fated, fixed . . ." her voice had gone dreamy.

It was Chamoun who was dreaming, he was sure, as the woman of his fantasies let him put his hands on her breasts, then guided his fingers downward.

If this was karma, then he did understand it—at least, his body did.

She kept her eyes closed, all the time. He didn't. He

179

wanted to watch her, to make sure he wasn't dreaming. And he was afraid someone would come along and find them. Why hadn't they gone inside?

The boat rocked gently under them as he lay her down on the deck. Her heart was beating nearly as fast as his. He said in her ear as he lowered himself onto her, "We should go inside to do this."

She pulled his head down to her. "Hush, this is better."

She liked the risk, he realized. His body liked it too—the desperation of his desire, its match in hers.

When the length of his bare body touched hers, he gasped with the pure pleasure of it. His pants were down around his ankles; hers, caught around her knees. Somehow, that wasn't an insurmountable problem.

At that moment, nothing was.

He found he needed the difficulty to keep himself from ending this moment too fast. He was halfway out of control, and she was a sex goddess, moving under him with a skill he'd never encountered before.

He couldn't help but lose the initiative to her—and everything else. He warned her, as best he could, and then gave in to his body's need for climax.

When he could see anything at all, and think anything at all, he saw her wide eyes and her open mouth, and heard her call his name.

Then they were both still in the bottom of her boat, fouled in their clothes, breathing hard.

Karma, she'd called it. Regret was what he felt. And guilt. And his backside was getting cold. His knees felt bruised and every muscle in his body was limp. He was drained and shaking. He knew he was heavy, on top of her.

He wanted to roll off her, but dared not offend. He tried to put his weight on his elbows. He reared up to look her in the face. "Did you . . . are you—"

"Yes, yes. Get up now." A swat on his backside punctuated her words.

He was suddenly embarrassed as she warned him to be careful not to soil her clothes. His neck was flushed; his hands shook as he dressed. He could hardly meet her eyes. It hadn't been more than a few minutes, yet now everything had changed. Was she satisfied? Had he impressed her the way she'd impressed him? He doubted it. He couldn't meet her eyes. His head was full of repercussions: he hadn't used any protection; had she? What about communicables, here where disease was rampant? And, most of all, had she liked it with him? Would she want him again?

He shot a look at her out of the corner of one eye. Everything was different now, all right. She was buttoning her blouse and watching him, and when she met his eyes, she said, "Next time, we'll make sure we have a bed under us."

Next time.

The very thought sent his mind reeling. Relief flooded him; his guilt trebled and a world of cares crashed down upon him. While his wife needed him, here he was, with . . . her.

She was telling him he needn't walk her to her door. She was telling him she'd call on him. And he was realizing that whatever merger-related contracts Vega Boregy and Chance Magruder were trying to negotiate with Nikolaev House had just been undermined.

He'd done it again. Chance's maneuvering was like spit in the wind, now. Rita Nikolaev had just cut her own deal with Chamoun Shipping, a deal he wasn't smart enough to anticipate, or even avoid.

The woman with whom he now shared a terrible secret hoisted herself lithely out of her boat and strode toward the mansion of her family without more than a casual wave.

Left alone, Chamoun felt as if he'd been caught red-handed in the act. He scrambled out of her boat and into his own. His wife was waiting. His life was waiting. Whatever he'd just done, that life and that wife had to be his utmost concern. But something in him knew very well that Rita Nikolaev's favors weren't the sort a man used once and then threw away.

As fast as he motored away from Nikolaev House, Chamoun couldn't outrun the knowledge that, whenever Rita called him, he'd come running right back again. If not her body, then his own guilty fear of exposure would see to that.

*   *   *

Cassie was in Vega's study, waiting with her father for Uncle Ito to arrive. Vega had been solicitous at first, full of fear that she'd been hurt.

Now her father was simply angry, and Vega Boregy's anger was something Cassie tried to avoid at all costs.

But what had happened to her this evening wasn't something one could pretend had never happened. So she kept trying to convince her father that the sharrh were a real threat, against which Boregy House must prepare to defend itself. And that the people of Merovingen-below were a part of that threat. And that Cassie had seen the future, as well as her own past.

Vega's skin was always pale; tonight you could see the engorged veins right through it. "I'm going to get that fool husband of yours, for this," he said as he paced. And more.

Cassie wouldn't hear of such trivialities. "If it weren't for Michael, I'd never have found out. Wait until Uncle Ito comes, father. Then you'll understand. Boregy House must become a fortress. We cannot count on the Kalugins to protect us, or on anyone else. We must have our own defenses, our own defense force. And we must be ready, when chaos reigns on the canals." She could see that scene again, even with her eyes open. And she could see another scene, one of her own future. The deathangel was still in her system, and her mind was full of truths yet to come.

By the time Tremaine Ito Boregy, the long-nosed Cardinal who was her uncle, arrived, Cassie was finished arguing with her father.

She sat, bedraggled and bemused, low on a brocade settee, her legs outstretched straight before her, watching her wiggling toes. When Ito came in, she spoke over her father's formal greeting and the cardinal's response. "Cardinal, hear me. I have seen the future and the danger that hangs like a sword over us all. You must heed me now, and in the future, or all we hold dear is doomed."

She didn't know from where such eloquence had come to her. But eloquent she was, as she warned Ito of the blood and fire to come, of treachery within and without, and lectured him on what steps Boregy House must take to withstand the fall of the Kalugins, which she foretold that night.

Ito pulled on his long nose and rustled across the room, hands hidden in his maroon robes. He knelt down before her and looked her squarely in the eye. He asked her one senseless question, and then another.

The answer to both of those came to her: "Treachery," she told him. "Treachery within and without. Trust no one but your own blood; look nowhere but to your own self. And prepare, Cardinal. Prepare!" She came up in her chair, a creature filled with fervor and revelation, and then slumped back suddenly, drained, and exhausted.

Ito straightened up and went to her father. "Vega," he said softly, "I don't understand what's happened here, but I can guess."

"It's Chamoun's influence," Vega Boregy grated. "I'm going to hang that boy out to dry—"

"It's karma. There are prophecies foretelling such an event, in the old writings. I never thought I'd live to see it. No one expected such a thing. She's a voice from heaven, Vega. Don't underestimate her power. You've a saint in your house—a creature who can see the future."

"Future, my ass. She's seeing deathangel hallucinations brought on by that trip you took Chamoun on. This is as much your fault, Ito, as—"

"It is my pleasure to take responsibility for this. We have a mantic seeress in this house, Vega, and the College, as long as she remains so, is virtually ours to command. Don't underestimate the temporal advantage of a spiritual advantage, Vega." Ito's eyes were bright as stars. "Just heed my advice, and this miracle will make yours the foremost house in Merovingen, and, if she's right, the eventual ruling house."

"Right? What could she be right about? You know there aren't any sharrh. Riots in the streets, memories of dying in flames; prognostications of things to come . . . It's all drug-induced nonsense, and I'm telling you, Ito, I hold you personally responsible for anything that happens to my daughter."

Vega looked over at Cassie. She was paying no

attention, it seemed. She was staring at her own hand as if something very interesting were in it.

"What has happened to your daughter, I say again," Ito intoned, "is a blessing. And it is karma. It was supposed to happen. Now I understand why Chamoun came into our lives, and everything else. We are firmly on the path to a crisis that cannot be avoided, but may be turned to our advantage."

"Will she be all right?" Cassie's father wanted to know.

"She'll be honored, revered, a numinous woman of historical importance, you dimwit." Ito rounded on Boregy. "I want her at the College tomorrow morning, first light. We must begin managing our gift."

"She'll be normal in the morning, one can only hope. All of this will be past and gone with a good night's sleep . . ."

Ito's scathing look silenced Vega's protestations. He looked again at his daughter and said, "What about her husband? Does the College still want him dead? Because I do."

"Not now," Ito said softly; "not yet. We don't know what effect that might have on her. As long as she wants Chamoun around, you must protect him like you would your own flesh and blood." Ito smiled bleakly. "The moment she's tired of him, or if he should displease her . . . that, of course, is a different matter. Tomorrow, then, first light?"

"What if she's back to normal?" said Vega insistently.

"She won't be," the cardinal replied. "But if she is, this event still has discrete significance."

"If I find out you're drugging her over there to make it happen again . . ."

"You'll be a part of whatever we do with this karmic blessing, Vega. A large and powerful, and eventually grateful, part."

The two men continued to hammer out their agreement while Cassie watched, uncaring, her mind years away and unconcerned. Her father would never hurt her. In a world where no one could be trusted, Vega was her single ally.

And since that world was a world whose future and past were as clear to her as its present, she was freed, at last, from fear. What would happen, would happen. Much of it, she would make happen. Karma was putty in her hands. Merovingen was hers to save—or to destroy. What was odd, was that she was the only one who knew it, as of yet.

When Michael sneaked in the water gate, it was nearly dawn. The last thing he expected was every light in Boregy House to be on, Cardinal Ito closeted with Vega, and Cassie wide awake in her room.

Her eyes still looked like those of a frightened cat. But those eyes filled with tears when she realized who'd opened the door to their bedroom.

She flung herself upon him, sobbing.

"What is it? Damn it, what is it?" He was sure she'd found him out, that she was going to start pummeling him and screaming for her father to throw the adulterer into a Justiciary cell.

"I missed you so. I need you so," she wept instead. "I have to tell you what happened, quickly. Quickly."

She led him, her trembling hand clutching his, to the bed. There she sat cross-legged and told him all about her regression, and about her encounter with Ito, and when she finally ran dry of words, she smiled at him beatifically.

"I don't understand," he said slowly. "You saw the future?"

"The karma of us all," she said, and tears came again to her eyes.

He was scared to death, again. Scared she was going to accuse him of trysting with Rita—if she'd seen the future, then she'd seen that, too.

But she didn't. She said, "Oh, Michael, please hold me. I'm so afraid."

He did, and she was shaking like a leaf.

"I'm going to the College tomorrow. The Cardinals want to interview me. And I'm still so sad about my lost baby. Michael, let's have a baby of our own, before everything is too confused. Before the riots. Before the flames—"

"Look here." He pushed her away, held her by the arms, squeezing hard. "You had a vision—okay. Maybe even a real regression, who knows? Mine was real enough. But, seeing the future? I doubt it. Old Ito just sees something in this for himself. Don't let them use you, Cassie. Whatever you do, don't let them do that."

"Let's have a baby, Michael," she said, not struggling in his cruel, tight grip.

And it seemed like a reasonable shot, given all the risks he'd taken tonight. If there was anything that would stabilize her, it would be that, he told himself. And if there was anything that would assure his position if his tryst with Rita ever came out, a Boregy heir was that thing.

He hoped he had it in him. Sleeping with his wife was one thing. Sleeping with the self-proclaimed prophetess of karmic retribution upon Merovingen was quite another.

Chance Magruder would get quite a laugh out of this, when Chamoun got around to telling him. Riots among the commonfolk of Merovingen were one of the goals of the Sword of God. But nobody'd thought that Cassie Boregy would help start them.

Or at least, Michael hadn't thought it. He hadn't understood what Magruder was up to, with the fireworks. Now he thought he did.

He didn't really understand what his wife was up to, either, as she crawled trembling into his arms, so demanding, so needy. He understood that he loved her, though. A few minutes with Rita had made that clear to him: losing Cassie was a risk Michael Chamoun was no longer willing to take.

If a baby would bring her to her senses, then he'd do his best. But the woman he was stripping with the utmost care wasn't the woman he'd left here, scant hours ago. As much as he tried to suppress the thought while he put his wife into their bed, Michael Chamoun was absolutely certain that nothing in Merovingen was ever going to be the same—not for him, not for Chance Magruder, not for the Boregys or the College. And not for Rita Nikolaev, whose smell was all over him as he started to make love to his wife.

CHAPTER XIII

TROUBLED WATERS
by C. J. Cherryh

"I got to go," Jones said to Mondragon one morning, poking at eggs that lay on her plate. Fine eggs. Fresh eggs. Nothing wrong with the eggs. But her stomach hurt and her nose was still running. "Mondragon, I got to get t' the water again. I can't take any more."

And he looked at her that way she knew he would. Desperate. And like it was his nightmare too. "It's sleeting, dammit. You've still got the sneezes."

"Look, I go out by bright noon, I go straight down t' Moghi's, I tie up there an' I ain't never left witnesses. I got my arm back, Mondragon! Anybody goes for me, they got my pole in their teeth, I ain't easy t' mess with!"

"There's *guns*, Jones. There's a shot from a bridge, there's—"

"They c'n get you the same way. . . ."

"They wouldn't. They won't, because *I'm* the one they want to lean on, not the one they'd use—"

"Well, then, they'd be damn *fools* t' shoot me, wouldn't they? Ain't nothin' they'd get outa you, then, would they? Nothin' cept you could go to anybody and tell ever'thing, 'fore they could stop ye, an' necks would stretch f' sure! So don't tell me they'd shoot at me! Ye're *scared*, Tom Mondragon, ye're scared, so ye're puttin' if off on me, and ye hold me here no diff'rent than the damn Meg—"

Oh, damn, no, don't say that.

His face was white and something went down hard when he swallowed.

"I'm *sorry*, Mondragon, I don't think that, I don't, I swear t' ye—"

187

"I'm trying to take care of you."

She put her head in her hands, elbows on the table, sick inside. Because he was so tired, his eyes had shadows that had nothing to do with enough to eat and shelter from the cold. He was thinner than the fever had made him, and more desperate.

But they had money again. The rent got paid. He came and went at odd hours, sometimes out all night, while she sweated and lost weight too and her food had trouble staying down, she was so scared, but she was canaler and she *kept* it down, you never lost a meal, never wasted anything, no matter.

But she couldn't stomach the damned eggs. She shoved the plate away, a quick push of one hand. "I'll eat 'em f' lunch," she said.

"Jones."

"I'm fine." She felt the water on her eyelashes. She swallowed hard and got her face under control and gave him an iron-jawed smile. "I'm fine, Mondragon. Just—damn fine. Don't worry 'bout me."

"Jones, . . ."

"Sorry," she said, and wiped her nose and her eyes with three passes of her arm. "Look, I'm still shook, is all. Ye know't. Ye said ye knowed."

"*Knew*, dammit." ·

"You knew." She watched him lean his head on his hand, rake it back through his hair.

"I'll go with you," he said hoarsely then. "You're right. I'm wrong. Just—I'll go with you. You wrap up. We'll go out to Moghi's, sit this morning, have lunch. You're not up to much, anyway."

"Alone," she said between her teeth. "Mondragon, I got *business with the Trade,* ye hear me. When I go, first time, I got to go alone. I got to talk to people. —Mondragon, I got t' make 'em understand!"

He looked at her, not understanding, shook his head in puzzlement.

"I got to talk to people plain, what happened, what didn't happen, I got to say it private, so's they know I ain't lyin'."

Still no understanding.

"Because I'd *say* it was nothin', if I was talkin' in front of you! You understand me?"

This time he did. He bit his lip. Nodded.

"But I won't worry ye. I won't go. I'll stay here."

"No," he said, like it was broken glass in his mouth. "You go, you do what you have to. You're right. I can't hold you. Not—the way you are. I can see that."

She sat and looked at him a long time.

"Hear that, mama?" she asked aloud. "Hear my man?"

The whole room felt warmer. The air felt freer.

"*Now* I'm loose," she said. She wiped her eyes, hard, with her sleeve. Not embarrassed. He had seen her cry before. But she bit her lip till it hurt, and stopped it. " 'M all right. I'll be all right. You ain't seen me be careful, yet. You watch me. I'll put the word out on those sherks. 'Body lays hands t' me or the boys or t' you, their guts'll be f' fishbait."

"I've respect for that. I *know* what you're saying. But you be careful naming names, Jones. Don't mention the Sword. Don't mention Kamats or Boregy or any of them. You could get *me* hung. Remember that. Be damn careful."

"Yey." She nodded once, sharply, her eyes still chilled with water. "I ain't that stupid."

"Jones, I'm telling you—everything I can. Don't do anything without telling me. Please. That's all I'll say."

It made her gut cramp, lying to him. "Damn sure. Just the simple word—there's somebody after ye. That we dunno. I ain't stupid. But ye got t' tell 'em somethin'."

"Megarys?"

Close to the truth. Real close. She felt it like a hook-pass. And smiled, tight-jawed. "Them. Yey. Accidents might happen there."

"Not you!"

"Ne, ne, no worry. Didn't I say?" She dragged the plate of eggs back in front of her and took into them, forcing the first cold bite down. But a body needed food, if a body was going on the water, in the winter wind. "But I wouldn't be surprised if they don't get a run o' real bad luck."

CHAPTER XIV

BY A WOMAN'S HAND
by Nancy Asire

The wind rattled the window of the College office and brought the world into focus again. Alfonso Rhajmurti stirred in his high-backed chair, shoved the book he had been reading to one side on his desk.

Not more than one hour past, he had sat in the center of a group of priests, their topic of discussion revolving around the ability of some folk to actually remember previous lives. Was this a special grace granted only to those whose karma was less than other people's, or was it something all humans could tap into, if given the proper keys?

He frowned, remembering. Ito Boregy, cardinal and College mover and shaker, was giving private—*private*, mind you—conversion lessons to a fellow named Mike Chamoun. Former Adventist down from Nev Hettek, and married to Cassie Boregy, this unlikely fellow (with certain help) had *remembered* a former life. And him a converted Adventist!

The resulting implications could prove interesting.

And so, the entire conversation had revolved around the prickly question of whether non-Revenantists could have lived former lives, and been caught up in the wheel of karma. *Or* did everyone live over and over again, with only certain people remembering other lifetimes?"

Rhajmurti, along with the other priests in the College, argued over concepts like this daily, that being their job. Though they taught mundane courses such as accounting, fine arts, management, law, and so forth, their primary vocation was religious. It was not unusual to find a large number of priests sequestered in a drafty meeting room arguing the fine points of karmic law for days on end.

Unbidden, the face of Justice Lee formed in Rhajmurti's mind.

Justice . . . or, more properly for the Revenantists, Justus. Former Adventist. Convert to Revenantism in order to gain patronage to the College. Rhajmurti rose from his chair and walked over to the window which still rattled in the cold north wind. What would Justice say if he knew that Rhajmurti would have patroned him even if he had *not* converted?

Rhajmurti frowned and ran a long, tapered finger down the window pane. Karmic debt. He had been arguing it earlier in the day with a group of students; now he faced such debt personally, as he had every day for the past nineteen years.

If only Justice did not look so much like Grandmother Lizbeth, it would be easier to deny there was ever anything more to the relationship than . . .

That's an unworthy thought. Rhajmurti turned from the window and stared at his unadorned wall, its starkness broken only by a small, tastefully scripted mantra urging patience. *He's my son, and I can't deny it. I haven't admitted it, of course, but I can't fool myself into thinking I'm untouched by karma.*

Justice's mother (he considered her his aunt) had been more than willing to go it alone after the boy's birth. She could always find a husband or a companion; children were no detriment, unless one had too many mouths to feed. But Rhajmurti had assured her he would care for Justice as best as he was able. She was Adventist, so his explanation of working off the karmic debt had fallen on deaf ears.

And Justice? Had he truly converted, or was he merely going through the motions to please his patron *and* gain acceptance in the highborn circles he aspired to? That remained a mystery Rhajmurti had never solved. He sought consolation by reminding himself that Justice had a genuine talent in rendering that should make him wealthy one day . . . that such a talent should not be squandered, despite being housed in an Adventist body.

Rhajmurti cleared his throat. Thinking about his

never-acknowledged son always made him feel guilty
. . . another evidence of the karmic connection. The
law of celibacy for priests was adhered to mainly because of such connection: the fewer the souls one was
tied to, the lower the sum total of karmic debt.
Rhajmurti would neither have been expelled from the
College, nor looked down upon by his peers; the only
outcome of acknowledging Justice as his son would
have been to draw direct scrutiny of those priests who
made it their business to keep track of other people's
karmic debt.

All this thought about Justice, karmic debt, and
previous lives had generated an appetite. Rhajmurti
took down his saffron cloak and contemplated the
poleboat ride to Kass and Hilda's tavern. He would be
cold, eat food that was wholesome but not spectacular, *but* more than likely see his son.

One of these days, Rhajmurti told himself, turning
off the lamp and leaving his small office, *I'll tell the
boy who his real father is. But not now . . . by the
Wheel! Not now.*

Justice settled back in his chair, pushed his plate
aside, and reached for his beer. Hilda had outdone
herself this evening: the silverbit—cooked to perfection; the greens smothered in some new sauce that
beggared description. And, a new keg of beer. If he
had a few more coins in his weekly allotment, he
would have sent to the kitchen for seconds.

Sunny stretched catlike, from the very tips of his
toes to his ears, to curl up tighter in a ball of gold fur
on the chair beside Justice. He smiled at the cat, and
reached out for the book he had brought along to
study.

The common room of Hilda's tavern was awash in
sound and light, but the noise level seldom bothered
Justice when he studied. If things got too noisy, he
could always go back to his room. He hoped he would
not have to do that, for he could stay warm out here,
courtesy of Hilda's oil stove, *plus* the body heat of the
clients around him.

A few minutes of staring at the same page augured
futility in trying to study. Justice laid the book down,

took another long swallow of beer, and faced what bothered him square on.

Denny. Denny and Raj. The whole episode. He liked Raj . . . truly liked him, but now Justice wondered what Raj was into. Advice was advice. You could either take it or leave it. That Raj had intended to hole up somewhere for two weeks and let this storm pass him by seemed the best alternative. But Denny's worried visit had raised serious doubts in Justice's mind.

Doubts about Denny, the canaler, Jones, and the mysterious fourth of that party—the man no one seemed willing to name.

Not that Justice wanted names. He was totally satisfied to know as little as possible about the entire thing.

But the fear in the boy—indicated something more than Raj had said. As for Marina Kamat, he knew the lady only by reputation. Granted, since he had started College he had found himself among the offspring of many of Merovingen's oldest Houses. He knew—on a speaking basis—most of those heirs to wealth and power. But, m'sera Kamat he did not know, more than her reputation. What she had done when she had found out that Raj had written the poetry in his friend's name. . . .

Justice shrugged. He had done all he could, had given Raj the best advice he had at the time. The entire situation was out of his hands now. Raj was safe—had dropped by to say so—a conversation painfully uninformative. One remembered a certain midnight errand—and other mysterious goings-on. . . .

"Justus."

The hoarse, nasal voice brought Justice out of his studies. He looked up: facing him from the other side of his table stood Krishna Malenkov.

Krishna. Justice's part-time tormentor; hightowner son of The Malenkovs, doomed by his father to live in this near-to-shabby rooming house close to the College on a monthly stipend that could not come close to meeting Krishna's needs. The stocky hightowner looked less than impressive now; the color of his nose rivaled the red of his shirt, and his eyes blinked slightly out of focus.

"Sit down, Krishna," Justice said, gesturing at a chair. "What's wrong?"

"I need some more of that medicine you sold me."

Justice lifted one eyebrow. "What did you do? Drink it like water? You had enough in that packet to get you through a week of the Crud."

Krishna's dark eyes wavered. "Dropped most of it," he admitted in what seemed a suitably embarrassed voice. "Had the shakes. Bad."

"Well, you *don't* look much better." Justice sighed quietly. "You still owe me for—"

"And I'll pay you back," Krishna snapped, lifting his chin and assuming a haughty expression. The impression was shattered in the next instant by a noisy, soppy sneeze. "There . . . you see?" Krishna drew a lace handkerchief from his shirt pocket and blew his nose. Several of the diners close by turned toward the noise, then looked away, offended. "I need it bad, Justus."

"Oh, all, right." Justice stood up, left his book open to guard his place at the table, and started back toward his room. Footsteps came from behind him; Krishna was following.

"Where do you get the stuff?" Krishna asked, as Justice unlocked the door to his room.

"Friend of mine. He owes me, too, and he's paying me in medicine."

"Huhn." Some of Krishna's old sarcasm surfaced. "Playing the lender, eh? Going to set up your own bank?"

Justice ignored the comment, got the lamp lit, and opened a drawer on his table. Pulling out a packet of Raj's herbal medicines, he turned to Krishna.

"There. See if you can keep from dropping it this time. I'm running low." He handed the medicine to his fellow student, hoping his voice did not reflect the lie. Raj had left plenty of medicine behind the day he had stopped by to ask Justice's advice. But given half the chance, Krishna would use up what supply Justice had.

"Thanks. I'll make sure you get paid back." Krishna

walked into the hall and turned left toward his own room.

Justice aimed a growled curse after the hightowner. *Sure you will . . . but in what year?* He shut the drawer and turned off the lamp. Senseless waste of oil, oil he had to provide himself, not only for the lamp, but for the heater. Fellow students complained that Justice had the coldest room in wintertime they had ever visited. Justice grimaced. Maybe so. But he was of no House to have the money to afford more.

Closing and locking the door behind him, Justice returned to the common room. His table waited for him, but it now had another occupant than the somnolent Sunny. Father Rhajmurti sat there, giving his order to Jason the waiter.

"Ah, Justice," Rhajmurti said. "I hope you don't mind if I join you."

"Certainly not." Justice sat down, closed his book, and turned to the priest. "May I help you, Father?"

"No. I've been sequestered in the College all day and needed a change of scenery. How are your exams coming?"

Justice shrugged. "I've been prepared for them all," he said. "Hard studying pays off."

A wide smile touched the priest's face. "Good lad. You haven't failed me yet. You get marks as good as any student I know. You've only one test left, right?"

"Two days from now. And it's going to be terrible. Accounting. Fah! I'm terrible with numbers."

"But you realize how much you need those numbers if you're ever to succeed as a painter, don't you?"

"Oh, yes. But that doesn't mean I have to *like* them."

Rhajmurti rubbed his chin. "You don't mind studying with other students, do you?"

"No."

"Good. I think I have a perfect partner in mind for you. She's a genius when it comes to accounting."

She. Justice lifted one eyebrow. "Do I know her?"

"You might. Sonja Keisel. She's in her third year, like you."

Sonja Keisel. The name rang a bell, but Justice could not bring a face to mind.

"Sure. I'll study with her. If she's as good as you say, I certainly won't be hurt by her help." He grinned and spread his hands. "And I need all the help I can get."

"Good. I'll be seeing her tomorrow. Should I set up a room for the two of you?"

Justice leapt at the chance to save even more on heating oil. "If you would. As long as it's not too much bother."

Rhajmurti nodded. Justice wondered briefly why the priest was going out of his way to help him prepare for a test. He knew himself in Rhajmurti's debt and had always tried to keep the scales in balance by performing to his best, but at times the priest's concern for his welfare seemed a bit out of proportion. If what the Revenantists taught about karma was true, then Rhajmurti was heaping up a powerful lot of it.

Oh, well. Justice had never turned down a gift given in friendship, and he was not about to start now.

The College still teemed with rumors of the incident in the harbor some weeks back. Justice heard the subject bandied back and forth among groups of students standing in the wide, drafty hallways. Was it the sharrh? Or—even worse, to some minds—was it the sharrists? Ancestors know, the sharrh seemed totally disinterested in mankind, as long as mankind avoided certain levels of technology. But the sharrists?

And all Justice knew was that he had had the fear of Something put into him when he had seen the lights and fire blooming over the harbor.

He shrugged, hurrying down the hallway toward the room where Father Rhajmurti had told him he would be studying with m'sera Keisel. His face felt hot, a reaction, he knew, that did not come from the exertion of his quick pace.

Ancestors! He had never been at ease around women!

Women he drew portraits of he did not find intimidating, or, if he did, he was able to sublimate the feeling beneath his concentration. Women priests who taught at the College impressed him with their learning and their expertise. And women he met in passing hardly bothered him at all.

But women of his own age, with whom he was expected to interact, put him in such a state of mind as to make him tongue-tied.

He could imagine Krishna off in some dark corner close by, snickering at it all.

He straightened his shoulders and hurried on. A late start this morning had forced him to forego breakfast if he expected to be on time. As it was, he knew himself to be late. The quick poleboat ride from Spellbridge to the College had chilled him; the icy wind still blew down the canals. What a condition to be in when he first met this hightowner lady.

And she, a genius in accounting.

He stopped by the door that led to the room where she would be waiting, straightened his coat, wishing it had been less threadbare. Drawing a deep breath, he walked into the room.

Only one person sat there.

Father Rhajmurti.

"Good morning, Justice," he said, gesturing to one of the chairs that flanked the small table he sat beside. "You're right on time, as usual."

Right on time? Lord and Ancestors . . . I'm late! Or . . . I think I am.

"M'sera Keisel should be here at any moment," Rhajmurti continued, seemingly unaware of the state Justice was in.

"Huhn." Justice sat down, arranging his book and papers in a neat pile before him. He turned to the priest, and risked all in one throw. "Father . . . you know I'm clumsy when I'm around ladies. Do I look all right? I want to make a good impression on her . . . she could make or break me to her House by what she thinks."

Rhajmurti smiled. "Don't worry about it. This is one lady who doesn't put much store in first impressions."

"No . . . I don't," said a voice from the door.

Justice looked up. A small, delicately built woman stood in the doorway, her black hair ruffled, and the expensive, fur-bordered cloak she wore shoved back over her shoulders. Her sweater was finely woven, the collar of her blouse tastefully decked with small jewels. Her trousers were of soft wool, worn tucked into boots the cost of which put those Justice wore to shame.

"I'm Sonja Keisel," she said, smiled disarmingly as she walked to the table, "although Father Rhajmurti has probably already told you my name."

"Justice Lee," Justice said, and stood to give her a slight bow. He gestured to the other chair. "Please, m'sera . . . be seated."

She set her books down and unfastened her cloak. "M'sera, be damned, Justus. If we're going to be studying together, I'll get sick of the title before the hour's out. Call me Sonja."

Justice swallowed, exchanged a quick look with Rhajmurti, and nodded. He took her cloak and hung it on one of the wall hooks next to his utilitarian coat.

"I'll leave you two alone," Rhajmurti said, standing and heading toward the door. "If you want to break for lunch, you know where my office is. We'll go together, if you like."

Sonja laughed softly. "We'll look you up then," she replied. "But I hope we'll be so deep in numbers that we won't notice the passing time."

Justice nodded again, afraid his voice would fail. Numbers? Lord and Ancestors! Sitting next to such a woman would tax the concentration of a yogi.

When lunchtime finally rolled around, Justice felt more pleased with himself and the situation. He had not disgraced himself, but had managed to keep his mind on his studies. He was, as Sonja said, hardly stupid; he simply had small aptitude for math.

She seemed to be totally relaxed around him, at ease with the situation, and more than helpful with her observations on the finer points of accounting. Yes, she knew he was an artist, studying under the patronage of Father Rhajmurti, but his lack of hightown birth bothered her not in the least. In the few breaks they had taken, she had told him some of her life in the Keisel household.

Her mother, Nadia Keisel, imported beef from the cities that lay north of Merovingen. Her family had held a monopoly over that trade for generations, and consequently, to say they lived quite well would have been an understatement. She had two older half-brothers born of contract marriages, but her parents had married before her birth.

Though she spoke of her family life in an easy tone of voice, Justice sensed something sad about her, a touch of the melancholic.

Now, hurrying behind her down the walkway on second-level Kass, Justice wondered what was troubling her, and if she would ever confide in him. A small voice laughed in his mind. *You? Confide in you? Surely she has better companions, ones who understand her station in life, more than a struggling artist with delusions of grandeur.*

He held the door of Hilda's tavern open for her and Father Rhajmurti, and followed them into the common room.

They were early, well before the sixth hour, so the true lunch crunch had not hit yet. No sooner had they started for Justice's usual table than Sunny came trotting across the room, golden tail held stiffly aloft, with just the slighest curl to its tip.

"Oh . . . she's gorgeous!" Sonja said, kneeling down to offer her fingertips for Sunny's inspection. Her dark eyes glittered in the lamplight as she looked up at Justice. "Is she yours?"

"He," Justice corrected. "No. He's not mine. He belongs to my landlady, Hilda Meier. She's also owner of this tavern."

"That cat might as well belong to 'im," a voice said from behind them. "Way he loves this man. . . . Huhn! Swear he takes after Justus here more'n he do me!"

Justice turned to face Hilda, who had come from her usual place by the kitchen door, drawn no doubt by the appearance of the definitely high-born.

"Will you be havin' lunch, m'sera?" she asked of Sonja, "or only somethin' t'drink?"

"Both," Sonja smiled, standing. Sunny had already passed judgment, despite mistaken gender, and was rubbing back and forth from Sonja's legs to Justice's.

Father Rhajmurti led the way to the table and seated Sonja, while Justice laid their wraps out on the fourth chair, making sure there was room for Sunny to curl up. Jason was at their sides immediately, ready to take their orders. Justice smiled slightly. He could not remember Jason moving so fast in months.

And lunch, when it came, put everything Justice had eaten in Hilda's for more than months to shame. Sonja had insisted on treating. And treat it was: whitetail, not silverbit . . . and very, very expensive. He glanced up at Rhajmurti, but received the slight headshake that said, don't question. So, with watering mouth, Justice began his meal.

He might as well have died and gone to heaven . . . or (with deference to the Revenantists) been born into the highest of all Merovingian Houses. The fish in its sauce was beyond description, the greens fresh and delightfully seasoned. And to drink—not beer, mind you, but wine . . . expensive, imported, slightly dry white.

Sonja ate as if she found nothing unusual about the meal and so, Justice thought, she probably would not. More than likely, such fare was a common sight on her table. He took a sip of wine, set his glass down, and covertly studied the woman.

Damn! There was a lot to study. He had liked her from the first words she had spoken, and she had not proved him wrong. Though possessing all the manners, class and style of her upbringing, she seemed totally unaffected by it all. That she would even consent to come to this place to eat said more than words could tell. Krishna ate here because he *lived* here, and because, if he could save on his meals, he could frequent the upper level bars and be seen in the "correct" company. Justice had the impression that Sonja would come back here to eat if she found the food and service good . . . come back unselfconsciously as she had entered the tavern first.

"Well, now . . . if it isn't Justus."

The drawling voice cut into Justice's warm feeling of contentment. He looked up from his plate: Krishna Malenkov stood a few paces away, hand on one hip, looking somewhat better than last night. The stocky hightowner sauntered forward, coming to a halt a pace away. "Father," he said, giving Rhajmurti a short bow. He moved to one side so he could see who else sat at the table.

Justice came close to laughing out loud at the change in Krishna's face.

"M'sera Keisel." All manners now, Krishna swept a graceful bow in Sonja's direction. "What are *you* doing here?"

The expression on Sonja's face was hard for Justice to read. She lifted one eyebrow slightly, and nodded her head in greeting the barest degree.

"I'm having lunch," she said in such a neutral, controlled voice that Justice would not have recognized it. "That should be obvious, don't you think?"

Krishna's face reddened. "What I mean to say, m'sera, is that it's surprising to find you here in this tavern when there are far more suitable places for one of your station to eat."

"Oh?" Sonja lifted one hand and beckoned to Jason who had never been more than a few steps away all through the meal. "I find the food and the company both excellent." She reached into her sweater and drew out four silver lunes. Justice stared at this wealth, so casually handled. "For the meals," she said to Jason, smiling, "and the rest for your fine service."

"Thank you, m'sera . . . thank you." Wide-eyed, Jason bowed several times, each bow lower than the last.

"M'sera—" Krishna began.

"Shall we return to the College, Father?" Sonja asked, ignoring Krishna as if he had not spoken. She pushed back her chair and stood. "We'll be late for our studies."

Justice rose to his feet, purposely keeping his face averted from Krishna's eyes. He extended Rhajmurti's cloak to the priest, and helped Sonja slip into her fur-bordered wrap. With a farewell scratch of Sunny's head, Justice shrugged into his own coat.

"So sorry to be in such a rush, Krishna," Sonja said, smiling an empty smile. "Perhaps we'll be seeing each other soon."

As he turned to follow Rhajmurti and Sonja from the common room, Justice throttled the childish urge to yell out for joy.

CHAPTER XV

TROUBLED WATERS

by C. J. Cherryh

It was tribunal, deep in Bogar Cut, under Bogar's foundations, a place where water was close and brick and pilings sent cold to the very bones. The candle on the slab of rock was the only light, except that gray that came dimly from Bogar Cut's shadow, noon-light, but overcast. Sleet again. Mist that slicked decks and stone.

Tribunal, canaler-law. And this time it was Jones who sat on the rock in front of the slab—not in any coat, not warm as Mondragon wanted her to be. She wore three sweaters, a pair of pants thick enough to keep the joints from chilling, and to keep her feet warm when she tucked them up with the poncho a skip-freighter wore on a day like this—still rich, as that went, but not the way a coat would mark her.

And alone. Damn well alone.

"What I got t' tell ye," she said. "—is what Megarys done. It wasn't f' slave-runnin'. It was pure damn blackmail. I be honest wi' ye. I tell ye ever'thing they done an' I tell ye right off they could o' done worse. But them that bought it done, that's my man's quarrel. Them that *done* it, done it to the Trade, and that's *my* quarrel. So if you tell me, ferget it, Jones, ye got what was comin' t' ye, I'll take it an' shut up and I'm sorry I bothered ye. I put it t' majority rule."

"Megarys ain't never bothered us before!" That was Mergeser, no friend of hers. "If 't wasn't f' yer hightowner they wouldn't o' bothered us now!"

" 'E ain't hightowner!" Sid Haney yelled. "Mondragon pulled wi' th' Trade t' fish us up when damn-'im Kalugin rode m' boat under! Jones' man's *Trade*, hear it?"

"Yey!" cried Tish Weller, and: "Yey," the murmur went around; and nobody, not even Mergeser, wanted to get aslant of parents whose kids and whose boat and whose karma was at issue.

"Thank 'e," Jones said, biting her lip. "Ye hear me, ne? Hear me out. I tell ye ever'thing. I don't leave nothin' out. An' ye gimme yey or not, whether I got Justification. But f' me, they laid hands on th' Trade. They got t' pay f' that. If ye think I was t' blame, ye pay *me*, an' ye tell 'em. But if ye think they was out o' line, what they did, then ye gimme leave, an' *I'll* put th' fear in 'em. 'S all I'm askin'. I don't ask the Trade t' do nothin' yet. Just cut me loose.

"We was at Moghi's. . . ."

CHAPTER XVI

BY A WOMAN'S HAND
by Nancy Asire

The early part of the afternoon sped by faster than Justice would have believed. His head spinning with numbers, rules, shortcuts, and the more esoteric twists and turns of accounting, he walked back toward Hilda's, the chill wind at his back, hardly noticing the cold. So, he had no aptitude for math. He had never been ashamed of admitting that fact until today. But with Sonja . . .

He shook his head. Warning bells rang in his mind, forbidding his thoughts from the direction they were going. He laughed shortly, mocking himself and his dreams. Sonja Keisel was far above the likes and dislikes of someone like him.

Damn! I'm a fool, thinking such things. How in the world could she even look at me with any other emotion than as someone who might be a—friend? Another laugh, equally bitter. *Keep your eyes on your path, Justice, or you'll trip yourself looking at the stars.*

He pushed the door open and stepped into Hilda's common room. It was nearing the ninth hour, a time when the tavern sat near empty, giving Hilda and her staff breathing room to prepare for the dinner-time crowds. Justice left the door, unbuttoning his coat, and headed toward the table he claimed as his.

Sunny, as usual, lay curled up in a chair . . . the same chair he had fallen asleep in during lunch. When Justice drew close, the gold cat opened one eye, yawned widely, stretched and fell instantly to sleep again. Justice smiled. Some things never changed. He set his book down, tossed his coat over the chairback next to Sunny, and sat down. He knew he should review what he and Sonja had gone over last, but her words seemed to be indelibly inscribed on his brain. For the first time in his life, he had no real fear of taking a test dealing with math.

Someone called his name. He glanced up and saw Jason standing behind the bar with a lifted mug in his hand. An early afternoon beer, especially after drinking the wine? Ah, why not. Justice nodded, settled back in the chair, fished three libby pieces out of his sweater in time to hand them to Jason, who set the full mug on the table. Justice took a long swallow, leaned back farther into the chair and contented himself with thinking about nothing.

It was useless. Every time his thoughts went one way or the other, they came to rest on Sonja.

I'm acting like some idiot thirteen year old! Lord! Just because she's one of the prettiest women I've seen in years, and just because she's hightowner and untouchable. . . . Damn! I can't spend my life wishing after what I can't have.

Justice sat up staighter, opened his book, determined to do something righteous. A soft thud sounded on the opposite side of the table; instants later Sunny had jumped up in Justice's lap, to stand kneading his front paws on Justice's leg. Idly scratching the cat, Justice turned a page, took another swallow of beer, and settled in for a long review while Sunny settled down for a nap.

"Justus."

He closed his eyes. Krishna—the one person he did not want to deal with right now. But ignoring Krishna never made him go away. Sighing softly, Justice looked up from his book.

"Mind if I join you?"

Justice lifted one eyebrow. Lately, Krishna had not been so polite. Another type of warning bell went off in Justice's head.

"No. Have a chair." Justice watched his hightowner neighbor settle in the chair opposite him. "Are you through with your exams?"

"Yesterday. By Rama! I'm glad that's over!"

"How do you think you did?"

Krishna shrugged. "Well enough, I guess, to keep

Papa off my back." He shifted in his chair. "So how do you know Sonja Keisel?"

Ah-h-h. Here it is. The real *reason Krishna wants to talk to me.* Justice reached for his beer. "Through Father Rhajmurti. I'd never met her before today. I've got an accounting test coming up, and she's a whizz at numbers. Rhajmurti thought it'd be helpful if she tutored me."

There. He had gotten through the entire speech without once losing control of his expression. Maybe he *was* adult enough to know he had no choice but to keep his mind off Sonja in any form other than as an acquaintance . . . maybe a friend.

"Oh." Krishna's gaze wandered over to the bar, but he shook his head when Jason gave the sign for a beer. "Just curious. You know she's a Borg."

Justice's heart did a curious little hop. "A Borg?"

"Her father's a Borg. Married her mother. She's a love child. She has two older half-brothers by contract marriages . . . one's a Borg and the other, a diNero. She lives over on Borg, you know."

Damn! Justice had known Sonja lived close to the College, but he had never guessed. . . . He knew m'sera Keisel operated the only legal source of beef and leather in town, and that she had married at last for love. He knew this, but had never questioned himself as to whom she was married to.

He had made it a practice never to pry into the doings of hightowners—he let *them* tell him what he was curious about. Though it kept him ignorant of many things he wished he knew, it also stood him in a beneficial light. When dealing with hightown Family, one's cause was best served if one seemed the total opposite of pushy.

And speaking of pushy . . . What the hell had possessed Krishna to sit down and unload Sonja's history? Justice rubbed his chin, grimaced at the roughness of sprouting stubble, and glanced over at Krishna.

"Oh, well. Whatever she is, she's damned good at math!"

That obviously was not the reaction Krishna had been waiting for. He frowned slightly, then leaned forward in his chair.

"How are your finances, Justus?"

"How are—" Justice blinked in surprise. "Why are *you* interested?"

"You know that medicine you gave . . . I mean, *sold* me? If you take enough of it, you'll get higher than the Angel."

Justice's chest tightened. He had been afraid of this happening after Raj had told him of the side effects. And leave it to Krishna to—

"If you can get your hands on more of this stuff, I've got someone real interested in buying it." Krishna's eyes glittered. "For a damned good price, too."

"Well. . . ." Justice stalled for time, trying to think of a brush-off he could give Krishna.

"You ever tried getting high on that stuff?"

"No." Justice met Krishna's gaze. "I take it only for the Crud."

"Oh, aren't we the goody-goody one?" Krishna put an exaggerated lisp in his speech, and waved a languid hand. "Campaigning for sainthood?"

"Hardly. I've got enough troubles coping without being high, that's all."

"I gathered. Well, *I* can think of better things to do with your medicine than give it out for the sniffles." Krishna's jaw set. "And, if you don't give me what you've got, you'll not like the outcome."

Justice stared. "I can't believe you're saying this to me, Krishna. Use your head, man! Selling drugs is damned dangerous. The town's in an uproar over the lights in the harbor, and every blackleg out there is just waiting for someone like you to pull a dumb stunt—to give them an excuse . . . *any* excuse!"

"I'm only going to say this once more, Justus. If you give me the medicine your friend leaves with you, I'll share the profit with you. If not . . ."

"What the hell do you think you can do? *Steal* it? You're crazier than I think you are!"

Krishna's dark eyes went darker. "Crazy, am I? Well, I suggest you check your supply of medicine when you get back to your room. You might find you have quite a bit less of it than when you left for the College this morning."

Justice shook his head, his mind trying to accept

what Krishna told him. Stealing? In Hilda's boarding house? He opened his mouth to call out to her, then shut it. What would he say? How could he *prove* Krishna had done it? Besides, where could Justice say he had gotten hold of the medicine? He would have needed money to buy it, money he obviously did not have. It was all too tangled, too firmly fixed in the gray areas of life that could not easily be explained away.

"You see," Krishna said, a cold smile touching his lips, "even *you* can't think of a way out of this."

"And if I refuse?" Justice asked, again stalling for time, damning his brain for its slowness.

"Ah? If you refuse?" Krishna spread his hands. "It's all very simple, Justus. I'll go to every one of my friends and tell them all kinds of things about you. Some of them may even be true. And when I'm done, there won't be an uptown House in Merovingen that will have anything to do with a down and out aspiring artist named Justus Lee." He shoved his chair back and stood. "Think about it, Justus. Think about it. I'll give you until tomorrow morning to have your answer."

Justice sat with his mouth open, remembered to close it at last. Krishna reached into his sweater, withdrew something small, and let it drop to the floor with an audible "clink." Leering at Justice, he turned away and stalked off across the common room toward the door that led outside. Justice shook his head, reached down with one hand, and stroked Sunny's side. The hand shook appreciably.

Now what did he do? Krishna had him over the proverbial barrel. And how the hell had Krishna gotten into his room? His heart sank. The extra key. He remembered it now . . . he had left it sitting on the table. And when Krishna had followed him to pick up another packet of medicine . . .

He picked up a flaccid Sunny, set him in a chair, and looked under the table. There, glinting dully in the afternoon light and the glow of the lamps, lay his key.

Justice closed his eyes, and fought against a mounting headache. He knelt, snatched up his key, then heaved himself back into his chair. No wonder Krishna had gone through his packet of medicine so quickly. He had not dropped it . . . he had taken most of it to see if he could get high. Finding that he could—and wonderfully so—he had then approached Justice for another packet, this one to sell.

"Damn!" Justice looked down at Sunny, who had started his afternoon bath. He had no one to turn to, no one to give him advice.

Except Father Rhajmurti. And considering the subject matter, that was a long shot at best.

Leaving the poleboat behind, Justice shrugged his coat collar up around his ears and quickly mounted the steps to the College. The afternoon seemed darker than it was, here on the east side of the ld building . . . darker and colder. Justice shivered, headed toward the doorway, and glanced once behind.

No one followed. He yanked the door open and stepped into the wide entry hall, a massive two-story affair, its walls covered with portraits of great founders of the College. He stopped for a moment, wary of slipping, his damp booted feet firmly planted on the white and black marble floor, and looked around.

Damn! Whatever had possessed Krishna to pull a stunt like this one? Justice had lived in the same rooming house as the hightowner for two years now, yet he had never seen Krishna do anything quite this stupid before. Did Krishna think himself above any kind of retribution? Or, that Justice had no recourse other than to bow to the demands of blackmail?

He grimaced, set off across the entry hall to the staircase. Several students he knew came walking down the stairs, books in hand, but obviously done with tests for now. Justice nodded to the students as he passed them on the stairs, and headed up to the second level where the classrooms and studios lay. He hoped at this hour to find Rhajmurti in one of them.

Constructed as an equilateral triangle, the College held most of its administrative offices on the lower level where access to shipping was easiest. The functionaries, the offices of the maintenance people, and the kitchens could be found here. The second level was given over to classrooms, each of the five major disciplines occupying its own space: Accounting/Management, Law, Medicine, the Fine Arts, and Religion.

Once dealing solely with the study of Revenantism, the College had branched out into other areas, for the priests were guardians of vast storehouses of knowledge. Somewhere, on the third level, where the priests lived and where few students ever went, lay the great Library; no one was quite sure what the Library held, but it was rumored among the students that books rested there that none but fully initiated priests could read.

At the top of the stairs, Justice turned to his right, and headed down the wide hallway toward the Fine Arts section of the College. He would more than likely find Rhajmurti there, unless the priest had returned to his room.

Justice saw only a few students in the rooms he passed, most of them musicians who practiced singly or together. The art studios lay on the north side of the College, where the light was best at all times of the year.

"Hey, Justus!"

He turned and saw one of his friends, Mikhail Rudenov.

"Hey, Mik! Finished with your exams?"

The fellow grinned, waved his flute above his head. "And glad of it! You?"

"One left. Accounting. You seen Father Rhajmurti?"

"Not lately, but I think he's down in the last studio."

"Thanks. I'll see you later."

"Luck to you!" Mikhail called out as Justice headed off in that direction.

Lord and my Ancestors! Please! Let him be there! If Rhajmurti had returned to his room, Justice would have to backtrack, go to the stairway that led to the third floor, and wait while one of the stairguards took a message to the priest that he had company.

He glanced into the studios as he walked past them: they sat empty, easels and painting supplies neatly arranged against the walls. He unbuttoned his coat, warm now that he was inside, away from the chill.

Father Rhajmurti sat by the window in the studio at the far end of the hall, wrapped in a light house cloak, for the room was large and had enough windows to make it chilly even though someone had lit the oil stove.

Not wanting to startle Rhajmurti, Justice knocked softly on the door jamb.

"Justice." The priest looked away from the window. "What are you doing here?"

"Can we talk privately?" Justice asked, glancing over his shoulder to make sure the hallway lay empty.

Rhajmurti lifted one eyebrow, gathered his cloak, and stood. "Of course. You've got a problem?"

"Understatement." Justice leaned back against the wall. "Where can we go that I can make sure we're not overheard?"

"That bad, eh?" Rhajmurti's dark eyes glinted in the fading light. "Come."

The priest led the way down the hall to a smaller studio, ushered Justice into the room, and shut the door.

"All right," Rhajmurti asked, sitting down on the edge of a counter and gesturing Justice to one of chairs drawn up close by. "What's wrong?"

Justice had heard those words "what's wrong" so many times from Rhajmurti he had lost count. "It's Krishna, again, Father."

"What's he done *now?*"

Justice drew a deep breath and launched into his story; as he spoke, he included all the details he could remember, down to the expressions on Krishna's face, and the nuances of the hightowner's voice. When he had finished, he sat watching Rhajmurti, and let the silence spin out.

And out.

"Vishnu!" The unexpected oath sounded strange coming from the priest who always seemed to be in such firm control. "He's really done it this time. Did he act odd when he was talking to you?"

"No odder than usual." Justice chewed on his lower lip. "No. I take that back. He was . . . well, wound up would be a good word for it."

"Wound up. Do you think he was high?"

Justice hesitated. "I suppose he could have been."

"Huhn."

Again the silence stretched out.

"Father—" Justice began.

"I remember you speaking to me about this Raj. Where does he get his medicine?"

"I'm not sure. All I know is that it works."

Rhajmurti rubbed his chin. "And, if taken in large enough doses, is a strong hallucinogen. No doubt there would be plenty of markets for him to sell it to." The priest began to pace up and down in front of Justice.

"What am I going to do, Father?" Justice tried to calm down, hearing his voice shake slightly. "He could *ruin* me with the Families before I even get started!"

"Hush." Rhajmurti raised a hand and kept pacing.

Justice shifted in the chair. He had no doubt that the priest fully understood exactly what Krishna had done. His greatest fear was that Krishna's position was so unassailable that even Rhajmurti could not think of a way out.

"He gave you until tomorrow morning to have an answer for him?"

"Yes."

"Hmmm." Rhajmurti stopped pacing and stood looking down at Justice. "I think I might have a solution. It all depends on exact timing, and on how sensitive you are to being seen in hightown company."

Justice blinked. "I suppose if I have to save my career before I *have* one, I'll do all kinds of strange things. What are you suggesting?"

"I'm suggesting that you and I take a short poleboat ride." The priest's face softened in a smile. "Over to Borg, I think."

Justice had visited a number of the homes of his hightowner friends, but nothing had prepared him for the luxury of the Keisel home on Borg. He, along with hundreds of others, crossed and recrossed the Borg Esplanade, that wide walkway which cut through the center of Borg to White; but what lay behind those small shops, and on the upper level would have boggled the minds of those who used the walkway.

Standing behind Rhajmurti, Justice tried not to gawk, or to look impressed. It was hard work. The Keisel home was split between the second and upper levels of Borg; its reception room (and consequently its address) was upper level. When Rhajmurti had rung the bell, a servant dressed in expensive livery had answered the door, and told them to be seated, that m'sera Keisel would be with them presently. No sooner had that fellow left, and Justice had joined Rhajmurti on a soft, comfortable couch, than another servant entered, offering them each a cup of hot tea to take the chill of travel from their bones.

Justice glanced around as he sipped his tea from a cup so thin he could see shadows through it. Oil stoves sat evenly spaced along the walls, stoves so disguised by facades they looked more like cupboards. For the first time in days, Justice sat in a room that held no trace of chill.

Damn! He thought he had seen riches before. He should have known when Krishna had said Sonja was a Borg what he was getting into.

The room was floored in burled wood—a pale, golden parquetry, inlaid with a soft red along the edges of the room. Electrics burned everywhere, the bright, white light hard to become accustomed to after oil lamps. The furniture, the rugs . . . the sale of only one of those items would have kept Justice in room rent for— He gave up trying to calculate it, and took another sip of tea.

As to why he and Father Rhajmurti had come calling, Justice had no real idea. He had questioned the priest about it, but Rhajmurti had told him no more than it was part of his plan to combat Krishna's blackmail . . . *if* the plan worked. After years of studying with Rhajmurti, Justice knew better than to question his patron when the priest seemed unwilling to talk.

And so he waited, trying to put the pieces of an unknown puzzle together. Why Borg? More precisely, why Sonja Keisel?

"M'sera Keisel."

The servant's voice brought Justice out of his musing. He looked up, saw her standing in the doorway, and rose. Bowing deeply, he wished he knew what to do . . . what to say.

"Justice," Rhajmurti said softly, from the depths of his bow. "Let me have a few moments alone with Sonja."

Justice swallowed and nodded. As he straightened, the priest stepped forward to meet Sonja in the center of the large room. Feeling definitely out of place and overly conspicuous, Justice backed up a few steps, hoping to blend in with the walls. Small chance that, dressed as he was in black.

The low murmur of conversation came from the center of the room where Rhajmurti and Sonja stood: the priest's deep voice blended with Sonja's lighter one, but Justice could not guess at the subject matter. He grimaced, seeing himself as she must see him: tall, slender, dark-haired, green-eyed, clad in serviceable but shabby clothes. Reeking poor. Or, if not poor, then far from even well off. With one of the jewels in her collar, he could—

"Justice."

He jumped at the sound of Father Rhajmurti's voice. The priest was beckoning him forward, a small smile softening his face. Sonja stood silent, her face much harder to read. Justice cursed his nervousness, then relented. Dammit, no! He had every reason to be nervous. His career was at stake.

Straightening his shoulders, he walked to their sides.

"I'm sorry to have been so rude," Rhajmurti said, "but I had reasons for wanting to talk in privacy. Now, those reasons aren't valid. We—" he gestured toward Sonja, "—have come up with a possible escape for you."

Justice could feel his eyebrows lifting.

"Don't look so surprised." Rhajmurti smiled a little, his dark eyes dancing. "Remember one of the laws of karma: what goes around, comes around, but not necessarily in the same coin."

Sonja laughed quietly.

"I've taken the liberty of explaining your problem to Sonja," Rhajmurti said. "Hearing me out, she agreed to help."

"Let me explain, Justus," she said, stepping closer,

the light glittering on the jewels she wore. "When I was growing up, I had many friends my own age. We were all tutored privately in our houses, but we did see each other frequently at parties. Some of my peers I liked, some I put up with, and others—well, to be honest, those others I could have dumped in the canals and not missed a moment's sleep afterward."

Justice listened to her, trying to figure out where she was going with this line of talk. Whatever she and Rhajmurti had agreed upon, it had amused her: her dark eyes sparkled in the light, and a faint flush colored her cheeks.

"Of those whom I could have cheerfully consigned to the canals, you may be assured Krishna Malenkov was one."

Refusing a poleboat ride home since Kass lay so close, Justice had left Rhajmurti and Sonja, exited onto the upper level of Borg, hurried down the stairs and out onto the second level walkway. Now, crossing Borg Bridge, he headed straight into the northern wind. Shivering, he gathered his coat closer with one chilled hand, burying the other deep in his pocket. If the weather got much colder, he would have to dig his gloves out from the bottom of his closet. He wanted to avoid this until the last possible moment, preferring to tough it out as long as possible. Gloves were not cheap; he had purchased his only two years ago, and they had nary a hole between them.

Despite the cold, folk were abroad on the bridge, coming home from work, or going off to market to buy the makings of supper. The people he met, however, went about their tasks without pausing to chat with a neighbor, or look in the doors of the shops still open. Even those talking about the lights over the harbor seemed to prefer doing that indoors. It was too damned chilly to dawdle.

Justice walked along, his head bent forward, wishing he had worn his cap. But when he had left Hilda's for the College, he had been in such a state of mind that remembering to put his coat on seemed (in retrospect) a major accomplishment.

And now, if things went right, he would not have to

215

worry about Krishna for a while. He smiled slightly, envisioning what would happen, caught himself day-dreaming, and focused on his path. The situation was serious, very serious, and the last thing he needed was to forget that.

He glanced up as he walked off Borg Bridge and into the twilight of the walkway that led around the back side of Kass. If things did not go as planned . . .

Damn! I've got to keep my mind in the present, or I'll give something away. Krishna's not stupid. He'll read right through me.

Hilda's sign, hung perpendicular to the tavern front, loomed up not all that far ahead. With his destination so near, Justice suddenly realized how cold he felt. He broke into a trot, weaving in and out of the foot traffic, aimed toward Hilda's door, and the warmth and comfort that lay on its other side.

The tavern grew noisier with each new arriving diner, but to Justice the noise was welcome. He sat at his table, Sunny curled up in his lap, and sipped at his beer. Now, though he knew he should be doing his last-minute studying, he sat with what he hoped looked like relaxed contentment, waiting for his dinner to be served.

Relaxed? Ha! He was anything but! For Father Rhajmurti's plan to work, everyone involved would have to be on time. There were few places to lurk inside the tavern, and fewer on the walkway outside.

Idly scratching Sunny's head, Justice looked around the tavern, again keeping his surveillance casual. No sign of Krishna. Lord! If Krishna decided to spend the evening out bar-hopping . . .

Jason came out of the kitchen and headed toward Justice's table. With a small sigh, Justice set out the money he owed for the meal, waited until Jason had started off again, and sat up straighter. Sunny lifted his head, sniffed at the smell of baked fish, and yawned. Obviously, Hilda had fed him and the other half-wild cats she watched over *before* the dinner hour.

With a quick look around the tavern (still no Krishna), Justice started his meal. He had brought his book with him, so he ate and read slowly, going over what Sonja had pointed out as being his weakest areas. He snorted a quiet laugh. Weakest areas? He had so few strong ones, everything seemed weak.

After the test tomorrow, if things went as they were supposed to tonight, Justice would have several days off to relax and do nothing. He had looked forward to this time as a vacation of sorts. Now, it might turn out to be time spent in a mad scramble to shore up the foundations of a career in the making.

He turned a page in his book, speared a bite of fish with his fork, and then paused, fish halfway to his mouth. Krishna stood a few paces away, arms crossed on his chest, watching.

Justice somehow kept the fish on its way without losing composure. Chewing slowly, he forced himself to meet Krishna's eyes, to keep expressionless. He must have been successful, for a brief look of anger crossed Krishna's face.

"Well, Justus," Krishna said, hooking a chair out from the table with his toe and sitting down.

Damn! I wish he'd at least vary his opening! "Well, Krishna," Justice replied, his heart pounding as he tried to match the hightowner's drawl. "Off for the evening, or are you having dinner first?"

Krishna did not reply, but sat staring at Justice as if he had expected some different greeting. This time, warned by Father Rhajmurti, Justice assessed the hightowner's physical appearance: still mildly high, though nowhere near to the state he had been in earlier.

"Oh, I think I'll hang around here for a while," Krishna said, leaning back in his chair. "In fact, I think I'll have my supper."

Justice breathed a sigh of relief, but forced an expression of momentary displeasure to his face. *Good. Now if everyone could only be where they were supposed to be, when they were supposed to be there. . . .*

Jason appeared at the table and took Krishna's order. Silverbit. The same dinner that Justice had ordered. *Huhn. That meant Krishna was still low on funds, or he had planned on a long night in the bars.* Justice kept reading his book, watching the hightowner from the corner of one eye. Krishna, for his part, merely stared, still waiting for something.

Justice thought he knew for what.

"Your test is tomorrow?" Krishna asked at last.

"Yes." Justice turned a page.

"Do you feel more confident having studied with m'sera Keisel?"

"Considerably." Justice kept his voice level and polite.

"It's a wonder she found the time to help someone like you," Krishna said, one eyebrow lifted in what bordered on disdain. "If she's as good as you say she is, she was probably bored to tears."

"More than likely," Justice replied equably. "However, she has manners, and was able to disguise her boredom."

Krishna reacted to this veiled insult by drawing himself up in his chair and squaring his shoulders. Justice pretended not to notice.

"Your meal, m'ser," Jason said, setting the plate and mug of beer before Krishna.

"What are you waiting for?" Krishna asked, looking up at Jason who stood politely by the table.

"Your money, m'ser," Jason replied.

Krishna waved. "Put it on my tab."

"I'm sorry, m'ser, but you've exceeded your allotment for this month. You father gave us express orders to . . ."

"Damn him!" Krishna dug in his sweater, and came up with the requisite coins. "There," he said, tossing the money on the edge of the table. "That should cover it. With a small bit for you and your service.

Jason's face never changed; he swept up the coins in a practiced hand, bowed his head slightly, and started back to the kitchen.

"So." Krishna turned to his dinner as though nothing had happened, though his ears had gone red. "Have you thought any more about what I told you this afternoon?"

Justice's stomach knotted. "Yes. I thought about it for a while, and decided I didn't like the idea."

"You didn't—?" Krishna's head jerked up. "Do you understand what you're doing to yourself? I can ruin you with a few words here and a few words there."

"I understand all too well," Justice said, taking a bite of his greens, struggling to keep his voice from shaking. *It's like a knife fight . . . you never know where the next move will come from. And you sure as hell better not let your opponent know what* your *plans are.* "Do you know you could go before the Justiciar for what you've done?"

Krishna's face went white, then red. "Prove it!" he snapped.

"Or have you considered," Justice continued, "that your father would be upset, to put it mildly, if he found out what you're doing."

"Prove that, too!" Krishna's head stuck forward, his jaw muscles clinched. "There's no way you can!"

From the corner of his eye, Justice saw Rhajmurti enter the tavern along with two other priests. Jason motioned them to an empty table sitting behind Krishna's back. Justice took a long breath, felt his gut quivering, and reached for his beer. Rhajmurti had come to the tavern to be present only in case of complete disaster. If possible, he was not to be included in what happened.

Ancestors! Let this end quickly! I don't know how much longer I can keep this up!

"I'll ruin you, Justus," Krishna said. "You won't have a chance of ever becoming more than an itinerant walkway sketcher. *I* know the hightown Houses and those who live in them. I'll—"

"And what will you tell them?" Justice asked, swirling the beer around in his mug. "How will *you* prove what you say?"

Krishna stared and, despite his anxiety, Justice had the urge to laugh. Things were definitely *not* going the way Krishna had planned. Rhajmurti's presence at the next table served as an anchor; Justice would have been unable to stay so cool if he had not known he would have eventual assistance. Now, if only—

"I won't have to prove anything," Krishna said. "I'm one of them. They'll believe me."

Justice shrugged. He forked another bite of fish, and then his heart jumped. Dressed in evening richness, subdued but undeniably elegant, Sonja walked slowly across the tavern toward Justice's table.

"Oh, Justus!" she said brightly, seating herself and turning her chair so that she sat partially blocking Krishna off from the conversation. "I'm so glad you're still here."

"Good evening, m'sera," Krishna said loudly, leaning sideways so he could see her face.

"Hello, Krishna," Sonja said in a distant voice, then, rushing on: "Justus . . . you could really help me out of a tough spot."

"After your assistance today, Sonja," Justice said, using her name instead of her title, "I'm willing to do anything I can."

Krishna, meanwhile, was doing an excellent fish imitation, his mouth opening and closing without a sound.

"You know the Governor's Winter Ball is coming up, and I have . . ." She gestured briefly. "I'd like you to be my guest, if you'd come."

Even though he knew Sonja would be saying those words, according to Rhajmurti's plan, Justice's throat tightened. The Governor's Ball! One of the greatest gala events of the year, and one to which only those of money and station received invitations. Someone like Justice could only *aspire* to attend it, and only if sometime in the future they might possibly have enough social status to be deemed interesting.

To receive such an invitation now, and to appear at that Ball in the company of someone like Sonja Keisel, would all but assure Justice of future employment by the hightown Families.

"Thank you, Sonja," Justice said, also thanking the Lord, along with every Revenantist god and saint he could think of, as well as his own luck. "I'd be more than happy to come with you."

"But . . . but . . ." Krishna had found his voice now. "You can't invite—" He gestured at Justice. "—*him!*"

Sonja turned her head as if she only now realized Krishna sat at the same table. "Oh?" she asked, her voice gone very formal. "And why not?"

"He's . . . he's a nobody! A nothing!" Krishna's

eyes had gone very wide. "If you want someone to go with," he said, "I'd be glad to take you."

"Why, thank you for your concern, Krishna," Sonja smiled, all frost and false politeness, "but, as you can see, I already have someone to accompany me."

"But . . ." Krishna shot a desperate look in Justice's direction. "You can't—"

"I'm a Keisel," Sonja said in a voice that rang of steel and ice, "and I can damn well do anything I *want* to."

Krishna's face had paled to near the shade of the white napkins. He glanced around the tavern as if seeking help, then shoved his chair back and stood.

"I'm sorry, m'sera . . . I must be going. Good evening."

And with that, Krishna turned and hurriedly headed for the exit.

Justice nearly fell out of his chair, he shook from relief so badly. He made a quick hand-sign to Rhajmurti, who had watched the entire incident, letting the priest know that his plan had worked. Sonja sat laughing quietly, her dark eyes sparkling in the lamp light. When Justice thought he had waited long enough for his voice to be steady, he spoke.

"Thank you, Sonja. You've just saved what small career I have."

She smiled. "From what Father Rhajmurti says, I don't think that's true. You have a brilliant career in front of you."

Justice felt his face go hot. "Anyway," he said, "thank you. And, if you want to withdraw the invitation, I'd—"

"And why would I want to do that?" Sonja asked, shoving Krishna's plate and beer mug to one side. She turned to Jason who had appeared like magic at the table, and ordered herself a meal of baked silverbit and a glass of wine. "Your fish looks good."

"It was . . . is," Justice said, moving the last few bites around with his fork. "It's cold now."

"When the waiter returns, send it back to the kitchen to be warmed up."

Justice grimaced. "I'm afraid my stomach's so knotted up that I wouldn't be able to enjoy it."

"Still nervous?"

"Look." Justice held out one hand: it shook noticeably. He grinned in spite of himself. "I'm not one to fall apart *during* anything . . . it's *after* I have to worry about."

Sunny stretched in Justice's lap, having slept through the whole production. Looking around, he decided nothing was happening of greater importance than another nap, so he buried his head under one outflung paw, and was instantly asleep.

"Seriously," Justice said, scratching Sunny's ears, his eyes meeting Sonja's, "if you want to go with someone else to the Ball, I won't—"

"I'm going with *you*, Justus Lee," Sonja said, lifting her chin. "Remember. I'm a Keisel. And what we Keisels want, we usually get."

CHAPTER XVII

NESSUS' SHIRT
by Roberta Rogow

The crowd in front of Ma Klickett's stall at canalside gathered to stare at the highly polished boat tethered to the docking-post. This was no ordinary skip, reeking of fish and worse dragged up from the Grand Canal; this was a private luxury-boat with the owners' Arms emblazoned on it, a man in dark green livery to pole it and another to escort the two m'seri into the tiny shop. Ma Klickett sat calmly, her fingers busy with the needles and the yarn, her eyes drinking in the sight, squat and dark on her little stool.

The two hightown women swished through the shop, filling it with their finery and their perfume. One was tall and fair, and one was tall and dark, and both wore many rings and tinkling bracelets and cloaks of heavy silk trimmed with fur.

"Are you sure this is the place, dear?" the fair one asked the other. "I mean . . . here?"

"Oh, yes." The dark one had that air of authority of one who always knows what's what and who's who. "M'sera Klickett, how do you do?" She extended a hand that had never seen the inside of a washtub of clothes, or the outside of a cooking-pot. "I was quite satisfied with the last sweater you made for me."

"Glad to hear it, m'sera." The rhythm of the needles punctuated her words. "See you brought a friend."

"I had to see where Ariadne got those simply fabulous sweaters," the fair one said with a laugh. "I never thought they'd come from here." She indicated the shop with a scornful shrug that took in the gray-brown walls and the wooden pegs, each with a hank of yarn.

223

Klickett's eyes widened a fraction, then flicked back to normal, unseen. "Each one different, each one made to order," she said. "And a song with each, if ye like."

"Really?" the fair m'sera drawled.

Ariadne frowned slightly. "M'sera Klickett's knitting is known throughout the city," she said. "I wanted to order three more sweaters: one for myself, one for each of my daughters. They've outgrown the last ones you knit. Children grow so fast, you know . . ."

"Aye, m'sera. They do," Klickett murmured, looking down. Her Little Jo would never grow, would never pole a skip with his father across the Grand Canal. . . .

The fair m'sera fingered one of the sweaters lying on the tiny counter. "These are quite inappropriate," she said. "Not at all fine enough, fit only for bargemen. Ariadne, I wonder that you dragged me down here!"

Klickett's eyes narrowed, but she never missed a beat with her needles. "If m'sera wishes, I've finer yarns in the back. I can show'm to ye. . . . 'Course it'll cost ye extra, fine-work like that."

"No matter," the fair one yawned. "Let's see them."

Klickett heaved herself off the stool with a grunt and waddled to the curtain that divided the shop in two. Behind the curtain she nodded at the two rangy women who were thumbing through the books tidily stacked on wooden shelves.

"Hightown clientele?" said the one with the long black hair and red head-band. "Soak 'em good, Klickett."

"They get what they pay for," Klickett said softly. She pulled a bundle down from the highest shelf. "Business, Rif. Don't come out till they're gone, hear?"

"Wouldn't soil our hands on 'em," said the other woman, shorter and curly-headed.

"They can be of use, Rattail. Just remember that." Klickett grinned and stepped out into the shop again. "Here y'are, m'seri. Finest of yarns, finest of colors. Never seen anything like this, hey?" She lifted up the sweater by its shoulders to display the iridescent colors that seemed to shimmer in the fading light.

Ariadne made an "ooooh" noise. Her friend's eyes gleamed, but the perfectly painted mouth was still petulant. "Anyone can knit this," she said. "I could find the same in one of the shops in the upper markets."

"Try it." Klickett shook her head. "This here's special yarn, spun fine, and mixed with a special down. The colors are part of the yarn. Got to be spun from one strand. Can't be got in the markets; can't be made—not by the Kamats, not by no one. Gotta know just what critter's hide makes the fur. Can't hurt the critters, either, or no more fur."

"Betsina, dear . . ." Ariadne sighed. "I hope you're not going to take it, because I want it."

Betsina's mouth took on a predatory curve. "Well, dear, it seems to me that I asked to see it first. And Pyotr can certainly afford it more than Farren can. . . . after all, a Deputy Prefect's stipend can't go too far these days, and there's no extra pickings in the Harbors Office."

Klickett's voice cut through the polite sparring. "M'seri, this here's a sample piece. Can't be sold. Just for show . . . But I can work yez up one to order, if ye like. Pick yer patterns, take yer measure, and come back in a week."

"Oh, but I must have it sooner than that," Betsina whined. "The Governor's Ball . . . I must have it for that. I'll even pay in advance!"

Klickett's round face revealed nothing. Ariadne glanced at the shop-woman, then at her friend.

"Cost yer a full piece," Klickett finally said. "Two days' work it'll be, an' nothing else for no one till it's done."

"An exclusive design, mind! No one else will have one before I do?" Betsina was gloating already, picturing the envious looks of the other women as she entered the Governor's ballroom clad in this gossamer wisp that almost seemed to float, so fine were the stitches and so open the lace pattern.

"No one else will have anything like it," Klickett promised.

The fitting, measuring and pattern-choosing took very little time. As soon as it was done, Betsina strolled out the door, laughing merrily; apparently she'd forgotten her promise to pay in advance.

Ariadne followed her friend out the door and onto the dock, feeling uneasy. She impulsively turned back and re-entered, staring for a moment at the two women who had emerged from Klickett's back room. They turned away, carrying books, appearing busy.

"Yes, m'sera?" Klickett drew her attention.

"I wanted to say . . ." the hightown woman began, then stopped, considered, and spoke again. "M'sera Betsina tends to get her own way. You may bring the sweaters for me and the children when you can. You will be paid, of course, on delivery."

"Aye, m'sera, and I thank you for the custom," Klickett said, but her eyes were on the door, on Betsina, as she spoke, and her look was far away. She scarcely noticed as Ariadne left.

Rif and Rattail looked at the door, then at each other, then at Klickett. "Hightown contacts?" Rif asked, quietly.

But Klickett didn't answer. She was thinking of that day, so long ago, when she had been on the Grand Canal with Big Jo and Little Jo. They had been enjoying a rare treat: a day of sunshine, and a full meal. Little Jo tumbled off the skip. They had reached out the oar to pull the boy in before he got too much of the poisonous water into him . . . canaler children learned to swim as soon as they could walk. Then that launch came roaring down at them, full throttle, with the hightown youths shrieking at the fun of running close on the canalers' boats. . . .

And Little Jo, right in the path of the launch, and Big Jo diving down to get the baby out of the way, and the girl in the front of the launch laughing and laughing, her fair hair blowing in the wind. . . . "Go, go!" in that same, petulant voice.

Klickett had never forgotten that empty laugh, that voice, that fair hair, nor that empty, pretty face. Now the face was painted and the hair was dyed, but the laugh was still as empty and the voice was still as shrill.

Ariadne and Betsina were poled off to their island homes. Rat and Rif stared after the departing skip.

"Getting up in the world, Klickett?" Rif asked. "No more room for our books?" She hefted the one she was carrying, displaying a page that showed an intricate knitting pattern. The text had very little to do with knitting.

"Oh, always room for another book, or another song," Klickett said. "Got a new one . . .

> Rat and Rif sing songs down in vile cafes,
> Help the poor folks out of their plights.
> They've got sacks of seeds of poison-eating weeds,
> Sown on dark Merovingen nights.

Rif's hand went to her nearest knife. "That's dangerous talk, sera. Some songs are better sung alone."

Klickett shrugged. "No one listens to me, dearie. I'm no professional singer; I just make 'em up for fun."

"Ha." Rat handed Klickett a few coins, and the books. "We'll bring some more tomorrow," she promised. "These look good. When can you get the new ones printed?"

"Gotta do this sweater first," Klickett told her. "Gimme three, four days. You'll get your book out then, no fear."

Rif shook her head. "I don't get you. You've got to hate them more than anyone. Now you make their fancy clothes, getting a toe into their circles. Why?"

Klickett picked up her knitting again. "Gotta eat, gotta have fire. Can't get 'em with books, not around here."

"Traitor," Rat said evenly.

Klickett shrugged. "You fight 'em your way, I fight 'em mine. Your books'll be ready next week, after I finish this little piece for m'sera Betsina. Her fine sweater'll pay for the paper and ink."

The women shrugged too, and left. Klickett closed the door behind them and shuttered the lone window. Then she pulled out the bag with the fine iridescent yarn, spun from the nests of skits, those ratlike creatures that infested the Flats up the canal past Zorya.

She made a few mental calculations, then pulled on her heaviest sweater, her thickest boots and the gloves with the fewest holes. Her tiny boat was tied under the dock, just big enough to pole one hefty but determined woman up the Grand Canal before darkness. She hung a lantern at her side and set out for the Flats.

The canals were almost empty at that hour; lovers weren't out yet, most business had finished for the day, night work hadn't started yet, the canalers were busy at dinner. She slid across the still waters, just another ragged woman on the canals, unnoticed. Once on the Flat, she struck a light and shone the lamp on the foliage that lined the bank. Skit-nests would be under the weeds.

She parted the grasses carefully. Skit-nest fur could be collected only in the breeding season; once the nest was empty, the fur would blow away or be matted into the soil. Skit-nests contained skit-pups, who were as nasty as their parents and even more inclined to snap, since they had yet to learn what was and was not edible. Klickett's gloves were badly slashed before her sack was full, and she was bleeding from a dozen needle-puncture bites.

Only one more chore to do. She picked her color-weed very carefully, then stepped back into the little boat and tied up her bleeding hands so the blood-smell would not attract any more skits, or anything bigger.

Once back in her shop, Klickett set about preparing her yarn. The pattern was easy: lace, of course, in diamonds-within-diamonds. Skit-nest fur would be soft, like floating down, barely settling on the soft skin of the hightown woman. It would need a little something else, something to bind it together. . . . Klickett's mouth tightened in determination. She had waited for this day, planned for it, and now there was no hesitation at all.

The next day found Klickett at her post, needles working away, in front of her shop. Rif strolled by and looked critically at the object taking form on the needles.

"Interesting," the musician commented, "But why the bandages around the fingers?"

"Got rat-bit last night," Klickett replied, counting stitches. "Gotta be careful of those little buggers . . . ten, eleven, twelve, over, slip, knit two together, over

. . . Got it!" She straightened out the piece, unwound more yarn from the sack at her feet, and started another row. With a sly look at Rif, she started to sing.

> *What d'ye do with a drunk Canaler?*
> *What d'ye do with a drunk Canaler?*
> *What d'ye do with a drunk Canaler,*
> *Ear-lye in the morning?*

Rif took up the chorus:

> *Dunk 'im in the Swamp and make 'im drink it.*
> *Dunk 'im in the Swamp and make 'im drink it.*
> *Dunk 'im in the Swamp and make 'im drink it,*
> *Ear-lye in the morning!*

It was an old song, but a popular one. There was a small crowd around the shop, mostly children but a few adults, and all grinned as they listened. Rif spoke quietly to one or two, who moved into the back of the shop and soon came out with small books in their hands, dropping coins into the box next to Klickett's stool. The knitted piece grew as the yarn wound out of the bag.

By dusk the first half of the sleeveless sweater was done. The second piece would be easier, then the beaded neck and the fine lace of the sleeve-edges. Klickett's needles worked faster at the thought of Betsina and this particular sweater.

Klickett had knitted steadily through the third day, with one eye out for the gaily-painted skip and the two m'seri. There were the usual customers, in and out of the shop, but no one from hightown. Perhaps she's decided against it, Klickett thought. Hightown women change their minds. . . .

Klickett wound the last of the yarn into her bag, and sighed. Time to close up, she thought. The sound of the skip nudging the dock made her turn sharply. This time Betsina was alone, except for the man poling the skip.

"Thought you wasn't coming, m'sera," Klickett said.

"I thought I'd never get rid of Ariadne," Betsina pouted. "But I wanted to see it first."

"And pay for it?" Klickett hinted.

Betsina stepped eagerly into the shop. Klickett lit the oil-lamp against the coming nightfall.

"Here she is," the stout woman said, laying the finished garment on the table. The irridescent yarn seemed to shimmer in the flickering lamplight, and the beads cleverly worked into the neckline emphasized the fragility of the design.

Betsina's mouth took on an avaricious curve. "Oooh!" She barely touched the delicate thing. "It's . . ." she realized that Klickett was watching. Immediately she resumed her cusomary petulant pout. "It's quite nice," she said. "I shall send my steward around in the morning with the payment."

Klickett shrugged and picked the sweater up by the shoulders. "I'll wrap it for ye," she said. Then, she added, almost as an afterthought," Ye'll be wearin' this with a liner? For if ye wish, I can line it for ye. 'T will take another day. . . ."

"But the Governor's Ball is tomorrow night," Betsina said. "I can't possibly wait. And a lining would spoil the effect . . . just wait until they see me in this!" She reached out an arm to see the shimmering yarn against her white skin. "Even that stick, Farren, will open his eyes!"

"Ah." Klickett nodded sagely. "But this yarn's sometimes a mite ticklish . . . 't were better if you wore something beneath."

"For propriety's sake?" Betsina's empty laugh rang through the tiny shop. "Really! You canal people! Such prudes!" She picked up the carefully-wrapped package and swept out of the shop, onto her own skip. The boatman poled her off into the night.

Klickett watched them go. She wished she could be there when that sweater was worn, but it was enough to imagine what would happen. If she had read the woman rightly, she would not heed the warning . . . but she *had* been warned. Even Mother Jane could do no more than that.

Klickett waddled back into her shop humming to herself. The rest would be in the hands of whatever gods were watching. . . .

* * *

It was a bright morning on the Grand Canal. Klickett was hard at work, outside her shop, while the local population used her dock as a fine vantage-point to watch the parade of barges and skips, all solemnly draped in purple and black ribbons, as they headed out to the Harbor.

"Nothing like a high-class funeral for show," commented Rif. "Give the people what they want . . ."

"They say she died slow and horrible," contributed one of the women on the dock, Some House's maid by the look of her outworn finery.

"She was warned," Klickett said to herself.

There was a step behind her. She turned to see Ariadne, dressed for the funeral, in a fine steel-gray sweater that Klickett had knit just that season.

"I thought I should tell you," Ariadne said softly. "I was asked where she got the . . . the garment."

"And?" Klickett's needles didn't miss a beat.

"You'd shown her something similar, but that she hadn't paid for it," Ariadne said slowly, "that, I know. . . ."

"Nor did she," Klickett said. "Nor would she have, ever, m'sera. She was a bad lot, she was. She done for my Jo, and she'd an eye to your man, too. 'Just wait till Farren sees this,' m'sera said, in this very shop."

"Did you know what it would do?" Ariadne asked.

"I heard about skit-fur," Klickett admitted. "All us on the Grand Canal knows better than to mess with skits. Didn't know what would happen, though. But it must have looked a treat."

"Oh, yes. It was quite . . . spectacular." Ariadne stared over the water at the largest of the barges, the one with the coffin. "She wore it with a pair of skin-tight trousers, as if she were a sixteen year old." The tall woman's mouth tightened in distaste. "And not a stitch under it, either."

Klickett glanced up. "Not even a bodice?"

"One could see . . . well, *all!*"

"And then what?"

Ariadne spoke slowly, seeing it all over again: "She was basking in everyone's admiration, and then she seemed to become uncomfortable . . . and then she started to feel some sort of pain . . . and had to be taken home. . . ."

"Yey, m'sera. I warned her, I did, to let me line it." Klickett's knitting needles seemed to pick up pace. She knew what would happen when the tiny barbed hooks of the skit-fur found their lodging-place in that soft white skin. It would be like a thousand thousand tiny needles pricking their way in, while the itchweed so carefully wound into the yarn would irritate the skin even more, and the little barbs would drive farther and farther, until they reached the nerve-endings, where the miniscule drops of skit-venom would begin their work. No, it had not been the easy death for that one, Klickett thought to herself.

"She had an eye to my husband, you say?" Ariadne's well-bred tones cut through Klickett's thoughts.

"She did."

"Then . . . perhaps . . . it was just as well things ended as they did,"

Or you'd have had her hide yourself, Klickett thought.

The two women watched as the cortege disappeared behind ordinary traffic, bound down the Grand Canal to the harbor proper.

"I thank ye for coming," Klickett said softly. "Were ye followed?"

"I doubt it. I took the foot-path from the bridge," Ariadne said. "I sincerely hope there will be no unpleasant aftermath for you."

"Or where would you get your sweaters?" Klickett said with a grin. "Ne, I'm in no danger. If the lady insisted on buying a shirt of skit-fur, and wearing it bareskin-under when she was warned . . . ?" Another eloquent shrug.

"They couldn't even get it off the body," came the voice of the lady's maid on the dock. "And she was all swole up, and blue with it, and her throat raw from screamin' in pain!"

"Ghouls," Ariadne said, dispassionately.

"Perhaps," Klickett said. "But she brought it on herself." Her powerful contralto voice rang out over the water, as the last of the cortege vanished around the bend and the crowd dispersed:

Way-hen, the water's risin',
Way-hen, the water's risin',
Way-hen, the water's risin',
Ear-lye in th' mornin'. . . .

CHAPTER XVIII

TREADING THE MAZE

by Leslie Fish

Waken in darkness to sounds of close water, far voices, sad birds' cries, the distant tapping of the undertaker's shop below opening for the day's quiet business. Not much noise on Coffin Isle.

And isn't that fitting, you creature of dark dreams?

Eyes open, eyes shut: no difference. The vision's still there: hawk-sharp face, dark wing of long hair, sardonic eyes and taunting smile. Long, slender, supple hands—of a musician? Acrobat? Thief? All those and more, and a body to match.

Rif, she calls herself.

Remember that first sight of her: poised on a dark roof, thieves' bag on her back, scaling-rope in her hands, caught in the act beyond all excuses. . . . Looking straight at you, right into the gun-muzzle. And she smiled. And saluted.

And dropped.

Twenty-five meters down, straight into the canal, you thought; better dead than captured, better dead her own way than yours, courage and resolution enough to catch the breath in your throat. Such purity, but no fanatic's grimness. Gone with a merry smile, and how in the cold Merovingen hell could that be?

Then the ear catching the whine of rope running through a pulley, remember that scaling-rope, and the snap of the line coming taut. The long fall changing to a long swing, swooping like a bird across the canal. Feet catching nimbly, just so, on the railing of a walkway full seven stories down. Perfect landing, the reckless beauty of it branding the eyes. Had she planned that, measured and calculated, before she climbed that

234

hightown roof? Or did it all run through her hawk's eyes just before she plunged? Either way, the artistry was beautiful beyond belief.

And she knew it. She stood there at the railing and reeled in her line, coiling it neatly around her arm, knowing full well that you saw her, had a clear shot, plenty of time to aim and any reason you needed to shoot. ("Right, m'ser. A burglar, caught breaking into Elgin House.") And she knew you wouldn't shoot, would stand there watching as she reeled in her line, tossed you another salute and disappeared into the walkway's shadows. She was right, and you never told anyone.

That was when you fell in love with her.

Caelum Alpha Halloran, you're a romantic idiot.

Black Cal sighed, pulled his eyes open and glumly sat up. Wan light straggled in through the shutters, showing dawn and little else. Normally that would mean nothing—his feet knew every centimeter of the floor—but today he needed to see something. He picked up the narrow mirror from the clothes-chest top, went to the window and pushed the shutter open to let a handspan of daylight in.

The weak light spitefully picked out his random scars and nakedness, but he ignored that. Nobody could see, nobody was looking—not at Coffin Isle with its so-apt business. Perhaps a dozen builders even remembered that there was an upstairs apartment over the lone shop on the narrow islet. If so, they would think the undertaker himself still lived there. Not so: the whole family had moved to more respectable quarters westward. Black Cal had arranged for the lease with the owner's blind old grandfather, using a false name, paying cash by mail-drop every first of the month. No one in all Merovingen knew he lived here. No one wanted to venture or look close, either. Privacy and silence: just what he wanted.

Black Cal studied himself in the mirror, in the merciless gray light. Long lean face and body and limbs, not a speck of fat anywhere. White scars everywhere, like ragged lace, over girder-stark bones and cable-long muscles. Bizarre, but not ugly. A hard-worked but well-maintained machine. Nothing but slight grim-

ness showing in the expression. The eyes, though . . .
Was that a flicker of yearning, of loneliness? A flicker
too much.

It's finally caught up to you. You're in love.

He gave a long resigned sigh, and put down the
mirror.

So, what are you going to do about it?

Black Cal turned back to the dark apartment, went
to the tiny washroom and scrubbed thoroughly, dried
off, went to the clothes-chest, pulled out the day's
clothes and got dressed.

And went out to look for Rif.

"Name?" said the bored census-clerk. He'd been at
this for days, and all the faces had begun to blur.

"Morgan Partera," said the gray-haired woman in
drab middletown garb. "And these are Niki and Rey."
She pointed to a pair of children, similarly dressed,
who giggled as if sharing some inane secret.

"Ages?" yawned the clerk, scribbling on the endless
forms.

"Thirty-seven, ten and eight." The woman sounded
equally bored, had probably been standing in line for
hours. "I sell cordage, live behind the shop, at Yan
North, Aisle B, Number 11, Suite C."

The kids giggled shrilly again. The woman gave
them a quick glare.

"Cordage merchant, Yan North . . ." the clerk repeated, scribbling.

The woman hiccupped, just once. The clerk didn't
bother to look up from his papers. The kids noticed,
peeked silently, and saw that the woman was staring
up at the walkway beyond the census-taker's station.
They stared too, puzzled, seeing only passersby and a
few people lounging at the railing. One of the loung-
ers, a very tall man dressed in black, seemed to be
looking back at them—but then he glanced away. The
woman turned her head, aimed her attention at the
clerk again. The kids gave up the mystery, and started
a half-hearted game of got-you-last.

"Is this going to take much longer?" the woman
asked, aiming light cuffs at the kids. "I've got to get
back to the shop."

"Just a minute, just a minute," the clerk grumbled, scrawling a last quick signature on an identity-card. "Here. Don't lose it. Next?" He shook out his cramped fingers and turned his attention to the next in line.

The woman hustled the two kids off down the walkway, toward a pastry-seller's booth just around the corner. The girl, seeing the payoff coming, clamored for a greenberry tart. The boy took up the howl, demanding a cream-cake.

The man on the walkway pulled himself off the railing and sauntered after them.

The woman saw him waiting as she turned away from the pastry-booth. She nodded once toward him, then snagged the kids' attention away from their treats. "Can ye get home a'right from here?" she asked.

"Yey, we're just down there," the girl pointed. The boy nodded preoccupied agreement, mouth busy with his cream-cake.

"Get on, then. See ye later." She gave the kids a parting pat, watched briefly as they strode off toward the nearest bridge, glanced automatically up and down the walkway, then paced over to the railing and took a slumped pose beside the waiting man. She said nothing.

"Hello, Rif," said Black Cal. "You don't look yourself today."

Rif scowled, wringing flakes of gray powder out of her eyebrows. "Thought my own mother wouldn't recognize me in this."

"I'm not your mother. How many ID cards have you picked up that way?"

"Nearly a dozen." Rif smiled briefly. "Must be a slow day if ye're busting folk fer that."

"I'm not." Black Cal looked away for a moment. "You just collecting ID's, or is there more to it?"

Rif shrugged. "Mostly just that. Also buggerin' the census. Make the town look bigger and tougher'n she really is."

"Tougher nut for Nev Hettek to crack?"

"Or any damn tyrant," Rif snapped, a glare of real outrage showing in her eyes. "Whadda ye *want*, Black Cal?"

Not this, he almost said. Instead he glanced at the strip of sky showing between the roofs. But what could he say to her? "That piece of info you gave me: I'm having some trouble using it."

"Piece . . . Oh, Tati's boyfiend? What's the trouble?"

"I can't trust my commander. Who do I tell it to?"

"Well, go over his head. Go all the way ter Old Iosef himself, if ye have to."

"Easier said than done." Black Cal dared to turn and look her straight in the eyes. "I'm not exactly well-liked up at the Justiciary."

Rif stared at him. ". . . nor the Signeury neither?"

"No. No friends in hightown." He studied his shoes.

"Damn," Rif whispered, making good guesses. "You're stuck out here alone?"

Black Cal nodded. The silence stretched.

"Hell," Rif finally muttered. "There's gotter be some way. Somebody in the net's gotter have a lead inter hightown. . . ."

"Find it for me. Find someone who'll use this right."

Rif gave him an odd look, but dutifully considered the problem. "Anastasi . . . Hmm, no. He'd be happy ter pull Tati down, but that's all he'd do. Wouldn't stop the Swords. Damn! Only Old Iosef himself would. but how d'we get 'er safely t'him?"

"You tell me." Black Cal grinned sourly. "I can't just walk into the Signeury and make an appointment."

"Hell, why not?"

"Because nobody there would give me one."

"Oh." Rif looked at him for a long minute. "So ye don't get far, nor make friends in high places, bein' the only honest blackleg in the city, do yer?"

"No, you don't."

"Ye need friends in hightown. Hell, who der we know what has any friends in hightown, let alone reliable . . ." Rif stopped, blinked a moment, and chuckled. "I suppose the back door gets yer inside as well's any other, maybe better."

"You know someone?"

"Maybe." A calculating smile twitched her mouth. "But she won't be easy, and—"

"And you want another favor done." Black Cal sighed. This wasn't what he'd wanted. Still, it was contact, and he'd play the game out. "Name it."

Rif took a deep breath. "Clear the permit fer Master

Milton's Magic Show ter perform on East Dike," she said, all in a rush.

Black Cal laughed in pure surprise. "Master who's what?"

"Master Milton's Magic Show." Rif punished her lower lip. "It's harmless, I swear. Just a bunch of entertainers, friends. Make some money, amuse folks, liven things up a little. That's all."

"That's all?" he gave her a warning look. *Don't lie to me. I don't like people who lie to me.*

"Harmless!" Rif insisted, daring him to think otherwise, but not giving anything away.

Black Cal drummed his fingers on the rail. "Then why can't Master Milton just go the usual route? Why do you need me?"

"Because . . . Because the only patron we could get was Old Man Fife." Rif frowned out at the water. "Ye know what rep he's got, and how his kids try ter stop him at every turn."

Black Cal sighed again. Couldn't anything in this world be simple? "No, I don't know. Tell me."

Rif gave him an almost-pleading look, thought a moment, took a deep breath and plunged ahead. "He's . . . what ye call 'eccentric.' That means he's willing ter try new ideas, play around with things, experiment. His kids're grown, married, and stuffy as a College bookroom. They're crazy on the thought that he'll spend all his money on toys and games, leave 'em nothing when he dies—not that they'd need it, the rich turds. But anyway, they've gone and bought some clerk somewhere in the Signeury, get ter hear 'bout anything big Old Man Fife tries ter do, anything needs official permits. They're blocking this, fer no better reason nor it'd cost the old man some money ter do it, and they don't want 'er spent."

Black Cal nodded understanding. "Which of his kids are in on this? What clerk do they pay, and where's the permit stalled?"

"Just Pavel and Rosita, both up in Sofia with their families. I don't know who the clerk is, or where the permit's gone—maybe pitched inter the water by now. Can ye find out? Do something?"

"Hmm. Why doesn't Master Milton just get himself a better patron?"

"Can't. Old Man Fife's the only one he could get ter, talk inter it."

"Why?" Black Cal threw her a sharp look. "And what's so important about this Magic Show, anyway?"

Rif rolled her eyes heavenward, then automatically checked for possible listeners, saw none. No excuse. She sighed. "The show . . . she's got lots of fireworks in 'er. Ends with a big fireworks display."

"Fireworks?"

"Theater trick, from Chattalen way." Rif groped to explain. "They're pretty fire-flowers, flashes of colored sparks, fire-trails, pretty light. They don't last long, and they take lots o' room fer proper safety— which is why they want ter do 'er on East Dike, but there's nothing like 'em while they last."

"I've heard of fireworks, once," Black Cal added up what he'd heard, what he'd remembered, and something that he'd been worrying about for weeks. "Like that sharrh-scare? Fires in the sky, you mean?"

Rif gave him a long, thoughtful look. "You got 'er. Like that, only smaller. Pretty and harmless—but she'll make people *think*." Then she held her breath, waiting to see if he got the rest of it.

He did. He smiled. Not his legendary hunter's grin that so few saw and lived to tell about, but something much gentler. On his face, it was an incredible sight. "So that sharrh-scare really was Swords' work? And this is the—your friends'—cure for it?"

Rif nodded solemnly.

Black Cal laughed softly, delighted. Damnation, but he liked the way the Janes' minds worked. If there was one faction in Merovingen's tangled politics that he could admire . . .

He stopped there, sobering fast. "Politics. I hate politics." He'd survived this long by, among other things, scrupulously avoiding anyone's politics. Why get involved now? On the word of a professional thief and admitted revolutionary? Because he liked the Janist style, and hers? Because he wanted her? Not good enough. "I need some guarantees," he said. "I don't work blind."

Rif rolled her eyes at that, remembering how well Black Cal could shoot in the dark. "Lord and Lady, what do ye want? How'm I supposed ter prove any o' this? My friends can't exactly go around leaving footprints, y'know." She paused, glanced nervously at him. "Ye asked, and I told. Everyone knows what happens ter people what lie ter *you*."

Black Cal looked away, shivering in the light breeze. He didn't want her afraid of him, complying out of fear. This was going all wrong. There had to be some way to change this, at least arrange to meet with her again, talk again, take another chance.

"Take me to meet these friends of yours," he said. "I want to see the fireworks, and who's handling them."

Rif sucked a hard breath and rattled her fingers on the railing. She'd only wanted a way around the clerical bottleneck; this was bringing Black Cal in too deep. He could shoot them all, bust them all, set back the Janes' plans by months that they couldn't afford. But if he agreed to help, as he seemed half willing to . . . Ye gods, what an ally he could make!

Besides, he already knew who some of the Janes were, and hadn't done them any harm. He'd helped with that water-purifying incident. He was notoriously honest, and none of the Janes had yet committed any crime in front of him.

Except, of course, for herself collecting fake IDs and falsifying the census. But he hadn't done anything about even that.

"Well, I can take ye ter meet Master Milton," she offered. It was a risk, knowing where she was to meet the crew next. Still, there would be only the one crew endangered, not the whole Jane network. And Milton's friends could take good care of themselves.

At worst, they might even be able to take down Black Cal.

Surprising, how that thought grieved her. Merovingen just wouldn't be the same without Black Cal.

"Set it up," he said. "Tonight, if you can. I'll go get the permit form."

Rif chewed her lip. "All right. Where can I find ye, and when?"

"Sundown. Foundry-Coffin Bridge."

"Sundown, then." There seemed to be nothing more to say. The ID card felt heavy in Rif's pocket, and the drying makeup itched unbearably. She got up, waved a brief farewell and ambled away, feeling his eyes on her back. Quick now, being late already, down to the tavern and its washroom to get out of this disguise, then off to the contact-point to hand over the ID cards, and then . . . Hell, enough ID-farming today. Let Rat take it all day. Next stop, Klickett's place.

Black Cal watched her go, sourly calling himself six kinds of an idiot. But no use: he'd gone and committed his word to this. He got up and headed off toward the Signeury to get the permit-form.

The last of the sun disappeared below the roofs, leaving the sky blue-gray with fast winter evening.

She's not coming, Black Cal told himself. *Good thing you picked a meet-point close to home. Short walk to your own door, own room, empty bed. . . .*

No, he'd be patient. It was barely sundown; give her time to get here. Dusk could last awhile, even at this time of year. Patience.

She's not coming. You've fooled yourself. He shifted his weight from foot to foot and stared moodily down at the dark water. *If she has any sense, she'll be halfway to the Chattalen by now.*

But he leaned on the bridge-rail and watched the water, knowing he'd stay there until it was too dark to see. Then he'd be sure. Then he'd leave.

A battered gray skip slid quietly around the Foundry corner. A woman in a long indigo cloak was poling it. She had long black hair, held back by a kerchief-cloth headband.

Black Cal remembered to breathe, then caught his breath again as she looked up, saw him, and smiled. He pulled himself away from the rail and went down to the tie-ups at the foot of the bridge. Rif bowed elegantly and waved him into the ancient skip. He got in without comment, not trusting his voice just now.

"Careful with those big feet," she grumbled, awkwardly turning the skip around in the channel. "Don't poke holes in this boat; she's not mine."

"Whose?" Black Cal managed to say.

"A little old blind lady what only uses 'er in the daytime. Now keep down."

"Where're we going?"

"North Flat, up the Greve Fork."

He couldn't find any comeback to that, nothing that wouldn't sound sarcastic. He couldn't think of the words that would turn the conversation the way he wanted it to go. It had been so long since he'd had to deal with such things, he was badly out of practice. He kept quiet all the way to the tip of The Rock.

North of The Rock, the wind off the clean water and farmland hit him like reproach. It was always a pain and vague sorrow to remember how much his city stank. *In more ways than one.* Black Cal brooded on the passing dark landscape as Rif poled her way up the deepening Greve Fork; North Flat to the right, combed with neat rows of planted fields, Greve Shore to the left, a bit wilder with its tree-thick windbreaks and orchards, a few small piers poking shyly into the water, almost invisible in the dark.

And there, far off to the left and ahead, the twinkle of a single lamp's light.

Rif grunted recognition, racked the pole and pulled out the oars. "Ye'll have ter help me with this," she said.

Black Cal duly took the other oar, and they pulled their way upstream and left, out into the deep channel and across it, side by side, saying nothing.

The light grew, revealing the edge of a tiny pier and a low-set small ship tied to it. Black Cal noted that the ship was like nothing he'd ever seen in Merovingen. Three narrow dark-painted hulls, set parallel with the central one leading, connected with an arrowhead-shaped main deck. A slender mast rose from each hull, booms shrouded with furled dark sails. There were small engines and rudders at each stern; she could fly under power or run silent in the wind. The thing couldn't have drawn more than a couple of handspan's depth, even fully loaded. She was clearly the fastest thing on any water, and not really designed for much cargo at all. A smuggler's dream.

At the moment, her crew of three—all dressed in dark nondescript sailor's shirts and pants—were busily unloading some oilcloth-sealed crates onto the pier, where a man in city clothing examined them for spillage and checked each one against a list in his hand. The man looked up as Rif pulled around the corner of the pier, drew close and began tying up. "Hoi, Rif," he called softly, drawing the attention of the sailors. "Ye're early . . . And who *is* that?"

"Follow my lead," Rif whispered to Black Cal, then called back: "He's the one I told ye 'bout, going ter get ye the permit. He wants t' talk ter ye. C'mon over." She scrambled up the short ladder onto the low pier, Black Cal stepping cautiously after her, and padded toward the man with the list. The sailors, trying very hard to look nonchalant, eased off the ship and climbed onto the pier behind the stacked cartons.

The man with the list stopped short, holding up the shuttered lamp as he saw who was coming. "B'Jane, Rif," he gawked, "That's a blackleg!"

The sailors tensed, ready to jump in any direction if they could only be sure which way was the right one.

"Sure is," Rif smiled wide and reassuring. "Master Milton, this is Black Cal."

"B-B—" The man almost dropped his list, fumbled after it, came up gaping like a fish. "You didn't say it was *him!*" he squeaked.

Black Cal sighed, and took a measuring glance at the sailors. They were looking at one another as if signaling, and one of them was easing around the crates to the left, sliding out of the lamplight's range. How predictible. Black Cal slowed his steps, kept a few paces behind Rif.

"I said he was bone-honest, and worked fer the city," Rif glowered. "Who 'n hell did ye think that meant?"

"But . . . I didn't think . . ." Master Milton floundered. He was a slender little man, built for skilled trade more than combat, and he clearly didn't want to get within Black Cal's legendary reach. "Lord and Lady, Rif, why a blackleg?"

"Who better, ter get inside the Signeury?" Rif snapped, hands resting on the hilts of her visible daggers. "He can be trusted, he's got connections, and he wants ter help."

"Why in hell did you have to bring him here? To-night?" A sweep of Master Milton's hand took in the cargo, the glum sailors and the obvious smuggler-ship.

"Because he needs ter know who he's trusting, that's why!" Rif snarled. "Ye fool, do ye think this is no risk fer him?"

Black Cal heard the soft running footsteps, just where he'd expected them. He dropped low, swung to the left and came up fast with a roundhouse backhand slam. It connected with a solid thump, a whoosh of fast-emptied lungs, a skidding slide, then nothing but empty wind. An instant later the sailor hit the water. The splash was loud and sloppy. Everybody else stopped to look—except Rif and Black Cal, who glanced at each other and shrugged. The sailor in the water sur-faced, spat, coughed, swore, coughed again, and started paddling doggedly for the ladder. Black Cal turned his attention back to the shocked Master Milton and the dismayed sailors.

"Is that the best you can do?" he asked through his best sneer. "Am I wasting my time with amateurs— or can you really take the Sword out of Merovingen?"

There was dead silence for several seconds, broken only by the slurging noise of the dunked sailor pulling himself back up onto the pier. Black Cal favored him with a measuring look. The sailor ducked away.

Master Milton recovered first. "All right, one thing we can agree on; we all hate Sword of God. Right?"

There was a quick chorus of affirmative growls, and another quick grin from Rif.

"Let's talk tactics," said Black Cal, padding toward Master Milton, who had the sense—and nerve—not to flinch away. "Exactly what's going to be in this fire-works show? How much room will you need? What kind of weather conditions? Where'll you seat the crowd?"

Master Milton actually smiled, pleased to hear some knowledgeable shoptalk. "We'll need a good hundred meters for safety," he began, patting the nearest of the crates. "That's why we wanted East Dike; put everybody on the street and the stairs, me at the foot of the pier, and the fireworks rack 'way out at the end, over the water. You want the charges, firing angles and ranges on all these?"

"Damn right," said Black Cal, taking out the permit-form and a note-pad. "Also timing, area, everything."

"All right." Master Milton sat down on a crate and began scribbling on the back of his list. Black Cal sat down beside him, glancing from paper to paper. The sailors looked at each other, wondering what to do next.

"Ye might finished unloading," Rif suggested.

The sailors shrugged, and did.

An hour later the skip was loaded to the gunwales, and Master Milton himself was poling it down toward the mouth of the Grand Canal. If he found the work tiring, he didn't complain. If Black Cal wanted to sit and talk quietly in the bow with Rif, that was none of his concern. He found Black Cal unsettling. By all means, let Rif deal with him.

"It's basically the Harbormaster's problem," Black Cal was saying. "I'll take it to his office once I've . . . dealt with the interference. That'll take maybe a day or two. Can you get me a connection to Old Iosef by then?"

"If you can do 'er, I can," said Rif. "Where'll I meet ye?"

"Same place as tonight." Black Cal looked away over the water, tapping his fingers on the gunwale. "Where're you heading now?"

"Back to Fife; put the . . . equipment in Old Man Fife's storeroom, take the skip back to Min's tie-up. Why?"

"Can Master Milton do it by himself?"

"Yey, I guess. Why?"

Black Cal didn't answer at once, seemed to be wrestling with himself. Rif decided that she was finished trying to second-guess him.

"Why?" she repeated. "There something else ye want?"

"Yes." He turned to give her a long look. "You."

". . . Can't believe I'm doing this," Rif muttered as she padded silently across the lightless bridge. "Coffin Isle?"

Black Cal gave her a worried glance. "You know this place?"

"Just ter speak of. There's nothing here but an undertaker's." Rif shivered. Who knew what kinks lurked in a mind like his? "Why here?"

"Home," he said. "I live upstairs."

"Mother of mercy." Rif shivered again. What kind of nerves did it take to live over an undertaker's shop? She hoped the place wouldn't smell too bad. She profoundly hoped Black Cal wasn't into necrophilia. She pulled her cloak tight around her, surreptitiously checking her knives, as Black Cal unlocked an unsuspected lower door.

Inside lay a dark stairway, and at the top another door. Rif checked for escape-routes while Black Cal worked the locks—two of them, she noted. The door opened on more blackness. He led the way inside and closed the thick door behind them. Both locks clicked again, and a chain rattled as well. No quick exit there.

Surprisingly, the place didn't smell bad at all. No formaldehyde, anyway; nothing seeping up ominously through the floor. The canals smelled better here than back home at Fife. Not bad, so far.

A match spurted, followed by the flaring of an oil-lamp. In the sudden soft light, Black Cal's face looked thoughtful, distant, and almost sad. Rif glanced around the apartment, strangely not surprised to see that it was meticulously clean and almost ascetically bare. There was one rug of unexpectedly good quality, one clothes-chest, one closet, one table and two chairs, nothing on the walls, plain curtains over the windows. Two doorways led off to a tiny kitchen and a not-much-bigger bathroom. The bed was a wide nest of thick quilts and oversized pillows, the only comfortable-looking spot in the main room. Rif wondered who had shared it last.

Black Cal took off his coat and hung it on a hook behind the door. Then he took off his gunbelt and hung it on the nearest bedpost. He sat down on the bed to tug at his boots, and Rif took the opportunity to pace briefly around the main room, raking in details.

Something winked in the lamplight on top of the clothes-chest, and Rif looked closer there. On top of the chest stood a mirror in a polished brass frame. Before it lay a clean white cloth, with a carved candlestick placed neatly in the center and a thick gold candle in it. Arranged around that, just where the candlelight would show them to best effect, twinkled two opal collar-studs, a strikingly beautiful rainbow-shell, and an ornamental dagger with an ornately sculpted handle and sheath. The blade, she noted, was made up of many layers of hammered steel with their edges stained flat black; it looked like shining, fine-grained white wood. The objects, she saw, were carefully posed on the cloth: a balanced composition. Rif stared at the arrangement for long moments, sure that this was a vital clue to the enigma that was Black Cal. She could solve the whole mystery if she could only ask the right question. Rif could think of only one.

"Why isn't your badge here?"

Black Cal shrugged one shoulder and looked away. "Doesn't belong there," was all he said. He tugged off his shirt and stretched it on the back of the nearer chair.

And you the only honest blackleg in Merovingen! Rif stared at him, understanding opening like a flower. She had the truth now, and it was simply unbelievable. "You . . . you always wanted to be an artist!" she breathed.

Black Cal dropped his hands to his lap and bowed his head. "No good at it," he said, so quietly that she could barely hear him. "Could see it, but couldn't do it. Only admire."

"Sweet Jane's mercy," Rif whispered, dropping her gaze to her fingers. Think of all the music in those hands, so easily done, as natural as breathing. Imagine those fingers gone. Imagine your voice gone. Imagine all that music inside you, and no way to let it out. Imagine having the soul of an artist—and no art. "Oh, Lord and Lady! Nothing ye could do? Nothing at all?"

"Only one thing." Black Cal pointed to the long, holstered revolver on the bedpost. "Only that."

Rif tottered to the bed, momentarily clumsy, and sat down beside him. She could understand now how Black Cal could shoot so fast, at easily fifty meters' distance, in deep-night dark—and still take down a

Sword agent with every sho~~t~~
spent every day with her gitar, ~~much time as she~~
done—year in and year out—wit~~much must he have~~
gun. ~~long-barreled~~

"Ye must be the best shot on th~~e~~
guessed. Another insight jumped. "Is . . .
became a blackleg?"

He shrugged again. "What else could I do h~~e~~
crook myself? I couldn't put up with all the intri~~g~~
Hunt pelts in the north? I'd be alone all year, and . .
I do need . . . human company."

Rif heaved a long sigh and leaned her head on his
shoulder. "Poor Cal. What did ye do ter get born
inter a mess like this?"

"I don't know," he half smiled, "But it must have
been something really spectacular."

Rif chuckled, and unfastened the clasp of her cloak.
"No half measures fer you, eh?"

"No half measures."

Late-morning sun flecked the water as Ariadne
Delaney, winter-cloaked and hooded to almost incog-
nito, slipped into Klickett's shop. A glance showed no
one else present but Klickett herself, needles working
steadily as ever. Ariadne coughed politely for attention, something she rarely felt obliged to do. "Ah,
Klickett, are my sweaters ready yet?"

The shopkeeper set down her needles with a genuine smile. "That they be, m'sera. Right under the
counter here." She reached down, fumbled a moment,
then came up with a paper-wrapped bundle. "Ye sure
of the size, and all?" She unfolded the paper, revealing fine-knit sweaters in several sizes and colors.

"Beautiful," Ariadne murmured, cautiously strok-
ing the fabric. It was feather-soft, liberally patterned,
the colors glowing like jewels even in the dim shop-
front light. "I've brought full payment, of course."

For an instant their eyes met, catching each other in
faint but knowing grins. Klickett laughed first. "Ah,
m'sera, it's a fine customer y'are. I'd not trade ye fer a
dozen, not from The Rock itself."

"I'm relieved to hear it." Ariadne smiled wider,
then caught herself. Downright shocking, this pleasure

...ntrigue. Dark knowledge of ...now adolescent. Still, this was so ...ifferent from the endless round of ...ocializing, the dull business of injecting ...ight flatteries into wary ears before making ...mooth suggestions about Farren's honesty, capa-...lity, hard work and fitness for better tasks. That was so tedious, and so rarely rewarding. This was ... well, *real*.

"Do ye care fer riddles, m'sera?" Klickett asked, rewrapping the bundle.

"Hmm? Oh, sometimes. What sort of riddles?"

"Political ones."

"Oho! Er, why, yes." Damn, there was a jolt of that really scandalous enjoyment again. But what harm could it do?

"Well now, suppose ye was a really-truly honest blackleg, but yer officers was all corrupt. That'd be hell, now, wouldn't it?" Klickett busied herself with tying up the package in string, not looking up.

"Oh, Lord, yes!" Ariadne was forcibly reminded of Farren, wearing his life and hope away at unrewarded work. Yes, he knew that particular form of hell. She often watched him suffer it.

"Well, suppose ye learned of a really dangerous piece o' corruption goin' on, very high-up in the gover'ment, rankin' second only ter Old Iosef himself."

"That far?" Ariadne felt her pulse quickening.

"Now remember, ye can't send word through yer superiors, 'cause it'd never get where it should go." Klickett finished tying, leaned on the counter and looked up, smiling ever so faintly. "How would a poor honest blackleg get personally ter Old Iosef, ter give'm the information?"

Ariadne held her breath. *This is it!* she thought, jubilant and appalled. This was her chance to get involved in something truly dangerous, fateful, important. And *real*. Think! Oh, think! "Why . . . I'd manage to get to some . . . social gathering where I knew he'd be. Then I'd arrange to be alone with him for a moment, and tell him there." No risk so far; everyone with political experience knew that this was the way accurate information was put, quickly, in the proper ears.

"Ah, but how would a lowly canal-side blackie get himself invited ter a hightown social?" Klickett's look was wry, ironic, knowing.

Ah, here it was: chance and choice. Ariadne paused for a heartbeat to reconsider—then dived for it. "Well, I suppose you'd need a reliable friend in the hightown who could . . . make certain you were invited."

"Aye, and that's a hard part in itself," said Klickett, smiling wearily into Ariadne's eyes.

"I'm sure some honest person would be willing to help," Ariadne smiled back. "It would require some . . . delicacy, of course."

"Hmm, so it would." Klickett fiddled with the last bow-tie on the package. "By the by, m'sera, I know of a fine musician would be just right fer entertainin' at a small party—a luncheon, say—nothin' formal or large. Quite good fer 'intimate gatherings' though, if ye're interested."

"Ah, really?" Ariadne smiled prettily, calculations rattling furiously in her head. "How convenient! I was just thinking of a small luncheon party I must arrange soon. A discreet entertainer would be perfect. Could I get in touch with your friend, say, tomorrow?"

"Surely, m'sera," Klickett beamed. "Just come by to my shop and leave word, say when and where, no trouble at all."

"I'd like to meet your friend first," Ariadne insisted. Time to take the lead in this discussion, lest anyone consider her weak-willed. "After all, one can't plan a proper gathering without knowing, ah, all the details."

"As ye like," Klickett agreed. "I'm sure my friend could come by tomorrow aft'noon."

"Shall we say, just after lunch?"

"Deal," said Klickett, handing over the package, beaming from ear to ear.

"Deal," Ariadne echoed, proffering the coins. They amounted to the full price for the sweaters, with a generous tip. She almost added more, out of gratitude for the opportunity offered, then decided in favor of caution. Yes, she must be very cautious now. But damn, she hadn't felt so . . . well, *alive* since her wedding.

Black Cal spent the early morning strolling through the Harbormaster's offices, casually inquiring who had charge of paperwork for temporary private use of harbor facilities. The search eventually led to the Public Affairs office, headed by an overclerk named Yelno. Black Cal observed the man from a distance, then quietly went off to the Bursar's office and looked up Yelno's home address. He spent the rest of the morning padding around the upper bridges that gave a clear view onto the Yelno family apartments. He watched until he spotted the elder Yelno son heading off on some errand that required fashionable dress. Black Cal followed him for most of the afternoon, observing from a distance.

At midafternoon he came back to the Harbor Public Affairs office, and this time went straight to Yelno himself.

"Get this permit signed and handed back to me in ten minutes," Black Cal said, smiling toothily in the overclerk's face, "And I'll forget that I saw your oldest boy picking a College professor's pocket today."

Yelno paled, but put on a good show of harrumphing and whuffling.

"It was a professor of Religion and Ethics," Black Cal added, unimpressed. "Lots of uptown connections. I'm sure he'd love to know who pinched his purse."

"All right!" Yelno caved in. "But look, it'll take more than ten minutes. The harbormaster—"

"Fifteen, then." Black Cal glanced at the office wall-clock. "Not a second more."

"Half an hour! Please!"

"Twenty minutes. Then I head for the College."

"All right! All right!" Yelno snatched the permit-form and scurried off with it. Black Cal hummed one of Rif's tunes and watched the clock. Yelno was back, sweating profusely, in just under nineteen minutes. The form was properly signed and sealed. "There," the overclerk panted, slapping the paper down on the counter. "But look, there's gonna be trouble from the family, y'know. Old Fife's crazy as a water-bug, and his heirs'll be yelling bloody murder about this. All the money he'll spend . . ."

"The heirs will be too busy with their own problems," Black Cal promised, flashing his wolfish smile as he tucked the paper in his pocket. He could guess now who did the spying for Old Man Fife's so-concerned children. "They'll have much bigger things to worry about than their Papa's fun—and so will you, if you tip them off and blow this bust for me."

Yelno retreated into terribly-compliant sweating jelly. Black Cal turned to leave.

"But why're you so concerned about the old man?" Yelno dared to ask, as the tall blackleg pulled away from the counter. "What's Old Fife's fun and games to you?"

"Helps me flush the game," said Black Cal. "Besides, I want to see the show."

Iosef Kalugin's office was huge, tastefully furnished, and wonderfully quiet. No sound intruded on the governor's concentration, except the clean wind through the barely-opened window and the ticking of the clock on the ornamental mantlepiece.

Still, Old Iosef considered as he set down his pen and rubbed his eyes, he could do with a little diversion right now. Checking copies of census-records against Tatiana's official reports was a dreary business. The discrepancies were greater than he'd expected, but no pattern had emerged from them yet.

Except, of course, that his daughter was unfit to rule a junkyard, let alone a city. She might, in time, make a competent battle-officer, but at the moment her talents fitted her for no better work than a common assassin. Iosef ran his fingers through his still-thick white hair and sourly considered the ironic fact that those who were most adept at seizing power were often the most incompetent at using it. *And vice versa,* he added, thinking of his elder son.

As if answering his unspoken wish, his secretary tapped discreetly at the office door. The governor smiled and called her in, guessing from the coded knocking that this was no troublesome crisis or even nuisance. M'sera Pardee, his confidential secretary of twenty-three years and more, padded to his desk and handed him a small cream-colored envelope of thick embossed paper. He smiled again as he took out the note, recognizing the seal, stationery and signature. Ariadne Delaney was, to his tastes, one of the most charming hostesses in the city. He always felt relaxed and entertained at her parties.

And yes, this was an invitation—to a small informal luncheon with m'sera Delaney, at her residence, day after next. It also promised "some delightfully interesting news."

How intriguing. Ariadne had far better sense than to waste a whole luncheon with him on some blatant advertisement for her husband, or on petty gossip. The woman had a fine sense of proportion, as well as taste. No, this would be exactly as promised: interesting.

He pulled out a sheet and envelope of his own personal stationery to pen a suitable reply.

It was late when Rif finished her last set at Hoh's, but still she chose to take the foot-tracks and bridges to Coffin Isle. No point letting even Old Min get suspicious, much less allowing some unknown pole-boatman to guess her destinaion. She used more than her usual care to be sure she wasn't seen or followed.

Coffin Isle was dark, save for the hint of lamplight behind the curtains on the upper story. She fumbled at the doorway for the hidden bell-pull. There was no sound she could detect, but a moment later the door whispered open. Even in the thick shadows she could make out the relief on Black Cal's face. He pulled her inside and shut the door behind her.

"Thought you weren't coming," he whispered, sliding his hands up her arms.

"Late night at Hoh's," she explained, reaching up for him.

That was all they said for the rest of the way up the stairs, and for an hour thereafter.

Eventually Rif pulled herself up from the tumble of quilts and pillows, and made a leisurely study of her astonishing bed-partner. He lay sprawled like a string-cut puppet in the rumpled bedclothes, still gulping air as if he'd run the length of the city and back, green eyes wide and soft and unfocused. He looked stunned, she thought—and no surprise, considering that long intense climax that had seemed to wring out his whole body. She'd seen men die with less struggle and frenzy. *How long,* she wondered, *has he gone without?*

Soft lamplight picked out his scars, as if he were covered with a fine, loose-weave, silver net. Those transverse lines on his forearms were easy to read; she had a few herself from blocking knife-attacks. The puckered, small, round marks were bullet-wounds. How had he survived that one in the chest? Ah, there: exit-wound under the arm—the bullet had turned on a rib. Lucky as well as tough, Black Cal.

Other marks were less explicable. Where did he get that chevron-shaped cut on his hip? Banging into a roof-corner, maybe? And who or what gave him that monstrous-long cut on the top of one thigh, leaving a small scar across his penis and continuing on the other leg? She ran a sympathetic finger down its length, pondering.

He flinched.

"Who did that?" Rif asked calmly. "He still alive anywhere?"

"Oh, no." Black Cal smiled. "He's probably drifted down to Dead Harbor by now. Pieces of him, anyway."

Rif laid her chin on his breastbone and blinked up into his deep green eyes. "Ye've paid one hell of a price f' yer art," she murmured.

"Yes." Black Cal squeezed his eyes shut for a moment, then shook off the mood. "Almost forgot something." He rolled to the side of the bed, reached for his coat on the chair and pulled a thick envelope out of a pocket. "Here," he said, handing it to her. "Master Milton's permit, with ten copies. Tell him to keep the original in a safe place and hand the others out to any blackleg who asks."

"Nice," Rif breathed, looking through the papers. "Hmm, I got some news fer you, too. She got up, went to the tumble of her clothes on the floor, stuffed the envelope into her shoulder-bag and came back with a folded piece of paper. "We got a lunch date almost clinched in hightown, day after t'morrow, this address. I got t' see the lady first, afternoon tomorrow, prove I can look an' act hightownish, seal the deal."

Black Cal chuckled. "sure you can act like a proper lady?"

"Sure." She cuffed him lightly on the shoulder. "I've acted before—and fer my life as well's fer my living. Can ye tell me anything about this lady, anything that might help?"

"Not really. Only that her husband's one of the few honest bureaucrats in-city, so he hasn't gotten far." Black Cal sighed. "You'll have to win the m'sera over by yourself. Sure you can do it?"

"Hell, yes. I listened to 'er carefully from behind the curtain at—well, at a friend's place. Ye can tell a lot from how somebody talks. Besides, Rattail's coaching me; lending me some fancy clothes too. I'll do 'er right."

"Hope so," said Black Cal, studying the note. "This is . . . a very hightown address, just short of The Rock itself. There's a lot riding on your performance."

"And yours, Black Cal." Rif gave him a long, somber look. "Tell yer story smooth and well. Old Iosef himself's coming to the party."

"Lord and Ancestors," Black Cal murmured, staring at her. "Rif, you're amazing."

"Ain't we a pair!" she laughed, snuggling into his neck.

"Damned right," he agreed, wrapping his arms around her. "Who would've imagined this?" *And,* the tactical corner of his mind added, *what they can't predict, they can't prevent.*

Ariadne entered Klickett's shop cautiously, first giving a quick backward look at the water and walkways to make sure she wasn't observed. She marveled at how quickly—and, dare one say it, happily—she'd adjusted to the mind-set of intrigue. Her boatman sat yawning at the tie-up, absently watching the small load of packages from her previous shopping, too thoroughly bored to remember half the stops they'd made that afternoon. There would be more tedious stops before he took her home. Nothing here to catch the attention, snag the memory, in the sight of a plainly-dressed woman going into a knitting-shop. She only hoped that Klickett's "friend" was equally discreet.

The interior was dim enough to make the eyes wait a few moments to adjust. Dimmer than normal? Probably. Yes, there sat Klickett, smiling acknowledgment, working her eternal needles. And there, an unfamiliar motion in a corner; just a young woman picking over some samples of yarn. Another shopper, or the contact she'd come to meet? The woman certainly didn't look like a blackleg. Perhaps a go-between?

"Ah, m'sera," Klickett purred, "Ye've come fer an order?"

"Possibly," Ariadne smiled, glancing toward the other woman. Smoothly, now. "But if you're busy with another customer . . . ?"

"M'sera Delaney, this is m'sera Alvarez—musician," said Klickett, not missing a stitch.

So, the game *did* have another level. Good, very good. "So pleased to meet you," said Ariadne, offering a polite hand and a genuine smile as she studied her new contact. Hmm, a medium-tall slender woman with long dark hair and sharp features, a generally athletic build and coordination to match, good polite smile and equally-acceptable handshake. Clothing quite acceptable: good-quality long overblouse in a rich but subdued maroon fineweave, matching tousers with fashionably-flared cuffs, modest but good-quality jewelry on the collar and cuffs, unobtrusive black shoes. An entertainer who could fit smoothly into a society gathering. Very good.

"Charmed, m'sera." The voice was perfect, too: accentless, faintly cultured, precise, just the right amount of warmth—and giving nothing away. In fact, the surface was so smooth that Ariadne could find no purchase on it. She'd have to make the first explorative move.

"Ah, do you play professionally, then?" Tsk. A weak move.

"Certainly," said Rif, actually enjoying the evaluation game, "Though I prefer to work in . . . more private circles."

Ariadne glanced briefly at Klickett, who only grinned.

No help there. No choice but to plunge ahead. "Marvelous. I wish I could hear you, er, perform."

"I regret I haven't brought my instrument with me." The intonation was ever so faintly stilted, hinting at a carefully-expunged accent, but the smile was letter-perfect. "Perhaps you could hear me sing at the College next month."

Actually, Rif smiled inwardly, she'd be singing in one of the taverns that students frequented, much to the annoyance of their professors. Not exactly a lie, but artfully slanted. Pity the Delaney woman didn't appreciate the illusion.

Still, Ariadne picked up enough significant facts to proceed. "Oh, you perform solo? Have you done the drawing-room circuit, perhaps?"

"Oh, on occasion," Rif tossed off, "but I've no appointments there at the moment." Perfect opening. Now wait for it.

Subtle offer, Ariadne considered. Yes, she'd do. Take the moment. "How wonderfully fortunate! I have a small luncheon gathering tomorrow, and I was just wondering what to do for the entertainment. Would you possibly be available . . . ?"

"Why, I'd be delighted," Rif purred. "Of course, I'll need to know when and where, how long to perform, what sort of mood to create . . . that sort of thing."

Ariadne maintained her smile without a twitch as she reached into her purse for a formal card. "Do come early," she added, "A good hour before noon, so we can go over the precise . . . arrangements."

"Certainly," said Rif, sliding card into a pocket.

Is that all? Ariadne wondered. *No mention of the . . . other?* For one horrid moment she thought she might have failed the test, wasn't to be trusted yet.

But then Rif added casually: "May I invite a gentleman friend?"

Ariadne blinked twice, but maintained her smile. "By all means, bring him with you," she said, reaching into her purse again. She took out a second card and handed it over, just in case the "gentleman friend" might need to come separately.

Rif acknowledged the subtlety with a beaming smile.

"Thank you so much," she said, tucking her second private passport away with the first. "Now I simply must run off to prepare. Tomorrow, then." With admirable speed, not losing an iota of poise, she swung an indigo cloak over her shoulders and swept quietly out of the shop. She left no sound of footsteps beyond the door.

Ariadne turned back to Klickett. "She's very good," she acknowledged.

"That she is, m'sera," the shopkeeper agreed. "Very talented."

"I hope she can perform that well in front of the governor," Ariadne let fall, secretly gratified by the rise of Klickett's eyebrows at the news. "And her friend . . . ?"

"Ah, he's the legendary Honest Servant, what needs no more skill than the plain truth, m'sera. You just tell 'm the right time ter drop the news."

"I'll give them an hour's briefing and practice," Ariadne promised. "It's very important to get all the details right."

"Hmm, true."

"You know, Klickett, I must confess I'm beginning to enjoy this."

"Lord help us all," Klickett muttered, "what've I gone an' set loose on the world?"

CHAPTER XIX

TREADING THE MAZE
by Leslie Fish

"First you pick out a good vantage-point." Black Cal waxed downright talkative with the two wide-eyed rookies. "Say, here, along this wall. This gives you a good view of the main door, and if you lean your head against the wall itself you can hear a lot that goes on inside."

The two neophyte blacklegs dutifully ground their ears against the wall of the Sofia Island apartment, wondering what the legendary super-blackleg was planning. One of them dared to ask: "How do you know there's anything to watch or listen for?"

"That's the result of legwork," Black Cal purred, watching the walkway outside the Fife-junior apartment's front door. "No substitute for legwork. You spend enough time patrolling the canals, watching carefully, and you see patterns. You also pick up gossip. You overhear things. In time you learn when and where things are likely to happen, and you arrange to be there. —Ah, hush now."

It was the old man's daughter Rosita, and no mistake, overfed and overdressed, flouncing merrily out the front door. Now if she missed seeing the poster. . .

No, she saw it. The thing was rather hard to miss, plastered as it was on the railing just opposite the doorway. Something new, big and bold and messy on the elegant railing. She saw it, all right. She stopped and came closer. She read it.

Black Cal, watching her expression, could almost guess which lines she was reading. "Master Milton's Magic Show! Outdoor Extravaganza! East Dike, foot of Pier 9! Room for All!" Puzzlement and annoyance there, deepening as she read through the date and time, turning to worry as she read the descriptions. "Magic! Music! Fireworks! The Greatest Show on Merovingen! Sights Never Before Seen!" Any second now she'd get down to the fine print.

Aha! She'd hit it! "A Rafael Fife Production." Oh, see the shock, hear the squawk. Right, she ripped the poster off the rail and went running back into the house with it, squalling loud enough to be heard without the ear-to-the-wall trick. Nonetheless, Black Cal pressed his head close to the plastered wood and signaled to the two rookies to do likewise.

They could hear the whole thing: the yells of outrage, the wails of what'll-we-do, the frantic—and silly—plotting. Oh, these two fools were never designed for conspiracy! They probably never even looked out the window to see if anyone was listening. Amazing. The two rookies' eyes grew round as they took in the clear, damning conversation.

"Why didn't your inside-man warn us?" Rosita wailed. "Why didn't he stop the permit, or lose it? Lord knows, we pay him enough!"

"Must've slipped past him," a male voice—Pavel—rumbled. "Or maybe Pop figured it out and counter-bribed him, or blew the whistle. *I* don't know. Maybe we should just rip all the damned posters down."

"What good will that do?" Rosita shrilled. "He's already spent the money, if it's gone this far. You know this'll get worse! How do we stop him from spending the money?"

"Oh, Lord, I don't know." Sounds of a frustrated fist pounding a desk. "All we can do is hope he drops dead soon."

"We've tried before," Rosita considered.

"And you know what happened. His damned boatman fought off the thugs. Can't do that again; you can bet Pop's always got bullyboys around him now. I can't afford to hire a top-notch assassin."

The rookies' eyes grew bigger and rounder. They pulled out pads and began scribbling notes. Black Cal only grinned, listening.

"Maybe we should try poison this time." Rosita sounded desperate enough to be utterly sincere. "Go visit him, drop it in his wine, leave the bottle in some servant's room."

"Rosita, that's disgusting. Blaming some innocent retainer . . ."

"But it would work."

"Hmm. Where could we get poison? Quietly?"

Both rookies were scribbling madly. Black Cal laughed to himself. If only all his cases could be this easy.

"We have some left over from the Cantry's," Rosita noted—as the rookies duly copied down the name. "I'll go get it."

"Make sure it's in a small enough bottle," Pavel called after her retreating footsteps.

"Yes, yes. And we'll go on foot, so the boatman won't talk."

The conversation ended in a thumping of moving feet, rattling of cabinet doors, whispers of cloaks being taken down and tied on. Nothing more to learn here. Chuckling softly, Black Cal led his two worshipful rookies around to the front door and placed them neatly on either side of it. He took up his own position farther down the walkway, just on the off chance that the two fools tried to run.

Ten minutes later, Pavel and Rosita Fife strode out their front door, cloaked and muffled for a long foot-journey across the city. They got all of two steps before the heavy hands fell on their shoulders, making them jump in unison.

"You're under arrest!" said the rookies together.

Smiling, smiling, Black Cal strolled up with the cuffs. "Folks," he purred, "you really ought to know your limitations."

The rookies made a fine show of handcuffing the dismayed Fife siblings, searching them, finding the fatal little bottle and stuffing it ceremoniously in an evidence-bag—all in front of a growing and appreciative crowd of neighbors and passersby. They were also hyper-efficient at marching the two prisoners straight down the shortest route—which happened to be the main walkway—to the Signeury, and swatting them righteously with batons when they protested too much. Black Cal brought up the rear of the little parade, content to let the rookies have their moment of honest glory. It all made quite a show for passing citizens, of whom there were many.

At the Signeury, the duty-officer took one look at the oncoming procession, and almost formally waved the handcuffed and disheveled couple into one of the better-quality cells. He had the forms ready and his pen out, clearly expecting this.

"How did you know we were coming?" Black Cal asked him. "We took the shortest route here. And how did you get the blue-ribbon cell clear so fast?"

"Aw, hell, Cal," the turnkey laughed, "we knew it this morning, when you took the rookies out."

"Really? Who told you?"

"Needed no telling. You only volunteer to train rookies when you're goin' out to bust hightown perps." The duty-officer gave a knowing wink. "The kids're too green to be bought up already, and there's too many of 'em f'r the perps' hightown lawyers to discredit. Real predictable, eh?"

Black Cal only laughed.

The sun was peeping out through the cloud-deck when the governor's small informal poleboat pulled up to the Delany slip. His lead boatman hopped out to secure the craft and follow the old man in, but Iosef Kalugin waved him back and strolled to the front door alone. He knew very well he was as safe here as on The Rock proper.

The door opened noiselessly, and a liveried doorman bowed him in. Inside, an immaculately-dressed maid took his coat, ushered him to the glassed-in east balcony, announced him at the door and discreetly vanished.

Ariadne rose to welcome him, dressed in a delightfully casual and form-fitting suit of heavy wheat-colored cotton, surmounted by one of those marvelous sweaters she almost always wore. She introduced him to the only other guests, and the governor's eyebrow—and estimation of his hostess—rose noticeably.

"Black Cal, no less," he smiled, shaking the tall blackleg's hand. "Of course I've heard of you. You're quite a legend, you know."

"I only hope I can live up to it, m'ser," Black Cal replied in that unnervingly quiet voice.

"And this is m'sera Alvarez," Ariadne neatly turned to Rif. "A musician, who'd like to entertain us today."

"Charmed," said Iosef, formally taking her hand. He noted the calluses, and the good-quality—if well-used—gitar held in the other hand. Yes, quite the professional. Ariadne always chose the best entertainment, always perfectly fitting to the occasion, even if the artists were sometimes quite obscure. Not that he kept track of the entertainment world, really; no time for it. "I look forward to hearing you perform."

"Delighted to oblige, m'ser." The woman smiled prettily and stepped back to her chair, discreetly pulling her instrument to the ready position.

So much for the hired help. That meant the only other guest here was Black Cal. He must have the "interesting news" that Ariadne promised. Intriguing, indeed.

"Shall we sit down?" Ariadne said, guiding them to a roomy arrangement of thick-cushioned wicker chairs, set about a circular glass-topped table.

Iosef sat, noting the unobtrusive comfort of the chairs, the understated elegance of the peach-toned tableware, the nice accents of tall potted plants that were actually thriving in the uncertain winter light. In fact, it was warm enough up here on the sun-heated balcony that he almost regretted having worn his woolen suit. Well, no harm to unbutton his jacket in this setting. Only Black Cal was watching him; m'sera Alvarez was tuning her gitar, and Ariadne was ringing a sweet-toned little brass bell for the maid. Iosef unfastened his jacket and pulled it open.

Drinks arrived, another of Ariadne's superb wine-and-fruit-juice concoctions, with a round of small spiced rolls and a cheese assortment. The entertainer took a ritual mouthful of her drink before commencing on a quiet romantic piece, very well played: a good background for light conversation, which Ariadne managed splendidly, as always.

After one and a half glasses of the fruit-punch, half a dozen assorted cheese canapés and the usual round of polite questions and answers about unimportant doings of friends and family, Iosef felt sufficiently assured to ask about the "interesting news."

"Ah, that you should hear from the source," Ariadne crooned, swirling her free hand elegantly toward Black Cal. *And pray he can say this right,* she added to herself. One hour's coaching might not have been enough.

All but forgotten, Rif switched to another song: a long classic ballad from the fabled Reconstruction era.

> *Honest Rowan was a hunter, good as any in the north.*
> *But the game were few and scattered. To the city she set forth.*
> *Who would have an honest servant? Ill the master that she found.*
> *Ill the day that wicked Tymann to his service had her bound.*

Black Cal fiddled quietly with his empty glass. "You know my reputation," he began.

"Oh, yes," Iosef encouraged. "Quite the legendary egalitarian."

"I'm interested in justice, actually." Black Cal looked up. "It's the law that sometimes gives me trouble. The two aren't the same."

"That's a rather widespread problem," the governor noted dryly. "I take it you've stumbled on an interesting conflict of interest."

> *'As I see you are a hunter, I command you hunt my foes*
> *In the streets about the city, in the alleys no one knows.*
> *Militiar and money-lender and the high priest I would choose.*
> *Go you forth and do my bidding. By your oath, you can't refuse.'*

"I've come across something too big to go public without ironclad proof," said Black Cal. "I can't get proof enough to push this past some, ah, prejudiced parties among my superiors."

"Too big?" Iosef leaned back in his chair, seeing where this led. "Politics, is it?"

"Politics," Black Cal agreed. "Very big politics. Very damned dangerous politics."

The governor nodded sympathy. Another police scandal, obviously. "How far up does the . . . problem go?"

"Right to the top." Black Cal locked eyes with him. "Your daughter's in it. In fact, she's half of it."

Iosef laughed. Tatiana again. What, something connected with her laughable mishandling of the census? Some juicy scandal with that Nev Hettek trade-pimp she was bedding these days? Another damned coup attempt? "Well, how bad is it?"

"Pretty bad." Black Cal shoved his glass aside. "I have some canalside sources who're refugees from Nev Hettek. Some of them recognized Tatiana's new lover."

"Indeed?" Oh, a household scandal, then. How bad could that be?

"He's not just pushing for Hettek trade. He's a very high-placed Sword of God agent, probably commander of all the other Sword agents in the city. Lord knows what he can do from his . . . new position. Lord knows what he's done already."

"In . . . deed." Iosef sat back to consider that. His own agents in Tatiana's offices and household hadn't learned this much. The implications were appalling.

> 'To the high priest Rowan went. 'Oh, Father, my
> confession take.
> I am sent to slay a priest, bound by an oath I
> cannot break.
> What now can an honest servant to an evil master
> do?
> I must bring your head to Tymann; for my target,
> ser, is you

"I can't trust my own officers with this," Black Cal went on. "Who else could I tell it to?"

"Yes, I see." The governor absently wiped his mustache with a napkin, plotting rapidly in his head. The one thing he did not doubt was that the information was good; Black Cal's reputation was legendary, and Ariadne's—though known only to a few—was equally sound. What a pity that the news had been obliged to take two steps, at least, and Lord knew how long, to reach him. He really needed more informants canalside. But remedy that later; for now, he would need every warm body to shadow and study the Nev Hettek man. Meanwhile, say something appropriate.

"Ah, yes. I find it distressing that there are no reliable routes whereby the, er, lower echelons can file complaints directly to the top of the system." Iosef hoped that didn't sound too pompous to his co-guest and hostess. It sounded laughably trite to him.

"That *is* something of a problem," Ariadne murmured.

"Yes, I've often thought that our time-honored patronage system had serious flaws." Oh, platitudes! Get out of here and deal with the problem at hand. The governor looked out over the water, apparently taken with the view. "Something really must be done about this." *Tatiana, you idiot!*

> *Out then sprang the high priest, angry, pistol*
> *drawn and spitting lead.*
> *Three times fast and sure he fired, and shattered*
> *wicked Tymann's head.*
> *'Go you free now, Honest Rowan, for your service*
> *here is done.*
> *Wicked master's honest servant, take the freedom*
> *you have won.'*

"Would you care for some more cheese?" Ariadne offered, neatly allowing for a change of pacing.

"Ah, no thank you, my dear." Iosef turned back to her, smiling his public smile. "A man my age really must watch his weight. In fact . . ." He drew out a gold pocket-watch and studied it briefly. "I really should go take my afternoon walk before heading back to work. Sorry to cut short this most excellent luncheon, but duty calls."

Black Cal glanced, bewildered, from one to the other.

Ariadne rang for the maid, who appeared with the governor's cloak almost before he'd pulled himself out of his chair. He made polite apologies and farewells all around, spending a few seconds longer with Black Cal. "Do come chat with me again some time, won't you?" he offered, pumping the taller man's hand. "I'm always happy to visit with the delectable Ariadne."

"Right," said Black Cal, catching the implication. *Meet here. No direct contact otherwise.* "Good health, governor."

"Ah, and to you, too." A last smile, and Old Iosef departed in an elegant swirl of cloak. They heard his footsteps gathering speed as he retreated through the house.

Ariadne held up a silencing finger, stepped quietly to the edge of the balcony and looked down. The other two followed her example. Below they could clearly see the boat-slip, Old Iosef's poleboat, and himself getting into it with uncharacteristic speed. They could all see his sharp command-gesture that sent the boat away at the best pace the polemen could make without drawing undue attention.

"You'll note that he isn't walking," said Ariadne.

"He's heading toward the Signeury," Black Cal added.

"Is that it?" said Rif, setting down her gitar. "Did he get it all? Will he move on it?"

"My dear," Ariadne smiled, "You can see that he's already moving."

Rif and Black Cal traded a look, a flickering smile of dawning hope, and the slightest brush of fingers.

Ariadne caught that, and marveled. So, even legends had a private life. How delicious. What an intriguing bonus to the afternoon's success. *I not only like political intrigue,* she realized, *I'm actually good at it!*

Instantly, she thought of Farren. She could open doors for him now. And what had the governor just said about needing more direct channels of information between the highest and lowest echelons? Who was in a better position to do it, to communicate with the vast ranks of the Shoeless? *Farren, my love, this will make your career.*

"Ah, well," she purred, dropping back into her chair. "My dear friends, if you have no pressing engagements, why not help me finish this excellent luncheon—and enjoy a small victory party?"

"Why not?" Rif grinned, looking at Black Cal.

He nodded agreement, guessing as well as she did where this could lead.

*   *   *

When the day burned down to lamplighting time, Tatiana Kalugin thankfully quit her office desk and its mountain of dreary reports. Time to go home, relax, change clothes and plan dinner with a certain merchant-captain. What a pity that she'd have nothing new or interesting to discuss with him tonight, but they could always amuse themselves in other ways. They could always play, over dinner, at inventing new embarrassments to spring on the pious old frauds of the College. . . .

As she passed the outer door, she noted that the usual man wasn't on duty. Corday, the night-shift guard, was there early.

"Where's Yovannan?" she asked in passing.

"Down with the Crud, m'sera," he said. "A lot of the staff have it."

"Hmm. Well, rework the roster. Just don't leave us short-handed up here." Thoughts elsewhere, she strode on down the hall.

"Aye, m'sera," Corday answered dutifully, watching her go. He waited a few seconds, then ambled to the nearest window and casually looked out. And rubbed his nose.

Down below, a waiting boatman caught the signal and scratched his ear in acknowledgment.

The guard went quietly back to his post.

Large outdoor entertainments were rare in Merovingen, particularly in the wet winter months, and therefore drew large crowds when they did occur. This one had been widely advertised, also. By sundown, the crowd on East Dike was huge. Fife-house retainers, selling tickets at the openings of the roped-off viewing area, rapidly filled their cash-boxes. Pushcart peddlers did a hot and fast trade in food, drink, drugs and souvenirs.

Old Man Fife, seated comfortably at the roped-off top of the central staircase to the dike's upper level, smiled benignly at the crowd. He was making a mint off this show, and his worthless brats would never see a penny of it.

Below him rippled the crowd, dress identifying everything from hightown to canalside. Pickpockets were busy there. So were the blacklegs assigned to crowd-control for the event; they'd asked surprisingly low bonus payment to do the extra work.

Black Cal strolled through the sea of bodies, stopping briefly to purchase two mugs of wine, looking as affable as anyone else in the audience. No one watching him would have noted that he had a specific goal in mind, but eventually his meandering footsteps led to the top of the northern stairs, far above the main body of the crowd.

Rif sat there, on the topmost step, one end of her indigo cloak stretched out almost accidentally beside her. Black Cal made sure no one was watching, and sat quietly on the spread cloak. He handed one of the mugs to Rif and leaned close.

"We won't hear much up here," Rif told him, "but we'll have the best all-around view, of everything."

"Right." Black Cal took a pull of the wine. Not bad at all. And the sky was clear, and the wind not bad, and the weather generally warm for this time of the year. "Master Milton couldn't have picked a better night."

"The Janist weather-scholars picked 'er." Rif eased a little more of her weight against him. "That's why the timing was so important, couldn't wait ter hunt up another patron. —Hey, she's starting."

It was time. Master Milton's four assistants came out to the edge of the surprisingly high stage they'd built on the pier's foot, and blatted noisily on cheap trumpets. The oversize sleeves of their gaudy costumes flapped in the light wind. The crowd cheered, then quieted and watched. The fantastically-garbed assistants picked up megaphones and brayed into the opening spiel of the show. The crowd listened awhile, chuckled a bit, mumbled softly with private comments and conversations.

Black Cal frowned. The show already looked cheap and tinselly to him, and not just to him, to judge from maybe ten percent of the crowd's reactions. The rest of the crowd seemed to like it, though. Too bad he couldn't hear the pitch from this distance.

The assistants retreated around the ends of the stage-curtain, and then the central portion opened to reveal

Master Milton, wearing a ridiculous sequined outfit. Behind him, what appeared to be an almost-equally-gaudy coffin lay on a cloth-draped bier. Leaning against it was a huge two-man saw.

"The sawing-the-woman-in-half trick, with all the trimmings," Rif purred. "The crowd ought ter eat that up."

The crowd did. Voices gasped and moaned appreciation as the saw cut noisily into the box, screeched in delighted horror as fake blood splashed out all over the stage, groaned and shivered when Master Milton pulled the two coffin-pieces apart to show the red-drenched ominous gap where the shapely female assistant's torso had been, then screeched in surprise when he made his Mystic Passes with the sparkly Magic Wand—and the two huge decorative urns on either side of the stage shot up sudden tongues of odd-colored fire.

"There's the first flash-paper," Rif noted. "Watch how he'll use 'em at the climax of every trick."

"Priming the pump," Black Cal guessed. "Getting the crowd used to fireworks."

The trumpets squawked, a noisy drum banged, the coffin opened up and the shapely female assistant jumped out smiling from ear to ear. The crowd roared and cheered while the troop took exaggerated bows. There was more inept-but-loud music while other assistants rolled out an oversized sea-chest.

"That's fer the trunk-vanish trick," Rif explained. "She'll have two flares o' flash-paper fer that. One when he makes 'er disappear, the other when he brings 'er back."

She was right. There were also loud drum-rolls while Master Milton poked big shiny imitation swords through the trunk's slats, and more fake blood ran out on the stage.

"I hope they don't slip on that crap," Black Cal yawned. "Does it get any sleazier than this?"

"Not much. They can't afford ter look too clumsy."

"Afford to?" Black Cal frowned at her. "Wait, Rif. All that effort for a show this cheap-looking . . . Are you telling me it's deliberate?"

"Hell, yes." Rif grinned. "Don'tcher see it? He's

using fireworks fer a style-trademark, fer a tinselly-sleaze magic show—and everybody that sees it links those two things together."

Black Cal felt his jaw drop.

"Ye see?" Rif insisted. "Get the crowd ter make the connection: fireworks equals cheap trick."

Black Cal stifled a whoop of laughter. "That's why the costumes look so silly? And the tickets are so cheap? And— Lord, it's brilliant! The style's part of the message. Every detail thought out. The sheer art— Rif, I love you!" He froze as he realized what he'd just said.

Rif thought it over for a handful of seconds, while onstage the trunk opened and the assistant hopped out. "What the hell, I guess I could love you too, Black Cal."

Almost shyly, he took her hand. "What a hell of a team we make," he said, watching the urns flare while Master Milton pulled all manner of ridiculous objects—including his shapely female assistant—out of a supposedly-empty barrel. "No one could expect anything like us. Nobody can predict us . . ."

"You an' me, Black Cal," Rif murmured, running her thumb across his long fingers. "Hell, we've got connections all the way from Tidewater ter The Rock, and we know every trick in the book between us. What in hell can't we do?"

Black Cal bent close and kissed her. Rif kissed back. They necked like teenagers all the way to the Grand Finale.

The crowd was ecstatic and restless when Master Milton, in a final horn-blare and drum-bang fanfare, turned his back to the audience—displaying a cloak patterned with sequined star-symbols—yelled his longest-yet mouthful of mystical mumbo-jumbo, and gestured theatrically at the horizon.

From the far end of the darkness-hidden pier, the first rockets leaped for the sky. The crowd gasped, shrieked, howled, and stared in fixed-eyed fascination at the whistling spark-trails that burst into multicolored fire-flowers. Master Milton smoothly continued his Mystical Passes. More rockets went up, bigger and noisier. Their thunder interrupted the growing noises of shocked recognition from the crowd. Whistle! Boom! Gunpowder stinks and rainbow spark-showers flooded the night.

"Now! Now comes the Roman-candle!" Rif had to shout. "Watch!"

At the end of the pier a tall fountain of gold, red and white sparks shot skyward, illuminating its accompanying black-powder cloud.

It also clearly picked out Master Milton's assistants at the end of the pier, running about with fuse-lighters on the ends of long poles, busily firing the wicks of fat rocket-tubes that sat in an orderly rack overhanging the water. By now, everyone could recognize the growing, acrid smell of gunpowder.

Everyone also saw one of the fresh-lit smaller rockets break free—accidentally?—from the rack and go bucketing across the pier. In the multiple spark-shower they saw one of the assistants chase after the runaway rocket, swatting at it with the end of his pole, until a—deliberately?—lucky blow booted the fugitive off the pier and into the dark water, where it hissed and sank to oblivion.

Master Milton continued to gesture theatrically and shout impressive gibberish, but no one was paying attention anymore. Crowd-voices stopped keening in fright and began rumbling and bellowing in recognition, relief and outrage. The words "sharrh" and "cheap trick" were repeated often and loud enough to be audible up to the top of the stairs.

"It's working!" Black Cal laughed like a kid. "They've caught on."

"We did it!" Rif sang. Then she caught at Black Cal and kissed him furiously.

The knowledge brought the crowd to action, but none of it unified. One batch of bravos tried to storm the stage—and discovered why it was built so tall. Confused blacklegs spotted them, saw something they could take action on, and swatted the mob back with riot batons. A larger section of the crowd condensed into a noisy brawl. Blacklegs waded into that, too. Smaller knots of onlookers—arguing, guessing, calculating, swapping theories—formed spontaneously all over the dock-level. One knot of religious opportunists tried to start up an obscure hymn. They were shouted down before finishing half a verse, and another brawl started. Quick-thinking lovers grabbed each other and ducked behind any available objects for quick sessions of frantic groping. A small gang of well-soaked drunks or druggies sat on the edge of a loading-dock, watching the whole spectacle with placid smiles. A wedge of mixed College students and priests struggled toward the nearest exit, eyes gleaming, some of them even jotting notes on their tablets as they fled. On the central steps, safely encircled by his defiant bodyguard, Old Man Fife laughed so hard that a few of his retainers worried about the possibility of heart attack.

Rif and Black Cal laughed until they fell over. They came up wheezing and gulping, to note that the stage-curtain had closed and Master Milton was nowhere in sight.

"Smart of him," Black Cal chuckled. "I hope he had the sense to shed those robes and jump off the pier."

"How'd you guess?" Rif panted. "Actually, the boat's waiting at the end o' the pier."

"Can he get safely out of town?"

"He ain't goin' ter. He'll show up in a couple days ter collect his money from Old Fife. Then the blacklegs'll catch 'im and take 'im ter the College t'answer lots of angry questions. No worries; he's got his answers all ready. He'll teach 'em lots about rockets while he's talking."

"Brilliant! Everybody learns, every detail planned. Damn, Rif, that's two Sword of God plots we've spoiled, in as many days."

"And more t' come," Rif promised. "Oh, the last salvo's coming up."

Black Cal laughed again. "What a crazy alliance we make. But hell, it works." He hugged her shamelessly. "Swords or sharrh, crooks or priests or politicians—all hell can't stop us."

"To the stars," she whispered against his neck. "All the way to the stars."

They sat sprawled on the top stair, hugging like a

pair of romantic kids, while the crowd roared and tangled below, and the last salvo of fireworks whistled and boomed and lit the sky like the blaze of day. Nobody noticed them at all.

EPILOGUE

TROUBLED WATERS
by C. J. Cherryh

The sky lit. Jones saw it go, figured every eye in Megary was turned toward *those* windows, the few windows there were at all in Megary.

And she skimmed right close to Ulger's side, silent as a whisper in the water.

Then she edged back to the crank. The pin was already in, securing the tiller. Awkward as sin to pole with the bar up and the engine fixed. But she had worked on that damn crank. She shoved it over and *this* time it caught on the first try.

Fast, now. No shakes. Get home to Mondragon, before he took to panic and started searching. He was out on his business. She was out on hers. It's all right, she had told the boys. Ye c'n go up, sit on the roof, watch th' show. A'right?

Maybe she had made it downstairs and away from the tie-up without the boys seeing at all. Probably not. Probably they had heard the boat moving and taken a look about then. But by then she was well away and *they* had to get off the roof.

The match flared, warm in her hands. The fuel-soaked rag was brighter.

Crash! The bottle broke on Megary's doorstep and fire blazed up.

A bullet spanged off something solid.

About the time she shoved the throttle wide, keeping low to the deck, the way she had run with Moghi's cargos with the harbor patrol in pursuit.

Fire in the sky.

They were ringing the bell somewhere by the time she was passing Calder Bend, and crowds were still thick everywhere this close to the harbor, people pointing toward the sound of the bell, with the big bell of the Signeury tolling—

Fire! Fire! Fire!

Not a big one. Megary would have it out in short order. Pity to scare folk.

But the first time it had been a dead fish, in Megary's fancyboat.

The next time that fancyboat had had its bilge-plug bunged right out.

And a window had gone. Denny wasn't the only one could shoot a stone.

Mondragon was going to raise hell about her sneaking off. But he knew, damn right he knew—he couldn't hold her.

And Megary—Megary was going to come crawling to the Trade, or do something foolish. She knew that, sure as she knew the waterways and the dark places and sure as they knew what it meant when things like this started happening to a House.

You could do a lot of things in Merovingen.

But nobody laid hands on the Trade.

APPENDIX

MEROVINGIAN PHARMACOLOGY 103
/OR/
"POISON IN JEST"

(An exerpt from the lectures of
Father Ignatius Singh, M.D.)

Young m'sers and m'seras, the subject I deal with today is one which, if it has not already impinged on your life and karma, is one that, as a doctor of medicine you will be dealing with on a regular basis. This is the subject of poisons.

Accidental poisoning is a fact of life on Merovin. Even after many centuries of life here, we are still finding new substances which are incompatible with human biology. That a great many of these discoveries are as a result of man's regrettable never-ending search for new ways in which to intoxicate his body and further complicate his karma goes without saying. The borderline between intoxication and toxemia is often a narrow one—and I point out to you that the two terms spring from the same root as evidence that this has been long known. We are fortunate that our bodies are as resilient as they are.

But accidental poisioning is not my topic; you have already covered that particular lesson under the heading of "emergency medicine and first aid." No, the subject of *this* lecture is deliberate poisoning.

For all of the outre toxic substances available to the poisoner of this city, you will find that in seventy-five percent of the cases he has resorted to the old favorites of arsenic, lead, strychnine, or cyanide. Why? It is quite simple; they are *still* the easiest to dispense, the most readily obtainable, the hardest to trace. The poisoner in this case will almost always be an amateur, rather than a professional. And in spite of the old saying that "poison is a woman's weapon," is as likely to be male as female. Administration will usually have been by ingestion, although there have been some ingenious cases of contact poisoning by means of irritation of the skin and subsequent application of the poison in a soothing ointment. I will not trouble you with the symptoms of these four old favorites; you will find them in your Toxicology text. To judge whether your client has been poisoned by one of these four, look for the following: an unhappy lover, a low-to-moderate level business rival, a contractual partner wanting out, hostile sibling rivalry, an aged and demanding parent. In short, look for someone with an emotionally based reason for eliminating your client, and access to your client.

The professional poisoner will use more sophisticated means, often administering the poison in several doses so as to counterfeit disease. Frequently the only clue that you will have will be the fact that *no one else* in the household is suffering from this illness. The motivation here will be one of three possibilities: political, economic, or emotional. Professional assassins are not inexpensive, *especially* those employing the more sophisticated means of elimination that poison provides, and you are unlikely to find them practicing their trade anywhere other than hightown.

In the case of a political motivation, there are three main sources of poisons: the sharrists, the Sword of God, and the Janists. The sharrists are the least subtle and are likely to use poison gas; you will *know* that your client has been poisoned. Here the main problem will be solved for you; if your client lives past the first twenty-four hours, it will mean he has enough lung-tissue intact to guarantee a recovery. Since the chemicals are volatile, they will eventually be purged simply by continuing to breathe. Inhalation of steam, particularly the steam from water in which threadstem is being boiled, seems to help. The Sword of God normally employs contact or injected poisons (most notably deathangel spines) and again, it will be obvious that your client has been poisoned. Their chosen toxins are most frequently neurotoxins; recovery is unlikely, but some physicians have had a certain amount of success in marginal cases by keeping the client very quiet and—when the toxin has reached the respiratory system—employing CPR until the effect begins to wear off. This will require having a half dozen assistants trained in CPR; I would suggest picking out several of the most trustworthy family servants and expanding their education should you find yourself employed in a politically active household. The Janists prefer to utilize ingested poisons, and they prefer subtlety as well. It is to their advantage that the death seem to be an Act of Jane. But if your client has been involved in action against Janists and suddenly falls ill, it would be wise to assume that he has been the victim of an assassination attempt. It is fortunate that most of the poisons employed by the Janists are native in origin; they are thus survivable. Use of purgatives, diuretics and emetics can be very effective and win your client's unending gratitude.

We now come to the unusual poisoner—

When an unusual poisoning occurs, the motive is usually revenge. When the poison causes great pain, it is especially wise to look for the motive of revenge. Most poisons of this nature are such that they require a specific antitoxin; often they are venoms of one sort or another. It is possible to save your client through the use of stimulants; particularly cardiac stimulants. It is quite likely, however, that brain damage will have occurred; you may wish to consult with your client's family on whether heroic measures are in order. For a culprit, look for one who will have contact with, but is not himself, a Janist—insofar as truly sophisticated employment of native toxins goes, the Janists have no peers.

Now—m'seri, this last piece of information is strictly confidential. It is to remain with you. The second most common poisoner using very sophisticated means is the ambitious family member. In this case, you would be wise to step back a pace and examine your options. Your oath as a physician requires that you do all in your power for your client—but you may serve a higher karma by throwing in with the rising power. The decision is between you and your conscience. You should be aware, however, that the ambitious family member may be capable of removing such an inconvienient obstacle as the family physician. You should also be aware that such a family member may approach you as the vector of his ambition. In the case of a crisis of conscience on your part, you must consider yourself bound to seek out your spritual advisors here at the College and inform them of your suspicions—or your certainties. We are your best protectors; we are your friends and instructors. We alone are in possession of the larger picture and can effectively guide your decision. And you must rely on us to guide such decisions for you.

Thank you for your attention. Class dismissed.

RAJ'S LETTER TO MARINA

(Page 1)

Most Gratious and Beautiful lady Marina Kamat—
Without ever intending to, I have Tricked you in a Cruel
and Unforgivible way. I, who you thought was only
the Hand that delivered Another's message to you, am
actually the True Writer of those messages. I let you
continue to believe the Lye, because I was too much of
a Coward to tell you the Truth, and because I selfishly
thought this would allow me to continue to see you. I
am a fool. I am Worse than a Fool. I am a Worm. I am
a Devil. I have No Right to Live. I am not Worthy to
sweep the water-stairs of your house. Please do not vent
your Just Anger upon that Other; he knows Nothing
of this, it is All My Fault. Let your Anger fall upon me.

(Page 2)

I know you must be feeling both Betrayed and Hurt; I
know you wish Never to see me again. Rest assurred,
Fair Lady, your Wish shall be granted. You will never
again need to Bear the Agony of chancing to Spye one
who has caused you such Pain. I, who should By All
Rites be thrown from the Highest Bridge in Merovingen
for the Suffering I have caused you, am making certain you will Never See Me Again. I am going where
you shall never follow, if God is Just.

(Page 3)

My punishment is in my hands; my punishment is
that Never Again shall I Look upon your Face, alas.
And that is Agony enough, Fairest Lady—oh believe
me, it is. It is an Agony that shall be with me through
all Eternity and Beyond. Although I should be Tosst
into a fire, although I should be Made to Suffer Forever, yet I should rather endure any Torture than
this—but because I have caused you even more Pain
with my Foolishness and Cowardice, I shall Endure it,

for however small time I have yet to live, and Beyond
that into Death Itself.

(Page 4)
It may be that you do not even yet Believe the Magni-
tude of the Fraud I have created. Therefore to convince you, I offer you this, the very last of my poor
Poems, that You may Read it and know that it came
from the same Damnd Hand:

(Page 5)
    O shining Lady, clear and bright,
    O you who turns to day my night,
    O ever-perfect, diamant light,
    Forgive me, if you can.
    I, who am mud beneath your feet
    I am a villian most complete
    I who have hurt a heart so sweet
    And then turned tail and ran.
    O do not turn your eyes away
    For you shall turn the blue sky gray
    I shall no more darken your day
    Let tears not stop your breath
    But if, despite of all my lyes
    There is forgiveness in your eyes
    Then as my sorrowing soul then dies
    I shall most welcome Death.
    Yours Forever,
    Raj

RAJ'S LETTER TO JONES

Dear Altair Jones;

I am Sorry more than I can say for Causing you such a great Deal of Trouble. I can only say that I'll Never Be in your Way Again. Don't get mad at Tom—it wasn't any of it his Fault and he never had anything to do with the Lady. Please take care of Denny when I'm Gone.

Raj

RAJ'S LETTER TO MONDRAGON

Dear Tom;

I am a Bigger Fool than you ever thought I was. I've gone and got Both of us in Trouble. And you didn't even know what was going on. I was writing Poems to m'sera Marina Kamat—she's the girl, not some girl in a boat, I didn't dare tell you because of what happened—anyway she thought they was Coming From You. She had me into House Kamat, and she talked at me—I thought she knew it was me, and she was so Nice, so Sweet, she gave me supper and she kissed me—it was Dark before I knew it, and she gave me a Note—I read it and then I figured out she Thought it was You, not me, that wrote the Poems. That's in love with her. And I didn't know what to Do—she promised me she'd see about sponserring me into the College, God, I want that almost as much as I love her—

And All I had to do was keep writing Poems and making like they came from You. I could see her and talk to her—I might get to be in the College, even, get to be a real Doctor.

But I knew it wasn't Right. And—I asked a friend for some Advice, he told me if she ever found Out she'd be Real Angry, as much with you as me, and that isn't Right At All. It isn't Honorable. I can't Live like that.

So I done my best to fix it. I sent a letter over to Kamat Telling the Truth. And I left this One for you, and one where Jones'll find it.

Now I'm Going Away, so I can't Cause you any more Trouble. Seems I'm better at that than anything else. So at least you won't have to worry about what I'm going to get you into next, not any more. I'm sorry, Tom,— but Sorry don't buy too much and it don't fix anything, either. Just, please, keep Denny out of Danger when I'm gone, if you figure I've ever Done anything for you.

Rigel Takahashi

MEROVINGIAN SONGS

PARTNERS

Lyrics by Mercedes Lackey ©1987
Music by C. J. Cherryh ©1987

Am
My mother worships money
  G
And my father worships work.
Am
My sister says that I'm a whore,
   G
My brother, I'm a sherk.
       Am   G
With such a loving family
               Am   G
There's no need to wonder why
C   G   Am   G
At sixteen I determined that
             Am   G Am
I'd break away or die.

Well, die is what I nearly did—
Out singing for my cash;
They threw a little money
But they threw a *lot* of trash.
I tried a little acting
'Cause the bug was in my soul,
But acting couldn't keep me fed;
I starved and then I stole.

Her name was Rif; she sang in bars;
Her hat was full of coin,
And she caught me quite red-handed
With what I tried to purloin.
She didn't call out for the law,
She didn't make a fuss—
"Rob from the rich to feed the poor—"
And, partner, that means us.

She taught me how to pick gitar
And how to pick a lock.
She taught me how to kill
And where to bluff, and when to shock.
But being partner to Rif
Sometimes is a royal pain—
A singer-thief; that's fine—But she's
An undercover Jane!

She's a crazy rabble-rouser
And she wants to save the world.
I think she'd challenge God himself
With rebel flags unfurled.
And I love her like my sister—(more!
'Cause I hate my sister's guts.)
But I'll be the first to tell you that
I think my partner's nuts.

So here we are out singing
In some dark canalside dive—
And all I want to do is somehow
keep us both alive.
Between the priests and blacklegs
trying to send us both to hell—
And the scrapes she gets us both into—Lord,
The stories I could tell!

She's a crazy rabble-rouser
and she's out to change the world
and with all she's dragged me into
I'm surprised my hair ain't curled.
But I wouldn't trade my partner Rif,
not for anyone I know—I
Sometimes think she might be right,
but, Lord! don't tell her so!

A SONG FOR MARINA

Lyrics by Mercedes Lackey ©1987
Music by C. J. Cherryh ©1987

   G   D
Look down on me, lady—
   G   D
Your window's so high,
    C   G
It's so hard to see you
      D   A
But still, I will try,
    C   D
It's dark by canalside,
    C   G
I know you won't see
    C   D
The one in the shadows—
    G   D
the shadow that's me.

Look down on me, lady—
Look down from above—
Although you don't know me
I'll tell you I love.
I'll write of your beauty
And watch you below
I'll love you forever
And you'll never know.

Look down on me, lady—
Oh won't you look down?
For if I were a king
I would give you my crown.
But I'm just a poet—
A fool at your feet—
Look down on me, lady—
Your smile is so sweet.

Look down on me, lady—
The stars in the skies
Cannot hope to equal
Your ever-bright eyes.
Alas, I've no fortune,
No future, no clan—
A look's all I'll get
So I'll take what I can.

INDEX TO CITY MAPS

INDEX OF ISLES AND BUILDINGS BY REGIONS

THE ROCK: (ELITE RESIDENTIAL)
LAGOONSIDE

GOVERNMENT CENTER THE TEN ISLES
(ELITE RESIDENCE)

THE SOUTH BANK   THE RESIDENCIES

Second rank of elite
41. White
42. Eber
43. Chavez
44. Bucher
45. St. John
46. Malvino (Adventist)
47. Mendelev
48. Sofia
49. Kamat
50. Tyler

Mostly wealthy or
government
51. North
52. Spellbridge
53. Kass
54. Borg
55. Bent
56. French
57. Cantry
58. Porfirio
59. Wex

WEST END   PORTSIDE

Upper middle class
60. Novgorod
61. Ciro
62. Bolado
63. diNero
64. Mars
65. Ventura
66. Gallandry (Advent.)
67. Martel
68. Salazar
69. Williams
70. Pardee
71. Calliste
72. Spiller
73. Yan
74. Ventani
75. Turk
76. Princeton
77. Dunham

Middle class
78. Golden
79. Pauley
80. Eick
81. Torrence
82. Yesudian
83. Capone
84. Deva
85. Bruder
86. Mohan
87. Deniz
88. Hendricks
89. Racawski
90. Hofmeyr
91. Petri
92. Rohan
93. Herschell
94. Bierbauer
95. Godwin
96. Arden
97. Aswad

TIDEWATER (SLUM)

98. Hafiz (brewery)
99. Rostov
100. Ravi
101. Greely
102. Megary (slaver)
103. Ulger
104. Mendex
105. Amparo
106. Calder
107. Fife
108. Salvatore

FOUNDRY DISTRICT

109. Spellman
110. Foundry
111. Vaitan
112. Sarojin
113. Nayab
114. Petrescu
115. Hagen

EASTSIDE (LOWER MID.)

116. Fishmarket
117. Masud
118. Knowles
119. Gossan (Adventist)
120. Bogar
121. Mantovan (Advent.) (wealthy)
122. Salem
123. Delaree

RIMMON ISLE (ELITE/MERCANTILE)

124. Khan
125. Raza
126. Takezawa
127. Yakunin
128. Balaci
129. Martushev
130. Nikolaev

MEROVIN

(first quarter — frontispiece map)

①

GREVE

Fork of the Det

NORTH FLAT
(Arable)

THE FLAT

Lagoon

2
NAVALE
COLUMBO
KALUGIN
9

3

BASARGIN
RAJ-WADE
KISTNA
ZORYA

6
DUNDEE
KUZ-MIN
CARSWELL
NARAIN

KROBO
KUMINSKI
ELGIN
38
BOREGY

ARCHANGEL
ITO
JUSTICIARY

LIND-SEY
VANCE

17
SPUR

CHAM
21
COL-LEGE
SIGNEURY
WHITE

DEEMS
Spur of Loop

BOIS
MANSUR
NORTH
SPELLBRIDGE
KASS
BORG
BUCHER

81
82
55
57
58

Grand

Grand

DET

THE FLAT

ESHKOW

ROM-NEY

DORJAN

Grand Canal

CHAVEZ

EAST DIKE

EBER

MENDELEV

DOCKS

MAL-VINO

41

45

SOFIA

KAMAT

TULER

NAHAR

VAI-TAN

SARD-JIN

FOUNDRY

109

110

114

HAGEN

MASUD

KNOWLES

119

* NUMBERS INDICATE ISLES AND BUILDINGS LISTED IN INDEX

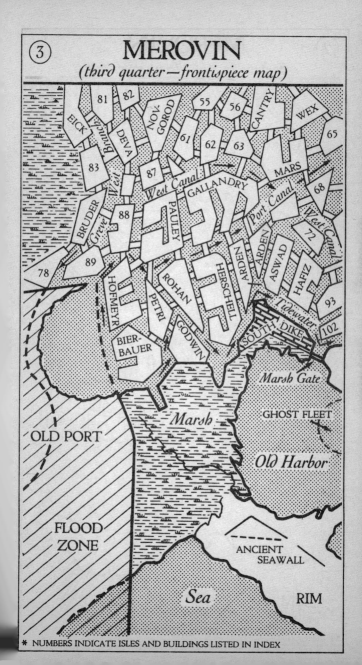

MEROVIN
(third quarter—frontispiece map)

③

81 82
NOV-GOROD 55 56 CANTRY WEX
EICK
BRANNY DEVA 61 62 63 65
83 87 MARS
WEST WEST CANAL GALLANDRY PORT CANAL 68
BRUDER GREVE 88 PAULEY 72
WEST CANAL
78 89 ARDEN
HOFMEYR ROHAN HERSCHELL ARDEN ASWAD HAFIZ 93
PETRI GODWIN SOUTH DIKE TIDEWATER 102
BIER-BAUER

Marsh Gate

GHOST FLEET

Marsh

Old Harbor

OLD PORT

FLOOD ZONE

ANCIENT SEAWALL

Sea   RIM

* NUMBERS INDICATE ISLES AND BUILDINGS LISTED IN INDEX

MEROVIN

(fourth quarter — frontispiece map)

④

Grand Canal

FOUN-DRY

NAYAB

FISH MARKET

MASUD

118

GOSSAN

65

Port WILLIAMS

PAR-DEE

CALLISTE

Snake Gut

SALEM

VEN-TANI

MANTOVAN

DELAREE

EAST DIKE

TURK

YAN

75

DUN-HAM

101

RAVI

MEN-DEZ

ULGER

FACTORY

CALDER

107

Old Grand

SALVATORE

RAMSEYHEAD

New Harbor

102

105

Tidewater

SOUTH DIKE

POGY GATE

RIMMON ISLE

DIKE

WHARF GATE

DEAD WHARF

124

125

120

GHOST FLEET

127

128

129

130

Dead Harbor

RIM

Sea

* NUMBERS INDICATE ISLES AND BUILDINGS LISTED IN INDEX

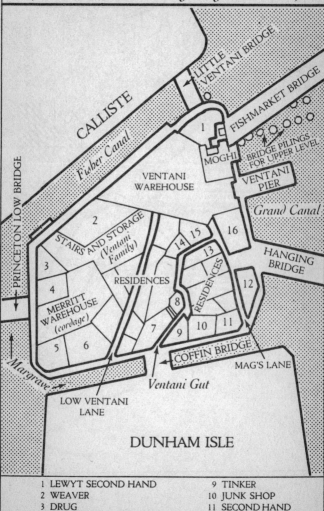

VENTANI ISLE
(Canalside Level showing Moghi's Tavern)

LITTLE VENTANI BRIDGE

CALLISTE

FISHMARKET BRIDGE

PRINCETON LOW BRIDGE

Fisher Canal

VENTANI WAREHOUSE

MOGHI

BRIDGE PILINGS FOR UPPER LEVEL

VENTANI PIER

Grand Canal

STAIRS AND STORAGE (Ventani Family)

2

RESIDENCES

14 15

13

16

HANGING BRIDGE

3

4

MERRITT WAREHOUSE (cordage)

RESIDENCES

8

12

5

6

7

9

10

11

COFFIN BRIDGE

MAG'S LANE

Margrave

Ventani Gut

LOW VENTANI LANE

DUNHAM ISLE

1 LEWYT SECOND HAND	9 TINKER
2 WEAVER	10 JUNK SHOP
3 DRUG	11 SECOND HAND
4 DOCTOR	12 SPICERY
5 CHANDLER	13 LIBERTY PAWN
6 FURNITURE MAKER	14 TACKLE
7 KILIM'S USED CLOTHES	15 MAG'S DRUG
8 JONES	16 ASSAN BAKERY

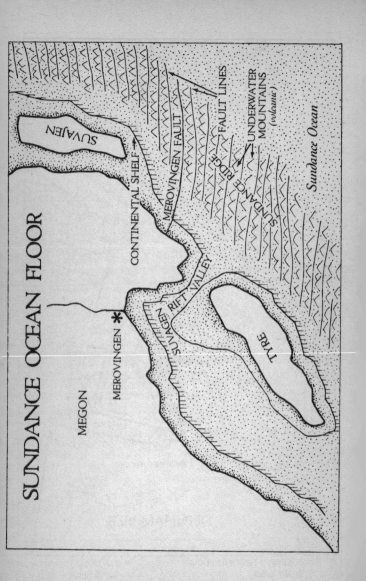

SUNDANCE OCEAN FLOOR

MEGON

MEROVINGEN ✱

SUVAJEN

CONTINENTAL SHELF →

MEROVINGEN FAULT

FAULT LINES

UNDERWATER MOUNTAINS
(volcanic)

SUNDANCE RIDGE

SUVAGEN RIFT VALLEY

TYRE

Sundance Ocean

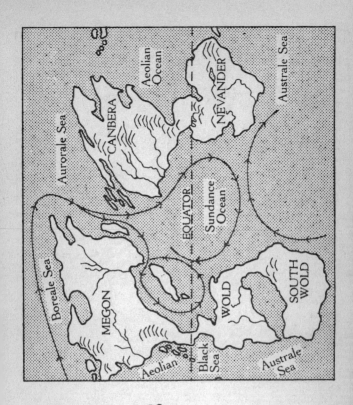

MAJOR EASTERN OCEANIC CURRENTS
(affecting climate)

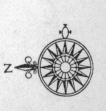

N

Aeolian Ocean

CANBERA

Aurorale Sea

NEVANDER

Australe Sea

EQUATOR

Sundance Ocean

Boreale Sea

MEGON

Aeolian

Black Sea

WOLD

SOUTH WOLD

Australe Sea

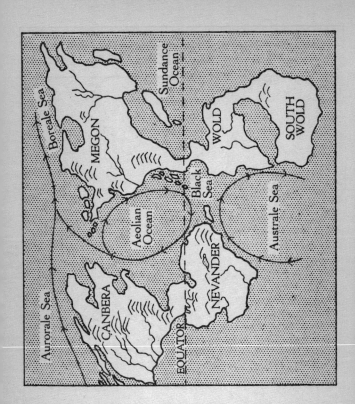

WESTERN

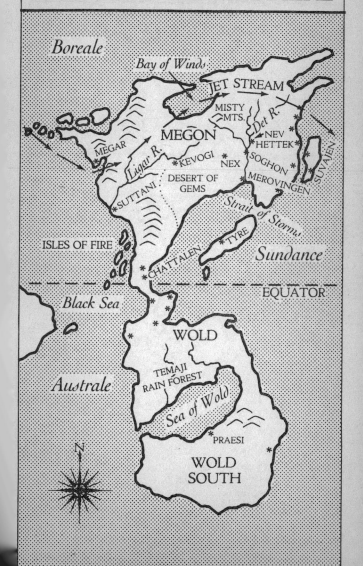

WESTERN HEMISPHERE

Boreale

Bay of Winds

JET STREAM

MISTY MTS.

MEGON

Det R.

NEV
HETTEK

SUVAJEN

MEGAR

Ligar R.

KEVOGI

NEX

SOGHON

SUTTANI

DESERT OF
GEMS

MEROVINGEN

Strait of Storms

ISLES OF FIRE

CHATTALEN

TYRE

Sundance

EQUATOR

Black Sea

WOLD

Australe

TEMAJI
RAIN FOREST

Sea of Wold

PRAESI

N

WOLD
SOUTH

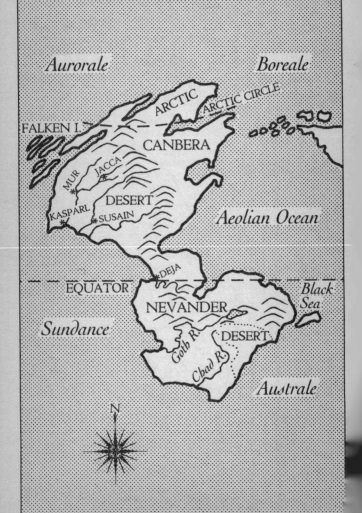

EASTERN HEMISPHERE

Aurorale

Boreale

ARCTIC

ARCTIC CIRCLE

FALKEN I.

CANBERA

MUR
JACCA

DESERT

KASPARL
SUSAIN

Aeolian Ocean

DEJA

EQUATOR

Black Sea

NEVANDER

Sundance

DESERT

Goth R.

Chad R.

Australe

N

DAW

More Top-Flight Science Fiction and Fantasy from
C.J. CHERRYH

Merovingen Nights
☐ ANGEL WITH THE SWORD   (UE2143—$3.50)

Merovingen Nights—Anthologies
☐ FESTIVAL MOON: (#1)   (UE2192—$3.50)
☐ FEVER SEASON (#2)   (UE2224—$3.50)
☐ TROUBLED WATERS (#3)   (UE2271—$3.50)

Ealdwood Fantasy Novels
☐ THE DREAMSTONE   (UE2013—$2.95)
☐ THE TREE OF SWORDS AND JEWELS

(UE1850—$2.95)

Other Cherryh Novels
☐ BROTHERS OF EARTH   (UE2290—$3.50)
☐ CUCKOO'S EGG   (UE2083—$3.50)
☐ HESTIA   (UE2208—$2.95)
☐ HUNTER OF WORLDS   (UE2217—$2.95)
☐ PORT ETERNITY   (UE2206—$2.95)
☐ SERPENT'S REACH   (UE2088—$3.50)
☐ WAVE WITHOUT A SHORE   (UE2101—$2.95)

Cherryh Anthologies
☐ SUNFALL   (UE1881—$2.50)
☐ VISIBLE LIGHT   (UE2129—$3.50)

DAW

SCIENCE FICTION MASTERWORKS FROM
THE INCOMPARABLE
C.J. CHERRYH